The LAND of the SILVER APPLES

Also by the Author

The Sea of Trolls
The House of the Scorpion
A Girl Named Disaster
The Warm Place
The Ear, the Eye and the Arm
Do You Know Me

The LAND of the SILVER APPLES

NANCY FARMER

A RICHARD JACKSON BOOK
Atheneum Books for Young Readers
New York   London   Toronto   Sydney

Atheneum Books for Young Readers
An imprint of Simon & Schuster Children's Publishing Division
1230 Avenue of the Americas, New York, New York 10020

Text copyright © 2007 by Nancy Farmer
Illustrations copyright © 2007 by Rick Sardinha
All rights reserved, including the right of reproduction in whole or in part in any form.
Book design by Ann Zeak
The text for this book is set in Edlund.
Manufactured in the United States of America
First Edition
2 4 6 8 10 9 7 5 3 1
Library of Congress Cataloging-in-Publication Data
Farmer, Nancy, 1941–
The Land of the Silver Apples/Nancy Farmer.—1st ed.
p.   cm.
"A Richard Jackson book."
Sequel to: The Sea of Trolls.
Summary: After escaping from the Sea of Trolls, the apprentice bard Jack plunges
into a new series of adventures, traveling underground to Elfland
and uncovering the truth about his little sister, Lucy.
Includes bibliographical references (p.)
ISBN-13: 978-1-4169-0735-0
ISBN-10: 1-4169-0735-1
[1. Bards and bardism—Fiction. 2. Druids and druidism—Fiction.
3. Saxons—Fiction. 4. Goblins—Fiction. 5. Elves—Fiction. 6. Mythology—Fiction.]
I. Title.
PZ7.F23814Lan 2007
[Fic]—dc22   2006031433

For Ruth Farmer

1916–2006

May the life force hold you
in the hollow of its hand

ACKNOWLEDGMENTS

Many, many thanks to my husband, Harold, for sharing my adventures on the Hollow Road.

To Richard Jackson, for his encouragement and help, and to Dr. William Ratliff, for providing me access to the Stanford University Library.

I also want to thank the members of our writing group: Margaret Kahn, Antoinette May, James Spencer, and Rob Swigart. There's nothing like a troupe of professional writers to pull you out of knucker holes when you fall in.

CONTENTS

CAST OF CHARACTERS

HUMANS (SAXONS)

Jack: Age thirteen; an apprentice bard

Lucy: Jack's sister; age seven

Mother: Alditha; Jack and Lucy's mother; a wise woman

Father: Giles Crookleg; Jack and Lucy's father

The Bard: A druid from Ireland; also known as Dragon Tongue

Pega: A slave girl; age fourteen

Brother Aiden: A monk from the Holy Isle

Father Swein: The abbot of St. Filian's Well

Brutus: A slave at St. Filian's Well

Father Severus: A prisoner of the elves

Hazel: A child stolen by hobgoblins

HUMANS (NORTHMEN)

Thorgil Olaf's Daughter: An ex-berserker; age thirteen

Olaf One-Brow: A famous warrior and Thorgil's adoptive father; deceased

Skakki: Olaf's son; shipmate of Thorgil

Rune: A skald

Eric the Rash: Shipmate of Thorgil

Eric Pretty-Face: Shipmate of Thorgil

Heinrich the Heinous: Nephew of King Ivar the Boneless

PICTS

Brude: Leader of the Old Ones

HOBGOBLINS

The Bugaboo: King of the hobgoblins
The Nemesis: The Bugaboo's second-in-command
Mumsie: The Bugaboo's mother
Mr. and Mrs. Blewit: Adoptive parents of Hazel

ELVES

Partholis: Queen of Elfland
Partholon: Partholis's consort
Ethne: An elf lady; daughter of Partholis and an unknown human
Gowrie: An elf lord
Nimue: The Lady of the Lake; a water elf

UNCLASSIFIABLE

King Yffi: Ruler of Din Guardi and Bebba's Town; half-kelpie
Man in the Moon: An old god; exiled to the moon
Forest Lord: An old god; ruler of the Green World
The Hedge: Aspect of the Forest Lord
Knuckers: They look like your worst nightmare.
Yarthkins: Also known as *landvættir*; spirits of the land. You really
   don't want to meddle with them.

The Song of Wandering Aengus

I went out to the hazel wood,
Because a fire was in my head,
And cut and peeled a hazel wand,
And hooked a berry to a thread;
And when white moths were on the wing,
And moth-like stars were flickering out,
I dropped the berry in a stream
And caught a little silver trout.

When I had laid it on the floor,
I went to blow the fire aflame,
But something rustled on the floor,
And some one called me by my name.
It had become a glimmering girl
With apple blossom in her hair
Who called me by my name and ran
And faded through the brightening air.

Though I am old with wandering
Through hollow lands and hilly lands,
I will find out where she has gone,
And kiss her lips and take her hands;
And walk among long dappled grass,
And pluck till time and times are done
The silver apples of the moon,
The golden apples of the sun.

—William Butler Yeats

The LAND of the SILVER APPLES

Chapter One

THE NECKLACE

It was the middle of the night when the rooster crowed. The sun had disappeared hours ago into a mass of clouds over the western hills. From the wind buffeting the walls of the house, Jack knew a storm had rolled off the North Sea. The sky would be black as a lead mine, and even the earth, covered with snow as it was, would be invisible. The sun when it rose—*if* it rose—would be masked in gloom.

The rooster crowed again. Jack heard his claws scratching the bottom of his basket as if he was wondering where his soft nest had gone. And where his warm companions had hidden themselves. The rooster was alone in his little pen.

"It's only for a while," Jack told the bird, who grumbled

briefly and settled down. He would crow again later, and again, until the sun really appeared. That was how roosters were. They made noise all night, to be certain of getting it right.

Jack threw back the heap of sheepskins covering him. The coals in the hearth still gleamed, but not for long, Jack thought with a twinge of fear. It was the Little Yule, the longest night of the year, and the Bard had commanded they put out all the fires in the village. The past year had been too dangerous. Berserkers had appeared from across the water, and only merest chance had kept them from slaughtering the villagers.

The Northmen had destroyed the Holy Isle. Those who had not been drowned or burned or chopped to bits had been hauled off into slavery.

It was time for new beginnings, the Bard said. Not one spark of fire was to remain in the little gathering of farms Jack knew as home. New fire had to be kindled from the earth. The Bard called it a "need-fire." Without it, the evils of the past would linger into the new year.

If the flame did *not* kindle, if the earth refused to give up its fire, the frost giants would know their time had come. They would descend from their icy fortresses in the far north. The great wolf of winter would devour the sun and light would never return.

Of course, that was the belief in the old days, Jack thought as he pulled on his calfskin boots. Now, with Brother Aiden in the village, people knew that the old beliefs should be cast away. The little monk sat outside his beehive-shaped hut and spoke to anyone who would listen. He gently corrected people's errors and spoke to them of the goodness of God. He was an excellent storyteller, almost as fine as the Bard. People were willing to listen to him.

Still, in the dark of the longest night of the year, it was hard to believe in such goodness. God had not protected the Holy Isle. The wolf of winter was abroad. You could hear his voice on the wind, and the very air rang with the shouts of frost giants. Surely it was wise to follow the old ways.

Jack climbed the ladder to the loft. "Mother, Father," he called. "Lucy."

"We're awake," his father replied. He was already bundled up for the long walk. Mother was ready too, but Lucy stubbornly clung to her covers.

"Leave me alone!" she wailed.

"It's St. Lucy's Day," Father coaxed. "You'll be the most important person in the village."

"I'm already the most important person in the village."

"The very idea!" Mother said. "More important than the Bard or Brother Aiden or the chief? You need a lesson in humility."

"Ah, but she's really a lost princess," Father said fondly. "She'll look so pretty in her new dress."

"I will, won't I?" said Lucy, condescending to rise.

Jack went back down the ladder. It was an argument Mother never won. She tried to teach Lucy manners, but Father always undermined her efforts.

To Giles Crookleg, his daughter was the most wonderful thing that had ever happened to him. He was forever cursed with lameness. Both he and his wife, Alditha, were sturdy rather than handsome, with faces browned by working in the fields. No one would ever mistake them for nobility. Jack knew he would be just like them when he grew up. But Lucy's hair was as golden as afternoon sunlight and her eyes were the violet blue of an evening sky. She moved with a bright grace that seemed barely to touch the earth. Giles, with his lumbering, shambling gait, could only admire her.

Jack had to admit, as he stirred up the hearth for one last burst of heat, that Lucy had been through much in the past year. She had seen murder and endured slavery in the Northland. He had too, but he was thirteen and she was only seven. He was willing to overlook most of her annoying habits.

He heated cider and warmed oatcakes on the stones next to the fire. Mother was busy dressing Lucy in her finery, and Jack heard complaints as the little girl's hair was combed. Father came down to drink his cider.

The cock crowed again. Both Jack and Father paused. It was said in the old days that a golden rooster lived in the branches of Yggdrassil. On the darkest night of the year he crowed. If he was answered by the black rooster that lived under the roots of the Great Tree, the End of Days had come.

No cry shook the heavens or echoed in the earth. Only the north wind blustered against the walls of the house, and Jack and Father relaxed. They continued to sip their drinks. "I *wish* we had a mirror," came Lucy's petulant voice. "I don't see why we can't buy one from the Pictish peddlers. We've got all that silver Jack brought home."

"It's for hard times," Mother said patiently.

"Oh, pooh! I want to see myself! I'm sure I'm beautiful."

"You'll do," Mother said.

In fact, Jack had more silver than his parents knew. The Bard had advised him to bury half of it under the floor of the ancient Roman house, where the old man lived. "Your mother has good sense," the Bard had said, "but Giles Crookleg— excuse me, lad—has the brain of an owl."

Father had spent some of his share on Brother Aiden's altar and a donkey for Lucy. The rest was reserved for that glorious day when she would marry a knight or even— Father's hopes rose ever higher—a *prince*. How Lucy would meet a prince in a tiny village tucked away from any major road was a mystery.

The little girl climbed down the ladder and twirled to show off her finery. She wore a long, white dress of the finest wool. Mother had woven the yellow sash herself, dying it with the pollen-colored washings from her beehives. The dress, however, had been imported from Edwin's Town in the far north. Such cloth was beyond Mother's ability, for her sheep produced only a coarse, gray wool.

Lucy wore a feathery green crown of yew on her golden hair. Jack thought it was as nice as a real crown, and only he understood its true meaning. The Bard said the yew tree guarded the door between this world and the next. On the longest night of the year this door stood open. Lucy's role was to close it during the need-fire ceremony, and she needed protection from whatever lay on the other side.

"I know what would go with this dress—my silver necklace," Lucy said.

"You are not to wear metal," Mother said sharply. "The Bard said it was forbidden."

"He's a *pagan*," Lucy said. She had only just learned the word.

"He's a wise man, and I'll have no disrespect from you!"

"A *pagan*, a *pagan*, a *pagan*!" Lucy sang in her maddening way. "He's going to be dragged down to Hell by demons with long claws."

"Get your cloak on, you rude child. We've got to go."

Lucy darted past Mother and grabbed Father's arm. "*You'll* let me wear the necklace, Da. Please? Please-please-please-please-please?" She cocked her head like a bright little sparrow, and Jack's heart sank. She was so adorable, all golden hair and smiles.

"You can't wear the necklace," Jack said. Lucy's smile instantly turned upside down.

"It's mine!" she spat.

"Not yet," Jack said. "It was given into my keeping. I decide when you get it."

"You thief!"

"Lucy!" cried Mother.

"What harm can it do, Alditha?" said Father, entering into the argument for the first time. He put his arm around the little girl, and she rubbed her cheek against his coat.

"Brother Aiden says this is St. Lucy's Day. Surely we honor the saint by dressing her namesake in the finest we have."

"Giles—," began Mother.

"Be still. I say she wears the necklace."

"It's dangerous," Jack said. "The Bard says metal can poison the need-fire because you can't tell where it's been. If it's been used as a weapon or for some other evil, it perverts the life force."

Father had treated Jack with more respect since his return from the land of the Northmen, but he was not going to be lectured by his son. "This is *my* house. *I* am the master," Giles Crookleg said. He went to the treasure chest with Lucy dancing at his side.

Father took the iron key from the thong around his neck and unlocked the chest. Inside were some of the things Mother had brought to the marriage: lengths of cloth, embroidery, and a few items of jewelry. Underneath were a heap of silver coins and a gold coin with the face of a Roman king that Father had found in the garden. Wrapped in a cloth was the necklace of silver leaves.

It gleamed with a brightness that was strangely compelling. Jack could understand Lucy's desire for it. It had been looted in a Northman raid, claimed by Frith Half-Troll, and had come to Thorgil the shield maiden. Thorgil fell in love with it, and this was most unusual because she scorned feminine weaknesses such as jewelry and baths. Then Thorgil, who valued suffering even more than silver, had given her beloved necklace to Lucy.

From the very beginning, the little girl had reacted badly to this generous gift. She claimed it came from Frith, who—Lucy insisted—had treated her like a real princess. And she became hysterical when Jack reminded her of the truth, that the evil half-troll had kept her in a cage and planned to sacrifice her. Jack had taken charge of the necklace then.

"Ooh!" cried Lucy, putting it on.

"Now we really have to go," said Father, locking the chest. He had lit two horn lanterns for the journey. Mother had packed several of her precious beeswax candles in a carrying bag. Jack poured water over the hearth, and smoke and steam billowed up. The light in the room shrank down to two brownish dots behind the panels of the horn lanterns.

"Be sure it's out," whispered Mother. Jack broke up the coals with the poker and poured on more water until he could feel only a fading heat in the hearthstones.

Father opened the door, and a blast of icy wind swept in. The rooster groaned in his pen, and a cup rolled along the floor. "Don't dawdle!" Father commanded, as though Jack and Mother had been responsible for the delay. Snow lay everywhere, and they could see only a few feet ahead by the dim lantern light. The sky was shrouded with clouds.

Father fetched the donkey for Lucy. Bluebell was an obedient, patient beast, chosen by Brother Aiden for her good character, but she had to be dragged from her pen on this night. She fought until Father smacked her hard and seated Lucy on her back. The donkey stood there, shivering and blowing steam from her nostrils.

"Good old Bluebell," crooned Lucy, hugging the animal's neck. The little girl was covered in a heavy woolen robe with a hood, and the robe hung down over Bluebell's sides. It must have given the donkey some warmth because she stopped resisting and followed Father's lead.

Jack went ahead with a lantern. It was slow going, for the road was icy where it wasn't covered with snow. Jack had to keep trudging to the side to find the posts that marked the way. Once, they wandered off course and knew they were wrong only when Jack bumped into a tree.

The wind gusted and the snowflakes danced. Jack heard a rooster crow, but it wasn't the golden bird sitting on the branches of Yggdrassil. It was only John the Fletcher's fighting cock that threatened anyone who passed by. They came to a cluster of buildings and turned at the blacksmith's house. "There's no fire," Mother murmured. The forge where iron bars were heated was as black as the anvil under the oak tree.

Jack felt a cold even deeper than the winter night. Never, in all his days, had he ever seen that fire out. It was like the heart of the village, where people gathered to talk and where you could warm your toes after a walk. Now it was dead. Soon every fire would be dead, including the two brown spots of light they carried.

More would have to be called up, using wood that had drawn its strength from the earth. For the need-fire had to be alive to turn the wheel of the year. Only then would the frost giants return to their mountains and the door be closed between this world and the next.

Chapter Two

THE NEED-FIRE CEREMONY

The chief's house was large and surrounded with outbuildings for livestock, storage, and a dairy. To one side was an apple orchard, now leafless and dark. Jack had often visited the chief since he'd become the Bard's apprentice. He carried the old man's harp for musical evenings and relished his position by the fire. Earlier, when Jack had been only Giles Crookleg's brat, the boy had been pushed to the coldest part of the room.

He had been given his own small harp, but he was not nearly ready to perform. His fingers, more used to digging turnips, did not have the practiced ease of his master's. The Bard said not to worry. The skill came with the years, and anyhow, Jack's voice was good enough to stand on its own.

Jack rapped on the chief's door with his staff, and Father shouldered his way in with Lucy in his arms. The hall was filled with the men who would take part in the ceremony. They needed to be strong, for the rite was difficult and might take a long time. The weak, the elderly, the children, and most of the women were huddled under sheepskins in their own dark homes. The Bard and Brother Aiden sat together by the still-burning hearth.

"May I put the donkey in your barn?" Father asked the chief.

"Sit down and rest, Giles," said the chief. "I know how difficult it was for you to walk here. Pega! Stir your stumps and attend to that beast." A girl sprang up from the shadows in a corner.

Jack had glimpsed her before. She was a silent creature who fled the instant you looked at her, and no wonder. Pega was woefully ugly. She had ears that stuck straight out through wispy hair. She was as skinny as a ferret, and her mouth was as wide as a frog's. Saddest of all, she had a birthmark covering half her face. It was said her mother had been frightened by a bat and that this was the mark of its wing.

No one actually knew who Pega's mother was. The girl had been sold as a slave very young and traded from village to village until she wound up here. She was older than Jack, but her growth was stunted. She was no taller than a ten-year-old. She had been bought as a dairymaid but performed any chore anywhere, for anyone who gave her an order.

Pega pushed her way through the crowd, looking for all the world like a frog struggling through tall grass. "I'll take the donkey," Jack said suddenly. He grabbed the lantern and set off before anyone could stop him. The wind tore at his cloak as he dragged Bluebell through the snow. He shoved her into the barn with the chief's cattle.

I'm an idiot, thought Jack, fighting his way back. He'd meant to pull the Bard aside and tell him about Lucy's necklace, but the sight of little Pega struggling to reach the door had struck him like a blow. He'd been a slave once. He knew what it was like to be utterly at the mercy of others.

I'll tell the Bard about the necklace when I get back, Jack decided. He knew the fire had to be kindled without the flint and iron they usually depended on. Metal was in the service of death—or, as the Bard put it, "Unlife." Tonight Unlife was at its most powerful. If it contaminated the new fire, the ceremony would be undone.

"Hurry!" cried the chief as Jack squeezed through the door. In the middle of the hall a plank of wood was laid into a groove on top of another plank, forming a large cross. Several men held down the lower piece and several more grasped each end of the upper one to saw it back and forth. Rubbing two sticks together to start a fire was hard enough. This was like rubbing two *logs* together.

Lucy had removed the woolen cloak to show off her beautiful white dress and the pollen-dyed belt Mother had made. Her glorious golden hair gleamed in the dim light. She held one of Mother's candles in her hand.

Jack didn't see the necklace. *Thank Heaven! Mother must have taken it,* he deduced, but then he saw a glint at the neck of the dress. Lucy had hidden it underneath.

"Now!" cried the Bard. Someone whisked Jack's lantern away and blew it out. The chief poured a bucket of water over the hearth. The coals hissed and crackled with steam. Jack felt the warmth die and the cold seep under the door around his feet. The hall turned completely black.

I have to do something, he thought frantically. He didn't want to yell across the room about the necklace. Father would get angry at him, and then everyone else would get angry at Father. A fight would break out. Conflict would sour the ceremony just as surely as metal. *Maybe silver won't matter. It isn't used in weapons,* Jack told himself, although he knew better. Any evil contaminated the metal. Frith Half-Troll had worn the necklace, and there were few more evil creatures than she.

He heard the *saw-saw-saw* of the plank being pulled back and forth. When one lot of men got tired, another group would take over. The Bard said it sometimes took hours to get a flame. The sound went on and on until Jack heard someone fall down. "Change sides!" cried the Bard.

"About time," someone groaned.

Men banged into one another in the dark, and John the Fletcher swore his hands had more splinters than the planks. The *saw-saw-saw* began again, and Jack smelled pine resin. He knew the wood was getting hot. "Faster!" roared the chief.

If I get close to Lucy, I can take the necklace without starting a fight, Jack thought. But as he wormed his way across the room, he got too close to the men. An elbow slammed into his stomach and knocked his breath out.

"Sorry, whoever that was," a man muttered.

"You're standing on my foot," someone else growled.

Jack blundered off, clutching his stomach. His sense of direction was gone. "Lucy!" he called.

"Jack?" she answered. Oh, stars! She was on the other side of the room. He'd got it wrong. Jack started to work his way back and blundered into the men again.

"Sorry," grunted someone. Jack was sure he'd got a black eye this time.

"Change sides!" shouted the Bard. By now Jack could smell smoke, and the men needed no encouragement to move faster. A spark appeared, then another and another. Jack saw a glow and a pair of hands crumbling the dry mushrooms everyone used as tinder. The flame blossomed.

"Hurrah!" everyone cheered. The chief fed handfuls of straw into it, and shadows danced along the walls. Lucy glided forth and lit her candle.

"Stop!" roared the Bard. Startled, Lucy dropped the candle, and it went out on the floor. "What's this?" the old man cried. It was rare that the Bard showed his true power, but he was showing it now. You could see exactly why the Northmen called him Dragon Tongue and took care to stay on his right side.

"You're wearing metal!" said the Bard, yanking the silver necklace up to the light. Lucy shrieked.

"Don't hurt her!" cried Father.

"And *you*, Giles, knew she had it," the old man said.

"It was to honor St. Lucy," Father protested.

"Don't give me that drivel! She cried and you gave in to her. Weak, impossibly foolish man! It was up to you to direct her. She's only a child. You have endangered the whole village."

Giles Crookleg recoiled, and Jack's heart went out to him even though he knew his father was in the wrong. Grumbles rose from the other men. "After all that work," muttered the blacksmith.

"My hands are full of splinters—and for what?" said John the Fletcher. Lucy burst into tears and buried her face in Mother's dress.

"We will not argue," the Bard said firmly. "The life force is not served by anger, not mine nor anyone's. We've worked with one heart, and it's possible that harm will not spread beyond this child." Father looked up, shocked. Jack was startled too, for he'd thought about only the need-fire being spoiled, not that actual harm would come to Lucy.

"We need another girl to pass the flame to the rest of the village," said the Bard.

"The baker has a girl and the tanner's widow has two," said the chief. "It will take time to fetch them."

"There's no need. We have someone here," came Brother Aiden's gentle voice. Till now the little monk hadn't taken part in the ceremony. It was, after all, a pagan rite. "There's Pega."

"Pega?" said the chief. "She's only a slave."

"More's the pity. She's a good child with a loving heart."

"But she's so—so—"

"Ugly," finished the blacksmith, who had two handsome grown-up daughters.

"Not inside," said Brother Aiden quietly.

"He's right," the Bard agreed. "Fate has not been kind to Pega, but the life force shines in her. Come, my dear," he said, holding his hand out to the terrified girl, who was being pushed forward by the men. "This night you will save the village."

"What about me?" wailed Lucy, who was still clinging to Mother's dress. "*I'm* supposed to be St. Lucy."

"Hush," said Mother, attempting to hold her in her arms. Lucy shoved her away.

"*I'm* the most important person in the village! *I'm* beautiful! *I'm* not a froggy slave!"

Father swept her up. He took the crown from her head and handed it shamefacedly to the Bard. He untied the yellow sash from her dress as she tried to kick him. "Sorry," he said in a strangled voice.

"Da! You can't let them do this," shrieked Lucy. "*I'm* Lucy! *I'm* the lost princess!" Giles Crookleg carried her screaming and protesting to the far end of the hall. Jack heard him promise her all sorts of treats if only she would be quiet and not cry and forgive him. Tears ran down Mother's face, but she did not leave her place by the fire. Even Jack felt shaken.

"Come, child," the Bard told Pega.

"You won't—beat me?" Pega said. She had a surprisingly sweet voice. Jack realized it was the first time he'd heard it.

"Never," promised the old man. "You are the bringer of light to the new year." He put the crown of yew on her head and tied the belt, dyed with the sunlit color gathered by bees, around the girl's shabby dress. Pega looked up and smiled. She *did* have an awfully froggy mouth, Jack decided, but there was no denying the goodness in her eyes.

The Bard took a candle—not the one Lucy had dropped on the floor—and handed it to Pega. "What should I do, sir?" she asked.

"Light it and hold it out so that others may take fire from you."

Pega obeyed, and one by one the men in the room lit their lamps. They left at once to kindle their own hearths or bring fire to those who were too ill or old to attend. Last of all, Mother lit her two lamps. "These are for you," she told the Bard and Brother Aiden, giving each of them four of her precious beeswax candles.

Pega, meanwhile, gazed at her candle in a kind of rapture. "I never had one of these," she murmured. "It's so soft and creamy. I believe it's the prettiest thing I ever saw."

"Then you may keep it," Mother said. "Put it out for now. It has done its work. When you feel the need, it will brighten your nights."

"I won't burn it. I'll keep it forever," Pega declared. "And when I die, I'll be buried with it."

"Don't speak of death on this night!" said the Bard. The girl looked so stricken that he patted her on the shoulder. "There, I'm only joking. We've put death behind us, thanks to you. It's time to be happy." He gently lifted the crown of yew from her head. He untied the yellow belt and handed it to Mother. Pega blew out her candle. With its light gone, something seemed to go out in her as well. The old, frightened look crept back into her eyes, and she looked down to hide her face.

"What should I do with this?" Mother pushed Lucy's discarded candle with her foot.

"I'll deal with it, Alditha," the Bard said. "Brother Aiden and I are going to sleep here. Are you staying?"

"We'd planned to, but—" Mother nodded at Father and Lucy huddled at the far end of the hall, then gazed at the chief scowling by the door. "Now may not be a good time."

So Jack took a lamp and went to fetch Bluebell. The donkey was even more unwilling to move this time, having found herself a warm nest between two cows. Jack pulled and smacked her on the rump until he had wrestled her back to the chief's door. Father came out with Lucy, but she screamed and refused to let go of him.

Jack saw, just before the door closed, the chief, the Bard, and Brother Aiden warming their hands at the fire. Pega was heating a poker to make them hot cider.

They started out, with Father carrying Lucy, and Jack hauling on Bluebell's rope. Light was building behind the heavy snow clouds. The long night was over and the sun was returning. The frost giants were retreating. The wolf of winter, though still healthy, would grow lean as the weeks passed.

Lucy stirred in Father's arms and said, in a sleepy voice, "You *will* remember what you promised me? I've been *such* a good girl."

Everyone slept late. Jack forced himself to crawl out of the warm sheepskins and return the rooster to his flock. The hens were huddled together in the straw of their enclosure. They barely stirred when Jack opened the barn door. Clouds blanketed the sky, and again snowflakes swirled on the wind. From the privy, Jack could hardly see his own house.

It was a day of rest, although no day on a farm was completely without work. Father coiled straw into beehives for use when spring came. He fastened sticks across the top for the bees to hang their combs and covered the basket with a tight-fitting lid. Mother spun wool.

Jack brought hay to Bluebell and fed the chickens, pigeons, and geese. Once there had been only chickens, but Father had increased his stock with the silver Jack had given him. The herd of sheep had grown from twenty to thirty. It was good to have more animals, but it also meant more work.

Jack trudged across the snow-covered garden to a tiny shed blanketed with turf. It was here Mother preserved her winter hives. Most had to be destroyed in fall because it was impossible to keep them through the cold, but Mother always saved five or six of her best producers. They were special bees, unlike the small, dark bees of the forest. They had come from Rome long ago, when Roman armies had ruled the land. The armies had gone, leaving behind the house where the Bard lived, a road going north through the forest, and the bees.

Jack crawled through the door of the shed and put his ear to the straw of the nearest hive. Its hum was low and sleepy. There were no sounds of distress or the chirps that meant the bees were starving. A faint warmth rose from the straw as if an animal slept inside. Jack smiled. He liked working with bees. He went from hive to hive, making sure they were healthy. Nearer spring, he would feed them bread soaked in cider and honey, to give them the strength to emerge.

Lucy slept till afternoon and came down in a rotten mood. Mother gave her breakfast and Father told her a story, but her sulks didn't lift for hours. No one talked about what had happened the night before.

Chapter Three

WASSAIL

"Fine weather," said Giles Crookleg, gazing up at the bright blue sky. The sun blazed along the icicles on the roof.

"Perfect," agreed Jack. He picked up a birch rod and a skin bag full of cider. Father already had his. Their feet crackled the icy covering of the road as they set out for the village. Jack saw crows sliding down a small, snowy hill, exactly like boys on sleds. They landed with a *whump*, flew back to the top, and slid down again. John the Fletcher's fighting cock was wearing itself out chasing another crow that kept landing within tempting reach and flying up again when the enraged rooster charged after it.

"Wake up!" Jack called to the leafless apple trees as they passed.

"Oh, aye. They'll wake up soon enough," said Father. "Both boys and trees improve with beating."

It was one of Father's usual remarks, but Jack refused to let it bother him. The air was too clear, too bright, too *alive*.

A noisy crowd of men and boys waited outside the chief's house. They all carried birch rods, and some of the boys chased each other in mock sword fights. Colin, the blacksmith's son, challenged Jack. They set off across the yard, slashing and cursing. "Vile barbarian, I'll have your head!" cried Colin.

"Sooner will it decorate my doorpost!" swore Jack. Colin was heavier than him, but Jack had learned a great deal about fighting from the Northmen. He soon had Colin on the run, shrieking, "No fair! No fair!" until a blast from the chief's hunting horn brought them to a halt.

The chief stood in his doorway with the Bard, who carried his blackened ash wood staff. Only Jack knew what power lay in it and where it had come from. His own smaller staff, won with great effort in Jotunheim, was stored at the Bard's house. Jack could practice with it there without listening to Father tell him about demons waiting to drag evil wizards down to Hell.

The boy felt a sudden rush of joy at the rightness of the gathering. It was good to be in the middle of a crowd with the sun shining and the air fresh off the sea.

The Bard held up his hand for silence. "The long night is past, and the sun has turned from walking in the south," he proclaimed in a ringing voice. "It comes toward us, bringing summer, but the journey will be long and hard. The sleep of winter still lies over the land. We must wake the orchards to new life."

The old man nodded to the chief, who spread his arms wide and cried, "You heard him! Let's go wake up some apple trees!" Everyone cheered and spread into the chief's orchard, slashing the trunks with birch rods.

"*Waes hael! Waes hael!*" the men and boys cried in Saxon. "Good health! Good health!" The Bard followed behind, his cheeks rosy with cold and his long beard and robes as white as the snow. After each tree was struck, he placed a morsel of bread soaked with cider in the branches, for the robins that would sing the apples back to life.

The villagers moved from farm to farm, blowing on wooden flutes and bawling songs at the tops of their voices. In between, they stopped to drink cider until most of the men were drunk. The last place they visited was Giles Crookleg's house because it was the farthest out of town. "*Waes hael!*" bellowed the villagers. Mother came out to greet them.

"*Waes hael!*" yelled the blacksmith, slashing none too accurately at the tree shading the barn. He sang in a loud, blustering voice,

> *Apple tree, apple tree,*
> *Bear good fruit!*
> *Or down with your top*
> *And up with your root!*

"It's not wise to threaten powers you don't understand," the Bard remarked, placing cider-soaked bread in the branches. The blacksmith belched thunderously and staggered off. "I'm glad this is the last of it," the old man said to Jack. "You'd think I'd be used to drunks, living with Northmen so long, but they still irritate me. And speaking of irritation, we have yet to discuss what happened during the need-fire ceremony."

Uh-oh, thought Jack. He had hoped to escape punishment.

"Yes, I see you understand what I'm talking about. You knew as well as Giles that Lucy had that necklace."

"I did try to stop her, sir, but Father—"

"You're thirteen years old," the Bard said sternly. "In the Northman lands you'd be considered an adult."

"Father doesn't think so."

"Well, I do. You've fought by the side of Olaf One-Brow. You've been to the hall of the Mountain Queen, seen Norns, and drunk from Mimir's Well. You vanquished Frith Half-Troll, something even I was unable to do. How much more growing up do you need?"

Jack wanted to say, *A lot,* but he knew that wasn't what the Bard wanted to hear. He was caught between two men, both of whom he'd always obeyed. Now the Bard was asking him to make a choice.

"I'm teaching you lore men would give their entire wealth-hoard to learn," the Bard went on. "There are few like me in the world. Each year there are fewer, and I have chosen you as my successor. This is a high destiny."

Jack felt ashamed for letting the old man down. The Bard had believed in him and had given him so much.

"There's more," said the Bard, gazing at the bright snowfields and blue sky beyond. "Something happened during the need-fire ceremony, and the wheel of the year was turned in a new direction. I can feel it in the bones of the earth. Change is coming. Enormous change."

"The Northmen won't be back, will they?" Jack hoped he didn't sound as appalled as he felt inside.

"Nothing so trivial as that," said the old man. "I'm speaking of something that will topple gods and spread its influence throughout the nine worlds for centuries to come."

Jack stared goggle-eyed at him. All *this* from Lucy wearing a necklace at the wrong time?

"I really must train that slack-jawed expression out of you—completely undermines your authority," said the Bard.

"But, sir, who could topple a god?" asked Jack. He knew, of course, that his own God was the enemy of Odin and Thor, and a good thing, too! Who needed bullies who told their worshippers to burn down villages? Less comfortably, Jack realized that Christians were opposed to his mother's beliefs in the powers that ruled the fields and beasts. And some of them even denounced bards.

It was all mixed up in Jack's mind. He was a good Christian—or tried to be—but he had been at the foot of Yggdrassil and had seen how everything belonged on it. What was wrong with the Christians having one branch and the Northmen another?

"I spoke too rashly. No one actually topples gods," the Bard said softly. "They are simply forgotten and fall asleep."

"That's what happened during the need-fire ceremony?"

"Not exactly." The Bard drew a pattern in the snow with the tip of his staff. It might have been a sunburst except that each ray had branches like a budding tree. It was the symbol on the rune of protection. "At the right time a very minor event—a hawk taking one chick and not another, a seed sprouting where it should not have grown—can have consequences that even the Wise cannot see. When Lucy failed the ceremony and Pega took her place, a profound shift happened in the life force. What this means has something to do with you three, but I don't understand it yet. All I ask is that you take your duties seriously."

"I won't fail you, sir," Jack said fervently.

"I hope that's true."

The old man frowned at the blacksmith, who had collapsed in the snow. Father knelt beside him in a fit of drunken remorse. "I should have been a monk," Giles Crookleg moaned, rocking back and forth on his knees. "No farmwork, no worries. I would have been happy as a monk."

"There, there," said the blacksmith sympathetically.

"Throw a sheepskin over those idiots before they freeze to death," said the Bard. He strode off, his white robe merging with the white snow so quickly, it seemed he'd vanished.

Chapter Four

THE SLAVE GIRL

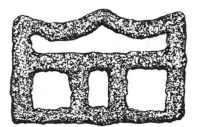

Mother and Jack had been cooking all day. He'd cleaned the fire pit outside, filled it with coals, and covered them with stones and wet straw. On top he'd placed a clay pot containing two plucked geese. With a covering of more straw and more coals, the geese had been stewing for a long time.

Father tied branches of holly around the door. As a Christian, he didn't believe in the old religion, but it didn't hurt to hang holly and repel unwanted gods, elves, demons, and other beasties that came out during the Great Yule. Some of the villagers also hung mistletoe, but Father said that was dangerous. Mistletoe was sacred to Freya, the goddess of love.

"I'm *bored*," said Lucy, poking at the fire pit with a stick.

"Do some work. Wash those turnips," Mother said.

Lucy made a halfhearted effort, but she left so much dirt, Jack had to wash them again. "Tell me a story," she wheedled Father, tugging at his sleeve.

"Later, princess," he promised. "I've got to get holly around the smoke holes. You never know what might come down a smoke hole this time of year."

"I'll do it," offered Jack. It hurt Father to climb a ladder, and even though he liked offering up his suffering to God, there were times when he was relieved to hand a chore to Jack.

"Ah, well. You might as well make yourself useful." Father sat down and put Lucy on his lap.

You're welcome, thought Jack. Once, it would have upset him to be treated so, but now he had a better understanding of his father. Giles Crookleg was not really a cruel man. He was merely a sad and disappointed one. His childhood had been harsh, and he saw no reason why Jack's should be any better. No one looked after his family better, Jack thought loyally.

The boy climbed up to the smoke hole at one end of the roof. He could look along the spine of the ceiling to the hole on the other end. A mouse squeaked indignantly and burrowed into the thatch. Jack attached the holly and climbed down.

Below, Mother was baking her special Yule bannocks in the ashes of the hearth. They were made of her best oatmeal, softened with honey and delicious goose fat. The edges were pinched out into points like the rays of the sun, and in the middle of each bannock was a hole. This was a charm to keep away trolls, who were common this time of year. Only the Bard and Jack had actually seen trolls, far away across the sea, but Mother said it didn't hurt to be careful.

By the time the sun dipped toward the western hills, the family was ready for the Great Yule feast. Father loaded Bluebell with baskets of roast goose, bannocks, and turnips. Lucy skipped ahead and Jack followed behind with a load of cider bags. Their shadows stretched long and blue across the fields of snow. The smoke of a dozen cooking fires blew across the road and made Jack's stomach rumble. He'd hardly eaten anything all day to keep room for the treats in store.

And he wasn't disappointed. The chief's hall was filled with trestle tables covered with food. There were rabbit pies and partridge pies and pigeon tarts and larks-in-a-blanket. There was smoked haddock and brined pork. Several kinds of cheese were displayed with barley cakes slathered in lard. For dessert they had baskets of slightly withered, but still good, apples. Families brought whatever they could afford, and those who had nothing, like the tanner's widow and her children, were welcome to take whatever they liked.

Every household had brought its special kind of cake: birlins made of barley-meal and mixed with caraway seeds, meldars coated with salt and snoddles that tasted of the ashes in which they were baked. But Mother's bannocks were rated the best because of the honey.

The most impressive dish was provided by the chief—a sheep's head split open so you could pick out bits of brain or tongue. It was served on a large wooden trencher with slices of mutton all around. At the outer edge was a festive border of boiled eggs, turnips, and onions, and a sheep's trotter at each corner for decoration. All together it was a wonderful display!

The villagers feasted until their faces were shiny with grease. One by one the smaller children fell asleep and were carried to an adjoining house. Pega stood guard over them and tended the small hearth fire there. Jack was glad to see she had not been forgotten. The chief's wife had given her a new dress. It was a hand-me-down, of course, but of decent wool and not too stained.

Early on, Pega had been allowed to take a trencher of food for herself. She hunched over and ate rapidly, as though she feared someone would take it from her. Jack felt again the pang he'd experienced at the Little Yule ceremony. What must it be like to be a slave forever? He'd been one a few short months and found it terrible.

Nor was Pega the only slave in the village. The blacksmith had two large and silent men to keep his fires going. All day they chopped wood, and at night they slept in a barn with the cattle. They had been sold by their father in Bebba's Town to the north, because they were of limited intelligence.

What did they think about? Jack wondered as he watched them feed in a darkened corner of the hall. They didn't talk, not even to each other. Perhaps they couldn't talk. *What must it be like, to be sold by your own father?* Jack thought.

When everyone had tucked away a last morsel of food, Brother Aiden told them the story of Baby Jesus. It was an exciting tale of angels and shepherds and of animals that warmed the infant god with their breath. Jack tried to imagine the great star that had drawn the kings of the East. What a sight it must have been!

Then the monk led them in singing "Angels We Have Heard on High" in Latin. None of the villagers spoke Latin, however. They could only hum along, but they made up for it later with *waes hael* songs. The blacksmith bellowed "The Holly and the Ivy" in his deep voice while his handsome daughters danced around the tables with their suitors.

The Bard sat in the shadows and listened. He hadn't brought his harp. The Little Yule and *waes hael* ceremonies belonged to him, but the Great Yule had been graciously offered to Brother Aiden. Jack was surprised by the friendship between the two men. Monks generally denounced the old ways, but Brother Aiden was different.

When he'd staggered into the village after the destruction of the Holy Isle, he'd gone mad with grief. At the time, everyone believed the Bard was mad too, but the old man's spirit was actually traveling in the shape of a bird. When the Bard's spirit returned, he took in the monk. "It's the least I can do after the trouble I caused," he explained.

Jack didn't feel as generous because Brother Aiden's care fell on him. It was his job to make sure the monk ate and exercised. He had to walk the man up and down the beach, all the while listening to his moans. Well, it *was* tragic, what had happened to Brother Aiden's companions, but no Northman would have complained so much about fate.

Every night the Bard played the harp and Jack sang while Brother Aiden sat by the hearth with a glazed look in his eyes. "Music is the very air of healing," the old man explained. "Aiden may not seem to be listening, but he is. His spirit is trapped in the burning library of the Holy Isle. With our help, it will escape." Gradually, the little monk's nightmares left him, and he was able to care for himself. The villagers built him a little beehive-shaped hut to live in.

Brother Aiden was touchingly grateful to the Bard and never once said a word about wicked pagans.

The Great Yule feast began to wind down. Wives packed up the remaining food and roused husbands from comfortable stupors. The blacksmith was carried home by his slaves, and more than one farmer was forcibly pushed out the door. Eventually, the hall emptied.

"Shall we go?" Mother said. She'd already wrapped Lucy in a woolen cloak.

"Not yet," said Father. "I have business to attend to. We'll wait until the Bard leaves."

Jack saw the Bard come alert—not that the old man was ever anything else.

"It may take a long time," Father explained. "I wouldn't want to keep you from your bed."

"That's quite all right," said the Bard.

"It will be boring."

"I'm seldom bored," the old man said genially.

Father frowned but turned brusquely to the chief. "It's about Pega."

"Has she done something wrong?" the chief said. He leaned back on his bench and stretched out his legs.

"No, no. It's something else. Tell me, is she healthy?"

What a strange question, thought Jack.

"As healthy as any child. She catches colds and so forth."

"Is she a good worker?"

"Ah!" The chief suddenly woke up. "An absolutely wonderful worker! For the size of her, she's amazing."

"Giles, what are you up to?" said the Bard. Now Lucy had awakened and eagerly pressed herself against Father's side.

"This is farm business," Father said.

"You have boys coming every day to help you," said the Bard. "What more do you need?"

"I plan to buy a few cows for butter and cheese."

It was the first Jack had heard of the plan. Father had all the work he could handle, even with the help of the village boys. That was an arrangement the Bard had worked out to free Jack for his apprenticeship. Father owned chickens, pigeons, geese, and thirty sheep, as well as the beehives and herb garden that were Mother's domain. During the summer he planted oats, beans, and turnips as well. How could he possibly take on cows?

"Pega's a valuable slave," said the chief.

"She's stunted and ugly. I'm surprised she doesn't turn the milk sour," Father said.

"On the contrary. She turns milk into fine yellow cheese," said the chief.

They were bargaining as though Pega were a sheep! Jack was so outraged, he couldn't trust himself to speak. He looked up and saw the Bard watching him intently.

"She looks weak. If I were a cow, I'd kick her out of the barn," said Giles Crookleg.

"She stares them down as well as any sheepdog," the chief replied.

"Giles," Mother said. "We have no room for cows."

So Mother didn't know about the scheme either, thought Jack.

"Be still," said Father. "I'll give you five silver pennies for the wench."

"Five!" cried the chief. "The skill in Pega's hands is worth at least fifty."

"For a sickly runt? I think not!"

"Observe her face, Giles. She has the scars of cowpox. She is safe from the great pox. I'll call her from the other house so you can see."

"Father," said Jack hesitantly.

"Be still. Dairymaids are well known for lung-sickness. Because of our friendship, however, I'll give you ten pennies," said Giles Crookleg.

"Father, buying slaves is evil," Jack said. A hush fell over the hall. All eyes turned to him.

"Excuse me?" said Father in a cold voice.

"He said, 'buying slaves is evil,'" Mother repeated.

Giles Crookleg rose to his feet. "How dare you oppose me!"

"There, there," the chief said hastily. "We have an expert on evil here. Brother Aiden, what's your opinion in this matter?"

He eats at the chief's table, Jack thought. *He won't say anything.* The boy's heart pounded and his face burned. He'd never opposed Father so directly or publicly. He hated doing it. But he knew how terrible it was to be sold like a cooking pot, to be discarded when you wore out.

"Slavery is wrong," said Brother Aiden in his gentle voice. Shock went through the room, although the Bard merely smiled. "It is lawful, as you know, but you were asking me about evil. My companions on the Holy Isle—those who were not slaughtered—were sold into captivity. Your own children were taken, Giles, and returned only by the greatest luck. How could you possibly want to own another human being?"

The hearth fire crackled and the wind fiddled with the thatch. Father looked thoroughly ashamed of himself. "I suppose—I suppose I don't," he said.

"Da, you promised me!" Lucy cried suddenly. "You said you'd buy me Pega if I'd be good! And I was!"

"So there we have it," said the Bard.

"Giles!" Mother gasped.

"I *did* want to start a dairy," Father said in his own defense.

"You promised me!" shrieked Lucy.

"Hush," said Mother, attempting to pull her from Father's side. The little girl clung to him, sobbing wildly, and Jack could see his father's resolve crumble.

"I gave my word," he said, putting his arm around his beloved daughter.

"I tell you what. I'll go down to forty pieces of silver," said the chief. He'd been startled by Brother Aiden's words, but Jack guessed he wasn't all that upset by them. Brother Aiden was always going on at people about sin.

"Thirty," Father said automatically.

"Giles, that's Lucy's dowry," Mother said.

"She'll marry well without it."

"Done!" said the chief.

Do something, somebody, thought Jack. He looked from Brother Aiden to the Bard and saw them looking back. At him. It was his task. He suddenly saw, in his mind's eye, Lucy throwing a tantrum at the need-fire ceremony and Pega taking the candle into her own hands. And he knew what his part in this had to be.

"I'll buy Pega for thirty-one pennies," said Jack. "And then I'll free her." He saw the Bard and Brother Aiden relax.

"What?" roared Father. "Where did you get that kind of money?"

"From the Northmen. I buried it under the floor of the Roman house."

"You *lied* to me? You withheld money for your own selfish uses? You're no son of mine, you disloyal whelp!"

"I'm not disloyal," Jack said wearily. "I suppose you won't believe me." He was shaking with nerves. His voice trembled and his heart ached within him, but he wouldn't back down.

"Leave my house at once!" shouted Giles Crookleg in a perfect fury. "Never return again!"

And Lucy wailed, "You promised me, Da. I was such a good girl, too!"

Chapter Five

THE FARSEEING CHARM

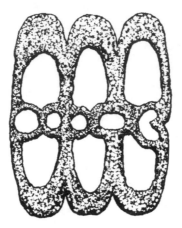

The old Roman house shuddered as the wind blew off the North Sea. Black ice covered the path outside, and cold crept in through a dozen cracks in the walls. Not for the first time, Jack wished the Bard lived somewhere else. But the old man said the life force was strong on the cliff. "It always is at the border of two realms," he explained. "The sea tries to capture the land, and the land forces it back. Between them is a great upwelling of power. It makes me feel quite young."

It makes me feel quite old, Jack thought bitterly. The cold and dark depressed him, and his heart was sore from being cast out by Father. Not a day went by when he didn't regret his rash action at the Yule feast. *I lost my home and family—*

for what? For a pesky girl who had glued herself to him like a hungry, yowling cat.

Jack couldn't really blame Pega. When he had grandly presented the thirty-one pieces of silver and the freeing was duly recorded by Brother Aiden, the chief had said, "Well, that's one less mouth to feed."

For the first time Jack realized what he'd done. He'd taken a scrawny, unlovable girl away from the only livelihood she knew. No one had a use for Pega as a paid servant. No one, in fact, wanted her around. She might mark unborn babies or make the sheep come down with foot rot. Who could tell what effect that weird birthmark on her face would have? Even Father wouldn't pay her a wage, not that Jack dared ask him.

"I will serve you all my days," Pega had announced. "You have given me freedom, and I'll never forget it."

She had followed Jack back to the Roman house. He didn't know what to do. He considered pelting her with rocks and was ashamed for thinking of it. He hoped the Bard would tell her to go away, but the old man welcomed her enthusiastically.

Now she was plaiting grass into mats at the other end of the house. She warbled like a little bird, and the Bard plucked his harp and smiled. *That's another thing,* Jack thought as he sank further into gloom. Pega's voice was remarkable. The Bard was enchanted by her, and Jack, try as he would to overcome it, was horribly jealous.

"Could you fetch some wood?" the Bard called. "I swear the frost giants are stamping around outside."

Right, thought Jack. *Give me the nasty work. Let Pega sit by the fire like a princess.* But he knew he was being unfair. Pega toiled from dawn to long past dark. She attempted any task you set her, even if it was beyond her strength. She worked, to be honest, like a slave. But it was different, she insisted, from actually *being* a slave. She never minded work so long as it was of her own free will.

Jack couldn't see the difference and thought her rather stupid.

He hauled driftwood from a back shed and nestled it in the coals of the hearth. Green and blue flames danced along the wood. "The colors of the sea," said the Bard.

"Is that because it came from the water?" Pega asked.

Of course, you half-wit, thought Jack.

"There's my clever girl," the Bard said. "Wood that has been at sea becomes partly sea. I have even seen trees turn to stone from long lying in the earth."

"Truly?" said Pega, her eyes shining.

"You could break an axe on them, for all they appear to be alive."

"I'm bored," said Jack. The Bard looked up sharply, and the boy regretted his outburst. Father always said the cure for boredom was hard work, so Jack expected to be handed another nasty chore. It had been a while since anyone had chipped the ice off the privy.

But the Bard put down his harp and said, "I think it's time for a lesson." Pega, without being told, fetched the poker to heat in the fire. "It's Brigid's Eve," the old man began.

"St. Brigid?" said Jack, who had heard of her from Father.

She had prayed to become ugly to avoid marriage. After her husband-to-be had rejected her, she became a holy nun. She had performed a number of entertaining and useful miracles. Her cows gave milk three times a day, and once, when a group of priests unexpectedly arrived for a visit, she changed her bathwater into beer.

"*Our* Brigid existed long before any saints," the Bard said. "She's one of the old gods out of Ireland. She taught the first bards how to sing."

Pega plunged the hot poker into the cider cups, and the smell of summer filled the room.

"She taught us the skill of farseeing," said the Bard. Suddenly, Jack no longer heard the storm blustering outside. He no longer felt cold or bored or even irritated by Pega, who had settled herself by the fire as though she really belonged there. The Bard was speaking of magic. And magic was what Jack wanted more than anything in the world.

"Farseeing is a matter of attention," the old man explained. "It's a matter of looking with particular intent, of peeling away the barriers between you and what you wish to know. I can't tell you how to do it. I can only tell you the steps. If you have the ability, and I think you do, you'll find the way. But be warned. You can become lost on this journey. Anger and jealousy can hide the path as surely as fog can cover a marsh. You can wander into darkness and never return."

The Bard looked into Jack's eyes, and the boy knew, sure as sure, that the old man had seen into his secret heart. He knew Jack resented Pega's presence. He was warning him of the danger this posed to becoming a bard. Very well! If that's what it took, he'd learn to *love* the pesky girl. "This is good!" remarked the old man, sipping his cider. "It's from your mother's hands, none finer."

For a while they sat in silence, watching the blue and green flames among the yellow. Pega gathered up the cups and put them away. Jack's and Pega's were cheaply made and easily broken. They were produced by the potter in the village. But the Bard's had a pale green glaze that reminded Jack of a cloudy sea and came from somewhere to the south.

"Can I do farseeing too?" Pega chirped.

Jack almost lost his resolve to stop hating her.

"This is not for you," the Bard said gently, and Jack's spirits soared. "You have your own talent, greater than you realize, but being a bard is a dangerous path and lonely. Your spirit craves a family and warmth."

"I'll never have those," Pega said.

"I think you will."

"No, never!" cried the girl with more anger than Jack thought she possessed.

"One thing you learn in a life as long as mine is never to say 'never,'" said the Bard.

"I'm sorry," Pega apologized at once. "I sound ungrateful and I'm not. I'd be happy staying here—and doing chores forever—and just being a fly on the wall."

"You're worth much more than that." The Bard patted her wispy hair, and she smiled, somewhat tearfully. "Now I'm about to teach Jack something important. Your job is to stay quiet. Do you think you can do that?"

"Oh, yes, sir! Anything!" Pega withdrew to her heap of straw in a corner, looking for all the world like a frog perched on a clump of weeds.

"You must curl your hands, Jack, to make what we call a 'seeing tube.'" The Bard demonstrated, curling his fingers around each of his eyes. "This helps you concentrate your vision. You walk sunwise around the fire and say to yourself:

I seek beyond
The folds of the mountains
The nine waves of the sea
The bird-crying winds.
I seek beyond
The turning of a maze
The untying of a knot
The opening of a door.
I am light, I am dark
I am both together
Show me what I seek!

"Say it over and over until you have traveled around the fire three times three. Then stand with your vision concentrated on the fire. Breathe deeply and begin again." The Bard put down his hands.

"That's it?" Jack asked.

"It's harder than you think."

"How many times should I do it?"

"I don't know," the old man said. "You won't succeed today or perhaps ever. If you're patient and have the gift, the way will open for you."

Jack would have liked more information, but that was how the Bard taught. He'd sent Jack out over the hills for months to observe birds and clouds without explaining why. All the while the boy had been learning about the life force.

The Bard repeated the charm until Jack had it right, for it was perilous to make a mistake. Jack understood this very well. He remembered what had happened when he tried to sing a praise-song for Queen Frith. All her hair had fallen out.

Pega sat solemnly on her clump of weeds. Her mouth was pressed into a thin line, and her ears seemed to stick out more than usual. Half her face was covered by the birthmark, making her appear to be half in shadow. She didn't make a sound.

"What should I look for, sir?" Jack asked.

"The sight will come to you, depending on what you most need. Later you can learn to bend it to your will." The Bard went to his truckle bed and lay down with his back to the fire.

What do I most need? Jack asked himself. *To see Mother.* She had been forbidden by Father from visiting him. The boy missed her terribly, and he felt deeply wronged. Father should never have tried to buy a slave, not after what Jack had told him about being carried off by Northmen. It was as though nothing Jack said made the least impression while Lucy's slightest wish was of overwhelming importance.

The boy made the seeing tubes with his hands, one for each eye. By some magic they came together to make one view that was somehow clearer and deeper. Jack gazed at the old pictures on the wall of the Roman house. A painted bird perched on a reed cane to which was tied a rosebush. Odd how he'd never noticed it was a rose before. He could see delicate thorns and a long sliver of light reflected on the cane. Where was the light coming from?

He turned and walked around the hearth, staring straight ahead and keeping the warmth of the fire on his right. The scene shifted from the bird to a shelf with bundles of dried herbs and on to the far end of the room, which was in shadow. Even that was interesting. He could see, just over the Bard's bed, a line of little holes where something had been attached. He'd never noticed them before.

Must repeat the charm, Jack scolded himself. He began chanting silently. It was difficult to keep track of the number of times he circled because he was only used to counting things he could see. The ever-changing scene made him slightly dizzy. Once, he blundered into the coals and burned his foot. When he had gone round three times three—hopefully—he turned to stare at the hearth.

Most of the green and blue flames had gone. It was a normal yellow fire, dipping and waving with an occasional snap of sparks. That was all.

Jack breathed deeply and began again. He performed the ritual until he got so sleepy, he lost track of how many times he had circled. He also thought he'd chanted *untying of a sheep* instead of *untying of a knot* the last time round. He banked the fire and went to bed.

Pega still watched the coals of the hearth with her bright little eyes and her ears sticking out, as though she could hear something far away. *Probably listening to bats,* Jack thought as he drifted off to sleep.

Chapter Six

THE LIGHT FROM FAR AWAY

It was lambing time, but this year Jack was not sent to hunt for newborns. Father had help from other village boys. Jack occasionally saw them dodging head-butts from the vicious black-faced ewes. He didn't miss the job—not one bit!—but he did miss coming home to Mother's cockle soup and bannock cakes. Lucy would run to hug him. He would sit down in his favorite place, and Mother would talk in her quiet way of something the hens had done or of a plant that had opened its leaves.

Jack wiped his eyes on his sleeve. He *would* not care. He was an adult now with important duties as a bard's apprentice. He had poetry to memorize, charms to learn, and fog to call up.

Pega did most of the household chores. She hauled logs from the beach, scampered over rocks in search of whelks, and picked weevils out of oats.

Whenever possible, Jack practiced his farseeing charm. Sometimes he thought he saw the fire dim. Sometimes the air dimpled like a pond with the first drops of rain. But always the vision cleared and Jack found himself back where he started. He continued to wonder about the source of the light shining on the painted cane. The Bard didn't ask about his progress, and Jack didn't volunteer any information.

Winter slipped away. A haze of green covered the hills, and the clouds turned from gray to white. Crickets began to chirp, and a warm wind blew from the south, bringing the first bees to the flowers. The bees reminded Jack of Mother and made him sad.

A group of Pictish peddlers arrived from Bebba's Town, leading their donkeys and blowing a horn to announce their presence. "They've got everything!" Colin, the blacksmith's son, cried as he delivered the daily shipment of bread. "They've got pots and knives and three-pronged eel spears and sewing needles! I'm to spy and find out how the needles are made. They won't tell Father."

"What else?" the Bard said.

"Boring stuff like parchment." Anything that wasn't made of iron didn't interest Colin.

"Parchment?" said the Bard.

"Heaps of it. Brother Aiden was bargaining for a piece." Colin handed the basket of bread to Pega and took his leave.

"I could use a bit of parchment," said the old man, considering. "Brother Aiden knows a secret formula for ink that never fades. I tell you what, let's pack a lunch and make a holiday of it."

But Jack didn't want to go. Father would be there, and the confrontation was more than he could bear.

"You'll have to face him sometime. You can't spend the rest of your life here," the Bard said.

"*I'm* not afraid of Giles Crookleg," declared Pega, dancing around. "I'm *free*, and he can't lay a hand on me."

"Oh, dry up," said Jack.

The Bard put on his white cloak. Pega decorated herself with a garland of flowers (which didn't improve her looks at all, Jack thought privately). She packed a basket with bread and cheese. "Sure you won't go?" the old man said at the door. "You could scare up a game of Bull in the Barn. It would do you a world of good."

Jack liked playing Bull in the Barn. A group of boys formed a ring around whoever was chosen to be the bull. The bull would ask each in turn, "Where's the key to the barn?" and each child would reply, "I don't know. Ask my neighbor." Until one of them suddenly shouted, "Get out the way you got in!" which was the signal for the bull to try to break through the encircling arms. It was a rough game that usually ended with someone running home, bawling at the top of his lungs. Jack enjoyed it, but he dreaded meeting Father.

"I'd rather stay," he said.

"Suit yourself." The Bard bade him a cheery good-bye,

and Pega skipped out with the picnic basket. Jack heard her warbling all the way down the path.

It was a bright, sunny day, but by contrast, the inside of the Roman house was dark. It suited Jack's mood. He'd been thrown out by Father, and now the Bard had deserted him. Jack took down his practice harp and played a few melancholy tunes to make himself feel more wretched. He thought about running away to Bebba's Town. The Bard and Pega would find him gone and be sorry. But another thought trickled like cold water down his spine: *Maybe they wouldn't miss me at all.*

After a while Jack went outside to work in the herb garden. *I should soak beans for dinner,* he thought, but he'd got used to Pega doing all the cooking. She made an excellent eel stew with barley, leeks, dill, and a touch of vinegar. It was unlike anything he'd ever eaten. Pega had been traded so many times up and down the coast that she had a large stockpile of recipes. The thought of eels reminded Jack of the spears Colin had been so excited about.

I should have asked the Bard to get one, he thought. He had a few silver coins left. Very few, thanks to Pega. At least she cooked and did her share of hunting. She had a peculiar skill in catching trout. She lay on her stomach by a stream and wiggled a finger like a fat worm. Sooner or later a trout drifted over, and she tickled it under the chin—did trout *have* chins? When it had fallen under her spell, she whisked it up into a bag.

Jack's thoughts kept coming back to Pega. She got into everything, like the mice during the harvest. To distract himself, he blew the hearth into life. He would practice farseeing, the one thing she hadn't managed to invade.

The flames were streaked with green and blue, and the fire rustled like a wind in a sail. Jack began the spell.

I seek beyond
The folds of the mountains
The nine waves of the sea . . .

He saw the painted bird on its reed cane. There were small daisies at the base of the rosebush and a fretwork of vines beyond. The leaves extended back into green darkness, against which the bird shone brightly. Its chest was puffed out with cream-colored feathers, and its wings were a lively brown. Jack thought it was a wren.

He circled three times three, paused, and began again. Boredom crept over him, and it seemed he had walked in this circle for years. He was hardly aware of movement anymore, only of the slow passage of images beyond the seeing tube. The room faded and suddenly—

Jack stopped. The bird was perched with its tiny claws fastened on to the cane. *It had a grasshopper in its beak!*

There had been no grasshopper before. Jack was sure of it. He couldn't possibly have missed such a detail. A long sliver of light gleamed on the cane. Jack turned to see where it was coming from and saw a small fire on an expanse of sand. Beyond lay the sea. Two boys were rolling over and over in a fierce fight. One of them had a bloody nose, and he was mouthing words Jack was sure were curses. Nothing could be heard.

The other boy seemed to be winning the battle. He thrust the first one into the sand and put his foot on his throat.

A man ran up. Jack's heart stood still. *It was Eric Pretty-Face! No one else had those horrible battle scars.*

Eric Pretty-Face pulled them apart like a pair of squabbling puppies and threw one in each direction. The boy with the bloody nose jumped to his feet and began screaming. The other one roared with laughter.

Turn, turn, Jack willed the boy who was jumping up and down and taunting his adversary. Then at last the boy did turn to show a triumphant, none-too-clean face.

Thorgil, thought Jack. He missed her—oh, heavens, how he had missed her!—and yet he hadn't been aware of it till now. The gray-green sea stretched out behind her, and a wind ruffled her chopped-off hair. All the excitement of sailing to the north came back to him. He could almost feel the deck move under his feet and hear the timbers creak. Somewhere a wind blew off a glacier from an ice mountain folded into itself.

"Jack!" Someone was tugging at his sleeve. The vision collapsed, and he was back in the Roman house. Pega was there, yanking on his arm, her froggy mouth opening and shutting as she spoke.

Rage swept over Jack. To have finally achieved his goal and have it snatched away drove him into a fury. He struck Pega across the mouth and sent her spinning. She fell to her hands and knees and scuttled out of reach.

"Jack!" cried another voice. The boy swung around.

"Mother?" he whispered.

"This is very, very bad," said the Bard, hurrying past Mother to lift up Pega. "Oh, my poor dear!" Her chin was dripping blood. She wasn't crying, only staring at him with wide, frightened eyes.

"Mother," Jack said again, dazed by what he'd just done.

"I came to fetch you home," Mother said. "Lucy's gone mad."

Chapter Seven

GILES'S SECRET

Jack followed his mother down the path. He was shaky, as though he were coming down with fever. He remembered his hand striking Pega's mouth and her spinning away. An ache in his arm told him how hard he had hit her.

"Why did you do that?" came Mother's quiet voice.

Jack didn't know why the rage had swept over him. It was just so wonderful to see Thorgil. He'd never expected to, not in this life or in Heaven. Girls like Thorgil didn't end up in Heaven, not even close. And then Pega spoiled it, coming between him and the vision.

"I suppose I'm jealous," Jack said.

"Of *Pega*?" said Mother, amazed. She had wanted to treat

the girl's injury, but the Bard had waved her away.

"Pega will recover more quickly with that boy out of here," he'd said.

That boy. Jack cringed inwardly. "I know it's wicked to be jealous," he explained, "but she sings so well and the Bard likes her so much. I'm not sorry I freed her," he went on hastily, "but I thought . . . somehow . . . she'd go away."

"Pega worships you," said Mother. "She tells everyone how wonderful you are."

"She won't now."

They walked on in silence. The path descended from the sea cliff to meadows drenched in wildflowers—cowslips, marigolds, and daisies. Jack and Mother forded a stream buried in ferns. Skylarks called to one another from high above the ground.

As they drew near the farm, Mother stopped. "I must explain," she said. "Ever since the need-fire ceremony, Lucy hasn't been right in the head. Oh, she behaves well enough around others. She can feed herself and talk, but she's become convinced she's a real princess."

"She went mad in the Northland too," said Jack.

Mother gazed at the farmhouse with its thread of smoke coming from the smoke hole. "Lucy has always been fanciful. So has Giles."

Jack could see it worried her to criticize Father.

"He knows what's real and what isn't," Mother went on. "Lucy doesn't. She orders us around like servants. She won't let her father touch her, says he's a peasant. It hurts him."

"I hurt him," Jack said. "What makes you think he won't throw me out again?"

"Your father is sorry for what he did. He won't admit it, but if you ask his forgiveness, he'll give it."

"He'll also thrash me."

Mother sighed. "He probably will." And then she added with a hint of mischief, "You could always offer up your pain to God." Jack was startled. Father went on and on about how pain was good for you and how you could offer it up to God. Mother had never contradicted him. It seemed she had her own ideas on the subject.

Why do I always have to be the one in the wrong? thought Jack as they continued on. But he knew he deserved a thrashing for striking Pega. What had possessed him to do such a thing?

Jack had not been home in months, and he was shocked at his father's appearance. The man's shoulders were hunched, as though he carried a heavy burden. His face was full of shadows. He crouched on a stool by the hearth and whittled a chunk of wood. It wasn't normal for Father to be indoors at this time of day. A farm in springtime wasn't a place you could ignore.

"What muck!" Lucy sneered, throwing a clumsily carved animal into the fire. "You'll never be as good as Olaf One-Brow. Never, never, never! He made me beautiful toys." She was dressed in her white Yule dress, now smudged with soot, and wore the necklace of silver leaves.

"Father?" said Jack, swallowing hard. Giles Crookleg looked up. "Father, I've come to apologize."

"So you should," said the man.

Jack forced down a surge of anger. "I was wrong to hide the money. It was disloyal and dishonest. I'm here to take whatever punishment you think fit."

"I'd say you deserve it." Giles reached into the heap of kindling and selected a birch rod. Jack mustered his courage. Father hit hard and thought anything less than six of the best was a holiday.

"You've been bad," Lucy announced smugly, wiping her hands on her grimy Yule dress. "I shall enjoy watching you suffer." Jack promised himself to take the silver necklace away the first time he got her alone. Father grabbed Jack's hair and raised the birch rod. The boy braced himself.

But instead of striking him, Giles Crookleg hurled the rod away and sank to his knees. "I can't do it! I can't do it!" he cried. He began to howl.

Jack was horrified. He'd never seen his father so distraught. "It's all right, Da," he said uncertainly.

"I shouldn't have lied," the man wailed. "It's my fault. Lucy's my fault. It was the sin of pride."

"You must lie down, Giles," Mother said, kneeling beside him. "I think you have a fever—yes, I can feel it. Come to the loft. I'll get you a healing drink."

Jack and Mother walked Father to the ladder. He climbed slowly and painfully with Jack behind in case he fell. Giles crawled into bed, still sobbing, and Mother brought him a tea of lettuce and willow to make him sleep. Presently, he went off to whatever dreams awaited him.

Jack sat by the fire, too stunned to talk. What had Father lied about? What sin had he committed?

"I did *not* give him permission to sleep," said Lucy, curling her hair around her finger and pursing her rosebud lips. "I shall have my knights thrash him."

Jack felt a tremor of dread as he looked at his sister. She had gone mad, and so, apparently, had Father. After what he'd done to Pega that morning, Jack wondered if he had too.

It was a long, depressing afternoon. A boy from another farm arrived to help with chores. Most of the black-faced sheep had been driven to pasture, but a pair of milking ewes remained. They tried to force their way through the fence the boys were repairing, to get at the peas and beans. When they failed, they chased poor Bluebell for sheer malice until she fell down with exhaustion. Jack had to shut her into the barn.

Ewes could leap onto a stone wall taller than a man, pause delicately with all four feet together, and spring to the other side. But a fence stopped them because they couldn't balance on the narrow top. Jack watched with satisfaction as the ewes attempted the leap and failed.

Jack ignored Lucy's repeated attempts to give him orders. He didn't think she was really out of her mind. She wasn't like Daft Tom, the miller's father, who had to be tied to a tree to keep him from harm. Lucy had simply hidden herself away, as she had when Queen Frith held her captive. With patience, Jack thought he could call her back.

I could try farseeing, he thought. *I found Thorgil. Would it be any different hunting for Lucy?* But it might be very different. Thorgil inhabited the same world as he did. In what strange realm was Lucy wandering?

Shortly before sundown the Bard arrived at the door of the farmhouse with Pega in his wake. "We'll sort things out, Alditha," the Bard told Mother. He frowned at Lucy in her smudged dress and at Father hunched by the fire. "You can stop staring, Jack," the old man said. "Pega's decided to forgive you." Jack saw to his horror that her mouth was swollen and she had a long cut on her lip.

"I—I didn't mean to hit you. I'm awfully sorry," he stammered.

"I've been hit harder. Dozens of times," boasted the girl.

"Well, um." Jack's wits were scattered by her response. "That's not good either."

"I, however, was not sure about forgiving you," said the Bard. "It's vile and shameful to hit someone who barely comes up to your shoulder."

Jack said nothing. What could he say?

"But I've been thinking about this family all afternoon. It seems nothing has gone right since the need-fire ceremony."

Silence fell over the room. The last long rays of sunlight faded from the doorway, and the hearth fire, by contrast, grew brighter. It was a mild spring evening with hardly a breath of wind. Jack heard a nightingale call from the apple tree by the barn.

"There were dark forces abroad that night," said the Bard.

"The door lay open between life and death, and it was of critical importance to have an innocent child receive the flame. Unfortunately, Lucy was not innocent." He gazed intently at the little girl. She stared back at him, untroubled by his concern. "At first I thought only Lucy was vulnerable to whatever crept through, but it seems she has passed it on. I should have guessed it when Giles tried to buy Pega."

"It's my fault! It's the sin of pride!" Father moaned, rocking back and forth.

The Bard glared at him and continued. "I've been worried about you as well, Alditha. You were forbidden to see Jack, but a loving mother would have sent messages to him. It seemed you had closed your heart."

"I hadn't! I swear," cried Mother. "But things were so difficult here."

"It's not like you to be cruel," the old man said, "yet you called Jack back, knowing Giles would probably beat him. This morning, when I saw what Jack had done to Pega, I was prepared to turn him into a toad *at the very least.* What were you thinking of, lad? You could have broken her jaw!"

"I—I wasn't thinking," Jack said. He wanted to crawl under a rock and never come out.

"I raised my staff, but Pega caught my arm. 'He's not like that,' she said. 'He didn't know what he was doing.' And I realized she was right. If it hadn't been for her, lad, you'd be hopping around a swamp right now."

"Thank you, Pega," said Jack humbly.

"It's the least I can do for someone who freed me from

slavery," Pega declared. "Besides, I've been hit by champions. Your blow wasn't even in third place."

Jack had trouble sorting out the compliments from the insults in that statement.

"Harm came to Lucy during the ceremony. It spread to Giles and then to Alditha. Last of all, it came to Jack," said the Bard. "It's like a fever in the life force. For all I know, it will infect the whole village."

It was entirely dark outside now, and a cool breeze began to stir from the hills to the west. Mother got up to close the door. The hearth cast a dancing light, and everyone's shadow stretched out behind him or her to make giant figures on the walls.

"Why hasn't anyone given me dinner?" demanded Lucy. The light glittered coldly on her necklace of silver leaves. While the hearth was warm and yellow, the light on the necklace had a blue quality that made you think of glaciers and frozen lakes.

"We'll eat later," said Mother.

"I want food now!" shouted Lucy. "I'm a princess, and I don't have to wait! Tell that froggy slave to get moving!"

Pega jumped up with her fists clenched. "You take that back! I'm no slave!"

"Froggy, froggy, froggy," taunted Lucy. Pega lunged, but the Bard blocked her path.

"That's how it begins!" he cried, raising his staff. Jack felt a wave of heat, and Pega sank down where she stood. The air rustled as though something was flying over the house on giant wings. The Bard lowered his staff, and the moment passed.

"That's how the contagion moves," the old man said. "It brings a fever and a rage. We must drive it off before it consumes all of us. The first thing is to get rid of that necklace."

"No!" screamed Lucy. "It's mine! It's mine! It was given to me by my real mother! I won't let any of you touch it!" She became completely hysterical then, and Father placed himself between her and the others.

"I won't let you hurt her," he said.

"Giles, you loon, we're trying to help her," said the Bard. "She was vulnerable during the need-fire ceremony because of that necklace. It must go." Mother, Jack, and Pega stood behind the old man. Jack felt somewhat hysterical himself. It seemed possible they would have to overpower Father, and the outcome of that wasn't certain. Father might be lame, but he'd been hardened by years of farmwork. He was as tough as an old oak tree and as stubborn as a black-faced ram.

"It's not her fault, see," Giles Crookleg said. "It's mine, from a lie I told long ago. I knew better—yes, I did—but I had the sin of pride. I was tempted and found wanting. Now the wages of sin have come upon me."

The Bard sat down on a bench and rubbed his eyes. "You're making even less sense than usual. I swear you're responsible for half the headaches in this village." The dangerous tension in the room ebbed away. Jack and Pega settled themselves at the Bard's feet, and Jack was heartily grateful they hadn't come to blows.

"You'd better tell me about that lie, Giles," said the old man, massaging his forehead. "From all the sin you keep going on about, I'm sure it's going to be spectacular."

Chapter Eight

THE LOST CHILD

"Lucy was only two days old," Father began, "but Alditha was sick with milk fever. She was unable to nurse the infant. Fortunately, the tanner's wife had just given birth to a child. I packed Lucy in a basket and carried her to the tannery, which, as you know, is on the other side of the hazel wood."

Jack knew the place—who didn't? Before the tanner had died two years ago, you could smell his workyard long before you could see it. He soaked hides people brought him in a great lime pit. After the hair had fallen off, he scraped the skins, soaked them in a sludge of bark to turn them brown, and packed them in whatever rotten fruit he could beg from farmers. He finished with a coating of pig and chicken manure. To say the place reeked like the back gate of Hell didn't even come close.

But it was a matter of life and death, Jack realized, for Lucy to be taken there. He half remembered her being gone. He'd been more concerned with Mother's illness at the time.

"The tanner's wife, bless her, nursed Lucy until Alditha recovered," Father said. "I went to fetch the infant home, and on the way back I saw that the ground of the hazel wood was covered with ripe nuts. It was a fine opportunity. That late in the season, the wild pigs had usually cleaned them up. I wedged Lucy's basket into the branches of an elder tree at the edge of the wood. She was well hidden there, sleeping like a little angel. I remember thinking how like me she was."

Jack, the Bard, and Mother all sat up straight. Pega, not being that familiar with the family, continued to watch Father with rapt attention. The others knew that Lucy was nothing like Giles Crookleg. That was the wonder of her. She was golden-haired and blue-eyed, as pretty as a sunbeam in a dark forest.

"I thought she'd be safe," mourned Father. "I thought nothing could reach her. I filled a bag with hazelnuts, and when I returned, I saw something move in the elder tree. I dropped the bag and ran. I heard the most terrible keening noise, worse than the howling of wolves. From all sides of the elder tree jumped a swarm of . . . *things*.

"They were like small, misshapen men, dappled and spotted as the grass on a forest floor. They moved around in a dizzying way, first visible, then melting into the leaves, then visible again. They scuttled around like spiders, passing a bundle from one to the other, and I saw—I saw—*that it was Lucy!*"

Father bent double, almost putting his head on his knees. Jack thought the man was going to be sick. He felt sick himself at the thought of that tiny baby being tossed back and forth. Mother had turned white with shock.

"What happened next?" asked the Bard.

Giles Crookleg sat up, his face twisted with pain. "I tried to catch them, but they kept weaving back and forth, tossing the baby between them. They sped off through the trees and up into the hills, away from the village. They went under branches so low, I couldn't follow and through gaps so narrow, I had to go around. I cursed my lameness. My speed was no match for theirs. They pulled away, going farther and farther ahead until they were only a blur in the distance. And then they were gone.

"Still I ran, calling and promising them anything if only they would give me back my child. But they never answered. There were dozens of trails in the forest, dozens of little streams and valleys. I searched one after the other until darkness began to fall. At last I returned to the elder tree. I knelt down under it and prayed to God for mercy, if not for me, for Alditha.

"And as I prayed, I heard the wonderful, warbling sound of a happy baby. I climbed up to the basket, and there, wrapped in a blanket, was the most beautiful infant I had ever seen. I knew God had sent her," said Giles Crookleg, his eyes alight with joy. He looked utterly transported, but as the moments passed with no one breaking the silence, the rapture faded from his face.

"I *hope* God sent her," he said.

It broke the spell. "Do you mean Lucy isn't my child?" cried Mother.

"I told you I wasn't," said Lucy comfortably. Of all the people in the room, she was the only one who wasn't dismayed. She stretched her arms like a cat and yawned delicately. "Da always said I was a princess."

"Why didn't you tell me the truth?" shrilled Mother. "I would have taken this Lucy, but I'd have searched for the other one. The whole village could have helped."

"Yes, well, you were ill. You were quite out of your head for a while."

"Not then! Not when you came back! I thought the baby looked different, but I'd only seen her briefly. Oh, Giles, how could you?"

"I was tempted and found wanting," Father said in a hollow voice. "I fell into sin. Don't think I haven't scourged myself for weakness!"

"Please stop offering up your pain to God," the Bard said wearily. "We have a serious problem, and it hasn't been helped by your deception." He walked over to Lucy and looked into her eyes. Mother had sunk to a bench. She hardly seemed to breathe. Jack felt he was in a bad dream. How could Lucy stop being his sister? But he had to admit she sometimes acted strangely.

"Who is she, sir?" he asked the Bard.

"That is a most interesting question," the old man replied. "I've seen changelings"—Father moaned and Mother caught her breath—"but never one like this. Changelings, poor things, are misfits in our world."

"Could I be one?" Pega said suddenly. Jack looked up to see her anguished face. It was half in shadow from the birthmark and half pale with fear. "I've often thought I was. The chief's wife has a mirror made of polished bronze, and I looked into it."

"No, my dear," the Bard said gently. "Changelings are always terrified because they've been torn from their rightful place. They fall into terrible rages and scream until everyone is driven mad. But changelings don't understand what they're doing, for they can't understand other people's feelings. You, my child, are not like that."

Pega's relief was so obvious, it was painful to watch.

"Lucy . . . ," the Bard said hesitantly, "*seems* to care, and yet her emotions flit by like sunlight on a stream."

"She cares for me," Giles said stoutly.

"When it suits her."

"Well, she's not a changeling, and that's that. Everyone loves her," declared Father.

"That's because I'm a princess," said Lucy, fluffing her pretty golden hair.

"I need to think about this," the Bard said, ignoring Lucy's adorable smile. "Such a fine spring evening shouldn't be spoiled with useless worry." The old man removed an oilskin packet from his carrying bag. It contained four excellent smoked trout that Pega had caught. Mother had already prepared barley cakes and a pot of parsnips mashed with a knob of butter.

Pega helped to serve dinner. She set to work as easily as she had in the Bard's house, and Mother thanked her warmly for it. *I helped too,* Jack thought. *I mended fences all day and chased evil-hearted ewes. No one paid the slightest attention to me. Nobody ever does. Good heavens, I sound like a whiny three-year-old. It must be that fever the Bard was talking about.* And he forced himself to look pleasant.

The Bard entertained them with a story about an island made entirely of ice, on which he had spent a week. He'd had a battle with a troll-bear floating on the same island and drove it into the sea.

Jack's thoughts kept going back to Lucy. She had always been different from the rest of them, so fair and golden-haired. It wasn't only her coloring. She moved in a way that made you glad. Her smile made you forget how irritating she'd been a moment before. Even Jack, who wasn't as besotted as Father, found himself laughing for no good reason when she chose to be pleasant.

The Bard and Pega stayed the night, for which Jack was grateful. He felt uncomfortable around Father. There wasn't enough bedding for all of them, so of course the Bard got the best of it. Jack and Pega made do with meager piles of straw, while Lucy, as befitted a lost princess, slept on a heap of fluffy sheepskins.

Jack woke before dawn, cold and irritable. The Bard was

already sitting by a lively fire and beckoned him to the hearth as though nothing had happened the day before. "I've been thinking about your sister," the old man said, poking the flames with his staff.

"I suppose she isn't really my sister," Jack said. In a way it felt as though Lucy were dead, though of course she was sleeping in the loft.

"It isn't a matter of blood ties, lad. All your life you've cared for her, and that makes her your sister in your heart. What concerns me is what *she* is capable of feeling."

The dawn chorus of birds was beginning—the whistle of robins, burble of wrens, and trill of thrushes. Beyond them all, in orchards and woodlands, crows called to one another as if reassuring themselves that their comrades had survived the night. Thorgil would have understood what they were saying, though she found their empty-headed chatter annoying.

"I saw Thorgil, sir," Jack blurted out. "When I was farseeing."

"You succeeded? Well done!"

Jack basked in the praise. He explained how he'd seen the painted bird sitting on the cane and how it suddenly had a grasshopper in its beak.

"That happens when the vision comes alive," the Bard explained. "You saw the bird as he was when the old Roman painted him."

"There was a light on the cane, and when I turned to find out where it was coming from, I saw a fire on a seashore. Thorgil was having a fight with a strange boy."

"That sounds about right," the Bard said. "Tell me, was the water to the east or west of them?"

Jack was suddenly swept with longing, and the vision strengthened in his mind. He saw the gray-green sea stretched out beyond the fire. The sun was rising above a fog bank far out on the water. And that meant—that meant—"The water lay to the east!"

The Bard nodded. Jack understood at once. The Northmen had crossed the sea again. What were they planning? Was Thorgil even now sailing down the coast with a band of berserkers?

The Bard put his finger to his lips. "We'll speak of this later." Jack heard Lucy complaining from the loft and Father apologizing. Pega sat up abruptly with straw dripping from her wispy hair. She sprang into action, storing bedding, lining up cups, and placing a poker in the fire to heat cider. Jack appreciated her efforts, but sometimes her incessant energy made him feel tired. Before Mother arrived, Pega had the iron pot, purchased with Jack's silver, on the hearth and was heating water for oatmeal. Father lurched down the ladder with Lucy in his arms.

"Where's my cider?" the little girl demanded. "I'm *dying* of thirst. I like my porridge with lots of honey."

"I'll help you," Jack said hastily, before Pega could drop the poker on Lucy's head. He took the skin bag and filled the cups. Mother took over the task of preparing oatmeal.

"I want to see Brother Aiden," she said, looking down at her work.

"Of course," Father replied meekly.

"Excellent idea!" said the Bard. "I have questions for him too. I'm fairly certain what those creatures in the hazel wood were, but Brother Aiden's opinion would be useful."

"I want to know where they live." Mother stirred the oatmeal without looking up. "I want you to find them, Giles, and bring our daughter home, and I want this to happen immediately, with no side trips to drink ale with the blacksmith. Do you hear me?"

It was so rare for Mother to give orders that everyone stared at her in amazement. People forgot she was a wise woman with knowledge of small magic and an ability to control animals by voice alone. She was using that voice now. No one spoke, not even the Bard. Jack felt the air tremble.

"Do you hear me, Giles?" repeated Mother.

"Yes, dearest," said Father. The air stopped vibrating. Everyone relaxed and continued with whatever he or she was doing.

Chapter Nine

BROTHER AIDEN

Mist was curling up from the fields and meadows as they walked to Brother Aiden's hut. Lucy insisted on riding Bluebell, though Jack thought it would have done her good to walk.

Brother Aiden was sitting outside, his face turned toward a flock of swallows wheeling in the upper air. He regarded them with an expression of such joy that Jack looked up to see if he'd missed something. They were ordinary birds swooping and twittering, but Jack noticed that they never strayed far from Brother Aiden's hut.

"They're worshipping God," said the little man, waking from his trance to greet his visitors. When Brother Aiden turned his attention from the sky, the swallows drifted away toward the hazel wood.

The chamber inside the beehive hut was dark and cramped, with a tiny altar topped by a small pewter cross. Father had made him a stool and worktable, as well as a chest to store supplies. When everything was inside, there was scarcely room for the monk himself. And so Father had built him a shed for cooking. Beside this neat little compound was a garden for herbs and vegetables.

When the weather was good, Brother Aiden dragged his table outside to work on a copy of the scriptures. He was working on it now, and his inks were lined up next to goose quills and brushes tipped with marten fur. He had only three pieces of parchment, but he worked so slowly, it didn't matter. The parchment was covered in swirling designs with odd little details like vines or snakes or eyes.

"Do they truly worship?" Father said in wonder, watching the swallows fly away.

"All things praise Him," Brother Aiden said. "When St. Cuthbert used to meditate in cold seawater up to his neck, the otters swarmed over his feet to dry them when he came out."

Jack was about to ask how something as wet as an otter could dry anything when he was silenced by a stern look from the Bard.

"We've come to you with questions," the old man said.

"I'll do my best, though you know I'm not greatly educated."

"You'll do," said the Bard, smiling. "Giles has just revealed that his girl Lucy isn't his." And he recounted the story of the elder tree and swarm of little men.

"Interesting," said Brother Aiden. "They sound like pookas."

"Pookas?" said Jack, to whom the term was unfamiliar.

"Or hobgoblins. They go by many names," said the Bard. "I thought of them too."

"I can't bear to think of my child being carried off by those—those *things*! Is she even alive?" cried Mother.

"My poor Alditha!" Brother Aiden grasped her hands. "We're a pair of fools, talking about your daughter as though she were only an amusing problem. I think it very likely your child is alive. Pookas aren't evil, just mischievous. They sometimes turn milk sour or knock holes in buckets. Nothing major."

"But what did they want with her?"

Brother Aiden and the Bard exchanged glances. "That's the only flaw in the theory," said the Bard. "I've never heard of pookas stealing a baby."

"If they did, I'm sure they'd be kind to it," Brother Aiden said.

Mother slumped down with her face in her hands, and Father, hesitantly, as though he expected to be rebuffed, knelt beside her. "I'll look for them. I'll offer them a ransom," he said.

"You don't know where they live." Mother's voice was muffled.

"That's where I might be of help," said the Bard. "There are ways into their land if you know where to look. And, of course, I do. Pookas live in caves under the ground, and I visited them often when I was a young man. They're fond of dark forests and mountains with rushing streams. The nearest place like that is the Forest of Lorn."

The Forest of Lorn, thought Jack. What a wonderful name! The very sound of it was exciting. He could almost see craggy ravines overhung with ferns. "Where is it, sir?" he asked eagerly.

"A few days' journey north of Bebba's Town."

"If the creatures lived that far away, what were they doing here?" said Father.

"You don't know pookas," the Bard said. "They'll run thirty miles to gather hazelnuts and be home in time for dinner. They're crazy about hazelnuts."

"If only I hadn't stopped in the woods," moaned Father.

"Well, you did, and that brings us to the second question," the Bard said. "Where did they get Lucy from?"

Everyone turned to her. She was picking wildflowers next to Brother Aiden's garden like any normal child. But then she thrust them at Pega and said in a nasty voice, "Weave them into a crown for me, froggy."

"Do it yourself, bedbug," retorted the girl. *Bedbug* was Pega's worst insult. She absolutely hated the bloodsucking creatures, having been locked into a hut swarming with them by one of her owners.

The Bard explained about Lucy's change of behavior since

the need-fire ceremony and the anger that had spread from Giles to Alditha to Jack.

"She might be possessed," observed Brother Aiden. "It's well known that demons are attracted to children who are indulged by their parents. The souls of children forced to endure hardships are too tough for demons to get their teeth into. They go after the tender lambs."

"Don't say things like that!" begged Father.

"I'm sorry. That's just the way things are," the little monk said. "Exorcism might do Lucy a world of good."

"She's not possessed!"

"Call it madness or a demon or whatever you like, something happened at the ceremony," the Bard argued.

"Oh, please stop," Mother broke in, and Jack was aware of how tired she looked. For the first time he saw strands of gray in her hair and lines on either side of her mouth. They must have been there before, but he hadn't noticed them. "Lucy draws away from us more each day. At first she only claimed to be someone else's daughter—little did I know how true that was!—but now she talks to people I can't see and repeats conversations I can't hear."

Jack saw that his little sister was talking to someone at that very moment. She was seated on the grass with the flowers she had picked scattered around her. She was looking at a spot just above Brother Aiden's herb garden. Her face was filled with joy, and she clasped her hands as though she were watching the most delightful entertainment.

"You didn't mention this before, Alditha," said Father.

"How could I, with you going on and on about demons?"

There was nothing in the herb garden except rosemary, mint, and sage, and a few bees hovering over the flowers.

"Lucy," said the Bard gently. "What do you see?"

She turned abruptly, her face contorted with rage. "Leave us!" she snarled. "You have not been given permission to speak."

"Then I ask permission," the old man said, and Jack wondered at his patience.

Lucy seemed confused for a moment. She turned toward the herb garden and back again. "You may speak," she said.

"I fear I cannot see your friends."

"That's because you're a commoner," said the little girl.

"Lucy!" cried Mother.

"It's all right. I'd like it very much, Lucy, if you'd give your friends my greetings."

The little girl turned toward the herb garden and spoke earnestly. Her lips moved, but no sound came out. The Bard came closer and watched the garden intently. Finally, she replied. "They say you are a foolish old man with hair growing out of your ears." Mother started to protest, but the Bard held up his hand.

"All true except the foolish part," he said. "Tell me, do these friends have names?"

"They don't like to give their names."

"What are they doing now?"

"Dancing—oh!"

For the Bard had thrown his cloak over the herb garden. He held it down with his foot. "Quick, Jack! Get the other end!" he shouted, but before Jack could react, a sudden fierce wind whipped the cloak back over the old man's head. The cloth wrapped itself tightly around his face. "Get it off me!" he cried in a muffled voice. Jack had to fight to peel the cloth away—it seemed to have a mind of its own!—but then it went limp and fell to the ground.

"I almost had them!" panted the Bard.

"You scared them off!" screamed Lucy. She threw herself down and rolled from side to side gnashing her teeth. When Father tried to pick her up, she struck him with her fists.

"They *were* demons!" Father groaned.

"We aren't sure of that," said the Bard, tidying his beard. "Personally, I think 'demon' is a ragbag category. There're sprites and boggarts, will-o'-the-wisps and pixies, spriggans and flibbertigibbets, not to mention yarthkins—wonderfully different beings. It makes just as much sense to refer to anything with wings as 'bird.'"

Brother Aiden knelt by Lucy and laid a hand on her tossing head. He said nothing, but somehow his touch calmed her as a good farmer's hand calms a frightened lamb.

"She's possessed, isn't she?" said Father.

"I'm not sure," said the little monk. "There's an abbot in Bebba's Town who specializes in such things."

"If you want my opinion, and of course you should," the Bard said, "an abbot wouldn't have the slightest idea how to handle Lucy's problem."

"What's the harm in an exorcism?" Brother Aiden argued.

"An exorcism is like using a boulder to kill a gnat." The

Bard paced around the herb garden as he thought. "It could do as much harm to Lucy as the gnat."

"We can't leave her like this." The little monk stroked Lucy's hair, but her eyes were still bewildered and unseeing.

"Bebba's Town is near the Holy Isle," murmured Father with a faraway look in his eyes. Jack knew he was remembering his visit there long ago, when the kindly monks tried to mend his leg.

"There's no one left on the Holy Isle," Brother Aiden reminded him. "The abbot, Father Swein, lives at St. Filian's Monastery. St. Filian's Well is famous for cures."

"Do you think it could fix my leg?" said Father.

"All things are possible with God, but the well's better known for afflictions of the soul. It might be just the thing for Lucy."

"It would be like going on a pilgrimage," Father said, that faraway look still in his eyes.

"A *pilgrimage*?" echoed Brother Aiden.

"We could go on to the Forest of Lorn," added Jack. All this while a strange feeling was uncurling inside him like a seedling reaching for the sun. He saw a ship leaning into a cold wind on a gray-green sea. Dark trees massed on the shore. *I should have learned my lesson by now,* he thought as the exhilarating sense of adventure grew. *Last time this happened, I almost wound up in a dragon's stomach.* The feeling was too strong to suppress, however.

Despite his joy at returning home from the Northland, Jack had found living in the village somewhat dull—not that he enjoyed bumping into trolls or being carried off by giant spiders. Far from it! But looking back, the trip seemed nicer than it had, in fact, been. *That's the nature of adventures,* Jack thought wisely. *They're nasty while they're happening and only fun later.*

"You could find my lost daughter," murmured Mother.

"Oh, very well," conceded the Bard. "I suppose I can be talked into a trip to the Forest of Lorn. It's years since I talked to pookas." He, too, had a distant look in his eyes.

All of them sat in a daze. A few hours before, their problems had seemed overwhelming. Now, in the bright spring sunlight with the swallows dipping and warbling, a plan unfolded in front of them. Father looked transported, and Jack realized he'd never traveled anywhere, except for that one trip to the Holy Isle. The Bard smiled, remembering things Jack could only guess at, and Jack saw himself walking through a magic forest full of little men.

"If we're going, someone has to pack," Pega said in her practical way, breaking into the reverie. Jack looked up. He couldn't remember anyone inviting *her* along.

"I'll have to look after the farm," said Mother. "I'll ask the tanner's wife and her two daughters to help me. They'll welcome the chance to move out of their miserable cottage."

"I wish you could come," Jack said, sorry to leave her with the work.

"I'm a wise woman," Mother said. "My place is with the fields, the animals, the bees, not a monastery. And besides, it will be a treat to have company to talk to of women's things— only, don't stay away too long!"

"It's settled, then," said the Bard. "I'll bring herbal cures to trade for lodgings, Giles can contribute candles, and Aiden his special inks. You're coming, aren't you, Aiden?"

"On a *pilgrimage*? With a visit to St. Filian's?" cried the little monk. "I wouldn't miss it for the world!"

Chapter Ten

THE PILGRIMAGE

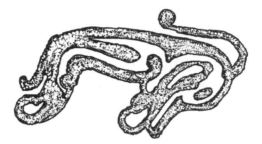

Jack hefted the eel trap and Pega the carrying bag as they set off for the stream. They slid down a grassy bank to where the water was deep and swift. Jack baited the trap with whelks and placed it in a dark side channel—the sort of place eels liked to hide. Then he and Pega sat down in the shade of some alders to wait.

"I'm really sorry I hit you," said Jack, looking uncomfortably at the cut on her lip.

"You went temporarily mad," said Pega. "One of my owners used to go insane once a month at the full moon."

"I'm not *that* bad," Jack said, nettled.

"It's all right. You can beat me up as much as you like. You freed me, so you've earned the right."

"I don't want that right! You're weird," Jack said.

"Not half as weird as your sister. She gets away with things only because she's beautiful."

Jack looked at Pega, surprised by the calm acceptance in her voice. The dappled sunshine spread a pattern of light and shade over her face, lessening the effect of the birthmark. On the other hand, it made her body look speckled. The way she was hunkered down didn't help either. He imagined her going *fiddip* and snagging a fly with her tongue.

"Do you mind . . . her being beautiful?" he said.

"Do you mean, am I jealous? Once, maybe. When I was younger, I used to go out on May Day morning to wash my face in dew. People said it made you pretty, but it didn't work on me." The stream rushed past, and a dark shadow flitted along the bottom and into the side channel. "Just because I'm ugly doesn't mean I hate beautiful things. There's an eel in the trap," she said.

They hauled it up quickly before the creature found its way out. Water splashed over their feet and clothes. It was a big one, three feet long and thrashing for all it was worth. Pega cut off its head with her fish knife and stuffed the still-writhing creature into the carrying bag.

"You're good at this," said Jack, who felt the air shudder with the eel's death.

"I once caught six in a row," boasted Pega. They threw the trap back in. After they had four, Pega loosened the skin around the necks of the eels. With a strong, quick jerk, she pulled it back over the entire body, like someone peeling off a glove. Then she cut the eels open and cleaned them thoroughly in the stream.

Back at the house she hung them, tail down, in a barrel over a smoldering fire. "This is something I learned from one of my owners in Edwin's Town," she explained. For three days and nights the eels dangled, dripping and perfuming everything with burning fish oil. But by the fourth morning they smelled delicious and would stay fresh for a long time.

Jack felt strange when Pega blithely talked about "one of her owners." She seemed to have been traded up and down the coast like an ugly dog. Edwin's Town was so far to the north, they didn't even speak Saxon there.

The weather was perfect when they set out. Birds were caroling from every field and tree. Brother Aiden informed the villagers they passed that they were on a pilgrimage, and everyone smiled and wished them luck. Pilgrimages were highly thought of, the longer the better. You could go to Canterbury or Rome or even Jerusalem, having glorious adventures on the way. Everyone respected you, and if you got martyred on the way, you went straight up to Heaven.

Giles Crookleg walked with his rolling gait, stamping along with more enthusiasm than anyone had seen in him for a long time. This was the life, he declared. He should have been a wandering monk. Lucy rode astride Bluebell, who was loaded with trade goods, as well as the Bard's travel harp. The Bard and Jack walked on either side with their staffs. To passersby, these appeared to be ordinary walking sticks, but with his, the Bard could make a wind blow an enemy off his feet or a bear fall asleep. He promised to teach Jack these skills when they reached the Forest of Lorn. Brother Aiden brought up the rear with Pega.

When they got to the top of a hill, the last place they would be able to see the village, they turned and looked back. It was a peaceful and satisfying scene. Threads of smoke came from a dozen houses, with an especially large plume from the fire pit where the blacksmith made charcoal. "I lay a protection on this valley," said the Bard. He chanted a spell in a language Jack didn't know. Brother Aiden blessed the village in Latin.

Jack squinted to make out his house at the other end of the valley. It shimmered in a warm haze rising from the fields, and from this roof, too, came a wisp of smoke. Mother was baking oatcakes. Not for her was the freedom of a jolly pilgrimage. Chickens and geese had to be fed, weeds pulled, and plants watered. Someone had to supervise the boys sent to help. Jack felt sad leaving her behind, but her joy would be great if he returned with his lost sister.

"I would not leave the village unguarded long," the Bard said now, shading his eyes and looking toward the sea. "Some say the dragon ships are moving again."

"Filthy pirates," said Father.

"May darkness fall upon their eyes. May storms tear open their sails. May they be stranded on the trackless deep with nothing to eat but the wind," said Brother Aiden. It sounded suspiciously like one of the Bard's curses and not the usual prayers the little monk intoned.

Jack was silent. He knew Thorgil was out there somewhere—burning and plundering, no doubt. He had tried to find her again with farseeing, but the vision had eluded him.

"Is it true they turn into wolves?" asked Pega.

Jack remembered Olaf One-Brow panting on the ridge above Gizur Thumb-Crusher's village. "Yes," he replied.

"We must go on," said the Bard. He led the way down the other side of the hill, and soon all trace of human habitation disappeared. Jack's spirits lifted. While he'd explored most of the land around the village, this was new and he liked it: No fields, no houses, and no evil-tempered sheep. Heather, gorse, and broom lay on either side, with woodlands crowding the valleys. The road was deeply rutted and crossed by streams. In some places it disappeared entirely. The king was supposed to maintain it, but Jack's village was of no importance and no one bothered to improve its connection to the outside world.

Just think! I might see a king, Jack thought happily. Bebba's Town was famous for Din Guardi, a fortress larger, older, and grander than any other in the kingdom. The royal court made its home there. Knights rode around on horses as grand as John the Fletcher's, and sometimes they engaged in tournaments for the entertainment of the locals.

I've already seen a king, Jack thought. *Ivar the Boneless, and what a disappointing wretch he was. A Saxon lord will certainly be more noble.*

Their progress was slow. Giles Crookleg, in spite of his enthusiasm, had to rest frequently, and the Bard also tired easily. Lucy demanded constant attention. She was cross about her travel clothes, which were sensibly roomy and mud-colored to hide the dirt. "You have to hide your presence from your enemy," Father explained. It was the beginning of a long, meandering story involving a giant called Bolster, whose wish was to enslave a princess to wash his clothes. At each stop Father pointed out a huge rock Bolster had thrown or a log he had used for a toothpick.

Jack didn't mind the slowness of their trip. The longer it took, the more he could soak up new sights and smells. They passed a rookery of crows, gathering in the late afternoon. The birds came from all directions, in ones and twos and threes, until they covered a giant oak so thickly, you could hardly see the leaves. The air was full of caws, warbles, hiccups, and croaks, and the Bard listened attentively, though he didn't reveal what he learned.

The pilgrims camped under an ash tree and ate onions, smoked eel, and travel scones. The scones had been made in a most unusual way. Pega had kneaded a dough of coarse wheat flour, butter, and salt. This she patted out onto a flat stone and attacked with a wooden mallet. She pounded and folded again and again until the dough was covered with little blisters and had a silky sheen. The scones were baked on a griddle and would not grow stale or hard, Pega said, for several weeks.

Now, under the tree with the fire snapping and the stars twinkling, the travel scones were as good as Yule cake. Even Lucy liked them. They drank cider, and Brother Aiden produced a sack of homemade ale, which Jack and Pega were allowed to taste. "You won't find that anywhere," said the Bard. "It's from a secret recipe. You'll never guess what's in it, my girl."

"I will so," said Pega, but her eyebrows raised with surprise when she tasted it. Jack couldn't begin to describe the flavor. It was like wind off a moor, the moon on a lake, a leaf uncurling in spring.

"This is incredible," he exclaimed.

Brother Aiden preened visibly. "One of my ancestors was captured by a Scottish king. He was promised his life, the hand of a princess, and a bag of gold if he would reveal the recipe. He preferred to die."

"That's what I call a serious cook," Pega said with approval.

"I feel like singing," announced Father, and at once he gave them a hymn:

> *Praise we now the Fashioner of Heaven's fabric,*
> *The majesty of His might and His mind's wisdom,*
> *Work of the World-warden, Worker of all wonders,*
> *How He the Lord of Glory everlasting,*
> *Made first for the race of men Heaven as a rooftree,*
> *Then made He Middle Earth to be their mansion.*

Jack was astounded. Father never sang! Not once in his life could the boy remember it happening, yet his father's voice was deep and good, a real bard's voice.

"That was written by Brother Caedmon long ago. You performed it extremely well," said Brother Aiden.

Father blushed like a child. "I learned it on the Holy Isle. No better place."

"No better place," agreed the little monk. "Give us more." So Father sang about the Creation and the naming of animals by Adam and the sailing of Noah's ark. He had memorized dozens of hymns. The wonder of it was how they had lain in his mind so long, waiting for this night.

"You do surprise me, Giles," said the Bard. "All this time I thought Jack got his musical talent from his mother."

"I learned the hymns of Caedmon because they were in Saxon and I could understand them," Father explained. "Also, because he'd been a farm brat like me."

"He used to run from parties, afraid someone would ask him to sing," Brother Aiden remembered. "Went out to sleep with the cattle. Then, one night, an angel came to him in a dream and taught him that first poem. We should all be so lucky!"

Father told them about how he'd been taken to the Holy Isle as a child so the monks could cure his deformed leg. They failed, he said, but they'd given him a glimpse into a world where all was orderly and beautiful. For the first time ever Jack heard his father speak without a trace of self-pity. He was simply happy to relive that supreme experience of his life.

The Bard struck up his harp and began a ballad they all knew about a rascally elvish knight and a clever village girl. He took the part of the knight and Pega was the girl. Then they all sang together, except Lucy, who had nodded off to sleep. Eventually, they all stretched out under the ash tree. The stars shone between the branches like fruit on the great tree Yggdrassil.

That night Jack dreamed of music so fair, he thought his heart would break, but when he awoke at dawn, the memory of it had vanished.

Chapter Eleven

THE LADY IN THE FOUNTAIN

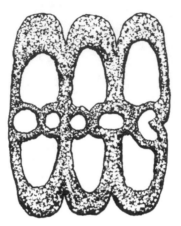

Bebba's Town more than lived up to Jack's expectations. The marketplace was crowded with tradesmen and animals. Rope-makers, tanners, and metalworkers displayed their wares. Woolen cloth, belt buckles, knives, iron griddles, and pottery lined the square, along with cages of wrens, finches, doves, and pigeons destined for someone's dinner.

"Jewels fit for a queen," shouted a metalworker, holding up a brooch studded with garnets as Lucy rode past on Bluebell. Lucy rewarded him with a smile. "By the Lady, she's a bonny lass," the man said to his companion, and they both gazed after her with admiring eyes.

Pega followed, her head bowed to hide her birthmark, but

there was no concealing her scrawny form. The metalworkers looked away, and one spat to the side, a way of averting a curse.

Next to a grassy lawn a man boiled onions in an iron cauldron. He fished them out with a pair of tongs and lined them up on a table. The Bard bought a dozen, and they feasted on hot, steaming onions sprinkled with salt.

"This is delicious," Father said, licking his fingers. "Who knew onions could taste so good?"

"It's the spring air," said the Bard.

"And the crowds," said Brother Aiden. "I love being surrounded by people. Look there. You can see the outline of the Holy Isle."

Jack squinted at the horizon and saw a pale shadow in the deeper gray of the sea. This was where Olaf and Rune, Sven the Vengeful and Eric Pretty-Face—and Thorgil—had slaughtered the innocent monks. It was hard to believe his friends had committed such atrocities, but they had. He must never forget it.

"How can one forgive people who are evil?" he said aloud.

If Brother Aiden was surprised by the sudden shift in conversation, he didn't show it. "We must forgive our enemies. If someone strikes us, we must turn the other cheek. Eventually, God's goodness will prevail."

That was all right if it only involved getting slapped, Jack thought. Northmen didn't just slap people, they cut off their heads.

"It's better not to get hit in the first place," the Bard advised.

"Now we must find a place to spend the night. You may like crowds, Aiden, but thieves and cutpurses like them too."

"We can reach the hostel at St. Filian's by afternoon," said the little monk.

"That's fine for the rest of you. Priests aren't happy when they see people like me on their doorstep," said the Bard. "I'll stay at Din Guardi. They don't like me there, either, but they're afraid of me."

The houses grew more humble as they walked. These were built low to the ground with sagging grass roofs. Small gardens huddled behind ramshackle fences. To the right the cultivated land gave way to sand, and beyond, rising from a rocky shelf jutting out to sea, was an enormous fortress.

Its towers were of dark, distempered stone, and it squatted like a patch of night on the fair coast. Most impressive was a hedge of ancient yew trees standing between the pilgrims and the fortress. The trees massed together so thickly, they looked like a wall and gave Jack an unpleasant feeling, though he didn't know why.

The Bard frowned as though he, too, found the view distasteful. "That is the fortress of Din Guardi," he said. "It has been there since time out of mind. They say one of the old gods built it."

"*Old* gods?" echoed Jack.

"The guardians of the fields, the earth, the trees. The ones who were here before people came. Most of them are asleep and better left so."

"Who lives there now, sir?" asked Jack.

"King Yffi."

"A real king?" said Jack, thrilled by the idea of a court with knights and horses and banners.

"He's a brute. Din Guardi is no place for children, and you're better off at the monastery." The Bard laughed. "But Yffi lays a fine table, and I like throwing him into a panic."

The road presently turned away from the coast and through a flowery meadow beside a rushing stream. They stopped to allow Bluebell to rest, and both Lucy and Pega waded into the water to wash the dust from their feet.

"This is where we part company," the Bard said. "I'll meet you here on the morning of the third day. That's more than enough time for Father Swein to winkle out a demon. And, Jack—"

The boy looked up at the man's sharp tone.

"Don't do anything foolish. Remember where your staff comes from and—well, you know what I'm talking about."

Jack understood, though he didn't think the Bard had anything to worry about. His staff, a copy of the old man's more powerful one, had called fire from the heart of Jotunheim. It still thrummed with power—faintly, to be sure, but still there. Jack had tried to do interesting things with it, such as lift a boulder into the sky or turn back the tide, but all he'd managed was to expel mice from a grain bin.

"We should follow him," Pega said as the Bard strode off.

"He can take care of himself," said Jack, annoyed that she'd thought of it first. "He battled Frith, Half-Trolls, and she was a lot more dangerous than this Yffi sounds."

"An adder is smaller than a wolf, but it can kill you just as dead," the girl retorted.

"There's St. Filian's," called Brother Aiden, pointing at a patch of white beyond a grove of pines on a hill. Behind the dark green branches Jack saw a wall of dazzling brightness that lifted his heart. As they drew nearer, he realized that it was a collection of buildings, all of the same shining hue.

"It's *beautiful*," he said.

"Aye, it is," Brother Aiden said, pleased. "The brothers paint it with lime to give it that color."

Jack gazed at the buildings in wonder. The monastery was buzzing with activity. Family groups waited to be admitted, monks bustled around shouting orders, slaves carried firewood. *Slaves?* thought Jack, amazed to find them here. Very soon Brother Aiden had them settled in the hostel, which was divided into stalls by movable partitions. One of the monastery slaves laid down dried heather for beds.

For all the beauty of the outside walls, the air inside was foul, no doubt due to the latrine at the far end of the building. The place was dank and cold, and the only light came through an open door.

"I didn't know monks were allowed to keep slaves," Jack said.

"Only ones who have lost their freedom through crime," Brother Aiden said. "Serving the church is supposed to improve their souls."

From what Jack saw, it seemed the church had an uphill battle. All the men were marked from earlier punishments—

whip scars, missing ears, slit noses. Two had withered hands, which Brother Aiden said had come from trials by ordeal. "They had to carry a glowing piece of iron nine feet or plunge their hands into boiling water to pick up a stone at the bottom," he said. "Afterward the wound was bound up. If it didn't fester in three days, they were considered innocent. These, clearly, were not."

Jack felt sick when he looked at the twisted flesh of those hands.

"It's a merciful punishment," the little monk explained. "Most thieves are put to death."

"There's nothing merciful about it," Pega muttered under her breath.

They joined a line outside the abbot's office, to make an appointment for Lucy's exorcism. A young monk sat at a table to write down names, the type of complaint, and the expected payment. Whole families accompanied sufferers, some to console them and others to restrain them. One man shouted obscenities and was tied into a blanket to keep him from hurting anyone.

Father held Lucy in his arms to protect her from the sight of raving lunatics. When they got to the table, the recording monk said, "I can see why you brought this one. She's ugly as sin."

"Not her," said Brother Aiden, putting Pega behind him. "The little girl. We fear she's possessed."

The recording monk smiled and reached up to touch Lucy's hair. "I find that hard to believe."

"She sees things that are not there and has delusions of being a princess."

"I *am* a princess," Lucy said, pouting.

"It seems harmless enough," the recording monk said, "but I'll put you down for half past matins tomorrow. What do you barter for her treatment?"

Brother Aiden brought out a small bag and withdrew delicate paintbrushes tipped with marten fur and bottles of brightly colored pigments. "I was the art master on the Holy Isle," he said.

"Oh! That means—oh, my! Father Swein will be so delighted. Are these the *secret* dyes?"

"They are."

Jack looked at Brother Aiden curiously. This was the first he'd heard of him being famous.

"I'll see you're admitted right away," said the young monk. "Shoo! Go away! Come back later," he told the waiting crowd. A pair of monastery slaves detached themselves from a wall and advanced menacingly on the patients and their families.

"Come in!" cried the young monk, unlocking a door. Brother Aiden, Jack, Giles, Lucy, and Pega found themselves in a delightful courtyard surrounded by high white walls and rosebushes. In the middle was a fountain bubbling noisily into a stone bowl. From there, the water spilled into a channel and disappeared through a hole in the wall.

"That's the real St. Filian's Well," the young monk informed them, "but it's too small to treat the mobs who come here. We've diverted the water to a larger pool. We can treat hundreds during the peak season." He disappeared through another door after bidding them to sit and enjoy the roses.

Father put Lucy down, and she ran at once to the bubbling spring. He hastily scooped her up again. "You can't play in it, dearest. It belongs to St. Filian," he told her.

"No, it doesn't. It's *hers*." She pointed at a spot near the stone basin.

"Hush, my lambkin, we don't want to make the saint angry."

Lucy settled into Father's arms and watched the spot. Jack wished the Bard were with them so they could trap whatever-it-was under the old man's cloak. He was convinced Lucy really saw something.

Jack approached the spring cautiously. He could see nothing except the sweet alyssum and lavender planted around the edge. The courtyard was heavy with perfume, and a haze of bees moved among the flowers. And yet something *was* there. He could sense a quickening in the air, a flicker of a creature too swift for him to see.

Jack's staff thrummed in his hand. His hearing caught at a murmur too low to understand but rising and falling as though it were speech. "Come forth," he whispered. "Reveal yourself, spirit of this place. Leave shadow behind and walk in the light of day. I call you by wood, by water, by stone."

The air beyond the fountain shivered and faded, as a meadow dims when fog rolls in from the sea. It was very like mist, except that it occupied only a small area. It drifted in a lazy circle, growing more distinct until Jack was able to see a shape condensing in the middle.

It was a lady dressed in white, an exquisite being whose feet made no impression on the flowers she trod. Her hair was pale gold and her skin was as fair as moonlight. She bent toward Jack's companions, beckoning them with her hand. Father couldn't see her, nor could Pega. Brother Aiden looked uneasy. Lucy watched with great attention.

The lady turned and saw Jack. Instantly, she thrust out her arm, and pain shot through Jack's chest as though he'd been struck with an arrow. The staff dropped from his hand. The sky arched overhead as he fell backward toward the ground.

Chapter Twelve

ST. OSWALD'S HEAD

"Does he have fits?" a man said nearby. Jack opened his eyes on the wooden beams of a low ceiling. Bunches of dried herbs dangled here and there.

"Never," replied Father. "Perhaps he's coming down with a fever."

"If anything, he's too cold. Were you bringing him for a dip in the pool?"

"Just my daughter," said Father.

"He probably only needs a hot meal. I'll have a slave bring soup."

Jack lifted his head. Pain shot down his spine. He saw a monk in a brown robe disappear through a door.

"Good, you're awake. How do you feel?" said Father.

"Like a herd of sheep ran over me." Jack found that any attempt to move swamped him with agony. "Where are we?"

"The monastery hospital. They've been more than nice to us! They moved us out of that smelly hostel and into the best guest rooms. We've been invited to dine with the abbot himself."

Father seemed more interested in their new status than Jack's health. *But I'm being unfair,* the boy thought. *This is the most exciting thing that's ever happened to him.* "Why are we getting special treatment?" he asked.

"It has something to do with those pots of ink Brother Aiden brought. They're made by a secret process known only to the monks of the Holy Isle and are as valuable as gold."

A slave arrived with a pot of lentil soup. "I'm to feed the lad—unless you want to do it," he said hopefully.

But Father was anxious to be off. There was a stained-glass window in the chapel, he said, and a fine herd of white sheep to see. An oak tree in the orchard had the face of St. Filian burned on it by a lightning stroke. Then they were going on a tour of the beer cellar. Imagine having so much beer that you needed a whole cellar to store it! A feast was being laid on that evening. It was a shame Jack couldn't come.

"Listen," said the slave after Father left, "I don't know what kind of mooncalf you are, but if you try to bite me, you're getting my fist for dessert."

"I'm not crazy," Jack said.

"That's what they all say." The slave spooned the soup into

Jack's mouth, not waiting to see whether it was swallowed before shoving the next dose inside.

"Wait! Wait!" sputtered Jack, jerking his head aside. His spine exploded with pain. He froze into position, fearful of any movement.

"What happened? Did you get thrashed?" the slave inquired. "They say thrashing cures everything. Got a sour marriage? Beat your wife. Got an idiot son? Knock sense into him. Father Swein says it works every time."

"You can't believe that rot," said Jack.

"Who am I to judge my betters? In five or ten years they might even beat goodness into me, though I doubt it. Are you ready for more food?"

"If you don't ram it down my throat!"

This time the slave was more careful, and Jack discovered that in spite of the pain, he was hungry. The stew was excellent, a thick pottage of lentils, leeks, and shreds of mutton. It had been days since he'd had anything so satisfying. "What's your name?" he asked the slave.

"Hey You, most of the time," replied the man. "My mother called me Brutus."

"Brutus? Is that Saxon?"

"It's Roman. And, yes"—the slave drew himself up to his full height—"the blood of conquerors flows in my veins. I am of the line of Lancelot, but as you see, I have fallen far from the glory of my ancestors. Father Swein says I'm fit only for pigsties."

Jack wondered what crime Brutus had committed to get

enslaved by a monastery. The man's arms were scarred by whips, and his nose had been broken. But a hint of nobility lay in his wide, intelligent face and gray eyes. "Someone I once knew," Jack said, "told me you should never give up, even if you're falling off a cliff. You never know what might happen on the way down."

Brutus laughed out loud. It was a surprising, joyful sound that completely transformed him. Suddenly, the scars and broken nose didn't matter. "I'd like to meet that fellow! He sounds like a true knight."

"You might not have liked him," said Jack, thinking of Olaf One-Brow's habit of chopping first and asking questions later.

"Might not have? Is he dead?" asked Brutus.

"He died in battle with a giant troll-bear. But he killed the bear," Jack added.

Brutus looked at him sharply. "There's more to you than meets the eye, mooncalf."

"I'm not a mooncalf," protested Jack, and provoked another laugh.

The meal continued pleasantly, except for Jack's grimaces of pain when he moved the wrong way. Brutus was full of tales, and he was clearly in no hurry to return to his chores. "How came you by this affliction?" he said at last.

Jack told him about the beautiful woman who had materialized out of mist. "When she thrust her arm at me, I lost my senses until I woke up here," he finished. "I'm not insane. I really did see her."

The slave sat very still, as though listening to something far away. The sounds of monastery life—wood being chopped, orders shouted, feet stamping—filtered in from outside. Then Brutus shook himself and came back to the present. "You weren't dreaming. You've been elf-shot."

The door flew open, and in came the monk who had treated Jack. "You lazy swine!" the monk shouted. "The cook's been waiting ages for his firewood. You deserve a double whipping!"

Brutus changed before Jack's eyes. He hunched over, and a half-witted expression crossed his face. "Begging your pardon, master," he whined. "You won't be angry with poor Brutus? He's such a poor excuse for a man."

"Oh, be gone with you," said the monk. The slave scuttled out the door.

The monk bustled about, fetching a threadbare blanket and tucking it around Jack. "I've been waiting for you to wake up so I can give you medicine. You're in luck. I happen to have soil from St. Oswald's grave on my shelves. Well, *one* of his graves." He showed the boy a pot of dark dirt that could have come from anywhere.

"This is from where they planted St. Oswald's head. The pagans buried parts of him all over the place after they martyred him. But the head ended up on the Holy Isle, so it's doubly blessed. I always think head soil is the best." The monk boiled water and picked odds and ends from the herbs hanging off the rafters. He finished by dropping a pinch of dirt into the cup. "There! If that doesn't cure you, nothing will."

He held the cup to Jack's lips. The tea tasted of chamomile with a strange mineral background. Oswald's head, no doubt.

"Why is Brutus a slave?" Jack asked when he'd choked down the last gritty bits.

The monk raised his eyebrows. "Has he been filling you up with tales about his noble ancestry? His mother was a miserable witch. When she lay dying of fever, she ordered her boy to drive off the priest with rocks. Refused the last rites, she did. Brutus set her body afloat in a little boat in the belief that it would take her to the Islands of the Blessed. He was condemned for witchcraft."

"For obeying his mother's last wish?" Jack said faintly. Choosing your afterlife seemed entirely reasonable to him. Not everyone was suited to Heaven—look at Thorgil—and the Bard always swore he would go to the Islands of the Blessed.

"No, no. Many fools believe in the Islands of the Blessed. Brutus was condemned for casting spells over women. They absolutely can't resist him . . . young, old, married, single— even the ewes follow him around the fields. We've spent years trying to thrash the magic out of him, but he's hopeless."

Jack lay awake thinking long after the monk left. The room was lit only by coals in the fire pit, and the herbs hanging from the rafters looked like bats. In the shadows on the far side of the room Jack saw his staff. He could imagine the monk's reaction if he knew how much magic it contained.

I have to be careful, Jack thought. *No wonder the Bard preferred to stay with King Yffi.* Jack's stomach began to churn.

Perhaps Oswald's head didn't like finding itself in his gut. Very soon the boy realized he would have to get out of bed or vomit over the blanket.

Jack's back exploded with pain as he rolled over and fell to the floor. He couldn't move. *Curse that lady,* he thought. *What business is it of hers to hang around the well? And why hurt me?*

Was she an elf? Jack recalled her pale gold hair and moonlit skin. Her eyes were like forget-me-nots in a deep forest. Everything about her seemed muted, but perhaps that was because she was enveloped in mist.

When the pain died down, he began to inch his way toward the staff—for no reason, really, only that it made him feel closer to the Bard. Right now he needed someone's friendship. The herb bundles looked like they were about to drop off the rafters and take wing. Oswald's head burbled in his stomach.

Eventually, he reached the wall. The staff felt warm, as though, in spite of the darkness, it still lay in sunlight. *"Ut, lytel spere, gif her inne sy,"* he whispered in Saxon. *Out, little spear, if it lies within.* He knew all about elf-shot. Mother had taught him a charm to remove it: *"Gif her inne sy, hit sceal gemyltan."* *If it lies within, it shall melt.*

He repeated the charm, and gradually, the warmth of the staff reached up his arm and flowed over his body. The pain withdrew until it was only a faint, glimmering echo. Then it went away altogether, and Jack fell into a dreamless sleep on the cold floor without even a blanket.

❖ ❖ ❖

"Oh, blessed saints, he's dead!"

The cry pierced Jack's comfortable sleep. He leaped to his feet, blinking at the distraught man before him. The monk sprang back. "Praise God and all His angels! The boy lives! Forgive me, St. Oswald, for doubting your miracle!"

"What miracle?" said Jack crossly. He'd been torn from the best rest he'd had since starting out on this pilgrimage.

"You," cried the monk. "On your knees, boy. We must thank Heaven." He pulled Jack down, and together they prayed. Jack gave thanks willingly, for by whatever means, his pain had vanished. Sunlight spilled through a window. The smell of bacon roasting over a fire drifted through the door. It was good to be alive.

"Wait till the abbot hears about this," said the monk, rising to his feet. "He's always saying St. Oswald isn't as powerful as St. Filian."

Still chatting, he led Jack down a hall to a door that he unlocked. Beyond was a musty-smelling room with gray stone walls, and at the far end was a faintly lit alcove. Jack felt a presence, just as he had sensed one by the well. A distinct impression of hostility hung in the air. *Oh no,* he thought. *I really don't need another elf-shot.* He grasped his staff and willed the creature to keep its distance. "This place isn't haunted, is it?"

"Certainly not! We exorcised that demon ages ago," said the monk, urging Jack on. "These holy relics are off-limits to ordinary folk, but as St. Oswald has chosen to favor you, I think he'd like you to see his."

His what? thought Jack. The alcove was filled with boxes carved with designs. On one a man struggled with a pair of serpents that threatened to devour his head. On another a woman's body ended in legs covered with scales. Instead of feet, she had fins.

In the alcove was a tiny window. Shards of colored glass—scarlet, apple green, and yellow—were fastened together with strips of lead. The morning sun lit them from behind, making them blaze like sparks of fire.

"Oh!" cried Jack, delighted.

"It *is* nice, isn't it?" agreed the monk. "Those are all the bits we were able to save from the Holy Isle. The window in our chapel is bigger, but the colors aren't as bright. There was nothing finer than that window on the Holy Isle. Here," said the monk proudly, tapping one of the carved boxes, "are St. Chad's sandals. He refused to ride horses on his pilgrimages, preferring to walk like a humble peasant."

"Perhaps he was afraid of horses," said Jack.

"Nonsense. Saints aren't afraid of anything. Here we have a lock of St. Cuthbert's hair. One of our monks had a dreadful tumor over his eye—big as a hen's egg, it was. The brother held Cuthbert's hair against his eyelid, and from that moment, the tumor began to shrink."

The monk held up one item after another, explaining their holy powers. Jack would have said *magic* powers, but he knew the monks were sensitive about that. Finally, the man brought out a chest made of sea ivory.

The cover was stained with something dark, perhaps

blood, Jack thought uneasily. He saw a carving of a man lying with his arms outstretched on a bed of leaves. Vines twisted around him like snakes, as though he were being devoured by foliage and would soon disappear altogether.

"This," the monk said reverently, "contains St. Oswald's arms."

"His weapons?"

"Oh, no. When the pagans chopped him up, the saint's pet raven carried off his real arms and hid them in a tree. It was one of Oswald's first miracles."

"You keep body parts in there?"

"Relics, my boy," corrected the monk. "Holy relics. Kings travel from far and wide to worship them. They pay us much gold for the privilege."

"How nice," said Jack, thinking, *Please don't open that box.*

"I'll take them to the chapel, and later we can burn a candle, to thank St. Oswald for his deliverance."

On the way the monk dropped Jack off at a small dining hall. Father, Brother Aiden, Pega, and Lucy were seated at a table laden with oatcakes and many other good things.

"You're cured!" cried Pega, jumping up to hug him.

"I'm so glad," said Brother Aiden, moving to make room.

"You should have been here last night," said Father, apparently forgetting that Jack had been paralyzed at the time. "We had mutton chops and chicken."

"And honey cakes," added Lucy.

"They flavored the meat with spices I've never heard of," Father said enthusiastically. "A black powder called 'pepper,' and a brown powder called 'cinnamon' from over the sea."

"They certainly eat well here," observed Jack, spearing a slice of bacon with his knife. *Or at least in Father Swein's dining hall,* he thought. He wondered what ordinary pilgrims got. Or slaves, for that matter.

Monks came and went. All of them were taller, fatter, and better dressed than Brother Aiden, who looked like a drab little sparrow in his threadbare robe. They heaped their plates with bacon, ham, oysters, and sardines, and they mopped up the gravy with fine, white bread slathered in butter.

"Was the food on the Holy Isle this good?" the boy asked.

"Oh, no," said Brother Aiden. "We had taken a vow of poverty. Our lives were simple. We hauled water, chopped wood, and tended fields. In our spare time we prayed. I was responsible for keeping order in the library. I fear the library here is neglected—manuscripts dumped on the floor, ink pots empty. I would not like to see the inks I brought dry up for lack of use."

Jack thought privately they would be sold to buy more bacon, ham, oysters, and sardines. "Did you own slaves?"

"Why—no," said the little monk. "Our abbot thought slavery was evil, as do I. But Father Swein is concerned with saving the souls of men who would otherwise have been executed. I would not criticize him."

A bell clanged in the distance. All the monks rose, some of them cramming a last oyster or oatcakes into their mouths before bustling out the door. Kitchen slaves shambled in to clear the tables.

"I believe," said Brother Aiden, "that it's time for the exorcism."

Chapter Thirteen

SMALL DEMON POSSESSION

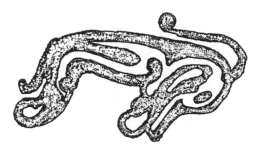

Father fussed with Lucy's hair. She was wearing her white Yule dress, which had been cleaned and brushed, and the silver necklace hung about her neck. "Is that necklace a good idea?" Jack said.

"Don't touch it!" the little girl shrilled. "You only want to steal it!"

"Dear child, he's your brother," Brother Aiden admonished.

"He's a thief!"

Father merely shrugged and gathered up his cloak. He lifted Lucy into his arms.

"I can whisk that necklace right off her," whispered Pega to Jack. "One of my owners taught me how to pick pockets."

"It would only make her wild," he replied. They followed Brother Aiden through the grounds of the monastery. A ragged line of people waited outside a door in a high wall, and for the first time Jack got a close look at those who came for St. Filian's blessing.

One boy drooled continuously—his tunic was soaked—and another twitched as though he had ants attacking his arms and legs. A thin, anxious-looking woman wept monotonously while her husband stroked her arm and murmured, "There, there." Presently, someone started screaming, and the whole line woke up with moans and shrieks. Family members stolidly comforted or wrestled—whichever was necessary.

Lucy shrank against Father's chest. "I don't like these people!"

"You won't be treated with them," Father assured her. "Father Swein has assured us a special audience."

Slowly, the line filed through the door. A monk stood outside with a checklist. "Jocelyn. Night terrors. Fee: A brace of rabbits. *Paid.*" He checked the item off a list. Jocelyn, who squeaked every time someone got close to her, was held closely by her mother. "Erkbert. Falling sickness and small demon possession. Fee: Two laying hens. *Paid.*" Erkbert walked meekly past the recording monk, followed by his equally meek wife. "Guthlac. Large demon possession. Fee: One cow in milk. *Paid.*" Guthlac, who was large himself, never mind the demon, had to be dragged through the door by his father and brothers.

"I want to go home," wailed Lucy.

"And so you shall, the minute you are cured," soothed Father.

"Just how do they exorcise people?" Jack asked.

"Sprinkle them with holy water, I expect," said Brother Aiden. "That's what we did on the Holy Isle."

By now they were at the door. "Lucy. Possible small demon possession. Fee: Five containers of Holy Isle ink—ah! It's you," cried the recording monk, smiling at Brother Aiden. He signaled to a large slave lounging against the wall. "Please conduct our esteemed visitor to the relic room. They're holding a small reception in your honor."

"But I wanted to observe the child's exorcism!"

"The abbot himself requested the celebration. It isn't every day we have the esteemed librarian from the Holy Isle as a guest. He'd be delighted, let me assure you, to have you stay permanently."

"But—," protested Brother Aiden as he was steered away from the door. Jack watched in dismay. He didn't trust these monks, and Aiden, small and humble though he was, provided some protection.

"Where was I?" said the recording monk. "Fee: Five containers of Holy Isle ink. *Paid.* In you go."

On the other side of the door was a jostling, moaning crowd. Beyond them lay a yawning pit with only the faintest glint of water in its black depths. A ladder was propped against its side, leading downward. Guarding the pit were the evilest-looking thugs the boy had ever seen, including Northmen.

"We're supposed to have a private consultation," protested Father. He turned back to the door, but it had closed. A gang of slaves positioned themselves before it.

"Get back with the rest of the loonies," snarled one of them.

"This isn't a place for a little child," cried Father, clutching Lucy to his chest.

"I want to go!" she wailed.

"You've got a choice, boss," said the leader of the slaves. "Line up nice and quiet with the other mooncalves, or get a dose of my special headache medicine." He smacked a cudgel against his meaty palm.

Father worked his way through the crowd, with Jack and Pega in tow. In the far corner of the courtyard he found a willow tree growing next to the wall. It had been cut down to allow the growth of a small forest of slender, new branches. Inside was a natural hollow just large enough for Lucy.

"It's like when we were hiding from Northmen," Jack whispered as she crouched inside. "You must be absolutely quiet." She nodded, making herself as small as possible. She remembered being dragged up by the hair and having a knife held to her throat.

"Can you climb that?" Father asked Jack.

"Me?"

"Get to the top and I'll hand you Lucy."

The willow branches were covered with fluffy yellow catkins that spilled pollen on Jack's face and made him sneeze. "Quiet," whispered Father. Jack swallowed and tried to ignore the tickle that rose in the back of his throat. He wormed between the willow and the wall, looking in vain for footholds. Every gap in the stones had been covered with white plaster. The branches bent beneath his weight and sprang up with a whoosh of pollen whenever he stepped off them. Any minute one of the slaves would notice. Jack paused halfway up, panting with exertion. "Hurry," urged Father.

He wriggled his way up the last stretch of wall and was relieved to see it was wide enough to lie down on. Through the catkins he saw a group of slaves approaching. Father and Pega crouched in the gap next to the wall while Lucy curled up in the hollow. The slaves trudged by, heading for the ladder in the well. They climbed down, one after the other. From the splashing and coughing, Jack guessed the water was deeper than it looked.

"Take this. The Bard said you must never be without it," whispered Pega. She carefully lifted Jack's ash wood staff through the branches. "It *tingles*," she gasped as he took the other end. It most definitely did. Jack almost dropped it in surprise. It was the strongest feeling of power he'd had since leaving Jotunheim. Several monks suddenly appeared and sat down on the grass in front of the willow.

What rotten luck! Jack couldn't possibly take Lucy now. *Go away,* he ordered them silently. But the men settled themselves comfortably for a stay.

Jack lay on the top of the wall, racking his brains for a plan. On the far side he saw the original St. Filian's Well, with its rosebushes and orderly flower beds. No lady in white, fortunately. *She must have been an elf,* thought Jack, remembering Brutus's remark about elf-shot. Jack had heard about elves all his life, about their beauty and eerie powers. Christians weren't supposed to believe in them, but Christians didn't believe in trolls, either, and Jack had seen those with his own eyes. He wished the Bard were here. The old man said that nothing was more enchanting than elf song at dusk. No bard could match it.

St. Filian's Well rose from a natural spring and was funneled through a hole in the wall to the black pit on the other side. Originally, Jack guessed, the water had meandered through fields. Or perhaps it had emptied into a lake. *What must the elf lady think of having her water stolen?* Jack thought. *Maybe that's why she's in such a bad mood.*

The slaves were herding the patients to one side, sending the families back out the gate. *If only we'd waited,* Jack thought regretfully. *We could have taken Lucy with us.* But the slaves might have forced her to stay, alone and unprotected.

The monks passed around a skin full of wine. "Good stuff," one of them commented.

"Spanish," another replied. "From that earl who asked St. Oswald to help pillage his neighbor."

"Did he help?"

"Of course. The neighbor was a pagan."

To Jack's amazement, the patients were being blindfolded. All submitted meekly except Guthlac, he of the large demon possession. He had to be thrown to the ground and tied up with rope. He twisted and roared and cursed and snapped, but the slaves soon had him done up as neatly as a caterpillar in a cocoon. Brutus was set to watch him.

Brutus. Jack didn't know what to make of him. He was admirable for obeying his mother's last wishes. On the other hand, he whined and groveled like a worm. As he was doing now before that tall monk in the spotless white robe.

"Afflicted ones!" cried the monk as a silence fell over the courtyard. "Your deliverance is at hand! St. Filian will lay his blessing upon you and drive forth those imps that bedevil your minds. They will resist. They will shriek into your ears and torment you with their filthy claws to gain mastery of your souls. But have faith. We shall be victorious. Sit on that one, Brutus," he added in a lower voice. "I swear, Beelzebub himself has taken up residence there."

"Yes, beloved master," said Brutus, planting himself on Guthlac's chest.

That must be the abbot, Father Swein, thought Jack.

The slaves led Jocelyn, she of the night terrors, to the edge of the pit. She moaned piteously. They stood her on the edge with her back to the water. "No, no, no, no," she wailed.

"That's only the demon talking," Father Swein assured the other patients, who were blindfolded and could not see what was happening.

"Please, oh, please," she begged. A slave shoved her brutally. She fell backward, screaming, into the pit. Jack leaped to his feet. Her cry was broken by a loud splash, and at once howls arose from below. It sounded as though all the fiends of Hell had risen from the depths and were fighting over the poor girl.

Jack, from his new height, could see down into the water.

The slaves were throwing Jocelyn around like a bundle of clothes. They submerged her, pinched her, pulled her hair, and slapped her face. Jack clutched the ash wood staff. He couldn't do a thing to help her.

"Pay no attention," intoned the abbot. "Satan is difficult to cast out, but St. Filian will overcome."

Jocelyn must have fainted, because Jack couldn't hear her cries anymore. She was carried, dripping, up the ladder and laid out on the grass. She seemed dead until a spasm shook her body and she vomited on the ground.

"Take her to the orchard and bind her to a tree," ordered Father Swein. "Her mother can collect her in the morning." There was not a scrap of pity in his voice. He might have been talking about a mangy dog.

Chapter Fourteen

THE EARTHQUAKE

One after another, the patients were backed up to the pit and shoved in for the slaves below to torment. Jack hated them, but he realized they were, after all, condemned felons with no experience of mercy. The monks were different. They cheered as though they were at a ball game and made bets over which patient would last the longest before passing out. Jack absolutely despised them.

The last to go was Guthlac in his cocoon of rope. No one had blindfolded him. It was far too dangerous to get near his snapping jaws. Two men dragged him to the edge and rolled him in. "Whuuuuuh!" roared Guthlac like an enraged bear as he went down. Not a bit of the fight was taken out of him.

Jack was delighted to see him sink his teeth into the first man who approached.

But then it went horribly wrong. The slaves dragged him under the water and continued their devilish howling while holding him down with their feet. Jack watched in stunned horror. He was seeing cold-blooded murder! Even the monks were shocked. "Father Swein! He's been down too long!" one of them cried.

The abbot slowly approached the edge of the well. He gazed over the pit, contemplating the scene below. "Bring him up," he said at last. The men swam aside. Guthlac rolled to the surface like a dead seal. He was too heavy for the ladder, so he was pulled up by rope. Brutus bent down to untie his bonds. "No need for that," Father Swein said.

"Master, he's dying," said Brutus, not stopping. "I can save him if I press the water out of him."

"You will step back."

"No, master," said Brutus. He turned Guthlac onto his stomach and began pushing on his ribs.

"You will step back." The abbot signaled to other slaves, and they pulled Brutus away. "This happens occasionally with the larger demons. Sometimes only death will drive them out. We have saved this man's eternal soul."

Brutus, as he had in the hospital, changed from a hero to a buffoon in the blink of an eye. "Begging your pardon, beloved master. Brutus is a half-wit, always was. He doesn't know dung from a dewdrop."

"That's true," said Father Swein as the slave proceeded to cower in a most nauseating way.

Jack felt dizzy with rage. These monks were as bad as Northmen. Worse, for they had no honor. They pillaged those who believed in their goodness and lived like kings with their fried oysters and sacks of Spanish wine.

"Who's that standing on the wall?" said the abbot. Too late Jack realized his mistake. In his attempt to see into the pit, he'd come out into the open.

"That's the lad St. Oswald cured!" said the monk who had cared for him in the hospital. "You're looking at a miracle, Father. Last night he could barely wiggle. I always said St. Oswald was powerful—"

"Be still," said Father Swein. "I remember he had a sister. Small demon possession or something. I haven't seen her yet."

"She left with the families. Father changed his mind," said Jack.

"You lie," the abbot said. *"I can see your father hiding behind the willow."*

At that, Giles Crookleg emerged. "I've changed my mind," he declared. "You can keep the Holy Isle ink. I'll take Lucy home."

"Oh, no, no, no," said Father Swein, smiling to hide the menace Jack saw in his eyes. "We can't have a demon trotting around, even a small, pretty one."

"Begging your pardon. Your treatment isn't suitable for a little child."

"Oh, but it *is*," the abbot said, amusement quirking his thin lips. "She'll feel so much better with that nasty imp out of her."

"I can't allow it. I'm sorry."

Father Swein signaled to his slaves. Father stood squarely in their path. Crookleg he might be, but he would not back down from a righteous fight no matter how many men opposed him. Jack had never been so proud of him.

"I can't allow it either," Jack cried, standing as tall as possible with his ash wood staff in his hand. The slaves guffawed, and Father Swein permitted himself a smile.

Pega burst out of the willow, dragging Lucy after her. "I'll lift her up to you, Jack. Grab her hands."

But Lucy—perverse as always—screamed, "Let me go, froggy! I hate slaves touching me!"

Pega dropped her at once.

"Pega—," Jack pleaded. But help came from a most unexpected direction.

Brutus was one of the men sent to subdue Father. When he caught sight of Lucy, he halted in shock. "Back! Back!" he ordered the others. "This is one of the Fair Folk."

"The Fair Folk are accursed demons!" thundered the abbot. "Obey me at once, or I'll hand you over to King Yffi!"

Brutus planted himself beside Father. "I'll not move an inch!" he shouted, once more the hero and not the buffoon. "My mother served the Fair Folk, and I shall do no less!" The slaves stared openmouthed at him.

"Move, you scum, or I'll have you all burned alive!" roared Father Swein. They surged forward and joined battle.

Jack knew Father and Brutus couldn't hold out against so many, and now the men in the well were swarming up the ladder. He trembled with rage at the treachery of the abbot. *Come forth,* his mind called as he grasped the thrumming staff until his knuckles whitened. *Break down these walls. Cleanse this foul place.* He didn't know what forces he was summoning, only that his cry sank into the deep places of the earth and echoed in vast, buried caverns that had never seen the sun. The staff shook in his hand. His hair crackled.

Thunder rolled through the ground. The stones groaned beneath Jack's feet, and a shudder caused everyone to stagger in the courtyard. Jack fell to his knees. A second quake sent rocks tumbling in clouds of disintegrating plaster. Jack saw St. Filian's Well split in two. Water burst out in a great plume and dashed itself against the wall. Jack was thrown onto the willow. He grabbed branches desperately as he fell down.

When he sat up, he saw a river foaming through a break in the wall. The flood was so huge, he couldn't hear the slaves screaming. He could only see their mouths opening and closing. Water cascaded into the pit, going on and on, not filling it up, but plunging into a freshly opened chasm at the bottom. It swept up poor Guthlac and carried him along. One tongue flicked out and caught Father Swein as neatly as a frog picking a single fly out of a swarm. With a scream, the abbot was dragged off.

Now, for reasons Jack did not know, the flow gentled and the foam subsided into a crystal arc of water. In the gap of the wall, standing on the arc as though she had no weight at all, was the elf lady. Brutus sank to his knees. Lucy clapped her hands with glee.

The lady held out her arms, and Lucy ran. Jack tried to catch her and so did Father, but he was too injured to stand. The elf lady swept Lucy up and, with a triumphant cry, leaped into the waters. The last of the stream slithered over the edge like the tail of a snake and disappeared.

Jack ran to the pit and looked down. The hole was black and bottomless, empty of any trace of life. And *dry*.

"She's gone. Drowned. Dead. My poor little girl," groaned Father, lying on the ground.

A few monks and slaves stood at the edge of the pit, and two slaves had been lowered on ropes to explore. Everyone else was either injured or milling helplessly in a daze through the rubble. Most of the courtyard walls had fallen down. Beyond them, Jack could see fallen roofs and smoke. "You think your loss is great?" wailed one of the monks. "We've lost our abbot. What shall we do? He was our guiding light!"

"To Hell with Father Swein," Giles Crookleg muttered.

"Where's that hospital monk?" cried Jack. He was worried about Father's injuries. The slaves had beaten him severely, and his crooked leg was bent at a different angle. Father had to be in agony.

"You tell 'em, Giles," Pega said. "I never saw a better cut-purse than that abbot."

"Can't anyone here set bones?" shouted Jack. But the chaos was more than anyone could cope with. Both inside and outside the courtyard, Jack heard moans and curses.

"I'll try," said Pega. "One of my owners—"

"I'll do it," said Brutus. He broke off several willow branches and squatted down beside Father. "This is going to hurt, sir."

"I don't care. She's dead. My poor, poor child!" raved Father.

"I don't think she is dead, sir. I saw the Lady take her."

"Lucy's drowned. We must pray for her soul. Get me onto my knees."

"You're not in any shape to be on your knees. Hold him," Brutus ordered two of the unhurt slaves. To Jack's surprise, they obeyed. There was something about Brutus, when he wasn't actually groveling, that commanded obedience. Jack gritted his teeth as he watched. If only he'd learned healing spells from the Bard instead of how to summon whatever it was that had just happened. Father screamed as Brutus moved the bone into place.

"Wish I could have used poppy juice," grunted the slave. "No time."

"Pain is good! I deserve it! It's all my fault!" cried Father before he passed out. Brutus seemed to be doing a good job, as far as Jack could tell. Father's leg was straighter and more normal than it had ever been. Brutus bound it to the splints with rope.

"There!" he said, sitting back. "I'm sorry to have hurt him."

"Will he—will he be all right?" said Jack.

"I hope so."

"You did a champion job," said Pega, inspecting the splints. "Where did you learn this skill?"

"From my mother," replied Brutus.

"Hoy!" shouted the slaves from the pit. They were quickly drawn up.

"Black as Satan down there," one of them said. "Can't go no farther without a torch. Without a *lot* of torches."

"Does the hole go straight down?" asked a monk.

"Turns to the side," said the slave. "Big enough for an army."

"And bone-dry," added his companion. No one said anything for a few moments after this announcement. The thought of a passage so big that it could hold an army was disturbing enough. *How can it be dry after all that water?* thought Jack.

"Oh no! The injuries are even worse here." Jack saw Brother Aiden, climbing over the rubble. He was followed by the hospital monk with a gang of helpers. "Move the injured to the fields," the little monk ordered. "No one sleeps inside tonight. The earthquake may return. Giles!" Brother Aiden bent down and felt Father's pulse. "He lives, thank Heaven. That's a handsome job of bone-setting."

"Brutus did it," said Jack.

"Really? I could use your help, young man. We've got broken bones all over. Did anyone die?"

"The water took Lucy, Father Swein, and a patient who was already dead," said Pega.

"Not Lucy!" cried Brother Aiden. "I knew about the abbot, but not the poor child. What a terrible fate!" The injured were being laid on planks of wood and carried away. Jack stood guard over Father to be sure he was moved carefully.

"Lucy has not drowned," Brutus said.

"You keep saying that. I saw her swept away, and believe me, nobody could survive that," Pega said. "It was the strangest thing, Brother Aiden. Lucy actually *ran* toward the water."

"She was called by the Lady," said Brutus, "and the Lady took her."

"I saw it too," said Jack.

What Brother Aiden was going to say was interrupted by the thunder of horses and riders galloping into the courtyard. "Company, halt!" bellowed a man in a helmet. The horses pulled to a stop, their heads tossing, their flanks wet with sweat. "Din Guardi shook like a rat in a dog's teeth, but it stood firm. We saw smoke coming from the monastery. Where's Father Swein? Good God! This must have been the center of the earthquake."

"The abbot is dead," said Brother Aiden, looking even more like a small brown sparrow beside the burly warriors. "I'm the art master from the Holy Isle."

"Ah!" said the horseman, obviously impressed. "It's good fortune you are here to step into his sandals. What caused this upheaval? Was it demons?"

"It was him!" shouted the hospital monk, pointing at Jack. "The slaves saw him just before the earthquake. He was mumbling charms and waving a wizard's staff. And to think I wasted St. Oswald's head on you," he said, shaking his fist at Jack.

Chapter Fifteen

DIN GUARDI

"It could have been worse," said the Bard, leaning back in the chair King Yffi had provided in his room. His feet extended toward a brazier full of coals near a deep, narrow window. A spring storm blustered outside. Rain occasionally splattered through and made the coals hiss. "It couldn't have been *much* worse, mind you, but worse." The old man sipped thoughtfully at the chamomile tea Pega had made him.

"It wasn't my fault," protested Jack. He'd spent the past night and most of the day in King Yffi's dungeon. Only Brother Aiden's appeals had released him. Jack's cell had been a dark, terrifying place hollowed out of rock, where he could hear the howls of unknown creatures and waves booming not far away.

"I warned you, just before I left: 'Don't do anything foolish.'"

"You did say that, sir. I remember," said Pega.

"Oh, be quiet," said Jack.

"Never use anger to reach the life force, lad," the Bard scolded him. "It turns on you when you least expect it."

Jack felt horrible. Because of him, St. Filian's Well had been destroyed and dozens of people had been hurt. Father wouldn't be able to walk for months and had gone mad with grief. Jack couldn't imagine how they were going to tell Mother about Lucy.

"King Yffi wanted to roast you over a slow fire—St. Filian's pays him well for protection—but I threatened him out of it." The Bard tranquilly drank his tea. The sun had set, and the long, rectangular window faded from silver to lead. The old man smiled as a swallow struggled into the opening and sat there, drying her wings.

"Thank you, sir," muttered Jack. Just because the king wasn't going to roast him didn't mean something else awful wasn't planned. Guards stood outside the door to make sure no one wandered.

"Yffi has an interesting decision to make," remarked the Bard. "I don't think he knows it yet."

Probably deciding how much pain I can endure, the boy thought.

Pega, busy as usual, had laid out a small table with bread and stew from the fortress kitchen. Jack noticed four trenchers and wondered who else was coming. Father was housed in Din

Guardi's infirmary, and the Bard said he'd been given poppy juice to calm his mind. "Giles has a long recovery ahead," the old man said. "I fear his leg is the least of his problems."

"Why are you treated so well, sir, when King Yffi is a Christian?" Jack asked, noting the richness of the room and its furnishings. "I thought they hated pagans."

"Yffi is like a wall covered with fresh plaster," explained the Bard. "He appears Christian on the outside, because it brings him wealth. Inside, he's the same brute who slew the rightful ruler of Din Guardi and enslaved his wife and child. Most creatures can be ruled by kindness, but now and then you meet one like Yffi who responds only to fear. Fortunately, I know how to supply it."

"But . . . ," said Jack, trying to sort out his thoughts, "I thought he was a king." In all the stories the boy had heard, such beings were noble from birth.

Pega laughed out loud. "You were hatched under a gooseberry bush. Kings are only successful thieves."

"That's not true!" Jack said hotly.

"There, there," the Bard said. "Not all rulers are corrupt, Pega, although your experience has taught you to believe it. Ah! There's Aiden. Now we can eat."

The little monk was wrapped in a wet cloak that steamed in the warm room. "What a day! I asked the monks of St. Filian's to clear fallen stones, and they replied, 'That's the slaves' job.' Everything was the slaves' job, I soon discovered. What do those men *do* all day? They certainly don't spend time in the library, and when I looked into the chapel, it was deserted." Brother Aiden unwrapped the cloak, transforming himself from a fat partridge into a skinny sparrow. Pega hung the cloak near the coals to dry.

The little monk produced Jack's ash wood staff. "I expect you'll need this soon, lad." Brother Aiden exchanged a meaningful look with the Bard. "The king's guards were afraid to touch it after they arrested you. Hot lentil soup! You're a wonder, Pega!" he cried before Jack could ask why he would need the staff.

They sat down to eat. The soup was flavored with onions and the new spice Father had called *pepper*. It was delicious! Jack thought he could eat pepper every day and twice on Sunday. The Bard saved a scrap of bread for the swallow in the window. She showed no fear whatsoever, but hopped forward and took the food from his hand.

When they were finished, Pega brought out a special treat she'd made in the fortress's kitchen, an omelet sweetened with honey. "If only Father Severus were here," Brother Aiden mused after they had settled around the brazier to bask in heat. "He'd get those lazy monks off their backsides. He could frighten a wolf into saying prayers."

"Who's Father Severus?" Jack asked.

"The man who saved my life," replied the little monk. "I was a starving child, lost in the Forest of Lorn. I remember eating bark."

"I've done that," Pega said brightly. "One of my owners—"

"Let him tell the story," said Jack, who wanted to hear about the Forest of Lorn.

"My memories are shadowy, but it seemed something was hunting me. I had made a nest in a tree like a bird. Father Severus had been sent into the forest to do penance, and he spotted my hiding place. I was afraid of him at first. I was afraid of everything, but he left food at the foot of my tree. Gradually, I learned to trust him."

"Were your parents dead?" asked Pega.

Brother Aiden sat back and frowned. "I don't remember. I can still speak their language." He said something in a whispery voice that seemed more like the wind blowing through a forest than human speech.

Jack's hair stood on end. "That's Pictish!" he exclaimed. He didn't understand the words, but their sighing, hissing quality brought back evil memories. He'd heard them in the slave market where the Northmen were trying to sell him. He remembered the small, painted warriors materializing from the twilight. Their skins seemed to writhe in the firelight. The pictures on their bodies—a wolf with a man's head in its jaws, a deer devouring a snake, a man being crushed beneath the feet of a bull—spoke of a world of pain. *They were like the drawings Brother Aiden made on his parchments.*

"You're a Pict!" Jack said, now understanding the monk's smallness.

"I am," replied Brother Aiden.

"How can that be? They're savages! They *eat* people!"

"Are you quite through?" said the Bard.

"I guess so," Jack said.

"Well then, I must say you've been insufferably rude. You know nothing of Aiden's people, yet you believe the worst of them."

"I saw them, sir. The Northmen were bartering slaves for weapons, and the Picts were feeling the captives all over to see how fat they were. They almost took me! It was horrible."

"And the Northmen's slaughter of the monks wasn't?" The Bard's eyes snapped with anger.

"Of course it was," Jack said, desperate to make the old man understand, "only the Picts were worse. Unnatural, you see. Even Olaf One-Brow hated them."

"The list of people Olaf One-Brow hated, and who hated him, would reach from here to the next village."

"I'm not offended," said Brother Aiden, unexpectedly coming to Jack's defense. "Many people find the Old Ones disturbing. Modern Picts are no different from anyone else. They wear clothes and live in houses. They speak the language of folks around them and marry their sons and daughters. The Old Ones . . ." Brother Aiden's voice trailed off.

"Live as their ancestors did a thousand years ago," the Bard finished. "Naked, painted, secretive, they come out only at night. People say light makes them weak."

"They've lived in darkness so long, it has made them fear the sun," agreed Brother Aiden.

"The Picts I saw were covered in designs," said Jack.

"I have a couple." Brother Aiden bared his chest to show an ornately decorated crescent moon intersected by a broken arrow. Beneath it was a blue line with five short lines crossing it at right angles. "You needn't be worried by me, Jack. I haven't eaten anyone in ages."

"I—I'm sorry," Jack stammered. He found it hard to associate the gentle monk with the savages he remembered at the slave market.

"This mark is how I got my name." Brother Aiden indicated the blue line.

"It's a rune," the Bard explained. "It means *aiden,* or 'yew tree' in Pictish. The monks of the Holy Isle thought it as good a name as any."

"Now I must attend to prayers," said Brother Aiden. He stopped by the window to say good-bye to the swallow. "I've often wondered where they go in winter. Some say they fly to Paradise," he said, stroking the bird's head.

"I'm curious," said Pega, holding out the warmed cloak for Brother Aiden to put on. "Why was Father Severus doing penance?"

"He had an unfortunate encounter with a mermaid—but I don't want to indulge in idle gossip," Brother Aiden said. "Tomorrow will be a long day. We should all get a good night's sleep."

"What's wrong with idle gossip? Would he prefer busy gossip?" fumed Pega later as she fluffed up her bedding. The Bard might be honored with a goose down mattress, but the courtesy didn't extend to Jack or Pega. The meager piles of straw would hardly take the curse off the stone floor. "I'll bet Father Severus fell in love with that mermaid," said Pega. "They say Sea Folk marry humans to gain souls."

"The Bard says they smell like seaweed," Jack said.

"Father Severus probably smelled like old boots."

"You don't respect anyone, do you?"

"That's not true," Pega protested. "I'm simply not taken in by frauds. Kings, nobles, abbots—they think they're so holy, mud wouldn't stick to their bums if they sat in a bog. But I admire good people—really I do—like the Bard and Brother Aiden . . . and you," she finished softly.

"Oh, go to sleep," said Jack, feeling uncomfortable with this sudden change of tone. He snuggled into his heap of straw and turned his back on her. The storm blustered outside. Occasional gusts of wind penetrated the narrow window and chilled his body. If only he had more straw. Or a sheepskin. Pega didn't seem to mind the cold, but she was used to ill treatment.

After a while Jack got up. The swallow was a dark blob in the corner of the window. Not even a child could get through that narrow space. From what little Jack could see, there was a long drop to the ground. He went to the door. The guards were curled up on the floor like a pack of wolfhounds.

Jack pulled the brazier to the middle of the room. If he couldn't sleep, he might as well make use of the time.

I seek beyond
The folds of the mountains
The nine waves of the sea
The bird-crying winds. . . .

❖❖❖

He chanted silently, circling the fire. Maybe he could see Lucy if she still lived. Round and round he went until the sound of the storm faded and the coals grew bright. A shudder rolled through the fortress.

"Don't do that," the Bard said sharply. Both he and Pega were sitting bolt upright. Cries sounded in the distance. "The forces you called up yesterday are still abroad. We don't want the whole fortress down around our ears." He got up and placed a poker in the coals. "Mint tea would go down well, Pega."

The girl set about fetching charcoal from an alcove. She built up the fire, filled cups from a wooden bucket, and sprinkled mint leaves on top. "I don't have honey, sir," she apologized.

"You're doing marvelously," the old man assured her. "We need the heat more than anything. My stars! You'd think it was December."

Soon they were sitting around the brazier with mint-flavored steam misting their faces. "What did I call up, sir?" Jack asked.

"An earthquake," the Bard replied.

"What *is* an earthquake?"

"A very good question. The Picts say it's the Great Worm and her nine wormlets burrowing in the earth. I've always thought it was an imbalance in the life force. An even better question is why it responded to you. What were you thinking when you called it, lad?"

"The first time I was angry at Father Swein. I mean, furious," Jack admitted. "I was grasping the staff so hard, it's a wonder it didn't break. It was shaking in my hands."

"I felt it too," Pega interrupted.

"Did you, now?" The Bard looked at her thoughtfully.

"I called—something—to come forth," Jack said. "I told it to break down the walls. And to clean up the place. For an instant I actually saw into the ground. There were caves like halls under the earth, pitch-black . . ."

"And the second time?" the Bard said softly.

"I was doing the farseeing spell. I only wanted to see Lucy." Jack felt hollow inside. Where was his little sister? Was she frightened by the dark halls he'd glimpsed? Or was she the prisoner of some monster?

"Long ago," said the Bard, folding his hands around his cup, "St. Filian's was not a well, but a lake. It was ruled by a powerful lady of Elfland—*the* Lady you heard Brutus speak of—and her nymphs. They had always been protected by the Lord of Din Guardi."

"Not King Yffi," said Jack.

"Not him. He slew the true king, and then he called in a group of renegade monks. They dammed up the spring that fed the lake, trapping the Lady in the courtyard with Christian magic. For years they've had a sweet little enterprise going there. The abbot of the Holy Isle complained, but nothing was done. Then Northmen destroyed the island. Too bad Olaf and his dim-witted crew didn't land here instead."

"Was the Lady truly unhappy?" asked Jack.

"In a tiny courtyard? Without the flocks of birds, the mists and reeds and wildflowers she loved? Of course she was. Even worse, she was aging. Elves live long in our world, but they prolong their existence by visiting Elfland, where time does not move."

"I suppose that's why she shot me," said Jack.

"She must have been brooding for years. When you broke open the pit— By Odin's eyebrows! That's it! How could I have missed it?"

"What, sir? What are you doing?"

The Bard dropped his cup and went to the window. He could just reach his arm through. The swallow chirped peevishly. "Don't worry, my friend. I'm only checking the weather," the old man said. "Hah!"

"What?" cried both Jack and Pega.

"Perfectly dry outside. Just as I thought. That was no ordinary storm."

"It was raining earlier," Pega said.

"The water poured out of the well and into that hole you opened up, Jack, leaving it *perfectly dry*." The Bard looked at Jack and Pega expectantly.

"But what does this have to do with—," Jack began.

"Think! All last night and today the sky's been streaming with rain. Now it's gone!" The old man folded his arms, looking immensely satisfied with himself.

Jack and Pega stared at him.

"Save me from slack-jawed apprentices! The Lady of

the Lake was emptying out the sky. She's taken all the water," explained the Bard. "It wouldn't surprise me if every well in this district has gone dry. And when King Yffi finds out, they'll be able to hear him bellow all the way to Jotunheim!"

Chapter Sixteen

KING YFFI

The swallow sang before dawn. She warbled and chirred as though she were holding a long conversation. Jack covered his ears, but it was no use. Cold seeped into his bones, and the straw had flattened into a thin mat. He sat up.

"You don't say," murmured the Bard.

Chirr, twitter, cheet, cheet, went the bird.

Pega was sitting up too, watching.

"The whole side of the mountain came down. That *was* an earthquake!"

Warble, churdle, coo.

"Your cave wasn't touched. Well, that's lucky, anyway. I'll see you in the Forest of Lorn, for we have much to discuss."

The old man sat back, and the swallow hopped to the edge of the window. She fluffed her feathers in the silvery light and flew off with a rustle of wings. "Good morning," the Bard said, standing and brushing the wrinkles from his robe. "I believe we'll have a fine, sunshiny day."

"Were you *talking* to that bird?" Pega asked.

"To be accurate, *she* was speaking to me. The earthquake caused havoc up and down this coast, and she wanted to know if another one was likely. I told her no."

"I didn't know swallows were so intelligent," said Pega. The Bard merely smiled, and Jack knew better than to ask him questions. The Bard never revealed anything unless he thought it was important. Jack often saw him talking to foxes, hawks, crows, and badgers, but he rarely passed on the information.

They breakfasted on bread left over from yesterday, soaked in cider to make it chewable. They had hardly finished when King Yffi's guards appeared. "Don't forget your staff," the Bard reminded Jack. They went down stairs that twisted round a central column. From this, Jack guessed they'd been in a tower. He'd hardly noticed when he was dragged up from the dungeons. The guards stamped along before and behind with not a glimmer of friendliness in their eyes.

The air in the passage was stale, and the floor was achingly cold. It seemed a place forever deserted by spring. Even in high summer, Jack thought it would be freezing. And sad. Cold could be cheerful, as when they woke the apple trees, but this was despairing. If Jack listened intently, he could—

almost—hear distant weeping. Or perhaps it was only his imagination.

King Yffi's hall was no less grim. It was large and sumptuously furnished, but the numerous torches along the walls did not lessen the melancholy that hung over the room. The king himself lounged on a gilded throne flanked by flaming braziers. He was a large man, taller and broader than any of his men. Most oddly, he was dressed in black from head to toe and his hands were encased in leather gloves. The only part of him visible were his eyes, sunk into his face like pebbles in a bowl of oatmeal.

A man knelt on the floor before him. Jack recognized Brutus in spite of the slave's eyes being blackened and his lip swollen. He'd obviously suffered for his defense of Lucy. "Brutus knows he's a wretch, noble master," the man groaned, banging his head on the floor. "He's as brainless as a March hare. He didn't mean to attack the nice monks—no, indeed—he loves them! But he was bewitched by a powerful wizard."

What wizard? thought Jack. Then he knew. Brutus was shifting the blame onto him! "That swine," Jack muttered.

"Patience," counseled the Bard. "There are worse things than being thought powerful."

"Aiii!" shrieked Brutus, throwing himself flat. "He's here! He's here! Please, master wizard, don't pull down this fortress! Don't crush poor Brutus under the stones!" He crept forward and kissed Jack's foot. Jack reacted at once. "Yiiiii!" screamed the slave. "He kicked me! He put evil magic into me. Brutus is going to soil his pants!" And he began passing gas noisily.

"Get him away!" shouted King Yffi. The guards dragged the slave to a far corner. Jack now saw that Brutus wasn't the only outsider present. Several monks, including Brother Aiden, stood behind the throne.

The room fell silent except for the flaring of the torches and Brutus's whimpers. "Wizards," said King Yffi at last, looking from the Bard to Jack. His eyes passed over Pega as though she didn't exist. "What have I done to deserve wizards?"

"Something good, no doubt," the Bard said.

"Nothing but ill luck has happened since you arrived," growled the king. "First the earthquake. Then the wells ran dry. My soldiers tell me the drought extends only a mile or two outside of Bebba's Town, but there's no way we can transport enough water for our needs. All because of *wizards*." Yffi's eyes fixed on Jack. "I ought to burn you at the stake."

"How about it, lad?" the Bard said genially. "Shall we knock down a few pillars to show them what's what?"

"Noooo!" shrieked Brutus from his corner. "Don't rain stones on poor Brutus!"

"I trust we can think of something else to do." Yffi cast a furtive look at the ceiling over his head.

"Getting the water *back* comes to mind," remarked the Bard.

"Indeed," said the king. He and the Bard stared at each other, and Jack was heartened to see Yffi drop his gaze first.

"Good!" said the old man. "Here are the facts as I know them: The Lady of the Lake fled with your water. (She would consider it *her* water, but we won't quibble.) At the same time she took Father Swein and this boy's sister prisoner. My advice would be to find her and promise to restore her lake. I'm sure she'll cooperate if we make it worth her while."

"How can we find her?" cried one of the monks. "She's gone down that dirty great hole where our well used to be."

"*I'm* not exploring it," one of the guards said under his breath.

"The monks say it's the mouth of Hell," another muttered.

"You'll go if I order you!" roared King Yffi, making everyone jump. "By St. Oswald's moldy arms, my kingdom is drying up! I'll send the whole army down there if I have to. I'll bring back that witch in chains!"

"Oh, dear," came Brother Aiden's gentle voice. "I'm afraid that won't work. The Lady of the Lake is a *water* elf. You can't chain water."

"I don't care how it's done!" shouted the king. "Use chains! Use a bucket! Put her in a jug for all I care! But I want her back on the job." He glowered at Jack. "You miserable wizard! I ought to feed you to my pet crabs—it's been weeks since I gave them a treat—but I have a better idea. *You* shall go down into that hole. *You* shall make the wells flow again. And if you don't, I'll weight your father down with rocks and drown him in the sea!"

Jack reeled with shock. He'd thought kings—Saxon kings, anyway—were somehow more noble than common folk. They were the guardians of justice. They wouldn't take revenge on a helpless man. But Yffi wasn't noble. He was only a vicious pirate who'd obtained his kingdom by murder. As Pega had said: Kings were merely successful thieves.

"I'll go with him," said Pega.

"It's too dangerous," said Jack.

She turned to him. Her grave expression gave her a dignity that silenced him. "I'm a free girl. I go where I will."

"Well, I'm not free, so you can't take *me*!" cried Brutus, scuttling across the floor on all fours. "Oh, no, no, no! You can't drag Brutus along. He's afraid of the dark. He'll die of terror!" He threw himself at King Yffi's feet, covering them with noisy kisses.

"Stop that!" roared the king, jumping up so quickly, he collided with a guard next to the throne. "I swear I've never met a more disgusting creature! You're going down that pit if it's the last thing I do, and I hope you meet something nasty at the bottom of it!"

Brutus curled up into a ball and began to howl.

"Take them away," cried the king. "I want them into that pit by nightfall—and post guards around the edge so they can't come sneaking back!"

"That went well," said the Bard as they were herded down the hall by a troop of grim-faced warriors. Yffi's men walked behind Brother Aiden, Pega, and Brutus, but they were careful to let the Bard and Jack take the lead. They were clearly uneasy at being so close to wizards.

Well? thought Jack. *I'd say it went absolutely foul.* They were going to be thrown into the mouth of Hell. If they didn't find water, Father would be drowned. *And we're stuck with him.* Jack glanced at Brutus, who was wailing monotonously. *If there is anything nasty down that hole, we'll never be able to sneak past it.*

"Things aren't as bad as they seem, lad," said the old man after the guards had shut them into the Bard's chambers. "Brutus has more to him than meets the eye."

Jack shrugged. In his opinion what met the eye was bad enough.

The slave stopped moaning the instant they were alone. "Good old Yffi," he declared, shifting easily from cowering worm to man. "He's as easy to predict as a sundial. Never passes up a chance to make people suffer."

"Creatures such as he live to spread misery," agreed the Bard. "Eventually, the misery finds its way back."

"Did you see how I slobbered over his feet? Lovely! Yffi hates slobber."

"You're certainly good at it," Jack said.

"Groveling is what kept my head on my shoulders all these years." Brutus winked cheerfully. "Just think! We're going on a quest. We'll have adventures. We might even meet dragons."

"I've met dragons," Jack said, who didn't like Brutus either as a worm or as a man. "Wringing your hands doesn't impress them."

"I'd never wring my hands," Brutus cried, drawing himself up to full height. "I'd *slay* a dragon, as all true knights should. I wouldn't say no to rescuing a princess, either."

Jack couldn't believe his ears. This was the man who, just minutes earlier, had been cowering on the floor like a whipped dog.

"It was important to make Yffi send Brutus along. You and Pega need someone to protect you," said the Bard.

Jack felt like he'd been dipped in icy water. "Aren't you coming?"

"Alas, no, lad. I'm not the man I was sixty years ago. Climbing down holes is no longer one of my skills. Besides, I'm needed here. The Northmen are on the move—not close yet, but you never know. The wells are dry, and I need to tell the villagers where to find water. And I must keep an eye on your father. He's been badly hurt. If I don't attend to his leg, he may never walk again."

Jack turned to Brother Aiden.

"Oh, dear. I hate to disappoint you," said Brother Aiden, bowing his head. "I'm taking over Father Swein's duties. The monks of St. Filian's are wandering about like little lost lambs. They need me to provide them with discipline and useful chores."

Jack had his own ideas about how lamblike the monks of St. Filian were, but he kept them to himself. His spirits sank through the floor. The only help he would receive was from a scrawny girl and a cowardly slave.

"Chin up, lad," the Bard said. "You may be young, impulsive, half trained, somewhat ignorant, and inexperienced— but I have faith in you."

"Thanks," muttered Jack. "I think."

They were interrupted by guards bringing food and supplies. "Eat up and pack the rest," growled the chief guard. "We'll be back at nightfall. It'll be dark, but"—he grinned, showing a mouthful of ragged teeth—"not as dark as where you're going."

The food consisted of cold oatmeal, day-old oatcakes, sour oat mash, and oat pudding (with suet). "I wish they'd picked out the weevils," said Pega, poking at the rubbery pudding with her finger, but no one else complained.

"Now," said the Bard as they sat around the brazier and Pega stowed the leftover food into sacks, "you can put your minds at rest. The tunnel is not the mouth of Hell."

"Are you certain?" said Brother Aiden.

"Absolutely! I have much experience with underground paths. Small ones are made by brownies, spriggans, and yarthkins."

What are those? thought Jack. All the same, he was enchanted by the idea of tiny, magical creatures burrowing around under his feet.

"Most large tunnels are made by elves. The Lady of the Lake has a close friendship with the Queen of Elfland, and I imagine that's where she's hiding."

"Have you been there, sir?" Jack asked.

"Oh, yes," replied the old man with a not-completely-happy expression on his face. "What bard would not want to hear that music? But . . ." He fell silent. Jack was surprised. The Bard was usually so confident. He could control winds and call up fire with his very words. It was for that the Northmen honored him and named him Dragon Tongue.

"Are elves as wonderful as the tales say?"

"Of course," the Bard said irritably. "They're elves, aren't they? Only . . ."

"They have no hearts. Good and evil swirl together in them, and they stand neither on the one side nor the other," said Brother Aiden.

"They're perilously fair, which even the wisest can mistake for goodness." The old man sighed. "Men have abandoned their families to starve, to follow after elves."

"Seems to me that's the men's fault," said Pega. "*I* wouldn't take after an elvish knight no matter how many times he snapped his fingers."

"You're still a child. You don't know," the Bard said.

"I suppose Elfland is where the Lady took Lucy," said Jack as a strange sensation fluttered along his nerves. "I suppose that's where we have to go."

"Yes," said the Bard without any enthusiasm.

"Hurrah!" cried Brutus. "We're going to have a wonderful, exciting, fantastic adventure!" His face was so transformed by joy, Jack forgot how spineless the slave could be.

"It *is* a quest." The boy sighed. The image of a ship sailing north on a foam-flecked sea with merry berserkers singing "Fame Never Dies" rose in his mind. He discarded the memory of smelly boots and sloshing bilge as unimportant. Such things didn't matter on quests.

"Excuse me, sir," Pega interrupted. "You said *most* of the large tunnels were made by elves. Who made the other ones?"

The Bard looked down at his hands. "Dragons."

"Dragons!" cried Brutus. "I'll slay them and rescue princesses."

"Oh, be quiet," said Jack.

"But that's highly unlikely here," the old man insisted. "The Lady of the Lake wouldn't take a path inhabited by dragons. Water and fire don't mix. Now let's get on with the packing. Time is short, and I need to explain the ground rules for visiting elves."

Chapter Seventeen

THE HALF-FALLEN ANGELS

"First, of course, you have to find elves," said the Bard, opening a large, ornately carved chest in the corner of his room.
Jack had not paid attention to it before—all houses contained
chests. Even the humblest cottage lacking chairs or tables had
a place to store valuables. This chest, he had supposed, held
bedding, crockery, and other day-to-day necessities. "Elves
don't welcome visitors except on Midsummer's Eve."

"You don't want to be around then," said Brother Aiden.

"Why? What happens then?" asked Jack, but the two men
ignored him.

"I've taught you to dowse for water—you've been doing
the exercises, haven't you?" The Bard removed a Y-shaped

stick from the chest and handed it to Jack. The boy nodded. It was, in fact, difficult not to find water around his village. Every time he practiced dowsing, the stick dragged him into a bog or sinkhole. Once, out of curiosity, he'd pointed it at the sea and was pulled right off a cliff.

"If you can track water, you should be able to follow the Lady of the Lake. Elf tunnels are littered with wood. They like carrying leafy branches with them when they travel. They build bowers to sleep in and don't bother to clean up afterward. You can use these for campfires, but don't build one near any black lumps you might find."

"Why? What are the black lumps?" Jack asked.

"Dragon poop. It's flammable."

"Elves are unbelievably trashy," said Brother Aiden. "I put it down to all the mead they drink."

"You can also use the discarded wood for torches," said the Bard. "Remember to check which way the smoke is blowing. Never go into a tunnel with no air movement."

"It will either be a dead end or a knucker hole," explained Brother Aiden. "You definitely *don't* want to explore a knucker hole. If the ground sucks at your feet, that's a bad sign."

"What's a knucker? Why does the ground suck at your feet?" cried Jack.

No one answered these questions. The Bard rummaged under sheepskins and spare cloaks for the items he'd apparently been storing since arriving at the fortress. It was like him, Jack knew. No matter where he found himself, the old man gathered herbs, odd rocks, sticks, and potions. These things might look like trash to others, but to the Bard, they quivered with secret power. Jack had been trying to develop the same skill, with mediocre results.

Meanwhile, Pega was packing oatcakes and skins of cider into carrying bags. She had her own little mesh bag with useful treasures, including the candle Mother had given her at the need-fire ceremony. Pega carried that everywhere.

Jack wondered if Mother had any idea what was happening to them. He knew she could learn things by gazing into a bowl of water. The Bard called it "scrying" and said that it gave you only hints. When Jack was in Jotunheim, Mother had seen him in the middle of a swarm of bees. Where or when was unclear. And Heide had seen Olaf One-Brow dying in a dark forest, when he was to perish in an open valley fighting a troll-bear.

The bags looked depressingly large, but Jack supposed he would be glad of them in the tunnel. Brutus did nothing. He hummed a happy little song and tapped the rhythm on his knees with his fingers. Jack promised to load him up with bags later.

"I think you're young enough to resist the lure of elves." The Bard frowned. "It's a curious thing, but this is one area where children are stronger than adults. They aren't as easily taken in by illusions, and elves, above all else, are masters of illusion. That's why they never come out into the light of day. Shadows, moonlight, mist . . . that's their natural element."

"You sound as if you don't like them," Jack said.

"Oh . . . I like them," the old man said. His eyes seemed

far away, as though he looked beyond the gray walls of the fortress into distances only guessed at.

"So what's wrong with them? What *are* elves?" Jack expected to be ignored again, but this time Brother Aiden answered.

"Long ago," he said, settling down in a way Jack knew signaled the beginning of a tale, "long ago they were angels."

Pega drew in her breath sharply, and Jack felt his world tilt to one side. Elves were *angels*? Father lumped them with demons, creatures to be hated and feared.

"It happened at the beginning of the world," said the little monk. "Adam and Eve had been driven from Paradise for eating of the tree of knowledge. Life was hard for them, poor sinners. Where once they had only to stretch out their hands to take honeycombs from the trees, now they toiled from dawn to dusk. Cold of winter and heat of summer tormented them. Dry winds withered their crops, and rain brought plague to their livestock. Even more terrible, one of their sons slew the other."

"That was Cain and Abel," announced Pega, who listened to Brother Aiden's tales every chance she got.

"Yes, my dear," the monk said. "Yet God did not entirely forget His children. He gave them good advice and He harkened to their prayers. Unfortunately, He was about to have trouble in His own home."

"Heaven," Pega said contentedly.

"Why don't you keep quiet and let Brother Aiden tell the story?" said Jack.

"Among the angels was a most beautiful and glorious being called Lucifer. Alas, he was consumed with jealousy and wanted Heaven for himself, and so he made war upon God."

"I didn't know such things were possible," said Jack.

"They aren't," said Brother Aiden. "Any fool knows God is all powerful, but Lucifer was an idiot. He recruited an army of other idiots and tried to take over."

Jack was enchanted by the little monk's tale, which was completely new to him. The angels sounded just like a pack of Northmen. Only, of course, God wasn't anything like Odin. "What happened next?" he asked.

"The battle was *very* short," said Brother Aiden. "Lucifer and his followers were tossed into Hell for all eternity, and I imagine the good angels had a victory feast afterward. Order was restored except for one little problem."

Pega, though she was listening carefully, was still tucking away odds and ends for the journey. A chunk of salt, fennel, sage, rosemary, and thyme were layered in a small parcel. Dried sea kale and fish filled a basket.

"I was writing down this very story in the village," said Brother Aiden. "God grant I return to finish it. There were the evil angels who followed Lucifer and the wise ones who followed God. But there was also a third group that refused to take sides. 'We'll wait to see how it comes out,' they said. 'We're angels and above such things as war.' They didn't realize that the very job of angels is to come down on the side of good. There's no room for moderates in Heaven."

A long red bar of sunlight came in through the narrow

window. The sun was setting, and for a moment all paused to watch. Jack thought about the hole that had opened up under St. Filian's Well: *Black as Satan down there,* the men exploring it had said. *Big enough for an army.* He wondered whether they'd ever see sunlight again.

"When the war was over," Brother Aiden continued, "God called this third group before His throne. 'Be gone from Heaven, you lukewarm cowards,' He said. 'You have lost your souls through indecision. Yet because you did not take up arms against Me, I will show you mercy. You will live among My children on earth and not be cast into Hell. Your years will be long and your powers great, but your path to Heaven will be hard. My mortal children have souls, but you must create yours through suffering and good deeds.'

"With that, the lukewarm angels were sent swirling down to earth like so many autumn leaves. They landed in meadows, mud puddles, and streams. All their finery was stripped away. Their wings were gone. Though they were still as beautiful as the dawn, they felt ugly compared to what they had been. Full of sorrow, they crept into the hollow hills, far from where human eyes could see them. And there they built their halls."

"So that's where elves came from," said Pega. She had finished packing, but her hands, never idle, were still busy whisking last night's straw into a tidy heap. "Even half-fallen angels must be happy."

"Not really," said the little monk. "The elves live long with many pleasures, but true joy is hidden from them. In the end they fade like rainbows when the night comes on, and they reach neither Heaven nor Hell."

"Nor are they taken into the life force to be reborn," added the Bard. "We bards have other tales of them, but all say the elves stepped out of the living stream long ago. They're only shadows—beautiful shadows. Most amazingly beautiful." The old man sighed.

"To gain souls, elves must agree to endure the sorrows of humanity—hunger, illness, pain, and death," Brother Aiden went on. "They have to do this willingly. No one can force them. Even then, an elf may not succeed, for he must also do good deeds. Kindness doesn't occur naturally to him. He could walk by a drowning child and not think to stretch out his hand."

"Wait a minute," said Jack as a thought occurred to him. "Brutus called Lucy one of the Fair Folk. Does that mean—"

"I'm afraid so," Brother Aiden said. "I suspected it all along. When I saw her dancing in the fields, when I compared her with the other village children, I knew there was a mystery about her origins. Now I'm sure of it. The Lady of the Lake would not have taken a mortal child."

Suddenly, everything fell into place for Jack. Lucy's selfishness, her lack of feeling for others, even her mad fantasies made sense *if she was an elf and not a human.*

"I suppose that explains why she was such a pain," mused Pega.

"How can I ever get the Lady of the Lake to release her?" Jack said, thinking of Mother grieving and alone on the farm.

Her true daughter was lost, her foster child cared not a whit about her. And if Jack didn't find the Lady of the Lake, Father wouldn't be coming home either.

"That's where Brutus can help you," said the Bard, breaking into the boy's thoughts. "He has skills few possess."

"Oh, sure! He can roll around on the ground and pass gas."

"Now, now. He hasn't had a chance to show his true worth."

Jack glared at Brutus, who was hunkered down like a large, untidy hound. The slave was practically panting with the excitement of being taken along on a quest. *If we do meet a dragon, I suppose he can take the edge off its appetite,* the boy thought uncharitably.

"As for weapons, he can use this," said the Bard. The old man rummaged in the bedding chest and pulled out a long bundle tied with rope. A sour stench washed over Jack. Brother Aiden and Pega recoiled.

"By the Lady, how did you find it?" cried Brutus. His eyes shone as he knelt to accept the gift.

"Poking around. Don't unwrap it yet," warned the Bard. "Yffi's been hunting it for years, tapping the walls for hidden chambers and so forth. Your mother was a wise woman as well as a queen. She knew he wouldn't think of something so simple as a pigsty."

"What is it?" said Jack, annoyed beyond endurance by the Bard's obvious respect for the slave.

"Shh. We must not draw the guards' attention."

And, indeed, the guards were at the door. They tramped

in and roughly ordered Jack, Pega, and Brutus outside. "Be gentle with them," begged Brother Aiden, which only made the guards smile unpleasantly and shove harder. But the Bard raised his staff and sent a swirl of bedding straw around the warriors' heads. Their smiles vanished instantly, for all knew the power of bards to drive men mad by blowing on a wisp of straw.

"You can ride with me," the captain of the guard growled when they got to the gate. Jack frowned, remembering how his hands had been tied and how he'd been forced to run behind the horses all the way to the fortress. But there was no point holding a grudge. The Bard's threat had at least ensured them decent treatment on the way back to St. Filian's Well.

Chapter Eighteen

THE HOLLOW ROAD

Darkness was falling swiftly as they rode out. It was not the gentle dusk of a seaside evening, for there was no mist to soften the air. No high, thin clouds caught the last rays of the sun, for there were no clouds. Night fell, rather, like an axe. By the time they reached the dense line of yew trees that stood between the fortress and the outside world, darkness was complete.

The trees spread out on either side in a thick, living wall. Only one iron gate formed an opening in that barrier, and it led to a long tunnel fringed with leaves. Jack had been too dazed on the trip to Din Guardi to react to it. Besides, it had been day. Now, with no light at all except the dim lanterns the king's men carried, the tunnel seemed endless. *Back, back,* thought Jack as the branches closed in.

The air was dusty and still. It caught in his throat. But more than that, Jack felt a resentment in the trees massed around them. *You think you're the masters with your scurrying feet,* the trees seemed to say. *We were here first.*

"Keep away," the boy cried as a branch swept across his face.

"Don't talk," said the captain of the guard.

Then they were out into the clean night air. A thousand stars spread across a moonless sky, and the men began to speak quietly. Jack felt blood on his face where the tree had struck him.

"Not so nice, eh, little wizard?" said the captain.

"What was that?" asked Jack, striving to keep his teeth from chattering.

"That was the Hedge. It's better than any wall."

"It protects the fortress?" said Jack, anxious to keep talking.

"I don't know about *protect.*" The man laughed harshly. "It keeps its distance from us, and we keep our distance from *it.* It has been there since time out of mind."

"It grew up when the Lord of the Forest laid siege to the Man in the Moon," came Brutus's voice from out of the dark.

"What do you know, you sniveling wretch?" snarled the captain.

"Nothing, noble master," whined the slave. "Brutus is as dumb as pig flop."

"Now look what you've done! You've started him up," complained one of the soldiers.

And for the rest of the journey Brutus moaned about how disgusting he was and how he was really, really, really sorry about it. It was extremely irritating, and more than once Jack heard a slap as someone attempted to shut the slave up, but nothing worked.

Burning torches outlined the black opening of the pit at St. Filian's. Slaves were constructing a fence around it under the nervous eyes of the monks. Jack noticed that the monks had St. Oswald's casket for extra defense. *Against what?* he thought. Yet he, too, felt a nameless dread. If the saint could repel whatever lurked below, he was all for it.

"Who's that?" asked Pega, peering at the portrait carved on the stained, ivory box.

"Good old Oswald," replied Brutus. "They always bring him out when the going gets tough." The saint was portrayed lying outstretched on a bed of leaves. Vines twisted around him like snakes. "That's a picture of his battle with the Lord of the Forest. Looks like the Forest Lord is winning."

"Silence, you heathen!" roared one of the monks, aiming a blow at the slave's head. Which, of course, set Brutus off on another fit of groveling.

A long rope with knots tied in it snaked over the side of the pit and disappeared into the dark. "How long must we stay down there?" Jack asked.

"You heard the king. Until you find water," the captain of the guard said.

Jack, like any farm boy, had much experience with climbing trees and hills. He had a good head for heights.

But he'd never been down a mine. The very thought of going under the earth now made him dizzy. It had something to do with being enclosed on all sides. It was like being swallowed alive.

"I, uh, I—" He gulped.

"I'll help you," said Brutus. He swiftly dropped all the carrying parcels over the side. Then he slung the boy, staff and all, over his shoulder and started down the swaying rope ladder. It happened so quickly, Jack only had time to stifle a scream and cling to the slave's arms like a cat trying to keep from being dragged out of a tree. At the bottom of the rope Brutus pulled the boy's fingers loose, swung him out, and let go.

Then Jack did scream—he couldn't help it. Almost at once he landed on soft sand and felt like an idiot. He looked up at the rim of torches and saw Brutus coming down with Pega in his arms. "If you've broken those cider bags, I'll never forgive you," she threatened.

"Don't worry, lassie. It's as soft as heather down there." Brutus jumped with a soft crunch on sand, and the guards pulled up the rope ladder.

"Hey!" Pega shouted. "How are we supposed to get out?"

"When the water starts flowing, you can swim out!" The captain and his men guffawed heartily as Pega let fly a string of insults.

"Pay no attention," said Brutus, gathering up the supplies. "They're sitting around like tadpoles in an empty pond. Soon they'll dry up and blow away."

"What about us? We'll dry up too," said Pega.

Brutus struck flint and iron, and lit a torch. It flared noisily, having been dipped in pitch, and settled down to a reddish flame. "It's true we may die on this quest, but there is honor in what we do, far beyond merely waiting for fate to overtake us."

The ruddy light shone on his face, marking out his strong cheekbones. Gone was the sniveling slave, and in his place was a man—rough and doglike to be sure—who might almost be noble. *Or at least until something scares him,* Jack thought. "I suppose we'd better get started," the boy said.

It was the hardest thing Jack ever did, walking into that long, black tunnel. Every nerve cried out to flee back to where he could see the ring of torches and the circle of stars beyond. But he would not show less courage than Brutus. He would not be outdone by someone who whimpered if a moth flew past his face.

So Jack walked ahead as though he hadn't a worry in the world. He did, of course. The tunnel led deeper under the earth, and the mass of rock overhead became that much thicker and heavier. It could collapse at any moment, squashing them as flat as fleas. Jack saw no reason why it couldn't.

They trudged for miles past dull limestone walls. Torches burned away and Brutus lit more. The ground was not only littered with discarded branches, but broken pottery, apple cores, fish bones, and mussel shells. Elves must have been trooping through the tunnel for years, and from the smell,

Jack suspected they buried their waste in the sand like cats. They were, as Brother Aiden had said, extremely trashy.

After a long while Jack and his companions came to a place where the passage divided in two. One path went to the left and the other, equal in size, to the right. A faint breeze wafted from both of them, so it was impossible for Jack to choose between them. But for the first time something new appeared on the walls. Knobs of gleaming, black material jutted from the limestone of the right-hand tunnel. "What's that?" said Jack, and was shocked by how loud his voice seemed after walking in silence so long.

"Some call it 'jet,'" said Brutus. "The Romans made it into jewelry."

Jack worked a knob loose. It was curiously warm and light. "Does it have another name?"

"My mother called it 'dragon poop.'"

Jack dropped the knob and dusted off his hands.

"That means we should stay out of the right-hand tunnel," Pega observed.

Jack unpacked the Y-shaped stick the Bard had given him. He held it out. Very faintly, he felt a stir in the wood and a corresponding tremor of energy in his hands. The water was far away down the right-hand tunnel. "Wouldn't you know it?" Jack muttered.

"By my reckoning, we've walked a quarter of the night away," said Brutus. "You and I could keep moving, but the lassie is clearly tired."

Jack had been so involved with his own worries, he hadn't

noticed the girl's exhaustion. "Oh! You should have said something, Pega. Of course we can camp here."

"I'm no weakling," she protested, but didn't suggest going on.

Brutus gathered wood and soon had a merry fire crackling—or as merry as a fire could be in a dark tunnel studded with dragon poop. He passed out slabs of oat pudding. "Drink as little as possible," he said, producing a bag of cider. "Who knows when we shall find water?"

"I think there's water down there," said Jack, pointing, "but it doesn't make sense. The Bard said a dragon wouldn't use a tunnel with water in it."

"It depends," said Brutus, his mouth full of pudding.

"And I suppose you know more about it than the Bard?"

"I might," said the slave with irritating confidence.

"One of my owners saw a dragon swimming in a lake," Pega offered. She picked the weevils out of her pudding and flicked them at the wall.

"He probably did," Brutus said. "Only *fire* dragons make tunnels, you see, but other kinds can use them—wyverns, hippogriffs, cockatrices, manticores, basilisks, Hydras, krakens, and, of course, Pictish beasts, which prefer water above all else." Brutus grinned boyishly as he warmed to his subject. "It's like a badger hole. The badger digs it, but foxes, rabbits, and mice use it once the original owner moves out."

"So we needn't worry about fire dragons," said Jack, "only wyverns, hippogriffs, cockatrices, manticores, basilisks, Hydras, krakens, and—and—what was the other one?"

"Pictish beasts," the slave said enthusiastically. "Mother found one and brought it home for a pet. It was newly hatched, no bigger than a cucumber, but it grew extremely fast. She got rid of it when it started devouring cattle."

The underworld was far more crowded than Jack had suspected. He didn't know what a Pictish beast was, but—going by the Picts—it was probably thoroughly nasty.

"I hope I didn't dampen your spirits," Brutus apologized. "Personally, I'm looking forward to adventures—my stars! I forgot the most important thing." He pounced on his bundle of supplies and withdrew the parcel the Bard had given him. The smell Jack had noticed earlier became stronger. He had supposed it came from the trash discarded by the elves.

"I thought this had been lost forever," said Brutus, unwrapping the noxious parcel.

Pega hurriedly moved to the edge of the firelight and cupped her hands over her mouth.

"Sorry, lassie. I forgot that most people don't like the odor of pig flop." Brutus strode up the tunnel and buried the wrapping under sand. "That smell takes me right back to my childhood. How I used to love mucking about with pigs, scratching their bristly ears, and riding on their backs. They adored Mother, naturally. So did I. To think they'd hidden *this* under their sty all these years." He drew the object from its scabbard, and Jack saw a flash of light. It was a beautifully made sword with a blade as bright as a setting sun. The scabbard flashed with gems—rubies, emeralds, and amethysts—and the belt to which it was attached was of bright green leather.

"An ordinary sword would have corroded, but not this," said Brutus. And, indeed, not a crumb of filth stained the wonderful object, nor a speck of rust. Even more surprising, the foul smell didn't cling to it either. The slave brought the sword down, dividing the fire in two. Sparks flew up in a dazzling cloud. "Behold Anredden!" he cried. "It was made by the Lady of the Lake for Lancelot. It is dedicated to her service, as am I!"

Sparks pattered all around, and Brutus's shadow loomed up taller and more glorious than the man who cast it. He sat down abruptly with the sword across his lap. The shadow shrank back to normal. "I'm sorry. It's ignoble to brag before you've earned your reputation, but it *does* feel nice."

Jack and Pega stared at him, openmouthed. "Who *are* you?" the boy said at last.

"I am the true ruler of Din Guardi, torn from my rightful inheritance by the treacherous Yffi. The Lords of Din Guardi have served the Lady of the Lake since time out of mind, and she in turn has protected them. But Yffi crept in with lies that my father unfortunately believed. Poor Father! Mother always said he was too trusting."

"Yffi killed your father?" said Pega.

"He came alone, begging for asylum. Father welcomed him, but all the while the traitor was planning his destruction. Yffi's army couldn't invade from the land. The Hedge allows entry only at one point and it is so narrow that you must pass through single file. The Hedge can't be entirely trusted either. Occasionally, a warrior enters the passage at one end and never comes out the other."

Jack's hand went instinctively to the scratches the yew branch had made on his face.

"Father guarded the sea, of course, but there was a third way to enter Din Guardi. There's a passage that goes deep beneath the rock, a terrible place where krakens nest and kelpies hunt. And there's a curse laid upon that way. Few survive the journey."

"Didn't your da know about the passage?" said Pega.

"Of course. He thought nothing would attempt it, but he didn't know Yffi. Have you seen his gloves?"

Jack remembered the king's heavy black gloves and clothes. Nothing was visible of the man except his eyes and the unnaturally white skin around them.

"Yffi is half kelpie," said Brutus.

"Crumbs! That's something I didn't need to hear," said Pega, hugging herself and looking at the dark tunnels stretching away from the firelight. "I did get a nasty feeling about him."

"If only Father had been as perceptive as you," Brutus said. "I don't know what horror led to Yffi's birth. Kelpies don't normally mate with humans. They eat them."

"You're giving me goose bumps," said Pega. "What's this kelpie thing?"

"A shape-shifter. Sometimes it appears as a beautiful horse, but if you attempt to ride it, it dives under the water and drowns you. Sometimes it looks like a giant otter and sometimes like a very handsome man. They say it can crush the bones in a woman merely by hugging her."

"I can see why women don't like them," observed Pega.

"By some means Yffi was produced, but the villagers cast the infant into the sea. He did not die, however. He was like a dolphin, able to swim from birth. He lived as kelpies do, by lying in wait and dragging his prey into the water. Being smaller than his kind, I imagine he was tormented by the others. Mother was unable to discover much about his childhood. She did learn that he crept up to houses after dark and watched people sitting by their fires. He learned their ways and how to wear their clothes, which he stole."

Jack, in spite of himself, felt sorry for the child Yffi. He hadn't asked to be born half monster. It must have been terrible watching the fires and knowing you'd never be welcome. And then returning to the water, where you weren't wanted either.

"Gradually, Yffi learned to be human," said Brutus. "He had to cover his hair, which was like an otter's, and his fingers, which were webbed and tipped with claws. The greenish teeth weren't a problem. Many knights have them."

Brutus paused to build up the fire. "I don't expect visitors, but it never hurts to be careful." Pega took out her eel-skinning knife and laid it within reach. "To finish the tale, Yffi stole a boat and passed himself off as a pirate. He soon became leader of a band, because even a half-kelpie is three times stronger than a man. But all the while he wanted to live on land, to be accepted and loved."

"Loved," murmured Pega. Jack was struck by the deep sadness in her voice. Looking at her covertly, he thought she could pass for half human herself, with her mottled face, undeveloped body, and wispy hair. Yet the Bard had firmly pronounced her human.

"Strange, isn't it?" Brutus said. "I think Yffi really wanted Father's friendship, but the kelpie part of him wanted blood. On the night of the invasion he swam out to the kraken nests and told them there was a ship sinking to the north. The krakens immediately went off in search of it. Then Yffi's men climbed up the tunnel to the dungeons. They swarmed through the fortress, killing all in their path. Father was cut down before he could reach his sword."

"But you and your mother survived," said Jack.

"Yffi wanted his new subjects to love him. That's why he only banished us to the pigsty and built St. Filian's Monastery, but he didn't really understand Christianity. St. Filian's was founded by renegade monks for profit, exactly what you'd expect from a pirate. Mother and I lived in constant fear of death. He was always threatening to feed me to his pet crabs. Now we should sleep. There's no telling how far we'll have to go tomorrow."

"I don't think I *can* sleep after that story," said Pega.

"Heroes often sing jolly songs to keep their spirits up while on quest," Brutus said.

"I'm too tired," said Pega. She held the candle Jack's mother had given her against her cheek, as if it made her feel safe.

So Brutus sang them a ballad about a knight tracking an ogre in a haunted wood. It had many a *hey!* and a *ho!* and a *dilly dilly down!* and was no doubt meant to put heart into you, but Jack found it depressing. Especially the way the *hey!* and the *ho!* echoed down the long, dark tunnels.

Chapter Nineteen

THE KNUCKER HOLE

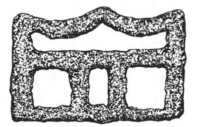

Brutus insisted it was morning when Jack awoke. He was already bustling around, toasting oatcakes on sticks. Pega was propped against a wall, looking the worse for wear.

"Nothing like warm oatcakes to start the day," the slave declared. Jack was allowed a few swallows of cider to wash them down.

"I dreamed of kelpies all night," said Pega. "Every time I woke up, I saw Yffi in the shadows."

"Mother used to say dreaming of bad things meant something good was about to happen," Brutus said.

"Like getting eaten by a dragon instead of starving to death." Pega was unusually ratty this morning, but Jack couldn't blame her. He felt ratty too. The walls were closing in and the air was stale. He felt the weight of the rock over his head.

"The more we eat, the less we'll have to carry," Brutus said brightly. "Mother always said there was a good side to everything, if you only took the trouble to find it." Humming maddeningly, he made up fresh torches and loaded up bags. Last of all, he strapped on the green belt with the sword Anredden.

When they were ready, Jack led them down the right-hand tunnel. It might be full of dragon poop, but it promised water. Somewhere. As they walked, the lumps of jet grew more numerous, and after a few hours they had to walk around heaps of it. "Look at that!" enthused Brutus. "There's enough here for a dozen dragons."

"Please don't talk," begged Pega. "I have such a headache." So Brutus whistled instead, a tuneless, breathy sound that soon drove Jack frantic.

"*Be quiet!*" he finally exploded. "Don't you understand stealth? Don't you understand caution? If there's a dragon within ten miles, he'll home right in on your miserable, incessant noise!"

"Somebody needs his nap," said Brutus, not in the least insulted. "Let's all take a break and chase those nasty jimjams away."

Jack slumped against a pile of dragon poop and fantasized about breaking his staff over the slave's head. Brutus passed around a sack of sour oat mash. Age had not improved it and Pega said it reminded her of rat droppings, but they didn't dare waste it. Jack was beginning to get dreadfully thirsty. He thought of waterfalls and rushing streams until he actually thought he could hear them. But if he concentrated, there was only the sluggish breeze. And, of course, Brutus.

"I know! I'll tell riddles," the slave cried. "There's nothing like riddles for sheer fun.

"Always I battle with wind and wave.
When under the sea, the rocks are my friends.
Lying still, I am strong. Wrenched loose, I'm defeated.
Tell me my name!"

Brutus waited expectantly, like a dog watching for a stick to be thrown.

"I don't *care*. My head hurts," said Pega.

"Wait. I think I can solve it," Jack said. "Wind and wave mean boats. And the part under the sea is . . . the anchor!"

"Very good," approved Brutus. "Here's another.

"Valued by all, I am brought from afar.
Gathered in groves, ferried from fields,
Wings bore me safely to lie under roof.
Tell me my name!"

"That's too easy. Honey," said Jack, who knew all about beekeeping from his mother.

"Here's a toughie.

"My house is noisy, but I am quiet.
When I lie still, my house yet moves.

Within it I stay. To leave it means death.
Tell me my name!"

Jack tried to work it out. "A snail's quiet, but so is its shell. A turtle? A chick in an egg?"

"It's a fish," said Pega. "A fish in a lovely, chattering, bubbling, water-filled stream—oh, bedbugs! We're going to die down here. We'll n-never see a s-stream again!" She burst into tears.

Jack was astounded. He'd never seen her cry before, not even when he struck her. He'd been so wrapped up in his own misery, he hadn't noticed how hopeless she'd become. He didn't know what to do.

But Brutus did. "There, lassie," he said, holding her and rocking her as though she were a baby. "The middle of a quest is always the hardest, but heroes come through. And we *are* heroes! They'll be singing about us as they do King Arthur and Lancelot, my ancestor. There were noble ladies, too, Morgan le Fay and Nimue, the Lady of the Lake. Actually, it's the same Lady of the Lake, for her kind live long, but the others wound up on the Islands of the Blessed, where it's always summer and sorrow never comes. My mother is there, for she was the Lady of Din Guardi as well as being a wise woman."

"I'm a Christian. I hope to wind up in Heaven." Pega laid her tearstained face against his chest.

"That's a grand place too, lassie. The point is, we live as bravely as possible and go to our just rewards. There's always hope, even in death."

"I like it when you call me 'lassie,'" said Pega, snuggling close.

"Then I'll do it often. Now I want you to drink some cider. You're far too dried out. We must go on, but you tell me if you get tired." Never had Brutus looked so noble, like a real king and not a sniveling wretch.

Jack promised to pay more attention to Pega. He knew she was capable of marching until she fell down dead, out of sheer mulishness. It was up to him to tell Brutus when she got tired.

They went on and on, with the dragon poop increasing until it formed pillars from floor to ceiling. They had to walk around them like trees in a forest. From time to time, Jack dowsed with the Y-shaped stick. Water was still ahead and growing nearer (he hoped). They rested often, though not often enough for Pega, who kept stumbling. Even Brutus's whistle had sunk to a slight hiss between his teeth. Jack's mouth was glued shut. He kept thinking of the cider bags. Surely, if they were going to die, it would be best to have one last, glorious drink and then sit down to await the inevitable.

"I hear something," said Pega.

Jack was so hypnotized by the crunch of their feet and Brutus's hissing, he hardly registered the noise. They all stopped and listened. *Eee eee eee,* said something not too far ahead.

"Is that a mouse?" whispered Jack.

Eee eee eee eee eee. The sound multiplied and spread.

Brutus drew his sword. Jack grasped his staff. They edged forward. The tunnel ended at an enormous hall like a bubble under the earth. The far side was hidden in darkness, and the ceiling was so high, it was scarcely visible. Brutus held up his torch. At first Jack thought he was looking at rock formations, but when one of the rocks stretched out a wing, he realized he was seeing bats.

Thousands and thousands of bats.

They clung to knobs of jet, jostling one another and squeaking peevishly when the light fell on them. Brutus laughed, a shocking sound in that empty hall. "By the Lady, it's only flitter mice. Hey! Flitter mice! You've got visitors." He waved the torch, and the bats rustled angrily. Something pattered down like dust.

"Oh, pooh! Lice!" cried Pega.

"Stop scaring them," said Jack, catching Brutus's arm.

"You're right, lad. I've been discourteous. It's their house." The slave lowered the torch and bowed. "We are but wayfarers passing through, gentle creatures. Please permit us to camp this one night. We shall be gone in the morning."

"Camp?" said Pega with longing in her voice.

"The sun is almost at the horizon, lassie."

"How do you know?" Jack said crossly. He was still brushing bat lice off his hair.

"I just do," Brutus replied. They searched for a campsite. Much of the floor was sandy but covered with the refuse of a large bat colony—tiny bones and guano. Wherever they looked, the creatures covered the ceiling.

"What do you suppose made those marks?" said Jack. A ropy trail plowed through the sand. It feathered out from a central, deeper furrow as wide as Jack was tall. When he tried to picture what could have made such a pattern, he imagined a blobby body with many snakelike arms pulling it along. It was not a welcome image.

"Whatever it is, I hope it stays away," said Pega. "Look at all this filth!"

On the far side seven more tunnels led outward, each one exactly like the others. "Oh, bother!" cried Jack, throwing down his carrying bags. "How are we ever going to find the right one!"

"Personally, I think this is a good sign. The hall is clearly an important meeting place," said Brutus.

"For what? Dragons?"

"Look!" cried Pega. With a dry, rustling sound, the bats detached themselves from the ceiling. They filled the air of the hall in a flickering mob, darting here and there, yet never colliding. "Oh! Oh! If bats fly three times around your head, it means you're going to die!" she moaned, crouching.

"They can't do it if you lie flat," said Jack, who had heard the same story. Both of them burrowed into the sand. Tiny bones crunched under their weight, and a fume of old guano enveloped their noses.

Brutus laughed. "Bats used to visit Mother all the time, and not one of them killed anything except a gnat. The sun has set, and they merely go forth to greet the night. Mark how they fly!"

Jack raised his head cautiously. The crowd of bats was smaller. Those that were left flowed into the tunnel on the extreme right. "They're going outside," he said as the meaning of it dawned on him.

"I spoke to them courteously, and they have shown us the path," Brutus replied.

But did it lead to Elfland? Jack didn't know. To be sure, he should inspect all the tunnels, but the lure of being outside was too great to resist. They could be free of the oppressive rocks. They could find water. "You can get up, Pega. They're gone," Jack said, having made up his mind.

"But they left their lice behind," she grumbled, brushing her hair.

Brutus suggested camping in the tunnel. The hall was too dirty, and not even he relished the idea of sleeping in an ominous space with openings snaking off in all directions. A fresh breeze met them as they entered. "This is nice!" said Jack. "Why don't we keep going?"

"The lassie needs rest," Brutus pointed out, "but I can go ahead and see how far the opening is."

"I'm not tired," protested Pega.

"You're practically falling over." Jack pulled her down to sit beside him. Brutus strode on with sword drawn, and they listened to his footsteps die away. The tunnel suddenly seemed much emptier.

"There's no branches on the ground here," said Pega, stifling a yawn.

Jack held his torch high. She was right. "If the entrance is near, we won't need more wood to build a fire."

"That's not what I meant. No litter means no elves. We're on the wrong path. Ohhhhh," Pega yawned again, and stretched.

"Maybe not," said Jack, who hated to give up the idea of going outside. What difference did it make anyhow? Once they found water, they could return.

Pega stood up, tottering on rubbery legs. "I've got to keep moving. If I lie down, I'll never get up again." She staggered against a pillar of dragon poop. "I say! There's a tunnel back here."

Jack was up at once. On the other side of the pillar was a dark opening. He held out the torch. It didn't flicker. "The air isn't moving. I think this is a cave."

"It wouldn't be a bad place to camp."

"If it's empty."

"We ought to look," argued Pega. "I'd sleep a lot better if I didn't have to worry about things creeping up on me. The ground is even soft . . . and sticky. *I can't lift my feet!*"

"Get out!" yelled Jack. Suddenly, he remembered what the Bard and Brother Aiden had said: *Never go into a tunnel with no air movement. It will either be a dead end or a knucker hole.*

"I can't! I can't! It won't let go!"

Jack put down the torch and grabbed her around the middle. He pulled as hard as he could, but he couldn't budge her. He heard a stealthy movement at the back of the cave, a sucking sound, as of something dragging itself out of deep mud.

"Keep pulling!" screamed Pega.

"Now *my* feet are stuck!" he cried.

Jack fumbled for the torch. He waved the flame back and forth at the cave. Something hissed and retreated. He couldn't see it clearly, but a lump of darkness at the far end seemed to flow down the wall.

"Brutus! Help! Come back!" Pega shrieked.

"It doesn't like fire," panted Jack, trying to stay upright as Pega clung to him. He looked around frantically for more wood and saw his ash wood staff. He dropped the torch. The staff was just out of reach.

"Don't leave me!" Pega screamed, hanging on to him. He had to tear her hands loose. He fell forward and landed with one hand on the ground and the other grasping the staff. He twisted around and pointed it at the cave.

By the dying light he saw a dark streak snaking across the floor. Several dark streaks. *Fire, come to me,* he called. He didn't have time to compose his mind or do any of the meditative things the Bard had taught him. All he had was raw need and terror. *Come to me, come to me, come to me!*

He reached down through the rock, expecting the sluggish response he got when calling fire in the village. But the magic was close to the surface of the earth here and eager to respond. Jack felt heat sweep toward him. "Run," he gasped.

"I can't," wept Pega.

A jet of flame shot out the end of the staff. Fire licked over the cave, and for an instant Jack saw a huge round body like a monstrous tick engorged with blood. Arms coiled from its sides, anchoring it to the rocks, and others fanned out across a floor deep in slime. They were almost touching Pega's feet. Then the flames engulfed them.

Jack wrenched her loose from the bubbling slime and staggered back. The heat was so intense, he was afraid to breathe. "The roof!" Pega cried. Jack looked up. In dozens of places the knobs of jet had caught fire. They burned furiously like a sky full of hot stars. The pillar before the cave went up with a sudden *whoosh*, making a blaze so dazzling, Jack was stunned. He felt Pega grab his arm. The whole tunnel was ablaze.

They ran. Sand stuck to the slime on Jack's feet and mired him down. He had a stitch in his side. He thought his knees would collapse, and still he ran, pulling Pega along. When at last they fell, gasping and coughing, to the ground, Jack could hear the roar of the flames behind them. A dire light flickered on the walls. "Is it coming?" Pega said fearfully.

Jack braced himself for another effort, but as the moments passed, the light grew no brighter and the roaring no louder. "The wind is blowing it away," he said. And, indeed, the fire drew air toward it so fiercely, a near gale moaned down the passage. A distant rumble told Jack that something had collapsed. "We can't stay here. Can you walk?"

"An hour ago I'd have said no," admitted Pega. "Amazing what mortal terror can do."

Jack nodded soberly. They went on again, slowly, with the

sand weighting down their feet. The light faded until it died away altogether, and they had to feel their way along the wall.

"The food's gone," Pega said.

"The cider, too," said Jack.

"I'm trying not to think about that."

"Would you believe it? I'm cold," said Jack. The wind had a touch of ice that went straight through him. His cloak had been with the carrying bags and was now ashes. "If we found wood, I could start a fire."

"Don't you dare!"

They trudged on, following the wall. Jack probed the ground ahead with his staff. His feet were scorched, and he guessed Pega's were too. He wondered what the bats would do when they tried to fly back up the passage. On the positive side, the fire must have cleaned out the wyverns, hippogriffs, cockatrices, manticores, basilisks, Hydras, and krakens. And knuckers.

Especially knuckers.

"Where do you suppose Brutus got to?" Pega said.

"I wonder," said Jack as all his bitter suspicions of the slave rushed back.

Chapter Twenty

THE ENCHANTED FOREST

"I wish I could light my candle," murmured Pega, lying on the sand.

"What candle?" said Jack, lying beside her. Exhaustion and thirst had finally overtaken them. Jack thought he could struggle on, but Pega was clearly at the end of her strength.

"The one your mother gave me."

"You still have it?" said Jack, surprised.

"Of course. It was given to me on the best day of my life. The day you freed me."

Jack knew she always carried it in a string bag tied to her waist. He thought it had been lost with all their other possessions.

"Your mother said, 'When you feel the need, it will brighten your nights.' And I said, 'When I die, I'll be buried with it.' So I shall."

Jack felt the prickle of tears. He was too dried out to produce them. "I'm surprised it survived the fire."

"Me too. It's slightly flattened." Jack heard Pega moving, and presently, he felt something brush his face. He smelled the honey-sweet wax. "Isn't that wonderful?" the girl said. "It's like being outside."

Jack remembered how Mother talked to the bees, telling them what was happening in the village. Bees wanted to know everything, she said, and for the first time the boy wondered if she was also listening to them. Mother sang when the weather was thundery, to keep the hives from swarming. *"Sitte ge, sigewif. Sigað to eorþan,"* she sang. *Settle, you warrior women. Sink to the earth.*

It was her small magic. It wasn't as impressive as the Bard's large magic, for he could call up storms and drive people mad, but it might be just as important. Jack hadn't thought of that before. Pega's candle, gathered patiently in field and meadow, had its own quiet power. It, too, had drawn fire from the earth.

He blinked his eyes. A pale, blue light hung in the distance. The hair stood up on his arms. He felt for his staff.

"Is it a ghost?" Pega whispered.

The blue light neither advanced nor retreated. It simply waited. *Is Brutus dead? Has his spirit come back to haunt us?* thought Jack. But, no, if it were Brutus's ghost, it would be moaning. The boy smiled in spite of himself. The light didn't move, but it became brighter. All at once Jack understood what he was seeing.

"It's the moon! I'm such a fool!"

"What?" Pega said drowsily.

"We're there! That's the entrance. Come on, Pega. You can make these last few steps." He pulled her up and half dragged her along the sand. When they got to the light, Jack saw it was falling from a hole at the top of a heap of rocks. That was why he hadn't seen it before. The moon had to be in exactly the right place to shine down.

"You go. Tell me if it's nice." Pega collapsed on the sand.

"I *know* it's nice. Come on!"

"Too tired." She sighed.

Jack knew he couldn't carry her. "I can't leave you here for a knucker to find."

"A knucker?"

"That thing we saw in the cave."

"That," said Pega with slightly more energy, "was a giant bedbug."

"It was a tick," said Jack, who hated ticks.

"It was a *bedbug*. A bedbug! I've seen thousands of them, only not so . . . huge." Pega's voice was edged with panic.

Jack thought for a moment. "There could be hundreds of them down here."

Pega grabbed Jack's arm. "You're making that up."

"It makes sense that there'd be more than one of them. Everything comes in pairs, and some creatures have a lot of babies."

Pega pulled herself up. "You'll have to help me," she said tensely. "I don't know if I can make it, but I'd rather fall and break my neck than . . ." She didn't finish, but Jack understood what she meant.

The rock pile wasn't stable. More than once a boulder shifted and sent a cascade of dirt and pebbles over them. More than once Jack and Pega had to cling to the side while they waited to see whether the whole pile would come down.

But at last they struggled out onto a steep hillside. They lay panting and stunned under a sky strewn with stars. A full moon hung overhead and painted the rocks with a lovely blue light. From below, where giant trees stretched their branches over unseen dark glades and meadows, came the music of a rushing stream.

The air was surprisingly cold, though its freshness made up for it. Jack had been in the fug of bat guano so long, he'd forgotten how good clean air could be. He breathed in long drafts of it, but as delightful as it was, it of course couldn't take the place of water. "It isn't much farther," he whispered to Pega.

Jack saw that they were halfway down a vast rock slide. An entire cliff had collapsed, sending stones and dirt all the way to the edge of a deep forest. The boy and girl slid down on loose gravel, occasionally coming to rest at giant boulders that stuck out like plums in a pudding. But it was far easier going down than up. The moonlight shone all around with a dreamlike radiance, so bright the hillside seemed to glow.

At the bottom they came to a narrow strip of meadowland before the trees.

"Ohhh," said Pega, sinking her scorched feet into grass. Buttercups, oxeye daisies, and primroses spread out in drifts, though their colors were hidden in the silvery light. Beyond, complete darkness loomed, and in that darkness the water sang.

"Do you think there're wolves?" whispered Pega, pressing against Jack.

"It doesn't make any difference. We have to go," the boy said. They edged through the cool grass, Jack in front with his staff at the ready. He heard nothing except the stream, yet he felt a watchfulness in the air. *I wish I had a knife,* he thought, but his knife had vanished with the rest of their supplies in the fire.

"It's so dark," Pega murmured.

Jack thought about shouting for Brutus—he must have come this way—but the watchfulness made him hesitate.

Only a dim echo of moonlight penetrated beyond the edge of the forest. Roots snaked around humps of moss, and branches twisted awkwardly. They seemed, to Jack's mind, to have frozen into place and were waiting for him to look away before moving again. He listened for the usual night sounds—frogs, crickets, or even an owl muttering as it glided after prey. There was nothing except the stream. "Well, here goes," Jack said.

He advanced carefully with Pega clinging to his arm. "We'll never find each other again if we get separated," she whispered. Jack thought it unlikely they'd get separated. She was holding him so tightly, he was sure there'd be a bruise in the morning. Once the light faded, they had to feel their way along with only the sound of water to guide them. Jack tripped over a root, and they both blundered into stinging nettles.

"Ah!" Jack cried, pitching forward. Pega's firm grip saved him. The ground was slippery with mud.

"There's *got* to be water," she moaned. Jack inched ahead on his knees. He saw a glimmer of light and recklessly tore away vines.

"Oh, sweet saints," Pega said reverently. The trees parted to show a rushing stream, marked here and there by slicks of moonlight. It flowed noisily over rocks and on into a broad channel, a dark presence slicing the forest in two.

Jack and Pega slid down the bank as fast as they could go and landed in the water up to their waists. The current was deeply cold. Jack didn't care. He drank until his head ached and his stomach cramped, but the water took away the pain in his feet.

Finally, they crawled back up the muddy bank and snuggled together like a pair of foxes in a tree hollowed by age. They were wet, cold, and very, very hungry, but the sound of water sent them to sleep as surely as if they were in the Bard's house with a fire snapping on the hearth. They slept through the night and the dawn as well. It was mid-morning before they stirred and saw the sun sending narrow beams of light into the forest outside.

"Where are we?" said Pega, shading her eyes.

"Here. Wherever *here* is," Jack answered, yawning. The air shivered with tiny midges dancing in the light that penetrated the forest. The stream tumbled nearby, and a carpet of wild strawberries covered the ground around the hollow tree. "Food!" Jack cried.

They picked the tiny fruit as fast as they could. "Mmf! This is good! More! More!!" Juice ran down Pega's chin and dripped onto her dress.

"You know," said Jack, sitting back after the first ecstasy of filling his stomach, "it's awfully early for strawberries."

"Who cares?" Pega wiped her mouth with her arm.

"It isn't even May Day. There should only be flowers."

"Then we're lucky," declared Pega. "Brother Aiden would call this a miracle." She began gathering strawberries again.

Jack was uneasy. Several things bothered him. The fire he'd called up in the tunnel had come too readily—not that he wasn't grateful. He didn't want to find out what knuckers ate for dinner when they couldn't find bats. But in the village fire-making was difficult. You had to clear your mind and call to the life force. You couldn't just snap your fingers.

The moonlight, too, had been odd. He'd been too tired to care last night, but now it came back to him. Everything seemed to *glow*. And now the strawberries. Not one of them was green or worm-eaten or overripe. "This place is like Jotunheim," he said.

"From what you've told me, it's a lot nicer than Jotunheim."

"Parts were horrible. Others . . . ." Jack's voice trailed off. There was no way he could explain the wonder of Yggdrassil to someone who hadn't seen it. "Anyhow, magic is what I'm talking about. It's close to the surface here, and dangerous."

"Dangerous?"

"Like when I called fire. I couldn't stop it."

Pega looked around. The trees were covered in thick moss, like sheep after a cold winter, and clusters of bluebells grew at their feet. The ground was a carpet of strawberries. Toward the stream was a swath of yellow irises. "All right. I agree. It does look a little too perfect. Are we going to have trolls stomping around demanding our blood?"

"Not here. It's too warm. But what," Jack hardly dared say it, "if this is Elfland?"

Pega's eyes opened wide. "Crumbs! It's pretty enough."

And wet enough, thought Jack. If ever there was a place the Lady of the Lake would love, this was it. "Brutus must be around somewhere. I wonder why he isn't calling for us," he said.

"We haven't been calling him, either."

"No," said Jack, once more aware of a watchfulness in the trees. Sometimes it seemed far away, concerned with other things, and sometimes it was right there next to them. "I haven't seen a sign of him, though he must be around. Unless he's dead. That would be a problem."

"It'd certainly be a problem for him," Pega said.

"I'm not being heartless. Of course I'd feel sorry if anything happened to Brutus, but we were counting on him. I suspect he's done something stupid, like challenge a dragon and got himself eaten."

"Inconsiderate of him."

"Do we keep exploring?" Jack said, ignoring her sarcasm. "We could wander for weeks. Or do we go back down the hole and choose another tunnel? The fire must be out by now."

"Go back down?" Pega turned very pale, and her birth-mark stood out like ink. "I wouldn't want to meet another of those—you know."

"Me neither."

"Well then."

They went back to the meadow. By day the hillside appeared an even greater ruin. A huge section of cliff had fallen, leaving a giant scar on the mountains above. The slide went halfway up and ended in rocks too rugged to climb. "This looks new," said Jack, shading his eyes. "I wonder if it happened during the earthquake."

They followed the edge of the meadow, fording little streams that poured out of the mountainside, keeping the grass to their left and the rocks to their right. Deer watched them gravely from the shadows of the trees, and red squirrels followed them with bright, black eyes. Voles, dormice, and shrews rummaged through the flowers, unworried by the appearance of strange humans. Even hedgehogs were foraging.

"That's another thing that just shouts magic," Jack pointed out. "Hedgehogs in daylight."

"I could catch those," Pega suggested. "You roast them coated in mud and the quills come right off."

"You aren't allowed to hunt in magic places," Jack said decisively.

"We'll need something. Those strawberries wore off hours ago." Eventually, Pega found a field of pignuts. She pulled them up and collected the round nuts on their roots. "I used to eat these when my owners didn't feed me," she explained. Jack decided they weren't too bad—like hazelnuts dipped in mud. Besides, he had nothing else.

The sun sank behind the mountains. Blue shadows flowed over the forest, and the temperature dropped. They hurriedly tried to gather firewood, but strangely, the forest produced nothing but a few twigs and damp leaves. The ancient trees clung on to every gnarled branch. "Doesn't anything *die* here?" Pega cried.

"Not if it's Elfland," Jack guessed. The light was fading, and his teeth chattered with cold. They would have to find shelter or freeze to death. They searched until they found a ring of trees so close together, the trunks formed a natural room.

"Can't you use your staff to call up fire?" Pega said, stamping her feet and rubbing her arms to keep warm.

"Even magic fire needs fuel. Somehow I don't think it's safe to burn these trees."

They were exhausted from walking, but sleep would not come. A chill came up from the ground, and neither Jack nor Pega cared to snuggle close to the roots. Jack was aware, though he couldn't say how, of a brooding *dislike* in the trees. They seemed to be making up their minds about what they might do with the intruders in their midst.

"That does it," Pega said, sitting up. "I've had it with those trees whispering."

"What whispering?" said Jack, jarred from what little comfort he had.

"Those sneaky sounds. Surely you heard them? I don't know what they're saying, but I don't like it. What did Brutus tell us to do when we were dispirited? Sing something cheerful."

"You mean his ballad about a knight hunting an ogre in a haunted wood? Remember how it ended?"

"Not *that* one," Pega said. "The one your father sang on the way to Bebba's Town." She immediately began Brother Caedmon's hymn, given to him by an angel in a dream.

Praise we now the Fashioner of Heaven's fabric,
The majesty of His might and His mind's wisdom . . .

Jack had to admit it was an excellent choice. For one thing, its soaring power put those whispering trees in their place. Jack couldn't hear them, but he didn't doubt that Pega could. For another, her voice was so marvelously fine. He'd been jealous of her at the Bard's house, but he knew even then he was being unfair. She wasn't a strong singer, yet her music filled the night. In the darkness you could believe you were listening to an elf lady.

Afterward they curled up together as they had in the hollow tree. No looming menace disturbed their sleep, and when they awoke, they found themselves covered with a blanket of the finest wool.

Chapter Twenty-one

THE GIRL IN THE MOSS

The little hollow was filled with a dim, green light. Jack could see sunbeams in the distance, but here the branches formed a dense mat. The air was heavy with the scent of lime flowers, and above, unseen, hummed a multitude of bees. For a moment Jack thought they had found their way into the Valley of Yggdrassil. But the hum wasn't frenzied as it had been there. It was merely the sound of bees going about their usual chores.

"Where did this blanket come from?" whispered Pega.

"Elves?" guessed Jack.

"Brother Aiden said elves were completely selfish. Someone else left this, but what kind of people creep up on you in the middle of the night?"

"Maybe Brutus found a village and borrowed some things," Jack said doubtfully. "I could shout for him, but—"

"It doesn't seem quite safe," Pega finished.

"He's *got* to be here somewhere. He probably went to the stream to fill the empty cider bags," said Jack. "He would have returned for us, unless . . ." *Unless he never got out in the first place,* the boy thought. But, no, they would have heard Brutus shouting if anything had gone wrong. It wasn't like the slave to go quietly into a knucker hole.

The trees weren't as threatening as they had seemed the night before, but they still made Jack uneasy. "This is an odd kind of wool," he said, feeling the fine, soft weave. From underneath, it was visible, but when he spread it on the ground, it vanished.

"It's magic," Pega said. "I've heard about cloaks of invisibility in stories. We'll have to be careful, or we'll lose it." She folded it up and put a rock on top to mark its position. "Look!" she cried. She pounced on what Jack had thought was a large mushroom bulging out of the tree roots. The top of it came off, and a delicious smell wafted through the hollow. "It's a pot and it's full of bread and the bread's still *warm*!"

Jack was by her side in a flash. "There's more," he said in wonder. Other mushroom-shaped containers revealed butter, honey, and golden rounds of cheese. The invisible creatures had even thought to provide wooden butter spreaders.

"Oh, thank you, thank you, whoever you are," called Pega. "I swear I'll do something nice for you, just name—"

"Hush," said Jack, covering her mouth. He knew from

stories that it was dangerous to make promises to things you couldn't see. "We're both extremely grateful," he said, formally bowing to the trees around. "We'd be really happy to share this meal with you."

But the forest was silent except for a faint breeze working its way through the branches and the bees humming all around. In the distance an unknown bird warbled and trilled.

Pega tore the bread apart and slathered it with butter and honey. She passed a chunk to Jack. "Do you think this food is enchanted?" he said, pausing with his hand in midair.

"I don't care!" Pega bit into her chunk and added, in a muffled voice, "You can wait to see if I turn into a grasshopper. At least I'll be a well-fed grasshopper."

Jack couldn't resist the smell of melting butter. He began devouring the warm bread, and it was even better than it smelled. The honey was as fragrant as a field of clover, and the cheese was sharp and wonderfully satisfying. He stuffed two rounds of it into his pockets for later.

When they were finished, they sat back in a kind of happy daze, too contented to move or talk. "We ought to wash our hands and faces," Pega said after a while.

"Hmm," said Jack. They sat a while longer, until the sound of a little, bubbling stream roused them. "I could use a drink," Jack murmured.

"Me too," said Pega. Time passed.

"We should move," Jack said. He forced himself to rise. The green stillness of the hollow lay heavily on his body and urged him to lie down again. *It's a fine old bed, earth is,* whispered a voice in Jack's mind. *You can pull the moss over you and sleep for a hundred years.* "Get up," cried Jack, suddenly alarmed. He dragged Pega to her feet and forced her to walk around. Once they were out of the hollow, Jack stamped his feet to get feeling back into them. Pega slapped her arms.

"What was that?" she said, her eyes wide and frightened.

"I don't know. The trees, maybe. I never trusted them."

They walked to the stream and washed their faces and hands. The cold water revived them.

"We mustn't get too comfortable," Jack said. "When I was in the Valley of Yggdrassil, I lost all track of time." He stopped and remembered the drowsy enchantment of that place. He'd still be there if it hadn't been for Thorgil. "We've got to remember our mission. Everyone's depending on us. We have to find the Lady of the Lake and bring the water back to Bebba's Town. King Yffi won't wait forever."

"That's funny. I completely forgot about Yffi." Pega waved her hand in front of her face as though brushing away spiderwebs.

"Magic does that. We have to keep reminding ourselves why we're here. We have to keep saying people's names. If I forget, you remind me."

Pega fetched her string bag and removed the candle Mother had given her. "Smell," she commanded.

Jack did so, and his head cleared at once. He remembered the village with its fields and houses. He saw the blacksmith fashioning a farm tool on his anvil, the baker pulling bread from his oven, and Mother sitting at her loom.

"You see," Pega said, sniffing the fragrant wax herself, "the need-fire came through this. It will light our way back home."

"You've learned more than I realized," said Jack gravely.

"I listened a lot. Slaves do," she replied.

They went back to the hollow to retrieve the blanket, but it was gone and so were the pots. "I suppose the owners took them," said Pega. "It's only natural. Now what do we do?"

Jack hung his head, trying to come up with a plan. "I wish I knew where we were," he said. "Maybe the Lady of the Lake is here, and maybe she isn't. Brutus could have found her, or he might have stumbled onto a dragon. We definitely can't go back down that tunnel."

In the end they kept on walking, keeping the trees to their left and the mountain to their right. They passed ghostly birches, aspens with leaves that twinkled in the wind, giant oaks with moss trailing like hair, and monstrous yews. The meadow through which they traveled was alive with small animals. Once, they saw a lynx watching them with round yellow eyes, and another time they crossed a stream where green butterflies drifted to and fro over banks of valerian.

It was a surpassingly beautiful place, yet ultimately, it was disappointing. They found no trails and saw no houses or the smoke that would come from houses. "Where are the people?" Pega said. In late afternoon they came to a rift in the trees where a tongue of rock jutted out of the mountain. They walked along the top.

"This wouldn't be a bad place to camp," Jack said.

"Too cold," said Pega. "Imagine how exposed we'd be."

"It's better than sleeping in the forest." Since that morning Jack had developed a dislike for trees. Roots snaked to the very edge of the rock as though trying to climb it. Moss humped up in patterns suggestive of buried bodies, though Jack guessed it was only more roots underneath. Suddenly, he saw a patch of white. "Look!" he cried.

"What is it?" Pega squinted against the dark shadow of the forest.

"It's a hare or a cat, curled up. No, it isn't! It's a face!" Jack began sliding down the steep sides of the rock.

"Wait for me," gasped Pega, sliding and tumbling after him. "It's a person! Someone sleeping in the forest, only he's covered with moss. Oh, it's terrible!"

Jack saw signs of a struggle, slash marks and turf pried up. Whoever it was had not gone down peacefully. He got to the site, pulled back a tangle of vines that were stealthily covering the moss, and shouted, so great was his shock.

"Thorgil! Oh, my dear! Thorgil! Wake up! I'll save you!" Her body was completely engulfed, but her face and throat were still clear. Jack tried to pull the moss up with his hands. It was thicker and stronger than any such plant he'd ever encountered. His fingers made no more impression on it than if he'd been trying to claw up stone.

"I can't find anything to dig with," moaned Pega, pulling at roots and yanking at the branches of a tree. "These are like iron! I can't break them!"

"I can try magic," Jack said, "but it might be dangerous.

Stand back, Pega. I'm not sure what will happen." Pega retreated to the edge of the rock. Jack rested his staff on the moss and tried to calm his mind.

What do I ask for? What do I say? he thought desperately. He was afraid to call fire. It might burst out and incinerate all of them. Even as he considered, he saw the moss creep softly up Thorgil's throat—*and recoil.*

It curled back, and flakes of ash drifted off in the slight breeze. The shield maiden's eyes were closed and her face was very pale, but the moss stirred gently over her chest. She was still breathing. Some power lay between her and the forest.

The rune of protection, thought Jack. He couldn't see it—it was invisible except for that brief time when it was passed from one person to another—but he felt its presence. The Bard had worn it when he passed through the Valley of Lunatics. Jack had carried it in Jotunheim and had given it up only to keep Thorgil from killing herself. It was pure life force.

Jack yearned to touch it. He didn't dare. The rune could only be given freely. It burned whoever tried to take it by force, as it was burning the moss now and keeping it from covering Thorgil's face.

He racked his brains for a solution. He knew how to call up fog and wind, find water, kindle fire, and (once) cause an earthquake. None of these would do him any good now. *If only I could wake her,* thought Jack. *She could will new strength from the rune.* He stroked her forehead and called her name, but she slept on.

"Can I help?" said Pega from the rock.

"You don't know magic," Jack said impatiently. He didn't want to be interrupted.

"I could sing."

Jack's head snapped up. Sing! Of course! What was the one thing most likely to rouse Thorgil to action? Without bothering to explain, he began:

Cattle die and kin die.
Houses burn to the ground.
But one thing never perishes:
The fame of a brave warrior.

"That's an odd thing to tell someone who might be dying," Pega said.

"Be quiet," said Jack. He went on:

Ships go down in the sea.
Kingdoms turn into dust.
One thing outlasts them all:
The fame of a brave warrior.

Fame never dies!
Fame never dies!
Fame never dies!

As he sang, the memory of the Northmen came back to him. They were in Olaf One-Brow's ship with a wind filling the red-and-cream-striped sail. Their lives were violent, they were thugs of the worst kind, foul, half crazy, and stupid, and yet . . . they were noble as well.

Jack began the song again, and Pega joined in—she was a quick study for music. *"Fame never dies! Fame never dies! Fame never dies!"* Thorgil's face lost its deadly pallor, and her lips trembled as though she was trying to join in. Her eyes flew open.

"Jack?" she whispered.

"You've got to live," Jack said, so delighted that he could hardly contain himself. Her eyes lost their brightness and began to close. "What kind of oath-breaking coward are you!" he shouted. "Is this an honorable death? Sleeping on a soft bed like the lowest thrall? Faugh! You deserve to go to Hel!"

"Jack!" cried Pega, shocked.

"Be still. I know what I'm doing. Thorgil Chicken-Heart is what they'll call you," he told the shield maiden. "Thorgil *Brjóstabarn*! Suckling baby!"

"I am *not* a *brjóstabarn*," snarled Thorgil, her face flushing red and her body quivering under the moss.

"Then live, you sorry excuse for carrion!"

The shield maiden's mouth contorted as though she had so many vile curses to utter, she couldn't get them out fast enough. The moss on her chest began to turn brown and flake away. The line of destruction moved down her arms and legs. She wrenched herself up and felt for her knife. Then weakness overtook her, and she collapsed to her knees, shaking violently.

"That's better," Jack said.

"Let me help you," Pega cried, bounding to Thorgil's side.

"No one . . ."—the shield maiden stopped and panted, so great was her exhaustion—"needs . . . to help me."

"Look at you. You can't even talk straight. 'Course you need help." Pega attempted to lift her, but Thorgil gave her a feeble slap.

"Leave her alone," Jack said. "Thorgil *Brjóstabarn* can crawl if she can't walk."

"Hate . . . you," said Thorgil, breathing heavily.

Jack went back to sit on the rocks. He felt as light as a sunbeam. "I'd get off that moss if I were you. Your choice, of course." Pega looked up at him in consternation. "I know you think I'm horrible, Pega, but I learned my manners from Northmen. They can hardly get through the day without ten insults and at least one death threat." Pega, after getting slapped—weakly—a few times, retreated to the rocks to sit by Jack.

Together they watched the shield maiden drag herself forward on hands and knees. Jack's heart, in spite of his harsh words, ached to see her struggle, but he also knew it was useless to interfere. Thorgil would have to rescue herself. Otherwise, she would feel humiliated and be even harder to deal with. Finally, she crept onto the lowest layer of stone, beyond the reach of questing tree roots.

"I . . . did it . . . ," she wheezed. "No . . . thanks to you."

Now Jack did scoot down to sit by her side. "You need water," he observed. "Wait here." He ran to a small rivulet trickling from the mountain nearby and filled his hands. Some of the water leaked out on the way back, but he managed to get a little into Thorgil's mouth. Back and forth he went, with Pega helping, until the shield maiden sighed and shook her head.

"Enough," she said.

Jack produced one of the rounds of cheese, and Thorgil almost bit him in her eagerness to get it. "Take little bites," he advised. "It's not safe to bolt your food after starving." But Thorgil paid no attention. When she was finished, she leaned back against the rock and closed her eyes.

"Is she going to faint again?" whispered Pega.

"I imagine she needs time to recover," said Jack. "I don't know how long she's been here." He noted that Thorgil's clothes were stained dark green and her boots were the color of tree bark. It was as though she'd been turning into part of the forest. Perhaps she had been.

"One of my owners refused to feed me for three weeks for spoiling one of his shirts," Pega remarked. She was huddled in a fold of the rock with her arms hugging her knees for warmth. The sun had gone behind the mountain, and the air had turned chill. "All I had was what I could find in the rubbish heap. You can't believe how good fish heads taste after three weeks."

Thorgil opened her eyes and looked straight at the girl. "You're a thrall," she said.

"What's a thrall?" asked Pega.

Jack swore under his breath. "Pay no attention. Northmen like picking fights more than bears like honey. Even their gods insult one another."

"'Thrall' means 'slave,'" Thorgil said in perfectly clear Saxon.

"I am not! Jack freed me!"

"I was a slave once," Jack said. "I'm not ashamed of it."

"You should be," Thorgil said with a wolfish smile.

You were too, thought Jack, but he bit back the words before they slipped out. Taunting Thorgil was a sport that had to be conducted very carefully. "Perhaps we should look for a place to sleep," he said. "Anyone want a bed of moss?"

"No!" Thorgil cried, which showed Jack how terrified she'd been. It wasn't like her to admit fear.

"I don't understand. We've spent two nights in the forest, and nothing happened to us until this morning," said Pega. "It's like the trees suddenly woke up."

"Or we ran into the wrong trees," said Jack. "I suppose some are good and some are bad, like people. Anyhow, we need shelter before it gets completely dark. I saw a cleft in the rocks earlier."

Chapter Twenty-two

THORGIL'S SAGA

The cleft turned out to be a tiny valley hidden in the side of the mountain. On one side of a stream was a shelf of rock wide enough to sleep on. At the upper end was an ancient apple tree so coated in lichen, it appeared almost silver. It was covered in white flowers that added to its ghostly appearance. For a wonder, it bore masses of pale yellow fruit as well. Or at least Jack thought they were yellow. The night was coming on so rapidly, it was difficult to tell.

"Do you think it's safe to eat them?" whispered Pega.

Jack climbed up to the tree. The air around it was filled with a wild sweetness unlike the flowers of the lime trees the night before. Those lulled you into sleep while these made you feel like something exciting was about to happen. "I think this is one of the good trees," he said.

Pega gathered some of the apples littering the ground. "Thank you kindly," she said, bowing to the tree.

Thorgil snorted. Jack guessed she thought it demeaning to say *thank you* to a tree. Once again, they could build no fire, but the air in the tiny valley was still and not too cold. They feasted on apples and the remaining round of cheese, with water from the stream. Pega sang a song about a fox and a hen who kept foiling the fox's plans to eat her. It had many verses, and both Jack and Thorgil joined in for the chorus. "My mother used to sing this when I was very small," said Thorgil.

"Mine too," said Jack, strangely moved. Thorgil almost never mentioned her mother, who had been sacrificed in the Northman lands.

"Mine too, probably, if I could remember her," added Pega.

They snuggled together for warmth and slept soundly in spite of the hardness of their bed. Jack woke in the middle of the night to see the full moon flooding down into the narrow valley. The apple tree shone with an unearthly brightness, and then it did, indeed, appear to be made of silver. *That's odd,* thought Jack, settling back beside Pega and Thorgil. *I could have sworn the moon was full two nights ago.*

Thorgil's shout awakened Jack and Pega. They scrambled to their feet and saw the shield maiden, knife drawn, staring at the apple tree. "Something was here," she said. "I saw it just as my eyes opened, but it disappeared."

Jack joined her in looking around. "What did it look like?"

"Hard to say. It moved so quickly. It was speckled green and brown, shorter than a man, and it had a face."

"Face?"

Thorgil smiled, as she tended to do when she had something unpleasant to say. "It was like a toad or a newt—wide, flat nostrils and a lipless mouth. I forgot to mention it was standing over Pega."

"Bedbugs!" cried Pega.

"It was stroking your hair."

"Stop trying to frighten her," Jack said. He climbed up to the apple tree and searched. There was nothing. Behind the tree the rock was seamed with many possible footholds. Whatever it was could easily have escaped.

"I swear by Odin I saw a creature," said Thorgil. Jack didn't doubt her. She was no liar, even if she took a malicious pleasure in frightening people. In a way he was glad she'd seen something. A giant toad was better than some of the things he'd been imagining.

"It's left us more of those pots," he said, kneeling by what appeared to be large mushrooms sprouting from the base of the tree.

Pega and Thorgil climbed up beside him. As before, the pots contained warm bread, butter, honey, and cheese. "This is a wonder," said Thorgil, letting the mouthwatering smell of bread waft over her face. "What magic brought these here?"

"I suppose our visitor left them," said Pega.

"I've heard that some creatures charm mud to look like food," remarked the shield maiden. "It turns back into mud in your stomach."

"Don't you ever have anything good to say?" Jack snapped.

Thorgil grinned.

They carried the food down to the shelf of rock by the stream and made a pleasant meal, with apples for dessert. "Now I want to know how you got here and how you got trapped in the moss," Jack told Thorgil. "I didn't ask you yesterday because you looked . . . tired." He'd been about to say *frightened*, but he knew that would only make her angry.

"We were on a quest," the shield maiden began.

"We?" queried Jack.

"Skakki, Sven the Vengeful, Eric the Rash—the usual crowd."

"And a boy I didn't recognize."

Thorgil straightened up in surprise. "How did you know that?"

"I'm a skald," Jack said airily. "It's my business to know such things."

"Then you can figure out the rest of it," snarled Thorgil.

"Please. I don't know beans," interrupted Pega. "I'd like to know what such a famous warrior is doing on our shores."

Jack mentally congratulated the girl for hitting on the one compliment likely to make Thorgil cooperate.

"We were doing our usual harvesting of cowardly Saxon villages," the shield maiden continued. She paused to let the insult sink in. Jack heroically kept silent. "But we had a tip about a secret passage into Elfland. Rune overheard it at the slave market—*you* remember the place, Jack."

"Go on," he said tensely.

"Skakki was bargaining with the Picts, and they didn't have enough weapons to trade for what we'd got. They offered to leave the shortfall on a deserted beach. Well, that kind of promise is worth about as much as a handful of dirt. But before Skakki said no, Rune pulled him aside. He'd been listening to the Picts argue. They didn't want to reveal the location of the beach *because a cave on it led to Elfland.* When Skakki heard that, he decided to take the chance."

"Why would you want to go to Elfland?" Pega asked.

"For the plunder, of course! They have silver and jewels, fine horses, too. We put ashore, and believe it or not, the weapons were there. We searched the beach, and Eric Pretty-Face found the cave—"

"Eric Pretty-Face?" said Pega.

"It's a Northman joke," Jack explained. "He has awful battle scars. His leg was practically chewed off by a troll." Pega's eyes opened very wide.

"But Rune had heard some lore about Elfland. Seems it isn't safe for adults, but children can get in and out," said the shield maiden.

Jack remembered the Bard telling him the same thing. *I think you're young enough to resist the lure of elves,* the old man had said. *It's a curious thing, but this is one area where children are stronger than adults. They aren't taken in by illusions, and elves, above all else, are masters of illusion.*

"Heinrich and I were chosen to go."

"That's the boy I don't know," said Jack.

"He was a nephew of Ivar the Boneless," said Thorgil. "He'd just turned twelve, and Ivar insisted we take him. You know how one person can simply ruin an outing? Heinrich had been spoiled rotten by his mother. He whined constantly. He wanted to be first on shore for the raids. He hogged the bog myrtle and demanded the first pick of plunder. *And* he insisted we call him Heinrich the Heinous, a title he had not earned. He was no more heinous than any other twelve-year-old, in spite of torturing thralls—"

"That's enough," said Jack, who didn't want to get into torturing thralls with Pega there. She was staring at Thorgil with frank horror. "Tell us about your quest."

"Heinrich insisted on going first to show off his weapons. Honestly! A sword, a spear, a shield, *and* a reserve shield when you're practically going down into a mine. How stupid can you get? Anyhow, on the second day Heinrich wanted to explore a side passage. 'You know what Rune said,' I told him. 'No side passages.' He called me a coward and went in." Thorgil swallowed and took a deep breath. Jack had an awful feeling he knew what was in the side passage.

"He—he called out that he was stuck," said the shield

maiden. "I was lagging behind with the supplies, and I heard Heinrich scream. I held up the torch and saw—" Thorgil broke off.

Jack and Pega waited. The shield maiden was clearly having trouble saying exactly what she saw. The sun had finally found its way into the narrow valley and roused a family of otters. They slid past on the stream, bobbed down, and came up with small silver fish in their paws. They were not in the least afraid of the humans on the bank.

"When I was very small," Thorgil said, gulping, "I found a nest of snakes while digging for wild garlic in the forest. They were slithering all over each other, hissing and baring their fangs. I ran home and was beaten for not fetching the garlic. That's what I saw in the cave, only this nest was much, much bigger. There were hundreds of serpents, and in the middle was Heinrich. They were wrapped around his arms and legs, and as I watched, one went down his throat. But before I could do anything, the ground started shaking! I've never felt anything like it. The rocks tumbled down, and I couldn't stay on my feet. Then something struck me from behind. When I awoke, the tunnel we'd come through had collapsed and a hole had opened up in the roof."

"And Heinrich?" said Pega.

"Gone. Buried behind the rocks." Thorgil looked down at her hands.

"He fell into a knucker hole," said Jack. "We were almost trapped by one too. It looked like a giant tick."

"No. A bedbug," Pega insisted.

"I swear by Odin it was a nest of snakes," said Thorgil.

"We're all probably right. I think a knucker looks like your worst nightmare," Jack said wisely.

Chapter Twenty-three

THE BUGABOO

By this time the sun was flooding into the little valley. All three children were depressed by Thorgil's tale, and Jack suggested they share the rest of her story later. He had filled his pockets with the excess cheese, which was fortunate, for the mushroom-shaped pots had vanished.

"It gives me the creeps to know that some creature can come and go without us seeing it." Pega shivered.

"It seems friendly," Jack said.

"Yes, but it won't come out into the open. How am I going to sleep with that thing tiptoeing around? And why was it hanging over *me*?"

"Perhaps you looked the most edible," suggested Thorgil.

"Stop that," said Jack. He was reluctant to leave the crevice in the mountains. It seemed so safe after the whispering trees and the shock of finding Thorgil half devoured by moss. But they had no choice.

They continued to follow the strip of meadow between the rocks and the forest. No one said anything. No one made the decision to go on. It was simply the easiest thing to do.

They passed groves of aspen, birch, alder, and ash, broken up by gnarled, lichen-encrusted oaks and lime trees that cast an eerie green shade. Presently, Jack noticed that the sun, instead of being behind them, was on their left. They had come to the end of the valley and were following the mountains around to the other side. Yet still there was no way out, and the rocks were still too steep to climb.

"I think this is leading us back," said Thorgil. "I had hoped to return to the ship, but the tunnel was blocked." They rested by a little rushing stream, and Jack passed around the cheese he'd taken. Much had happened since he last saw Thorgil, and he told her first of his return to the village and of the Bard's travels in the body of Bold Heart.

"That was Bold Heart?" cried the shield maiden. "That stupid bird told me he was the Bard, but I assumed he was lying. So many birds do."

"You can understand birds?" said Pega.

The shield maiden nodded curtly. Jack remembered she didn't like understanding them. She said they reminded her of a mob of drunk Northmen and never shut up.

"What's that one saying?" said Pega, pointing at a finch warbling on an elder bush.

Thorgil listened. "He's saying, 'I'm itchy. I'm itchy. I'm itchy.' And that one's saying, 'So am I. So am I. So am I.' The one on the beech tree is singing, 'Bird lice, bird lice, we've all got bird lice!'"

"Knowing does kind of take the fun out of it," decided Pega.

They traveled on. Jack told Thorgil about Lucy's madness, the destruction of St. Filian's Well, and Brutus's disappearance.

"*You* caused the earthquake?" cried Thorgil when he got to that part.

"I didn't mean to. I was angry. The Bard says never to do magic when you're angry."

"That's a wonderful skill!" exclaimed Thorgil. "You could cause an avalanche to fall on your enemies. You could wipe out a whole village."

"Oh, bother," muttered Jack. He'd forgotten how bloodthirsty she was. But on the whole they spent a pleasant day swapping tales and reminiscing about their adventures in Jotunheim. Jack didn't notice until late afternoon that Pega had said nothing for a very long time.

He looked for a place to spend the night, but this time he found no friendly side valley. They'd have to camp on the rocks or go under the trees.

"I will not go under the trees," Thorgil said.

"Frightened?" said Pega waspishly.

"Only *thralls* are afraid," the shield maiden hissed.

"That's lucky, because there are no thralls here," retorted Pega. "As for me, I'm going to find a nice, soft little bed of moss. I suppose you'd prefer to cower on the rocks."

"Pega!" cried Jack. He was surprised. It wasn't like her to pick fights.

But Thorgil merely grunted. "I choose my battles. I don't care to wake with a monster leaning over me."

Pega stamped off to the trees, though not actually under the branches, Jack noticed. Thorgil found a smooth shelf of rock. "This makes no sense," Jack told her. "We have to stay together."

"Then let her come here," the shield maiden said.

"I'm not moving!" called Pega.

Jack looked from one to the other, trying to think of a way to bring them together. He couldn't understand why this argument had suddenly surfaced. "At least let's tell stories or something. I'm not sleepy yet." Grudgingly, the girls met halfway between their chosen camps. It wasn't a good place, being somewhat marshy, but Jack was grateful for whatever he could get. What could have caused this problem? he wondered. You expected ratty behavior from Thorgil—the time to worry was when she was being nice—but Pega had always been eager to please.

"I know one story I'd like," Pega declared. "I'd like to know why a *famous warrior* ended up covered in moss."

"It's a fair question," admitted Thorgil. "I'd rather answer it before it gets dark."

After the earthquake, the shield maiden began, she'd

climbed up to the hole in the roof. It was such a relief to be outside, she decided to look for water before returning. "I found a stream and then set about getting food," she said. "All my supplies, except for this knife, had disappeared in the rock slide. I thought hunting would be difficult, but the animals were amazingly tame. Stupid, in fact. They practically lay down and asked me to kill them."

"Oh, Thorgil," said Jack. "That should have told you this place was magic. Don't you remember the Valley of Yggdrassil? Killing those animals was forbidden."

"I was *hungry*," Thorgil said with some irritation. "In my opinion a fawn that sits down in front of someone who's hungry is committing suicide."

"You didn't—," said Pega.

"Of course I did," said the shield maiden. "Then I couldn't find firewood to cook it. I tried to tear off branches, but the trees here must be made of iron. All I could do was hack off a few twigs. When I returned to the fawn, it was gone. I felt something watching me."

"Crumbs!" said Pega, hugging herself.

"It wasn't like anything I've ever encountered, not like a human, animal, or troll. It was cold. Like a tree. I could feel its thoughts. It wasn't angry. It merely wanted to get rid of me in that slow, patient way trees have when they ooze sap over an annoying beetle."

Jack shivered. He remembered the casual way the Hedge surrounding Din Guardi had put out a branch to scratch his face.

"I had the strongest desire to lie down. I knew—I knew," said Thorgil, her voice suddenly husky, "that if I stayed, I wouldn't have the strength to resist. So I started running. To be more exact, I went mad."

"Berserk?" Jack guessed.

"Going berserk would have been fun. All that hacking, chopping, and pillaging . . . Ah, well." Thorgil sighed. "What I felt was panic."

Jack nodded. He knew she hadn't been able to go berserk since drinking from Mimir's Well.

"I simply ran . . . and ran . . . and ran. When I stopped for breath, the trees closed in around me, so I went on until my legs collapsed under me. I stabbed the moss and screamed to keep *it* away, but *it* had all the time in the world. At last I could fight no longer and lay down. I could feel roots creeping around me and moss stealing over my arms and legs. Its thoughts were like decaying leaf mold—oh!" Thorgil shuddered violently. Jack put his arms around her.

He braced himself for a blow—Thorgil wasn't exactly keen on sympathy—but the shield maiden was too overcome to object. After a while she shook him off and gave him a fierce little smile.

By now the valley was in shadow. Stars were beginning to appear in the deep blue sky, and a cold dampness seeped from the meadow. "Which is it to be?" said Jack. "The trees or the rocks?"

Pega hunched over, looking more than ever like a large

frog in a small pond. "After that story I don't want to get close to the trees either," she said, "but I want my own rock."

"I don't know why you're in such a snit," said Jack sharply. Thorgil's story had upset him more than he cared to admit. "You want to be alone? Fine. Get your own personal rock. We'll stay here."

He felt guilty about letting her go, but he was tired and didn't want to spend half the night arguing. Thorgil had found a protected place between two boulders. They curled up side by side and talked about Jotunheim. The shield maiden went to sleep, but Jack stared up at the sky between the boulders and tried to make plans. He heard Pega sobbing quietly.

Oh, bedbugs, he thought, using one of Pega's favorite swearwords. *I'd better go over there.* Then he heard another sound. At first it was a murmur, like a distant stream, but it grew. Jack's heart stood still. The murmur separated into voices that were almost, but not quite, clear. Pega had fallen dead silent.

Jack stood up carefully. A full moon cast an eerie light over the hillside. He saw Pega sitting not far away, and all around her the rocks flickered as though something was running over them. *Beautiful lady,* the voices sang. *Fairest of the fair. Never weep for we are with you. We adore you. We love you.*

"Jack?" croaked Pega, so terrified she could hardly speak.

"Thorgil," Jack whispered. He knew he would need her help. The shield maiden shot straight up with her knife drawn, ready for action.

"It's that thing I saw this morning, only there's more of him," she said.

"We're coming, Pega," said Jack, staff poised at the ready.

We mean no harm, the voices whispered. *The lady weeps and so we came. Fairest of the fair. We love you.*

"They're touching me," squeaked Pega.

"You're frightening her," said Jack.

You hurt her, the voices said accusingly. *You drove her away and she wept.*

"I did not. She wanted to be alone."

Not her. Not her. Her loneliness called to us. Cruel mud man.

"Jack, get them to stop touching me," wailed Pega.

"You heard her," said Jack. "Whatever it is you're doing, stop it at once."

"Shall I attack?" whispered Thorgil.

"Not yet. Look, you really are frightening her," called Jack. "Why don't you come out in the open so we can see you?"

Lovely one, is that your wish? The voices sounded like wind in trees.

"Yes! Keep your hands to yourselves," said Pega. Then, like water that suddenly becomes still so you can see into its depths, the creatures appeared. There were hundreds of them! They formed a dense ring around Pega but, fortunately, not too close to her. Jack couldn't think what to do. How on earth was he going to make all those creatures go away?

They were like small men, dressed in clothes that blended with the rocks. Their skin was covered in blotches, and they had large, sleepy-looking eyes. Their noses were two slits above a wide, lipless mouth, and their hair—what there was of it—was plastered over damp-looking foreheads. They had long fingers that were flattened unpleasantly at the ends.

"Kobolds," whispered Thorgil beside him.

"You've seen them before?" he said in a low voice.

"They infested Olaf's ship on his trip up the Rhine. He had to get a wise woman to drive them out."

"Are they dangerous?"

"No," said Thorgil. "They only play pranks and steal things."

"Steal things!" cried a voice behind them. Both Jack and Thorgil jumped. One of the creatures was standing far too close for comfort. "Steal things! I like that! After all the nice things we've done for you—bringing you food and keeping the Forest Lord busy at the other end of the valley."

"Olaf also said they were touchy," added Thorgil.

"I'm sorry," said Jack, bowing politely. "We didn't mean to insult you. We're extremely grateful for your help."

"Hmf!" said the creature.

"Could you ask your companions to let our friend go? She's really upset."

"We aren't doing anything to her. *You're* the ones who made her feel unwelcome."

"Yes, well, we're sorry about that, too. Couldn't you let us go to her?" asked Jack.

"Nobody's stopping you," sneered the creature.

Jack and Thorgil approached the ring. It opened to let

them through and closed behind them. Jack was aware of hundreds of froggy eyes watching him. He felt their hands flutter against him, like being buffeted by clouds of moths.

"I can see why Pega was upset," said Thorgil, jabbing at an invisible stomach with her elbow.

"Oh, Jack! Jack!" Pega cried, flinging her arms around him when at last he reached her. "Why are they all here? Why are they watching me? What *are* they?"

"Thorgil says they're kobolds."

"Not quite correct." A larger and more lavishly speckled creature suddenly popped up beside Pega, and she screamed. "'Kobolds' is what we're called in Germany. Here we're known as hobgoblins. Some also refer to us as brownies, fenoderees, or, my personal favorite, bugaboos."

"You're a bugaboo?" Pega said faintly.

"Dear lady, I am *the* Bugaboo, the ruler of this place."

"And I'm his Nemesis," said the creature who had been talking to Jack and Thorgil earlier.

"Hurrah for the Bugaboo and his Nemesis!" cried all the other creatures, dancing around so ecstatically that they popped in and out of sight.

"What's a nemesis?" growled Thorgil. She was not taking the incessant interest of the hobgoblins well. She kept slapping little hands that were trying to feel her clothes, her hair, her skin. This didn't do the slightest good. The creatures merely giggled and came straight back.

"Every king has to have a nemesis," said the Nemesis, puffing out his chest, "to tell him when he's wrong or being stupid or lazy. Otherwise, he gets too full of himself. Don't you have them?"

"I don't think our kings like to be criticized," said Jack.

"Well, *of course* they don't! Criticism is supposed to hurt. Otherwise, it's no good."

"Our kings," Jack said, "kill people who make them angry."

A shocked silence fell over the gathering. "Did he say 'kill people'?" murmured one of the creatures.

"We don't approve of it, but it happens," said Jack.

"Perfectly disgusting," said the Nemesis, running his long fingers through his hair. "I must say, I'm not surprised. Mud men are savages at the best of times."

"Now, now. We mustn't be rude to our guests," protested the Bugaboo. "We're perfectly delighted to have visitors. So little happens in the valley, especially since that awful rock slide. You must come back to our halls for a party. We have one every night."

"There you go, sucking up as usual," grumbled the Nemesis. But he joined the others in herding Jack, Thorgil, and Pega along the rocks in the brilliant moonlight.

Chapter Twenty-four

A PROPOSAL OF MARRIAGE

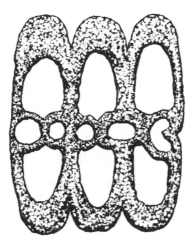

They walked on, surrounded by the mob of hobgoblins with no chance of breaking free. They hugged themselves against the cold, and their breath came out as mist. Presently, they came to a path paved with round, transparent pebbles. The moon was reflected inside each pebble so that it appeared to be a path of raindrops shimmering in the night.

"What magic is this?" said Thorgil, halting. Several hobgoblins bumped into her.

"No magic. They're moonstones," the Bugaboo explained. The shield maiden immediately knelt down and scooped some up. But they dissolved into water in her hands.

Jack had been trying to remember stories about hobgoblins.

He recalled that goblins (who were surely related) had a bad reputation where children were concerned. "We should be going on our way," he told the Bugaboo. "We're most grateful for your invitation, but we're on an important quest and have no time to visit."

"Nonsense. You have all the time in the world," said the hobgoblin king.

"I'm afraid not. My father is being held prisoner. He'll be killed if we don't return as soon as possible."

"Look at the moon," the Bugaboo commanded.

It was full and very bright. *It was full last night, too,* Jack thought again with a whisper of alarm.

The Bugaboo's eyes were large and dark under their sleepy lids. The moon was reflected in them, as it was in the pebbles. "Night after night it rises, always perfect and never moth-eaten as it is in your world. The elves call it the Silver Apple."

"But how—," began Jack.

"When the elves were cast out of Heaven, they were given the power to hold back time. The wheel of the year does not turn in the Land of the Silver Apples."

"You mean time doesn't pass here?" said Pega. She was pressed close to Jack and hadn't lessened her grip on his arm since they'd begun walking.

"That's right, my little dewdrop," said the Bugaboo, chucking her under the chin. Pega hid her face on Jack's chest.

"Less talk and more walk," grumbled the Nemesis.

The tide of hobgoblins swept on, carrying Jack, Pega, and Thorgil along as effortlessly as leaves in a stream. The path curved around and about giant boulders, going steadily up until it ended at a door in the side of the mountain.

"This is ill fortune. We'll be at their mercy inside," said Thorgil.

"It might be all right," Jack said doubtfully. "They *have* been feeding us."

"Fattening us up, more like."

The Bugaboo rapped on the door. Many locks were turned and chains withdrawn. It was flung open by a gloomy hobgoblin carrying a spear. "About time! Dinner's burned to ashes," he complained.

"That's my son," the Nemesis said proudly. The roof and sides of the passage beyond were covered with softly glowing mushrooms, and the air was filled with a pleasant, earthy aroma. Jack wondered whether you could eat the mushrooms. He was terribly hungry by this time. *It probably isn't safe to eat things that glow,* he decided, but they did smell delicious.

They came to a second door, which was opened by another, even more insulting hobgoblin. "That's my other son," the Nemesis said with a chuckle. "He can turn milk sour just by looking at it." Jack halted in amazement at the scene on the other side.

An enormous cave stretched as far as he could see. Overhead, fires burned in midair like lost stars. Jack tried to make out what they were, but they were too far away and too changeable. He cried out in surprise when some of them darted down and hung flaring over the arriving mob.

"Will-o'-the-wisps," explained the hobgoblin king. "They're always curious." Thorgil shook her fist at them, and they darted away.

The path went down into a cluster of handsome little houses with thatched roofs and enclosed yards. Hobgoblin women in long dresses bustled about pots. Babies waved little arms from cradles. Everywhere creatures spun wool, gardened, hammered wood, wove baskets—all the things normal people did in a village. It was wonderfully cheering to Jack. In the distance he saw fields with animals. It was like an entire world tucked away in the heart of the mountain.

The Bugaboo strode along, nodding grandly to his subjects, who cheered him. Behind him, the Nemesis kept up a constant stream of jibes.

"Look at those fools," he said. "You'd think they were welcoming the Forest Lord. He's one of the old gods, but you're only another hobgoblin who sleeps late and loafs the rest of the time. It's not as if you've ever done anything clever."

Jack knew he'd get angry if someone kept taunting him like that, but the Bugaboo sailed on blithely. His people really seemed to like him. Now and then someone yelled, "Go for it, Nemesis! Give us your best curses." And the Nemesis would bow in return. They were a very odd folk.

The returning mob fanned out, going off to different houses until only the Bugaboo, the Nemesis, and the children were left. They arrived at a large hall with a forecourt enclosed by an earthen wall covered with mushrooms. The mushrooms had obviously been planted with an eye to color, for they formed patterns in red, yellow, purple, and white.

A flock of hobgoblins streamed into the forecourt, shouting greetings and hopping up and down with glee. A large woman grabbed the Nemesis and kissed him soundly on both cheeks. "So you're back, you old rapscallion! I suppose you didn't think of me once," she said.

"Why should I? It was a relief to get away," replied the Nemesis, kissing her back. He produced a dainty bouquet of violets from his pocket.

"I suppose these are crushed," she sniffed.

"I hope so," her husband said, although Jack thought the flowers looked fine.

An older woman fussed over the Bugaboo. "You didn't run into trouble, did you, Buggiekins?" she asked.

"No fear, Mumsie! The Forest Lord is as predictable as moonrise. He was busy getting tree roots to work on the rock slide."

Mumsie suddenly noticed Pega. "Now I know why you were so late!" she cried. She whisked Pega into an enthusiastic hug, which the girl struggled to escape. "Feisty little darling, aren't you? Come along with me. We'll get you out of those rags and into something nice."

"Jack!" wailed Pega, fighting desperately.

"Please, sir," Jack appealed to the hobgoblin king, "she's afraid."

"*Is* my little forest flower shy?" crooned the Bugaboo

fondly, extricating her from his mother's arms. "*Is* she a dear little fledgling peeping over the edge of her nest?"

"I'm not a flower! I'm not a stupid bird! You're strangling me!" Pega shouted.

The king put her down and stood back, grinning widely—a hobgoblin could grin very widely indeed, Jack observed. Pega immediately ran and flung her arms around the boy so tightly, he could hardly breathe.

"I see I have shown a lack of courtesy," the Bugaboo said, bowing formally. "I had not realized you were her brother. I would never have associated such beauty with—well, you mud men can't help how you look. The point is, I should have asked your permission first. Dear boy—Jack's the name, isn't it? Dear Jack, would you grant me the sublime honor of courting your adorable sister and of hopefully winning her hand in marriage?"

"*Marriage?*" shrieked Pega.

Jack looked from one face to another. Everyone was smiling, and the women were giving soft little hoots of encouragement. "Um . . . er . . . ," Jack said, his mind racing wildly.

Pega sank to the ground and burst into tears as though her heart would break. The hoots vanished instantly. A flock of will-o'-the-wisps darted down to watch. "I thought," she gasped between racking sobs, "I thought I'd overcome it. All my life I've feared to look into a stream, to see my face staring back. I've seen everyone turn aside and spit when they saw me. No master kept me if his wife became pregnant, for fear I would mark the child. I tried not to care. I prayed for understanding. Why? Why was I cursed with such ugliness? What had I done to deserve it?"

She rocked back and forth. No one moved. Jack, Thorgil, the hobgoblins, even the will-o'-the-wisps seemed paralyzed by such grief.

"Brother Aiden told me I had a beautiful soul and that in Heaven I would shine like the morning star. And then Jack freed me from slavery." Pega looked up, her blotchy face transformed by adoration. "I vowed to serve him all my days and never, never to indulge in self-pity again, but I did not dream of such cruelty! I'm not a flower. I'm not a baby bird. No one could want to marry me except as a joke."

The Bugaboo hunkered down next to Pega and attempted to take her hand. She pushed him away. "Please don't cry, my little toadstool. I meant no joke. I don't even have a sense of humor."

"He's right. He couldn't get a cackle out of a jackdaw with the stories he tells," said the Nemesis.

"I was drawn first to your voice," said the Bugaboo. "I thought it was the Elf Queen invading our land and went out to—um, well, never mind what I was going to do. We've never got along with elves. But when I saw your face, I fell in love at first sight. 'It's the moonlight,' I told myself. 'In the daylight she'll look like any other mud woman.' But the sun only revealed more loveliness."

Pega looked up. Her face was wet with tears, and she wiped her nose on her sleeve. She was trembling with emotion. "You've been spying on me all this time?"

"Yes! And who would not?" cried the Bugaboo.

Pega laughed weakly. "I guess—to you—I look pretty appetizing."

The hobgoblin king grinned, stretching his rubbery mouth to its widest. His speckled face beamed with joy.

"Oh, Lord," said Pega, looking down again.

Jack decided it was time to step in. "I may not be her brother, sir," he said, "but I'm most definitely her guardian. In our lands courtship proceeds slowly. The lady needs time to get used to her suitor." Jack knew this wasn't true in real life, but he'd heard of such things in stories.

"Marriage is a trap," Thorgil interrupted. "The minute any girl gets tricked into it, she loses everything. She loses the sweet joys of battle and of braving wild storms in search of good pillage. She spends her life doing degrading tasks—cooking, weaving, sewing, scrubbing—all the while chasing after smelly little brats. There is no honor in this. You and I need to have a talk, Pega."

Everyone stared at the shield maiden. Finally, the Bugaboo said, "The Forest Lord should have taken this one. But I do understand the rules of courtship. Forgive me for being impulsive, my darling mugwort." He took Pega's hands, and this time she was too dispirited to reject him. "I will wait for you as long as it takes. For the rest of my life, if necessary."

All the women present hooted with pleasure, and one or two wiped her eyes. Pega merely looked depressed.

"And now it's time for dinner!" cried the Bugaboo to cheers and applause.

"Finally," grumbled the Nemesis.

The hobgoblins scurried around, setting up trestle tables and hauling out trenchers, knives, and spoons. They set out what appeared to be giant acorn cups, flattened on the bottom so they would not tip over. Jack picked up one and examined it.

"From the Forest Lord's own oak tree," explained Mumsie.

"Without his knowledge, of course," said the Bugaboo.

"You keep talking about the Forest Lord," said Jack. "Who is he?"

"One of the old gods," replied the hobgoblin king. "He was here first, with the Man in the Moon, the Wild Huntsman, and the yarthkins."

"He hates men for their slaughter of his children," Mumsie said. She looked very solemn, and Jack saw that she was not the ridiculous creature she seemed, but someone deep.

"His children?" the boy asked.

"The trees, the grass, the moss, as well as the beasts and birds. The Forest Lord rules the green world. For those who harm his subjects, he has an abiding hatred. That's why he tried to take your friend Thorgil."

"What's that? What are you saying?" Thorgil said, suddenly waking up.

"You killed the fawn that trusted you," the Bugaboo's mother replied, not in the least cowed by the shield maiden's anger. "No one hunts the Forest Lord's creatures in the heart of his kingdom, not even us. What the animals do with each other is according to his laws. The fawn would have fled from a wolf, but not from you. Such a betrayal of trust sent a shudder through the forest. All the animals became a little less trusting. It was like an assault on the Forest Lord's realm."

"You knew Thorgil was in danger, and you left her to die?" Jack had begun to like the hobgoblins, but to leave someone helpless to be slowly eaten by moss . . . that was barbaric.

"She had earned her fate." Mumsie's eyes, so like pools of dark water, showed no trace of regret.

"We saved the other one," said the Bugaboo, perhaps wanting to lighten the grim mood that had overtaken the festivities.

"One of your stunning examples of stupidity," declared the Nemesis. "He was being dragged into the river by vines— served him right for trying to hack through them. He thanked us by complaining that we were being too rough."

"Wait," said Jack as a happy thought occurred to him. "His name wouldn't be Brutus?"

"I see you know him," said the Nemesis.

"Know him?" said Pega, for the first time moved from her moody silence. "He's my friend."

"Oh, dear! I wish we'd kept him," said the Bugaboo.

"What did you do with him?"

"Nothing bad," the hobgoblin king replied hastily, attempting to put his arm around her. Pega wriggled away.

The Nemesis laughed nastily. "We gave him what he wanted. Be careful what you ask for, I always say. Brutus wasn't a bit grateful. 'Oh, no, no, no. Brutus doesn't like this, no, he doesn't,'" the hobgoblin said in a credible imitation of the slave's voice.

"You've hurt him," accused Jack, rising to his feet. He'd been driven frantic by the man's complaints and incessant whistling, but he didn't wish him harm.

"Never! We saved his life!" cried the Bugaboo.

"I was the one who sent him packing," the Nemesis gloated. "His Royal Idiocy wanted to keep him as a guest, but it's my job to make sure order is kept in this kingdom. You could see the havoc Brutus was going to cause. He's a descendant of Lancelot, and every man of that line knows how to cast spells over women."

"Please tell us where he is." Jack saw the Bugaboo glance at the Nemesis and the latter shake his head.

"He wanted to get out, so I put him out. Heaven knows where he ended up," said the Nemesis.

"The food's going to be spoiled if we wait much longer," Mumsie interrupted. She signaled to her helpers to bring food. Jack thought about protesting, but he was extremely hungry and poor Pega looked ready to faint.

The dinner was better than Jack had hoped: creamy lentil soup with dense slabs of bread flavored with dill. Fire-roasted turnips swam in fragrant, melted butter, and great wheels of cheese were passed around. Most notable of all were the mushrooms. Boiled, deep-fried, pickled, baked in pies—there seemed no end to their variety. Jack hadn't known so many existed or were safe to eat. "Are you sure—," he began as a purple fungus was plopped onto his trencher like a massive steak.

"Sure of what? That it's delicious? Yes!" said the Bugaboo, tucking into his fungus.

"Mud men are always afraid of our mushrooms," the Nemesis observed. "Mind you," he added, "mistakes *have* been made."

Jack sipped his drink from the giant acorn cup. It tasted faintly of pine needles, but it seemed to be water. Unusually fresh water. It was cold—a welcome thing in a courtyard surrounded by many torches. It didn't make Jack sleepy— not exactly—but he felt his thoughts slow. He studied the acorn cup. It was handsome indeed, a bright brown you could sink your gaze into, going deeper until you could see into the heart of it.

"I think you've had enough," said Mumsie, taking the cup from him. Jack was surprised to find himself lying facedown on the purple fungus. He sat up, confused. Mushroom juice dripped off his chin.

"Hah! Can't hold his water!" crowed the Nemesis.

"Now, now. Mud men—excuse me, *humans*—often have trouble with it," the Bugaboo said. He ordered Jack's cup refilled. "You'll do better with ordinary cave water," he said kindly.

Jack tasted it. It was chalky and not especially good, but it didn't send him into a trance.

"The other was meant as a treat," Mumsie explained. "We take it from the Forest Lord's own pool, when he's busy elsewhere, of course. It makes you think long, slow thoughts like a tree does. Quite refreshing, like having a holiday."

"I drink nothing that comes from the Forest Lord," said Thorgil, pushing her cup away. Her face was pale, and Jack guessed that she was remembering the moss.

"Easily remedied," said the hobgoblin king. He ordered both Thorgil's and Pega's cups refilled with cave water. Jack noticed that several creatures at the table were staring fixedly with small smiles (small for hobgoblins, that is) on their faces.

"It is not wise to drink something that renders you defenseless," observed Thorgil, also looking at them. "Your enemies could creep up on you."

The Bugaboo wriggled his ears with mirth. "Dear me! We have no enemies."

"Everyone has them," said Thorgil.

"Not us. We're universally liked."

"Then why do you post guards at your gates?" the shield maiden persisted. "Why do you secure your doors with many locks? And why do you go about invisibly?"

The laughter died away. The torches at the edge of the courtyard flared, and a pair of will-o'-the wisps darted down to explore the sudden silence. "There *are* elves," the Bugaboo said.

Chapter Twenty-five

FROG SPAWN OMELET

"The elves steal our children," explained the king. "You have to understand that elvish life is centered on pleasure. They cannot bear to spend one minute without entertainment, and they have to keep coming up with new amusements because they're so easily bored. Once, long ago, they decided it was fun to switch our babies with human ones. I believe you call them 'changelings.'"

Jack remembered the Bard talking about such things. *Changelings,* the old man had said, *are always terrified because they've been torn from their rightful place. They fall into terrible rages and scream until everyone is driven mad.* Jack thought, *Well, why wouldn't they?* A human baby suddenly waking up surrounded by hobgoblins would go wild with terror. It must be just as frightening the other way around. "Do the elves give you our children?" he asked.

The Bugaboo sighed deeply, and the hobgoblin women cooed in response. It sounded like a flock of pigeons whispering to one another. "They turn human children into pets. It's considered stylish to have a toddler on a leash. He can be dressed up in funny costumes or trained to do tricks. Toddlers are more clever than dogs, but they're not as durable. Eventually, they fall into despair—lack of love does that. When a child is no longer entertaining, he's left in a forest for wolves to dispose of."

"How terrible!" gasped Pega.

"My father once left me out for wolves to devour," Thorgil remarked.

"I'm not surprised," said the Bugaboo. "The greatest sorrow of our lives is the loss of our sproglings—that's our word for 'children.' There's not a family here who hasn't lost one or two little ones. We try to plug up the tunnels. We post guards and lay traps, but the elves always find a way in."

Hobgoblins had an unnerving habit of blinking their eyes one at a time, not both together as humans did. When they were upset, as the Bugaboo was now, they not only blinked rapidly, but erratically. Jack got dizzy watching him.

Something was hovering at the back of Jack's mind, something important he had to remember, but the warmth, the rich food, and perhaps the effects of the Forest Lord's water had dulled his wits. He was also extremely tired. Pega was nodding off, and even Thorgil jerked her head up in an effort to stay alert.

Dessert was an enormous steamed pudding wrapped in cloth. Jack vaguely remembered eating some. What he'd taken for plums were purple mushrooms.

After dinner the hobgoblins cleared the tables. Jack watched them in a kind of daze. He knew it would be polite to help, but all he wanted was to sleep. Soon a pack of hobgoblin youths led him off, and Pega and Thorgil were taken in another direction.

The sleeping hutches were hollows scraped into the earthen floor of a small side cave. There was one cave for boy hobgoblins, he was told, and another for girls. The adults slept in their own houses, along with the sproglings. The hollows were lined with the softest imaginable wool, and the youths curled up inside them like bunnies.

Jack found he couldn't stretch his legs without sticking his feet out over the edge, but this was a minor problem. He was so tired, he could have slept on a bed of stinging nettles. The sound of snores filled the cave like the grunts of bullfrogs in a summer pond. The wool smelled strongly of mushrooms and perhaps hobgoblins.

Jack sat up and rubbed his eyes. Giant frogs were leaping around him, belching the way frogs do when they are happy. Then he saw that they were hobgoblin youths. A cluster of will-o'-the-wisps hovered near the top of the cave.

"It's morning! It's morning!" cried a youth, landing near

Jack's hutch. "Time to sing and dance and make merry!"

Jack crawled out of the nest. His head ached, and he was in no mood to dance. The hobgoblin youth bounced up and down invitingly, making him queasy.

When he stood up, he was at once the center of attention. He was patted and prodded with sticky fingers until he wanted to punch the next creature that touched him. "Where's my staff?" he said, searching the ground next to his hutch. It was second nature for him to carry it at all times. It was the most important thing he owned, and he knew he'd had it when he went to sleep. "Where's my staff!" he repeated.

Instead of answering, the hobgoblins grabbed his arms and legs and soared away in a series of ecstatic leaps. "Sing and dance and make merry!" they shrieked. Jack struggled to get free, but their hands were surprisingly strong.

"Let me go!" Jack yelled.

"Mud men need to play," one of his captors told him. "They're far too gloomy, always talking about sin. They must enjoy life!"

"With singing and dancing and making merry!" warbled the others.

"Put me down!"

A horn sounded in the distance, not the thrilling hunting horn John the Fletcher sometimes winded, but a nasty blatting noise.

"Breakfast!" screamed the youths. They streamed out of the cave, dragging the boy along. The horn blatted again. The tables were covered with steaming dishes. Thorgil and Pega were already there, looking disheveled and grim. On the roof of the Bugaboo's hall a hobgoblin puffed himself up like a bullfrog. He let the air out through his nostrils, which could be squeezed open and closed at will. It was this that produced the ugly sound Jack had heard.

"Do you know what those sneaks did last night?" raged Thorgil. "They stole my knife! Ohhh, there was something in that food. My ears ring like a dozen warriors clashing their swords."

Jack felt strange too. The cave swayed gently when he tried to focus on it. "They took my staff."

"That proves their evil intentions. I told you it was ill fortune to be trapped in this cave. They're fattening us up."

"They didn't take my candle," said Pega, holding up the string bag she carried with her.

"Why would they want that?" said Thorgil. "You aren't going to cut anyone's head off with it."

"I don't think the hobgoblins plan to hurt us," Pega insisted. "After all, they let Brutus go."

"That's *their* story. For all we know, they've picked his bones clean." The shield maiden glared belligerently at the hordes of hobgoblins gathered to celebrate breakfast. They hooted and drummed on the tables as they waited for the food to arrive. Presently, the Bugaboo and the Nemesis appeared.

"What a splendid morning, my little dewdrop," the Bugaboo exclaimed as he sat down next to Pega.

"If you say so." She edged closer to Thorgil.

"I *do* say so. In fact, I'll say it again. What a splendid, absolutely perfect morning!"

"When he goes on like that, you know it's going to rain rats and frogs before sundown," said the Nemesis.

Mumsie and the Nemesis's wife came out with trays and were greeted with cheers. "We're in for a treat," the Bugaboo announced. "Mumsie has made us her special frog spawn omelet."

"Hurrah!" shrieked the assembled hobgoblins, stamping their feet. Thorgil clapped her hands over her ears.

"Frog spawn omelet?" Pega murmured.

"Made from the very freshest eggs," the king said, placing a quivering green slab on her trencher.

"They'll really make you hop," the Nemesis said, carving another slab for Jack. "Do you get it, ha-ha? Frogs? They'll make you hop?"

"I get it," said Jack. He had trouble focusing his eyes.

"Well, you aren't laughing. You mud men have no sense of humor."

"I don't feel like laughing," said Jack, beginning to lose his patience. The incessant noise was getting on his nerves, and he felt sick. "I told you we had an important quest to fulfill. The Lady of the Lake has run off with the water in Bebba's Town. Our task—one of our tasks—is to bring her back."

"That's the same whiny story Brutus told. Ask me if I care," the Nemesis jeered.

"You don't understand! My father's being held hostage.

He'll be killed if I don't return the water. Oh, why won't you listen!" The conversation around the table stopped. Everyone turned to look at Jack, and Pega snatched away her hand, which the Bugaboo was attempting to hold. Jack rose and bowed to him. "We're grateful for your hospitality, sir, but we can't stay."

"Don't be silly. You've only just arrived," said the hobgoblin king. "We have dozens of things planned to entertain you: fungus fairs, motley sheep shearing, hopping contests, and glee club performances. We can't possibly think of letting you go."

"And we can't possibly think of staying. There's one more thing: Where's my staff and Thorgil's knife? We had them last night, and you took them!" Jack had dropped all pretense of being polite.

The hobgoblins puffed themselves up and hissed like angry cats. "You're accusing us of stealing? Us? Your benefactors?" screamed the Nemesis, bouncing up and down on his bench.

"Not exactly," said Jack, dismayed by the anger he'd provoked. "Perhaps you were just borrowing them."

"I've told you once and I'll tell you again: Time does not pass here," growled the Bugaboo. "This realm is the Land of the Silver Apples. We fortunate beings who live within its borders do not age unless we venture into Middle Earth. When you leave—*if* you leave—you can enter the stream of life at the exact point you left it. You can carry on with your quest then. Now apologize to Mumsie. You've made her quite ill with your insults."

Jack was confounded. He understood now that they were prisoners. He could see himself and the girls spending months here, even years. Would they grow old? *Could* they grow old?

"I'm waiting," said the Bugaboo, tapping his foot.

Jack swallowed the angry words he longed to hurl at him. They were trapped in this cave without weapons or allies, and their only hope of escape lay in keeping the hobgoblins friendly. Somehow, given time—and they had plenty of *that*, Jack thought bitterly—they could discover the exit Brutus used.

"Of course I apologize, Mumsie," said Jack, clenching his fists in frustration. "I never meant to hurt your feelings. Your frog spawn omelet is delicious."

"Now, that's really going too far," muttered Thorgil, but Mumsie grinned, and the good humor around the tables was restored.

Chapter Twenty-six

THE MAELSTROM

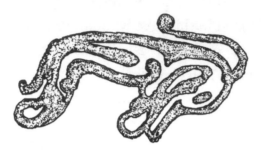

Jack, Thorgil, and Pega trudged along in varying moods of gloom. They had spent weeks exploring the cave, always dogged by a pack of hobgoblin youths. They were allowed some freedom, but they were never left entirely alone. Thorgil's frequent bursts of temper caused the youths to hang back out of range of her fists.

Swarms of will-o'-the-wisps filled the upper reaches so that it was almost as bright as day inside the mountain. But not quite. Something was missing from the light. Jack felt it, though he didn't know what it was. No leafy plants grew here, no grass or even moss. Instead, the humans and hobgoblins passed through vast fields of mushrooms. Some were as tall as trees with darkness pooled at their base. Even the shadows were wrong. They kept shifting as the will-o'-the-wisps darted around.

The mushrooms were of every imaginable shape and color. They filled the air with a damp, musty smell that Jack found oppressive. He had learned, through Pega's instructions, not to eat certain fungi. The red spotted ones gave you nightmares, the round purple ones he'd mistaken for plums dulled your wits. The Bugaboo warned her about toxic mushrooms when he remembered and was most apologetic when he forgot. "Humans and hobgoblins don't eat exactly the same things," he had explained. "We, for example, dare not touch parsnips. One mouthful makes us itch for a week."

Suddenly, something punched Jack in the stomach. He folded up on the ground, gasping for breath. "What was that?" cried Thorgil, reaching for her knife and not finding it. "By Thor, I feel naked without weapons!" She tore up mushrooms and hurled them at the invisible enemy.

"It's the motley sheep," called one of the young hobgoblins. "Look for shadows that shouldn't be there."

Pega knelt by Jack. "You'll be all right in a moment," she said softly. "I know how miserable it is to have the breath knocked out of you."

"Where are these wretched beasts?" demanded Thorgil.

"I . . . hate . . . sheep," wheezed Jack, cradling his bruised stomach. It took him several minutes, but he was finally able to detect collections of smudges hanging in midair. "Why would anyone keep an animal he can't see?" he asked.

"It's for the motley wool," explained the hobgoblin. "It conceals us when we go abroad in the world. You should see the cloaks we make—or, rather, you *shouldn't* see them." The youth laughed heartily at his own joke. He bounced away from a collection of smudges that was sneaking up on him.

When Jack had recovered, they went on. They were in the deepest part of the cave now, far from any hobgoblin dwelling. Side passages branched off in all directions. It might take years to explore all of them, Jack thought morosely, and who knew what creatures might be lurking in the shadows?

They walked past columns of limestone that glittered eerily in the light of the will-o'-the-wisps. Glowworms dangled on glistening threads. Giant cave spiders scurried into the shadows. "Those remind me of knuckers," said Pega, shuddering.

"We cleaned out most of the knuckers," offered one of the young hobgoblins. "The rule is, if a will-o'-the-wisp won't go inside a tunnel, you'd better stay out too."

At last they arrived at a black lake filling the farthest end of the cave. Here were no mushrooms or any other form of life, and the will-o'-the-wisps refused to venture over its dark waters. The lake stretched on into ever-increasing gloom until it fell into profound shadow. Jack instinctively disliked it.

"I wouldn't sail on those waters," remarked Thorgil.

"The Bugaboo thought you'd like this," a hobgoblin youth told Pega, pointing at a shelf of crystal jutting out over the lake. It was as clear as glass and no thicker than a crust of ice.

"It's . . . impressive," said Pega. Jack knew she was feeling the same unease he was.

"Walk on it," suggested one of the youths.

"No, thank you," said Pega.

"It's safe as long as you don't jump up and down." The creature trotted out onto the shelf and back again. With each step, the crystal chimed a different note. The water shivered in response. A pattern of wavelets rose and formed lines that radiated from the center like the spokes of a wheel.

"That *is* pretty!" said Pega.

"You can get all kinds of patterns if you walk in different ways," the hobgoblin said. But still Pega hesitated.

Thorgil, scorning caution, strode out boldly and stamped her foot. "No!" shrieked the hobgoblins, scurrying for the rocks. A single, musical note boomed through the cave. It grew louder and louder, the water heaved, and the center began to sink. The whole lake began to turn.

"Come back!" shouted Jack. Thorgil stood on the crystal with the waves foaming around her boots.

"It's a maelstrom!" she cried, laughing.

"Get out of there!" Jack ran out on the crystal and dragged her back. Now the whirlpool—or *maelstrom*, as Thorgil called it—was in full spate. It roared like an angry beast, going round and round as the black hole in its center deepened. Jack couldn't see into it. He didn't *want* to see into it. He was too busy climbing rocks and helping Pega to higher ground. The hobgoblins gibbered with fear from their perches.

Then, gradually, the water slowed. The roaring faded, and

the gaping hole vanished. Only a faint sheen of ripples showed where the whirlpool had been.

"By the nine sea hags, that was a fine adventure!" exulted Thorgil. "This cave is getting me down. Nothing ever happens here. Each day is like the one before, and the same stale jokes are told over and over."

Jack had to agree. It was all too easy to slide into an endless routine that dulled you as much as the mushrooms he was learning to avoid.

The hobgoblin youths crowded around Thorgil, wringing their hands. "Never stamp on the crystal. Oh, no, no, no," one of them moaned. "We only tap it, to see the pretty waves. No stamping. Never."

Now that the lake was calm again, the hobgoblin youths went off to play. They tapped and stroked the crystal shelf to produce beautiful cascades of music. It was a fine performance until they spoiled it by singing. They puffed up like the hobgoblin who had called them to breakfast and produced the most horrible wailing sounds.

Jack, Thorgil, and Pega retreated behind a barrier of limestone, to shut out the worst of the noise. Pega shuddered. "The Bugaboo calls their music 'skirling.' I think it's worse than the howling of hungry wolves when you're alone in the forest."

"Worse than howling wolves?" echoed Jack. There was something familiar about those words. For days now, certain memories had been hovering just out of reach. "My stars! That's what Father heard when my sister was stolen!"

And now Jack remembered Father's description of the little men—dappled and spotted as the grass on a forest floor. They moved around in a dizzying way, first visible, then melting into the leaves, then visible again. They had been wearing motley wool cloaks, Jack suddenly realized! "Hobgoblins stole my sister!" he cried.

"I thought the Bard called the kidnappers 'pookas,'" said Pega.

"He also called them hobgoblins. How could I have forgotten?"

"My head's been in the clouds too. It's those wretched mushrooms. Do you think they still have her?" said Pega.

Thoughts whirled in Jack's mind. His sister could be hidden anywhere in this enormous underground world. And if he could find her, how could he get her out? For that matter, how could he rescue himself, Pega, and Thorgil? "I don't know where to begin," he said.

"Why not simply ask the hobgoblins where your sister is?" said Pega.

"*Ask?*" cried Jack and Thorgil.

"They mean us no harm."

"No harm? They only disarm us and keep us prisoner!" said Thorgil.

"I've learned a great deal from listening to the Bugaboo and Mumsie," explained Pega. "I think they genuinely want us to be happy. They may pretend to dislike humans and call us 'mud men,' but secretly, they admire us. Haven't you noticed how much this place resembles one of our villages?

Hobgoblins copy everything we do. They have the same clothes and houses, the same pastimes and occupations. They can't grow flowers in their gardens, so they plant red, yellow, and green mushrooms instead."

Jack listened with amazement. He'd spent so much time searching for ways to escape, he hadn't paid attention to the hobgoblins. The cave *was* a copy of a village. Why have houses with thatched roofs in a place where no rain fell? Why wear hats—as the hobgoblin men did when they gathered mushrooms—when there was no sun?

"Why do they want *us*?" he asked.

"Because we're the most interesting thing that's happened to them in ages," Pega said. "You must have seen how dull life is here. Nothing ever changes. Mumsie says that's the bad side of living in the Land of the Silver Apples. There's a sameness that eats away at life even as it preserves it. Each day repeats itself endlessly until the inhabitants go into a trance from which they can't be roused. The hobgoblins visit Middle Earth regularly to wake up."

The horrid skirling had ended, and Jack could hear the hobgoblin youths anxiously calling their names. "We'll ask about my sister tonight," he decided. "Pega can soften up the Bugaboo first with her singing."

Chapter Twenty-seven

HAZEL

That night Pega gave them "The Jolly Miller" and "The False Knight," followed by "The Man in the Moon," a song Jack hadn't heard. The Man in the Moon came down to gather wood for his hearth, leaning on a forked stick as he searched. It was an odd tale and somehow disturbing. Jack wondered where she'd learned it.

"I have sometimes spoken to the Man in the Moon," remarked Mumsie when the song was finished. "He has much lore for those who can bear his company."

"He really exists?" said Jack, who had supposed it was only a legend.

"He's one of the old gods. He's doomed to ride the night

sky alone, and being with him is like being lost on an endless sea with no star to guide you. He visits the green world only during the dark of the moon, and his conversation is both cheerless and disturbing."

"I wish you wouldn't talk to him," said the Bugaboo. "You cry for hours afterward."

"Knowledge is always gained at a price," said Mumsie, her eyes blinking serenely. "I gather news of the wide world from the swallows that visit the forest outside. It's the only way the Man in the Moon can learn of it. In the dark night only owls are abroad, and they're both stupid and surly."

Jack's eyes widened. He remembered the Bard talking earnestly to a swallow in the window of Din Guardi. "Are you—a bard?" he asked cautiously.

Mumsie laughed. "Nothing so grand. I've learned a few things from the Wise, but I'm far too lazy to commit my life to such study."

Jack didn't believe her. There was nothing at all lazy about the Bugaboo's mother. It seemed she knew much that she didn't care to reveal.

"I think we need something cheerful to make up for tales about the Man in the Moon," said the king. "Give us 'Caedmon's Hymn,' Pega my dear."

She smiled and obeyed. As her perfect voice soared up to a mob of entranced will-o'-the-wisps, hobgoblins began to appear from nearby houses. They came in twos and threes until a dense ring of them surrounded the courtyard. When

Pega finished, they all sighed like a wind blowing through a forest.

"You darling!" cried the Bugaboo. "I can't tell you how happy you've made me. Ask for anything and it shall be yours."

"Now you're in for it," said the Nemesis. "She won't be satisfied until she's got your heart and liver."

"First I have to tell you a story," began Pega. "Long ago Jack's mother gave birth to a little girl. Unfortunately, she was so ill, the baby had to be cared for by another woman. Later, when Jack's mother had recovered, his father went off to fetch the infant, and on the way home he stopped to gather hazelnuts."

At the mention of hazelnuts all the hobgoblins sat up straight and looked attentive.

"He put the infant's basket into a tree to keep it safe, but then a terrible thing happened. A crowd of little men swarmed up the tree and stole her. Jack's father tried to catch them, but they were too swift."

"There you go again," grumbled the Nemesis, "accusing us of stealing."

"I didn't mention you," retorted Pega. "But you're right. They were hobgoblins. Jack's father went frantic with grief, and he knew his wife would be heartbroken."

Mumsie dabbed at her eyes with her apron. Several women cooed in sympathy.

"Amazingly, when Jack's father went back to the basket, there was another baby inside. It was a beautiful child—a thoroughly selfish one, it turned out."

"Lucy isn't that bad," Jack protested.

"She could use improvement," Thorgil said. "She ought to be beaten frequently, as I was, to develop character."

"I'm not finished," said Pega, frowning at the shield maiden. "Jack's father took the new infant home and never told anyone what happened for years. Now I'm coming to my request." She put her hands on her hips and looked directly at the king. "I want Jack's sister returned so we can take her home."

Absolute silence fell over the gathering. Dozens of shiny, black eyes stared at Pega, and nothing moved. Even the will-o'-the-wisps were frozen. Then Mumsie sighed deeply. "I knew no good would come of it," she said. "I told you, 'Don't copy the elves. They're bad to the bone.'"

"But, Mumsie, I only wanted to give them a taste of their own medicine," protested the Bugaboo. "I took one of their brats and found an unguarded cradle to leave her in. I thought it would teach the elves how it feels to lose a child."

"It didn't teach them a thing," said Mumsie. "It only gave us the problem of what to do with the baby you took from that cradle."

Jack hardly dared to breathe. Had his sister been handed over to the elves to become a toddler on a leash?

Mumsie clapped her hands, and a young hobgoblin came up to her. "Go to the Blewits' house and fetch the human child," she ordered.

Jack sighed in relief. The hobgoblins *did* have his sister and they were bringing her to him now! Events were moving so fast, it made his head spin. What would she look like? What kind of life had she led? A dozen questions occurred to him, but he was too overwhelmed to speak. And so was everyone else.

In the distance Jack saw a male and a female hobgoblin coming down a path that led from a rocky ledge. In front danced a girl still too far away to see clearly.

The crowd around the Bugaboo's hall parted. The woman hobgoblin was sobbing, and her husband had his arm around her. The girl suddenly halted and ran back to them. They hugged her, each taking a small hand to lead her forward. She was much smaller than Lucy—the size of a four-year-old, per-haps.

"This is your sister," Mumsie said to Jack. "We named her Hazel."

The girl looked up at Jack in utter amazement. "A *mud man!*" she cried. "And there's more? What a treat! Where did you get them?"

"I never told her the truth," wept the woman hobgoblin.

"None of us did, Mrs. Blewit," said Mumsie.

Hazel danced from Jack to Thorgil to Pega. "This one's pretty," she said, pointing a chubby finger at Pega.

"Told her what?" Jack was finding it difficult to speak. Hazel was the exact image of Father, right down to his sturdy body and determined expression. Her eyes were gray, not violet, and her hair was brown, not golden as afternoon sunlight. She didn't float like thistledown. She bounced like a puppy on oversized paws. No one would ever mistake her for a lost princess.

But she was pretty in her own way, with round rosy cheeks and thick, healthy hair that sprang up on her round head.

"We never told her that she's not a hobgoblin," said Mumsie.

Jack was astounded. How could Hazel not know she was different from the other children? She must have looked into a stream or noticed that her arms weren't speckled. But she was very young, and small children might not notice things like that. "Hazel," he called. She ran to him, and he knelt down beside her. "Hazel, I'm your brother."

"No you're not!" She giggled.

"We're alike. Our hair, our eyes, our bodies are the same. Look at your hands. Your fingers aren't long and thin. They aren't sticky at the ends. You're a mud girl."

"I'm a hobgoblin, silly, like Ma and Da." She pointed at the Blewits. "I don't like you, but I like *her*." Hazel went back to Pega, who lifted her in her arms.

"Oof! Heavier than she looks," Pega said, putting her back down again.

"She's spent her whole life with the Blewits. They lost their only child shortly before we acquired her," Mumsie said.

Stole her, you mean, thought Jack. He didn't say it aloud. He didn't want to start an argument now.

"If time doesn't pass here," he said, reasoning it out, "Hazel should still be an infant. But she isn't. How is this possible?"

"Do you think we'd keep her shut up like a bird in a cage?" Mr. Blewit said indignantly. He was a thin, gloomy-looking hobgoblin with permanently hunched shoulders. "A sprogling needs fresh air. We often take her into the fields of Middle Earth."

"And we love it there, too," said Mrs. Blewit. "We are creatures of Middle Earth, not the Land of the Silver Apples. Sometimes we long to visit the mountains of our youth even though it means we shall age."

"Many hobgoblins refuse to leave their homelands," added the Bugaboo. "Kobolds, for example, are perfectly happy in the dark forests of Germany, and brownies cannot be lured from their hearths. We are the only ones who have come here."

Jack watched Hazel, his mind numbed by the reality of her. She looked human, but she behaved exactly like a hobgoblin. She hopped like one, hooted like one, and gleeped like one. "Gleeping" was a particularly nasty sound the hobgoblins made when they were happy, halfway between a croak and a belch. Hazel was doing it now. "We'll have to get used to each other," Jack said.

"Fortunately, we have lots of time," Mumsie said.

"All the time in the world," added the Bugaboo.

"No, we don't," said Pega. "I asked for Jack's sister to be returned so we could take her home."

"You can't take my baby!" Mrs. Blewit suddenly burst out. "I've cared for her all her life and I love her so! Oh, no, no, no, you can't be so cruel."

"We can wait a few days," said Jack.

"A day, a month, a year—it won't make any difference," wailed Mrs. Blewit. "I'll love her just as much then as now.

Oh, my darling, my tadpole, my wuggie-wumps, they're going to take you away!" She hugged Hazel, and the little girl began to cry.

"You can't have her and that's flat," growled Mr. Blewit, smacking his fist against his palm.

"She's *my* sister," cried Jack.

"Stop it right there," said the Nemesis, coming between the two. "Great toadstools, Blewit, you're acting like a mud man."

"I'm sorry, Nemesis, but it goes against the grain," apologized the hobgoblin. "When we lost our little one, Hazel was the answer to our prayers. I can't give her up."

"Let's all take a deep breath," the Nemesis advised. "It's almost time for bed, and I'm sure we'll see things more clearly in the morning. Mumsie? Did I see a basket of apples in the kitchen this morning?"

"You did indeed," the Bugaboo's mother replied. "They're from the Forest Lord's best trees (he was busy with the rock slide at the other end of the valley). They've been roasted and dipped in honey."

"Excellent! I'm sure it will do Hazel good to see everyone friendly again. It's very bad for sproglings when their elders quarrel." The Nemesis's eyes were as deep and tranquil as forest pools, and he had a calming effect on everyone.

Jack wondered who actually ruled this kingdom—the Bugaboo, Mumsie, or the Nemesis? Or did they work together at the jobs they did best?

Hazel stopped sobbing and settled down in Mrs. Blewit's lap. She stuck her tongue out at Jack.

Chapter Twenty-eight

ST. COLUMBA

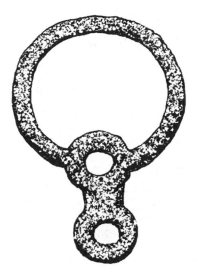

They sat around the tables drinking cider. The taste was slightly vinegary, but Jack found it deeply satisfying because it came from Middle Earth, not the Land of the Silver Apples. It had come from trees that had slept all winter and were wakened by boys and men shouting *waes hael*. The chopped-up apples had been fermented in vats of ordinary water. But they had been left slightly too long, and the cider had turned just that little bit sour. It was this imperfection, the evidence of change and time, that Jack relished.

The Bugaboo was gazing moodily at will-o'-the-wisps, and Pega was playing peekaboo with Hazel. The little girl had worked herself into a state of hysteria, bouncing up and down like a sprogling and gleeping when Pega uncovered her eyes. *Dear Heaven,* thought Jack, *how am I ever going to get used to her?*

Turning to the Bugaboo, he asked why there was such enmity between hobgoblins and elves. "The elves hate us because we have souls," the king explained.

Jack listened in fascination as the Bugaboo retold Brother Aiden's story of the war in Heaven and of how God cast out the angels who wouldn't take sides. "For long years we lived peacefully with elves," the Bugaboo said. "Or, rather, they ignored us and we stayed out of their way. They built the Hollow Road to avoid the Forest Lord. He wasn't above trapping an unwary elf caught hunting in his realm.

"Then the Picts landed in boats and straight off began chopping down trees. The Forest Lord took a terrible vengeance. He asked his brother, the Man in the Moon, to rain madness on their women. Some hurled themselves off cliffs, others drowned themselves in the sea. The men fled underground, where, in the secret places of the earth, they encountered elves.

"They were awestruck," continued the king. "Or, I should say, they were *enthralled,* which is a much more serious affair. Most of the Picts came out of hiding and bartered for wives from the Irish across the sea. A few stayed behind."

"The Old Ones," said Jack.

"They worship the elves like gods and bring them slaves."

Jack and Thorgil exchanged a startled look. Jack remembered the slave market so long ago, when the Northmen had tried to sell him and Lucy. He remembered the small men who had seemed like shadows from the forest. Their bodies writhed with painted vines, and their voices hissed like the wind through pine needles. Their leader had wanted Lucy, but Olaf One-Brow had protected her.

"I thought they ate their captives," said Thorgil.

"Once they did," the Bugaboo said. "Now slaves unsuitable for elf service are sacrificed to the Forest Lord. The Old Ones seek his friendship, but they delude themselves. The Forest Lord will never be their friend. His hatred is eternal. Slaves are taken under the trees in the dark of the moon. What happens to them there is something I don't care to describe."

"I think I know," said Thorgil, who had turned deadly pale.

"Who wants a roasted apple?" said Mumsie. The hobgoblins eagerly held out their bowls. Mumsie ladled out the steaming fruit drizzled with honey, and a helper topped them with cream. The warm and spicy smells raised Jack's spirits after the depressing history of the Picts. There had been a gloomy monk among the slaves they had bought from the Northmen. Jack wondered what his fate had been.

The hobgoblins competed to see how many apples they could stuff into their cheeks. The winner managed ten— hobgoblin cheeks were amazingly stretchy. Hazel had to be pounded on the back because she tried to mimic them. *My stars, even I think of her as a sprogling,* Jack realized. He tried to lure her to him by holding out a roasted apple. She fled at once to Mrs. Blewit's arms, and he felt both sad and jealous.

"The Picts were followed by the Celts, Britons, Romans, and Saxons," continued the Bugaboo, tossing the apple cores over his shoulder. "You never saw anything like the Roman army! They swarmed over the hills, clanking and stamping and bawling orders. They cut down trees, built roads, and heaved up walls. If the Forest Lord got a few of them, there were always more behind. He was left only a few untouched stretches of trees, and it weakened him. He draws his strength from them, you see."

"Now we're coming to the good part," interrupted the Nemesis. "The arrival of St. Columba."

"My ever-so-great-grandparents saw him arrive," the king said. "He came over the sea from Ireland."

"In a little coracle," added the Nemesis, his eyes blinking in a soothing rhythm. He clearly liked the story of St. Columba. "The waves should have dashed it to pieces, but it floated along as peacefully as a gull. Columba spoke to the Picts of strange things called 'mercy' and 'pity.' The Picts laughed merrily and tried to murder him, but Columba blew a wisp of straw into the air."

"He was a bard!" cried Jack. "That's how they drive people mad."

"Whatever he did, it scared the living daylights out of the Picts. They fell on their knees and begged him for this new thing called mercy. So Columba poured water over their heads, and they all became as docile as lambs."

"My ever-so-great-grandparents concealed themselves in motley wool cloaks to listen to the saint's sermons," the

Bugaboo resumed. "Then, as now, hobgoblins were not welcome in mud men's houses. They followed Columba as he walked from village to village, always keeping out of sight. And one dark night my ever-so-great-grandfather got up the courage to approach his window. 'Please, mud man,' he whispered. 'What magic did you use on the Picts?'

"'Come in by the fire so I can see you,' said Columba. My ever-so-great-grandfather edged through the door, expecting to be pelted with rocks, as was the custom. But Columba only laughed. 'You're a rare one,' he said. He gave my ever-so-great-grandfather a cup of cider and asked him many questions about mercy and pity. He was impressed with my ever-so-great-grandfather's answers. 'I see you've been listening,' Columba said approvingly. My ever-so-great-grandfather admitted to eavesdropping at windows.

"The upshot was that Columba called all the hobgoblins together and baptized them. They stood on the banks of Loch Ness, and one after the other, Columba popped them in. It took seven days and seven nights. At one point a kelpie surfaced and ate a few hobgoblins, but the saint drove him off."

"Kelpies! That's the part I hate!" the Nemesis broke in. "They'll do anything to get at us—climb trees, burrow into the earth, hurl themselves off cliffs. I can't bear thinking about it!" He had turned pale, and his whole body quivered. Mumsie and the Nemesis's wife settled on either side of the distraught hobgoblin, cooing and stroking him until he recovered.

"He lost his parents, aunts, and uncles on a picnic at

Loch Ness," the Bugaboo whispered to Jack. "We all try not to mention the K-word around him. To finish our history, Columba assured our ancestors that they now had souls in tip-top condition. And since that time the elves have been our bitter enemies."

Chapter Twenty-nine

BETRAYAL

Jack was curled up in his sleeping hutch. It was the middle of the night, not that this made a difference. Without sunlight, things tended to run together. He heard the various bleeps, bloops, hisses, and groans of the slumbering youths.

The opening of the sleeping cave glowed. A will-o'-the-wisp had come down to the opening, which was odd in the middle of the night. Jack turned his back, dully watching the movement of shadows on a nearby wall. Will-o'-the-wisps hardly ever stayed still, and so neither did the shadows. Suddenly, arms reached down and wrenched him out of the hutch. Something clamped over his mouth and eyes. He struggled and kicked, but his assailant was too strong.

Jack felt himself rushed along, as when the youths performed their morning leaps, but this was not accompanied by cries of joy. Whatever held him traveled in complete silence. Jack's head cleared instantly. His apathy vanished.

What had captured him? It wasn't a dragon. Not hot enough. Or a troll. Not cold enough. A kelpie? Not wet enough. That left wyverns, hippogriffs, cockatrices, manticores, basilisks, Hydras, krakens, and Pictish beasts, about which Jack knew little. *Could it be a knucker?* He remembered the loathsome body like a monstrous tick engorged with blood. Arms coiled from its sides, anchoring it to the rocks, and others fanned out across a floor deep in slime.

Jack began struggling in earnest, but it did him no good. He heard something hiss, and his arms and legs were clamped even harder. *I'll wait till it stops,* he decided. *I'll fight it then.* He forced himself to think rationally. It couldn't be a knucker. Not slimy enough.

Jack's blood was singing and his heart pounded, but amazingly, he wasn't afraid. It was a relief to have something happen after so many days of monotony. He understood Thorgil's joy at awakening the maelstrom.

The headlong flight jolted to a stop, and the creature let him go. He saw shadowy forms around him and attacked. He headbutted one of the shapes in the stomach, causing it to shriek and fall. He turned swiftly to pull the legs out from under another, and just as quickly, he grasped an arm and swung a creature around to collide with more of its kind. But there were too many. They swarmed over him, pinning him down.

"Festering fungi! This one's as bad as the other!" growled a familiar voice. The battle fury in Jack's mind vanished. He lay on a bed of squashed mushrooms with the blobby shapes of hob-goblins sitting on his arms and legs. A pair of will-o'-the-wisps, barely enough to dispel the gloom, hovered overhead.

"I hope you're satisfied, mud man. You've made Blewit lose his dinner." The Nemesis loomed against the dim light, and Jack heard someone hacking and spitting. It must have been Mr. Blewit he rammed in the stomach.

"If you ambush someone in the middle of the night, you can expect trouble," said Jack.

"Oh, we've had nothing but trouble since His Royal Idiocy invited you," the Nemesis said. He signaled, and the hobgoblins allowed Jack to sit up, but they still held him.

"It was a good fight," said Thorgil from not far away. "You would have made a decent berserker." She was being guarded as closely as he.

"Thanks," he said.

"I acquitted myself well too," the shield maiden replied. "Knocked out two of the little sneaks and crippled a third."

Jack saw Pega sitting nearby. "Are you all right?" he called.

"As well as can be expected for someone who's been pulled six ways to Sunday."

The Nemesis sniffed derisively. "That's what you get for driving our king off his head."

"I never did such a thing," Pega retorted hotly. "He was the one who pursued me."

"Oh, I've seen your mincing little ways, charming him so

he forgets his duties. You asked him to hand over our Hazel and break the Blewits' hearts. Well, I won't have it."

"If you intend to murder us, at least let us die with weapons in our hands," said Thorgil.

"Murder?" The Nemesis bounced up and down with rage. "Do you think we're mud men? We have souls and we take care of them, thank you very much. We're simply going to move you on."

"To Middle Earth?" said Jack.

The hobgoblins laughed—or they at least made the noise that showed they were amused. To Jack, it sounded like someone choking on a piece of gristle.

"Oh, no," said the Nemesis, catching his breath and blinking his eyes rapidly. "We're going to give you exactly what you asked for and send you to Elfland."

"Elfland?" echoed Jack, hardly daring to believe their good fortune.

"Why not?" said the Nemesis. "I tried to get the Bugaboo to do it straightaway. He was too besotted with Lady Temptation there."

"I never tempted him!" protested Pega.

The Nemesis signaled again. The hobgoblins let go of their prisoners, scampering out of reach before Thorgil could react. They climbed the rocks and sat there, blobby shadows in the half-light. Mr. Blewit, still holding his stomach, joined the Nemesis.

"Look, I'm sorry I hurt you," Jack said. He had no ill will against the melancholy hobgoblin, who only wanted to keep a child he looked upon as his own. "Why didn't you wait until we could talk things over?"

The Nemesis came close enough for Jack to see into his dark eyes. "It wouldn't have made a difference. Losing Hazel a year from now would be just as painful."

"What kind of future can she possibly have here?" Jack said. "She's not made to spend half her life underground. What happens when she grows up? Someday she's going to look into a pool and know she's not the same as the rest of you."

"We'll tell her it doesn't make a scrap of difference!" said Mr. Blewit.

Jack couldn't think of an answer to this. Hazel had never accepted him and ran when he tried to approach her. She might not accept Mother, either.

"There's no point in arguing. Hazel can't go," the Nemesis said flatly. "Anyhow, she's terrified of elves."

"Are they really so bad?"

"Worse!" Mr. Blewit hunched his shoulders as though warding off a chill. "*You* won't be able to see it. Mud men never do. It's the *glamour*, you see. Makes everything look wonderful, but it's all lies."

"Then why, since you hate elves so much, do you live next door to them?" demanded Jack. "You despise them. They steal your children. The Bugaboo said there's not a family here who hasn't lost one or two little ones. It seems to me that if you lived next door to a pack of hungry wolves, you'd either kill them or move out."

The hobgoblins looked away and several of them shuffled

their feet. Jack thought they looked shifty. Or guilty. It was difficult to tell in the dim light. Finally the Nemesis cleared his throat. "We have been weak," he admitted. "First we were drawn to elf music and then as time passed—or rather *did not pass*—we experienced immortality. Oh, I know!" He waved away Mr. Blewit's objections. "Our motives were pure. Who wants to see one's parents grow old and die? But we made an evil bargain."

"Then why not go the whole hog, move to Elfland and be done with it," said Pega, brushing mushroom spores off her dress.

"And live with those liars?" Mr. Blewit cried.

"Looks to me like you've done a good job of lying to yourselves without anyone's help," she retorted.

"No," the Nemesis said slowly. "Blewit is right. The power of Elfland to deceive is dire. Its influence radiates over the entire Land of the Silver Apples, but it is strongest at its core. Here, at least, we have not turned away entirely from the world. We still feel joy and sorrow, but Elfland is hollow. It is a living death."

"Bedbugs! You don't half try to scare folks," said Pega.

"Let's get moving," said the Nemesis. The shadows that lurked at the edge of the light now closed in. Jack braced himself for more unpleasantness, but the hobgoblins merely urged him along. There were more of them than he had realized. They came out of the dark and crowded behind the humans. Jack felt their long fingers fluttering at his back.

It was possible to see only a few steps ahead in the glow of the two will-o'-the-wisps. Pillars loomed up and fell behind. The heavy odor of crushed toadstools rose from beneath their feet, and an unseen river flowed somewhere to the right.

Presently, the land broke off at the edge of a lake, with only a transparent shelf of crystal extending over its dark depths. Jack suddenly became aware of the hobgoblins' intentions. "You're going to drown us in the whirlpool!" he cried.

"As usual, you accuse us of your failings," said the Nemesis. "This is the way into Elfland. Don't pull those long faces at me! You asked for it and now you're going to get it."

"We're even returning your weapons," said Mr. Blewit. He unwrapped a bundle and presented Thorgil with her knife and Jack with his staff. Jack was delighted to hold the smooth, dark wood in his hands again. He eagerly sought the life force but felt only the faintest echo of it.

"Thorgil, what do you sense in the rune of protection?" he asked.

The shield maiden put her hand to her neck and frowned. "Nothing—no, that's not true. There's something. It's like a chick trying to break out of an egg."

"That's what I was afraid of," Jack said. "Something is blocking the life force here." He gazed at the dark water with dislike. The feeble glow of the will-o'-the-wisps had little power to light it.

"Enough of this nitter-natter," growled the Nemesis. "We must conclude our business before the Bugaboo wakes up. Toadflax and Beetle Grub! Awaken the whirlpool!"

Two burly hobgoblins ran out on the crystal shelf and

jumped up and down, making it emit a clashing noise that swelled until it seemed the very cavern would collapse. The whirlpool formed instantly, yawning like a grotesque mouth.

The hobgoblins ran back, and before Jack could react, they tore Pega from his side and threw her in. "You monsters!" Jack shouted. Pega's screams faded swiftly as she was sucked into the maelstrom. He didn't think. He only knew he had to save her. He threw himself after her.

Chapter Thirty

ELFLAND

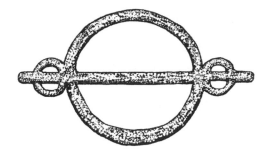

The water foamed around him, and he had just a glimpse of the shore before he fell into darkness. He swirled around with his back in the water and his face to the black *nothingness* at the center. He could breathe. He did this automatically. But the deadness enveloping him was appalling. He wanted to die, to do anything to escape. He could do nothing. Round and round he went until his senses reeled and all thought fled.

For a long time Jack was carried along. Gradually, the whirling motion slowed until he moved no more swiftly than an autumn leaf wafting down from a tree. At last the motion stopped, and he dropped onto a grassy meadow.

"Oh, Jack!" wept Pega, flinging herself onto him. "Are we dead? I sure hope this is Heaven."

Jack stared up into a starry sky made luminous by a full moon. There was no sign of the whirlpool, no sign of anything above him except a summer night. Trees lifted silvery branches at the edge of the meadow, and a nightingale sang not far away. He smelled flowers, marvelous flowers sweeter than newly opened roses. A breeze brought him the cooler odor of mint.

"No mushrooms," Jack murmured.

"What? I hadn't noticed." Pega sat up and breathed deeply. "You're right! There's not the tiniest smidgen of mushroom. It's wonderful!"

Jack continued to stare up at the sky. It was filled with a thousand winking, blinking stars. Some were blue-white or yellow. Others gleamed red and apple green. All were brighter than the stars of Middle Earth, but perhaps that was because this place was so perfect.

Perfect. That was the quality that hovered over this world. No flaw dimmed its perfection, no misshapen branch in the trees or harsh note in the nightingale's voice. No unpleasant odors floated on the breeze. The grass was soft and thick—not wet as grass usually was in the middle of the night, but misted with enough coolness to be delightful.

"It might be Heaven," Jack said. A thump made him sit up.

"By Balder's backside, that was foul!" swore Thorgil.

It can't be Heaven, Jack thought with a twinge of disappointment. *Thorgil wouldn't be here.* "Thorgil?" he called.

She came immediately to his side. "Seen any enemies?"

"No. Just look at this place," Jack said. The shield maiden turned to observe the silvery trees, the meadow, and the stars. A fold of earth not far away concealed a stream. Its light chatter was etched on the night air. Slowly, gracefully, a flock of deer emerged from under the trees and walked toward them. Their skins, unnaturally bright under the moon, were flecked with white, and their delicate hooves stepped noiselessly. Even Thorgil was struck dumb by their beauty.

The deer passed by and went down into the folded earth. Jack heard their feet splash in the water.

"At least we won't starve," said the shield maiden.

"Oh, Thorgil, haven't you learned anything?" said Jack. "You can't hunt until you know it's allowed."

They all fell silent then. It was enough to lie under the stars and to watch the great moon—surely larger than in Middle Earth—ride the air.

Jack tried to go over all that had happened since they had left the village. They had traveled to St. Filian's Well and on to Din Guardi. There was the Hedge and a tunnel. Something had had happened in the tunnel, but he couldn't quite remember what. And then they were in a forest. Thorgil appeared, or had she been there all along? Jack dimly recalled a cave full of mushrooms with—who *had* been living in that cave?

It was fading now. It didn't matter, really. This was such a beautiful place, who would want anything else?

❖❖❖

Jack awoke with sunlight shining on his face. He blinked and found that it didn't hurt his eyes. It was gentle, like the sun on days when peat fires veiled it.

The forest was no longer silver, but a lively green. Drifts of flowers covered the meadow, and the deer were cropping the grass. "Isn't it nice?" said Pega. She'd been up awhile, for she had gathered a heap of apples. They were large and golden, and—Jack soon discovered—honey-sweet.

Thorgil fingered her knife and watched the deer. "I *know*," she said. "I mustn't hunt them. But wouldn't they taste good roasted over coals?"

"Let's find out who owns them first," said Jack. They watched the birds as they ate. Some were green with long, rose-colored tail feathers. Others were a blue so perfectly matched to the sky that they disappeared when they flew. Their voices filled the air with joyous music.

"What are they saying?" Pega asked Thorgil.

The shield maiden shook her head. "I don't know. It's only noise."

"Nice noise," commented Pega.

"Yes, but I should be able to understand them."

"Do you know what else is strange?" said Jack. "There's not one single honeybee."

"There're butterflies," observed Thorgil, and indeed, the meadow thronged with them. They were so large and magnificently colored, it was difficult to tell them apart from the flowers.

"My mother keeps bees," Jack said. He knew this, and yet, when he tried to picture the farm and its hives, he couldn't. It was as though a mist had risen up in his memories. "Mother says bees carry the life force from plant to plant."

"That's interesting," said Pega, not sounding interested at all. She was making a wreath of flowers, her clever fingers weaving them into a kind of crown. Jack saw, with a trickle of fear, that none of the blossoms were familiar. They were beautiful—everything here was—but strange. Almost daisies, near marigolds, could-be buttercups, much-too-large lark-spurs covered the meadow.

Jack reached for his staff, willing the tremor of power into his hand. There was nothing. *It is dead, like the whirlpool.* "This place isn't real!" he cried.

"It feels real," Pega said, pulling up some of the grass.

"This is the glamour Mr. Blewit was talking about."

"Who?" murmured Thorgil.

"You know. The guy with those blobby creatures who threw us into the whirlpool." Yet even as Jack thought it, the memory came apart. As he struggled to pull it back, he heard the most wonderful sound in the distance. It was a thrilling, clear-voiced hunting horn. And with it came the baying of hounds, if you could compare that ecstatic noise with the racket ordinary dogs made. It was a celebration of summer, green trees, and running. It was pure joy. And just when Jack thought it couldn't get any better, he heard the voices.

There was no describing *them.* Jack was intensely musical.

He had one of the finest voices in Middle Earth, but he was nothing compared to the elves. They weren't even singing. Their ordinary speech was more melodious than any earthly song.

Deer burst from the trees. The horn sounded again, and appearing from the green darkness came a mob of beaters. They ran before a band of horsemen, thrashing the bushes with sticks to drive the prey. They were small men, naked except for loincloths. They were covered in swirling designs like the shadows of the forest so that it was hard to tell them apart from the trees.

They were Picts.

These weren't the peddlers who roamed the roads of Middle Earth, selling metalware and pots. These were the Old Ones who inhabited Jack's nightmares, the ones who had bargained for Lucy and who conducted secret ceremonies under the moon.

The Picts halted, uttering loud hisses. The horsemen pulled up their steeds and called to their hounds. "What have we here?" cried a glorious voice. Jack looked up into the fairest face he had ever seen. The man's golden hair was bound by a silver crown. His tunic was the green of beech leaves and his cloak the deeper shade of ivy. A broad-chested Pict with a shaggy beard and drooping eyebrows grasped his horse's bridle as the animal tossed its head.

"Leave off, Brude. You're frightening him," said the horseman. "Well, strangers! What are you doing in our realm? To what do we owe the pleasure of your company?" He smiled, a flash of perfect teeth that made Jack feel unaccountably happy. Behind him jostled other riders. Their steeds were nothing like the sturdy battle horse John the Fletcher owned. These were no broad-hoofed animals with shaggy coats and tails cut short to avoid burrs. They were as graceful as deer. Their eyes were intelligent, and their manes and tails shone like silver.

Elf-horses, thought Jack with a shiver of recognition. Olaf One-Brow had looted one during the destruction of Gizur Thumb-Crusher's village.

As for the riders, Jack hardly dared lift his eyes to them. Their beauty was dazzling. Both men and women rode in the company, dressed in varying hues of green, and all were without the blemishes that plagued mortal men. Here were no crooked teeth or flawed faces, no marks of illness, accident, or famine. Suddenly, Jack saw his companions in the light of these perfect beings. Thorgil was coarse, and Pega—poor Pega!—scarcely seemed human. As for his own looks, Jack had no illusions.

"Has the cat stolen your tongues?" the huntsman cried merrily.

"Do not mock them, Gowrie," said one of the women. "They are but newly arrived from Middle Earth, though I wonder at the small one. She has the look of the changelings."

"She is human, dear Ethne," replied the huntsman. "I detect the stench of mortality."

"Then they must be brought to our halls," declared Ethne. "The queen will surely want to see them."

The company rode off with a winding of horns and crying of hounds. Brude and the Picts remained behind. "You commmme," Brude hissed, as though human speech came to him with difficulty. His followers grasped their beating sticks and formed a guard around Jack and his companions.

Chapter Thirty-one

THE DARK RIVER

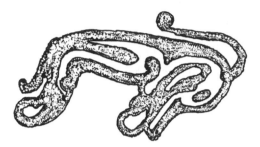

It should have been frightening, but Jack was too enchanted to worry. The forest through which they were passing was lovelier than anything he'd ever seen. Each tree was perfect in its own way yet different from every other tree. Each opening revealed an unexpected delight. A waterfall poured over a white cliff, a pool was dotted with flowers big enough to sit on, a field of daffodils—or something like daffodils—stood as tall as your head. Jack looked eagerly for the next revelation. He scarcely noticed the sullen band of Picts or that he wasn't free to wander.

An eagle took to the air from a distant cliff. Its wingspan dwarfed any bird of Middle Earth and its claws could easily have carried off an elk. It screamed a challenge, yet even this cry was delightful and not alarming.

"It's as large as a Jotunheim eagle," Jack murmured.

"But different," added Thorgil, sounding half asleep.

"Browner. Bigger." Jack found it difficult to describe what set the eagle apart.

"Like something from Yggdrassil."

Jack was jolted awake. The eagle was nothing like a bird that would perch on the Great Tree. It was too perfect. It would never drop a feather or get its feet covered in mud. Yggdrassil's creatures were awe-inspiring but not immune to change. Nothing living was. Jack felt a whisper of the fear he had experienced in the whirlpool.

"What's wrong?" said Pega.

The whisper went away. Jack willed it to go away. "Just a stomachache. Must have eaten too many apples," he said, smiling.

A Pict nudged him with a stick, and he moved on. They passed a tree entirely covered with butterflies and another hung with vines so delicate, they were like shreds of mist.

The forest ended, and everything suddenly changed. Before them was a dark river—or perhaps it was a long, thin lake, because the water didn't move at all. The path vanished underneath it and reappeared on the other side. It actually did disappear. You couldn't see into the water, nor did it reflect the sky or shore. It was simply a band of darkness blocking their way.

The Picts halted, obviously taken by surprise. They gestured at the barrier with hisses and growls, and Brude's voice rose above the rest. He wanted to go on; it was clear from the way he waved his arms. Jack thought the water hadn't been there long and probably wasn't deep. He probed with his staff. The water swirled sluggishly, creeping up the wood toward his hand. Jack retreated at once.

"We could easily swim that," Thorgil pointed out.

"I'd rather walk," said Jack, watching oily ripples spread out from where he'd stirred it.

Finally, Brude prevailed, and the Picts once again formed a guard. "Go," Brude commanded, poking Jack with his stick.

The children held hands, forming a human chain, with Jack in front, followed by Thorgil and Pega. Two Picts led them, carefully feeling the way. The rest brought up the rear. The first part was only ankle-deep. Jack breathed a sigh of relief and tried to ignore the tendrils of water exploring his legs.

The river became deeper. Now it came to his knees, and Jack noticed something odd. You could always feel real water against your skin. Not this. "Go!" Brude said, with an edge of panic.

Suddenly, one of the leading Picts stepped to the side and vanished like a fly popping into a frog's mouth. He went down without a splash, and his comrades broke into a run. They fought past the children, shoving and hissing, and scrambled up the farther bank, where they immediately started fighting among themselves.

Jack and Thorgil were abandoned in the middle of the lake. "Where's Pega?" cried Jack.

"She fell over!" Thorgil said. "When those pigs went by, they knocked her down!" Jack looked around, hoping to see movement in the water. There was nothing.

"Commmme!" roared Brude from the farther bank.

"No!" Jack shouted back. She had to be somewhere. How long could she hold her breath? "Pega! Move your arms! Stand up! Try to jump!" But the lake stayed perfectly still. They felt around the bottom with their feet, and it was Thorgil who found her, lying just under the surface. Unconscious, but alive.

They inched along, carrying the girl between them. The water came up to Jack's chest, and he wondered if he could swim in this—whatever it was. He didn't like the idea of it touching his face. The Picts watched sullenly. *They could help,* Jack thought, *but they won't, the swine. They didn't even try to rescue their comrade.*

Finally, they clambered out into a shimmering sea of grass and laid Pega down. Jack bent over, hands on knees, panting. He felt as though he'd run a mile. Thorgil stretched out on her back, equally overcome.

"We have to get the water out of her," gasped Jack, staggering over to roll Pega onto her stomach. But when he pressed on her ribs, nothing happened. He rolled her back. She was pale as chalk.

"She's breathing," said Thorgil, kneeling beside them.

Jack fished out the candle Pega carried in her string bag and held it to her nose. She shuddered and moaned. "I was dreaming," she whispered.

"You're awake now." Jack was trembling with relief. She had looked so dead!

"Terrible dream," the girl said.

"Don't think about it. Look at the meadow instead."

Thorgil helped Jack raise the girl. They both supported her, for Pega was so overcome, she had no strength left. Gradually, she roused and sat up by herself. They gazed at the perfect blue sky, the meadow, the birds that caroled as they flew.

It was a beautiful place, quiet and somehow secret. The grass bent before a breeze, rippling like a live sea. Beyond the hateful river, Jack could still see the forest. The trees were utterly flawless. Together they formed a mass of greenery more lovely than anything in Middle Earth.

The Picts herded Jack and his companions onward. It wasn't an unpleasant journey. Grassland gave way to orchard, and everyone gathered fruit from the trees. As before, nothing was quite like Middle Earth, but the fruit was so delicious that Jack didn't care. The apples were silvery, like tiny moons hanging among the dark leaves. The smell alone was enough to make you happy, and when you ate them, you didn't need anything else.

On the other side of the orchard they saw a palace in the distance. "Elfhame," growled Brude, gesturing with his stick. Jack had seen the hall of the Mountain Queen in Jotunheim. It had been magnificent, carved out of ice and haunted by mists, but Elfhame was more fair.

Graceful towers were joined by magnificent arches. The walls were covered with climbing roses, and irises and violets formed purple shadows under the trees. Or at least they resembled irises and violets. A path led off to a fountain around which were men and women frozen in the middle of a dance. Jack stopped in his tracks. "Have they been turned to stone?" he said in a low voice.

"Olaf One-Brow used to carve animals from wood," Thorgil said, touching one of the statues with her finger. "I think this is similar, but—" She paused, frowning.

Jack understood her confusion. Olaf's animals covered the ceiling and pillars of his home, where they watched its inhabitants like friendly spirits. They weren't perfect. You'd never mistake them for the real thing, and yet somehow the giant's soul had flowed into his art. You could imagine his bellowing laugh behind the squirrels, ravens, and wolves that decorated his hall. These statues, beautiful beyond belief, were dead.

Jack gasped.

"What is it?" cried Thorgil, her hand going to her knife.

"That tree," he whispered. Pega turned to see what had startled him. It seemed a normal tree until you got close enough to see the fruit was actually honey cakes.

"Good!" grunted Brude, shoving them out of the way. He and his followers gathered around and stuffed their mouths. Thorgil also waded into the fray, jostling, fighting for position, and gorging herself with equal abandon. Jack was uncomfortably aware of similarities between Northmen and Picts.

The tree was soon picked clean. But when the warriors stepped away, their faces all sticky with sweetness, more fruit swelled up on the branches. So of course they had to go back for seconds. Eventually, the Picts and Thorgil slumped to the ground, bloated but apparently happy.

Pega delicately plucked a honey cake with her fingers. "Would you like one, Jack?"

He stared at the tree with dislike. "How can you have honey in a place with no bees?"

"Who cares?" said Thorgil, sprawled on the ground.

"I do. Bees are the servants of the life force, and if they're not here, this tree doesn't exist. I don't know what you've been eating, but don't be surprised if it makes you sick."

"You really don't know how to have a good time." The shield maiden belched richly.

"There's another thing," Jack said. "Father used to tell Lucy a tale about a honey cake that fell on the ground and put down roots. It grew into a tree. Well, here's the tree! Father made up that story, but this is a place where impossible things happen. The flowers are too big, the fruit too sweet. I say it's glamour, and it's all a lie."

Pega put down her cake without tasting it. Her face looked strained and tired. "When I fell into that—that river, I thought I was going to die. I couldn't move. I couldn't scream. All the fields and flowers were gone. It was dark . . . dark . . ." The girl covered her face with her hands.

"It was a bad dream. Don't think about it." Jack was concerned by her obvious distress.

"It was real! It's hard to remember, everything's so pretty here. You don't *want* to remember." Pega hurled the honey cake into a bush. "Elfland had vanished, and all that was left was a cave full of bones and filth. I think that's what this place really is, only the glamour hides it from you. There was no hope. No warmth. No love." She burst into tears.

Something in Pega's words woke a memory in Jack's mind. He and Thorgil had been waiting for the Norns in the hall of the Mountain Queen. Voices gathered in the distance, coming nearer and whispering of a world of loss so terrible, you would run mad to think of it. All that was bright and brave and beautiful would go down to defeat. You could not stop it. You could only watch it die. And Jack remembered his answer to such despair: *I serve the life force. The Norns' way is only one leaf on the Great Tree. I do not believe in death.*

Chapter Thirty-two

LUCY

Jack was about to tell Pega about the Norns when a horn sounded from within the palace. Voices called, a host of them. The front gate opened, and out came the prettiest, merriest people Jack had ever seen. They were dressed in all the colors of the rainbow.

Some danced like the figures in the fountains, and some played harps or flutes. Others tossed rose petals into the wind and sang with voices so fair, Jack thought his heart would break. Beauty and longing overwhelmed him until he scarcely knew whether it was joy or pain he felt.

Jack was transfixed. He could not have moved if a shower

of silver arrows were raining down on him. Everyone else seemed as stunned as he.

The company drew near, and Jack recognized the huntsman called Gowrie. By his side Lady Ethne carried garlands of flowers. "Welcome!" she cried, presenting the garlands to Jack, Thorgil, and Pega. Brude craned his neck hopefully, but she passed him by. "Welcome to Elfhame! Come heal your earthly cares. All joy lies within, where Partholis rules with Partholon, her consort. Come, weary travelers, to join our revels!"

Jack found himself surrounded by the company. He felt outrageously happy and smiled at Ethne, who smiled back, instantly winning his allegiance. She was so radiant! He had never known anyone so fair. She drew him on effortlessly.

The Picts followed behind like a pack of hungry, ill-favored hounds.

Jack walked in a dream. Wonders led to more wonders. The gate of Elfhame was a single arc of gold framed in a wreath of emerald vines. The doors were of silver. Pillars soared up inside to a dark blue ceiling spangled with a myriad of lamps.

Elves stood on either side, dressed in robes trimmed with fur and shot with gold. Little dogs with jingling bells on their collars danced around their feet. One dashed up to Pega, bared its pretty teeth, and darted away.

Some of the ladies had toddlers on leashes. These kept falling over and whimpering. One of them sniffled constantly, and its owner rapped it sharply on the head with a fan.

Jack and his companions were swept on through several rooms, each more magnificent than the last, until they reached a hall with a floor of glass. In the center of the air burned a miniature sun. Jack turned his face up in wonder, to feel its mild warmth.

"Come on," urged Ethne, laughing. Jack followed her onto the glass. *It's like walking on water,* he thought, for beneath the transparent floor was a lake full of golden-scaled fish that glittered as they swam. The elf lady took his hands and swirled him into a dance.

Thorgil probed the surface with her foot before stepping on it. "I do not fear this," she announced.

"Of course not!" cried Gowrie, pulling her on. Pega halted at the edge and then walked stolidly after the couples. Jack glanced back to see that no one had chosen her for a partner. He let go of Ethne and hurried back to her.

"Come on, Pega," he said kindly, holding out his hand. Her look was so grateful, his heart turned over. She had almost been a queen in the realm of the hobgoblins. Now her ugliness was painfully obvious. He tried to copy the elves' steps, but Jack wasn't a good dancer, and of course no one had ever bothered to teach Pega. All he knew were highland flings that were more like jumping up and down until you ran out of breath.

But then Ethne joined them, and her magic turned them all graceful. Round and round they went, with the miniature sun overhead and the golden fish beneath their feet. It was intoxicating. It was like the best days of Jack's life rolled into one. He was so happy, he laughed out loud.

Then they were at the other end of the hall. Jack staggered to a halt, his heart pounding and his body clammy with sweat. Pega collapsed against him. Ethne was still as fresh as a daisy.

Before them rose a dais bearing four thrones. At the right end sat the Lady of the Lake. Jack remembered her, all right. His back tingled where she'd shot him. In the center were a tall woman in golden robes and a tall man in silver. At the other end, in a throne hardly bigger than an ordinary chair, was Lucy.

"Lucy!" cried Jack. The Lady of the Lake raised her hand threateningly. A man Jack hadn't noticed rose from the floor near the Lady's feet.

"Good for you! You made it!" Brutus said, bounding from the dais. No longer was he dressed in the rags of a slave. He wore a splendid gold tunic under a crimson cloak. The great sword Anredden hung from a belt flashing with diamonds. "Don't speak to your sister yet," he said. "There are courtesies we must observe in this place." He grabbed Jack's arm and pulled him down to bow to the thrones. Thorgil and Pega followed suit.

"Brutus—," began Jack, both exasperated and delighted to see him. What *had* the untrustworthy slave been up to all this time?

"Manners, lad," said Brutus. "Noble Partholis and Partholon, these are the companions I told you about," he said, making another, exaggerated bow to the dais. "They have come to marvel at your splendor. I implore you to veil your face, Partholis, so they won't be blinded by your beauty."

"You're as honey-tongued as always, heir of Lancelot," said the queen, laughing. "How do you put up with him, Nimue?"

"His compliments ripple like a babbling brook," said the Lady of the Lake, smiling. "They are as various as its waves, and as inconstant."

"You wound me, mistress! I am ever faithful," cried Brutus, smacking himself on the chest. "The fountains that gladden my soul run dry. I am distraught! I perish with grief!"

"Don't perish yet," Nimue said with a giggle. "We have a party on tonight."

"Is that the thrall you lost? He seems completely insane," murmured Thorgil to Pega.

"You get used to it." Pega grinned with delight.

"We welcome you, friends of Brutus," Queen Partholis said, rising from her throne. "We offer you our goodwill and hospitality. Make free with all the pleasures of Elfland and find comfort in its halls and gardens." Her voice was like summer rain falling on parched soil. Jack could have listened to it for hours.

"We are most grateful, Your Noble Highnesses," said Jack, giving almost as florid a bow as Brutus. He felt silly, but he supposed it was the thing to do.

The queen laughed again, a silvery ripple that made Jack smile in response. "Lady Ethne advised us of your arrival, and so we have prepared a feast." She clapped her hands.

Thralls poured out of side chambers with tables and

benches. More followed with steaming trays of swans, venison, jugged hare, suckling pig, and many things Jack didn't recognize. Oysters and whelks made a border around a giant salmon on a platter so huge, it took six men to carry it. Tiny larks, scarcely a mouthful each, were heaped in crystal bowls. And of course there was every kind of pudding, pie, trifle, syllabub, and flummery imaginable.

All this time Lucy pouted on her throne, kicking her feet back and forth. Jack recognized that behavior. It meant she was cross because she wasn't the center of attention. He tried to catch her eye, but Brutus stopped him. "Patience, lad," warned the man. "Wait till their highnesses are busy elsewhere."

Jack was seated at a long table with Pega on one side and Lady Ethne on the other. Thorgil was placed with Gowrie, the huntsman. The two immediately began discussing ways of dismembering game.

Brutus loaded a plate with food and climbed onto the dais. "Oh, fie!" he said, crouching by the Lady of the Lake. "Such delicate hands were not meant for cutting up partridges. Allow me to put morsels of food into your pretty mouth." Nimue blushed and giggled. Jack wondered how the slave got away with such nonsense.

"*She's* stuffing herself, all right," said Pega, gesturing at Lucy. "Any decent sister would have spoken to you."

"She's probably enchanted," Jack said.

"Pooh! She's no different than she ever was. And how did they get this feast ready so quickly? I know how long it takes to pluck swans. What's this monstrosity?" Pega held up a pigeon with six drumsticks.

"Generally, if I don't know what something is, I don't eat it," said Jack.

Thorgil took the pigeon, ate all six drumsticks, and pronounced them delicious.

Jack looked around the hall. He saw no old elves, and there were almost no elf children. About a dozen toddlers on leashes crouched at their owners' feet. Jack turned away, sickened, and wondered if they still remembered their parents. He couldn't think of a way to free them.

He saw that all the thralls were human, for the elves did nothing for themselves. They called a thrall to bring them a spoon on the other side of a table rather than reach for it. The humans toiled endlessly, carrying dishes, cleaning up spills, and running to do some peevish elf's bidding.

Any one of them could have come from Jack's village. They were ordinary folk who'd had the bad luck to fall asleep on an elf hill and follow strange music in the night. The Bard had said how dangerous that was. Once you were lured in, you might not reappear for years.

Brude and his followers had not been invited to the feast. They waited at a doorway, snuffing the air and jostling one another. *Good dogs. Stay,* thought Jack with grim satisfaction. The Picts weren't even as important as the thralls.

His thoughts shifted to and fro, one moment despising the elves and then, turning to Lady Ethne beside him, enchanted once more. She asked him many questions about

Middle Earth, of families, farming, and—most surprisingly—of monasteries. Jack knew little about monasteries, except for St. Filian's.

Ethne had heard of the place. Wasn't it awful how they had trapped poor Nimue in the fountain? Father Swein had sprinkled holy water around the outer walls. When Nimue had tried to cross it, she came up in the most dreadful rash.

Ethne's voice was like a lively stream pouring down a hillside. Jack was enthralled by it. He barely noticed Pega on his other side.

"Now's your chance," said Thorgil, poking him with a drumstick. Jack looked up to see that Partholis and Partholon had left the dais. They were making a ceremonial tour of the hall, greeting their subjects and being bowed to in return. Brutus had completely engrossed Nimue's attention. Lucy was unguarded.

Jack went to the platform and touched his sister's foot to get her attention. "We've come to take you home," he said in a low voice.

Lucy frowned. "Do I know you?"

"I'm your brother. Don't play silly games."

"I don't have a brother." Lucy kicked at him.

"Have it your way, but you do have a mother and father who miss you terribly."

"Oh, *them.*" Lucy shrugged. "My real parents are here, or at least Partholis is. She can't remember which one is my father."

Jack wanted to slap her, but he held his temper. "We've

come all this way to rescue you. You're probably under a spell and can't remember how nice it was at home."

"Oh, I remember! Lumpy beds, ugly dresses, and the same oatcakes day after day after day." Lucy leaned forward, and Jack saw, with a sinking feeling, the necklace of silver leaves.

"Can I see that?" he said, thinking that this might be the thing enchanting her.

"Don't touch it! Thief!" Lucy jumped from her throne and ran to the Lady of the Lake, who gave Jack a venomous look before turning back to Brutus.

"Spoiled rotten" was Thorgil's opinion when Jack returned. "I always said a good thrashing and a night outside with the wolves would have been good for her."

"You may be right," Jack said glumly.

Partholis and Partholon finished their tour and mounted the dais once more. "Now for an after-dinner treat," announced the queen. "I would bid our dear visitors to give us a song or some such entertainment to repay us for our hospitality—not you, Brutus. We would not want to give Nimue cause for jealousy."

Brutus grinned wolfishly. Thorgil cursed under her breath, and Pega looked terrified. "I'll do it," Jack offered. He knew the others weren't used to performing, and he'd appeared before far worse audiences. He'd sung for blood-thirsty berserkers. At least these people weren't going to hack him to bits if they weren't amused.

The thrones were moved to one side. Jack climbed onto

the dais, and the elves watched him intently. They seemed eager to listen, and yet Jack had a sense that there was something malicious about their attention. No matter. They couldn't be nastier than Frith Half-Troll, who had the power to freeze a man's blood in his veins. "I give you the saga of Beowulf," he began.

Jack had a good voice and he knew it, but the effect was not what he expected. The elves seemed disappointed, although the queen was polite and Ethne smiled encouragement. When he was finished, everyone clapped halfheartedly. "I've heard that story before," said Partholis, "from a mortal called Dragon Tongue."

"The Bard?" said Jack, startled.

"Ah, he was a cheeky devil," said the queen, smiling at the memory. "I quite adored his golden hair."

Partholon stirred himself for the first time. "He was a scoundrel of the first order."

"You didn't like the attention he paid to me. You're *jealous*," said the queen, delighted.

"Nonsense. Everyone pays attention to you. It makes as much sense to worry about moths dancing around a light. Dragon Tongue made off with some of my best magic," grumbled Partholon, and sank into silence again.

The elves clamored for another story. "By Odin's eyebrows, don't look at me," said Thorgil. "I'd rather take a spear thrust than make a fool of myself." But Gowrie led everyone in calling for the shield maiden. And so Thorgil, who wasn't all that opposed to showing off, climbed onto the dais.

The problem was, Jack thought, she really didn't know how to tell a story. She rushed through the action and had to go back and explain things. She had moments of poetry, but her voice was so harsh, you thought you were being sworn at. On the good side, she was better than Sven the Vengeful, who forgot the point of jokes, and Eric Pretty-Face, who always shouted. Other Northmen would have enjoyed her performance very much.

Thorgil spoke of Olaf One-Brow and his battles. It was a saga that could go on for a long time. Olaf had fought many battles. But partway through the first tale, about how the giant had rescued Ivar the Boneless from the Mountain Queen, someone burst out laughing.

Thorgil halted. This tickled the elves even more, and they began nudging one another. "Go on," one of them called. The shield maiden continued, but the undercurrent of laughter returned, and soon everyone was infected with it.

"Isn't she priceless?" an elf lady whispered.

"That *voice*. It just makes you want to howl," said another.

Thorgil's face turned red, and she yelled, "Listen, you toad-eating lops. I'm talking about the bravest man who ever lived, and if you don't like it, you can take a flying leap!" The whole hall erupted with laughter. Elves pounded the tables and fairly wept with glee. The shield maiden drew her knife. Brutus leaped to his feet.

"I think that was a wonderful performance," he cried, putting himself between Thorgil and her intended targets. "Let's give this gallant warrior a hand." The elves broke into a storm of clapping and cheers. Brutus swiftly steered Thorgil back to her seat.

"They *liked* it?" she said in bewilderment.

"Absolutely. Brought tears to their eyes," said the slave.

"Of course they did," said Jack, knowing that what the elves really enjoyed was Thorgil's lack of talent.

"Let's have the little hob-human," Gowrie shouted. This was considered extremely witty, and everyone started laughing again.

"I can't go up there," Pega said, shrinking into her seat.

"Hob-human! Hob-human! Hob-human!" chanted the elves, drumming the tables, and Queen Partholis rose to quiet them.

"This *has* been a party," she said with a pretty smile. "I'm afraid you have to perform, child. They simply won't settle down without it."

"I can't," Pega moaned.

"Please, Mother," said Ethne, rising from her seat. "The child is overcome by fear, and it would be cruel to insist."

Partholis frowned. "You may be my child, Ethne, but you have more than a little taint of humanity. I say she performs and that's the end of it."

To Jack's surprise, Ethne put her arm around Pega and whispered, "I'll stand with you."

"We'll all stand with you," said Jack. "Don't worry. If you falter, I'll take over." Trembling, Pega allowed herself to be lifted to the dais. Thorgil and Brutus stood behind her as a protective guard, and Ethne took her hand. Jack murmured, "Give them Brother Caedmon's hymn."

So Pega began. Her voice was almost inaudible at first, but she quickly recovered. She loved music as much as Jack did, and once she got going, she forgot everything else. Her voice rose through the hall with those sublime notes that had so impressed the Bard and enchanted the Bugaboo. It was as though all the beauty missing in her body had concentrated in this one skill.

Praise we now the Fashioner of Heaven's fabric,
The majesty of His might and His mind's wisdom,
Work of the World-warden, Worker of all wonders . . .

It was the hymn given to Caedmon by the angel. You could see the glory of Heaven and the wonder of the earth as you listened to it. It was a celebration of life beyond even what Jack could call up with his staff. It humbled him to admit this, but it was so. He was so caught up in the song that he didn't notice, at first, the reaction of the elves. They were absolutely silent.

They were stunned.

Jack woke up when he heard a sob. An elf lady had buried her face in her hands, and several others wept quietly. "Oh, make it stop," groaned the lady. The men were crying too. Jack knew why, and, of course, this was why he'd suggested this particular hymn.

He'd been disgusted by the elves' taunting of Thorgil and

Pega. He knew they only wanted to make fun of humans. No mortal could possibly compete with them, and these bored, jaded—what had Thorgil called them?—toad-eating fops merely wanted entertainment. Well, they'd got more than they bargained for. This hymn came straight from Heaven, the one thing elves couldn't have. It had to remind them of it. Pega's perfect voice had been a nasty surprise too. Jack smiled grimly. This was the sort of revenge you needn't feel guilty about.

"*Stop!*" a voice shouted behind them. Pega halted. Partholon was standing over Partholis, who had fainted.

Ethne screamed and ran to the queen. "You scheming mortals!" roared Partholon. "You've brought sorrow to this hall that has not seen grief for an age! Brude! Take the humans to the dungeons! I'll decide on their fate later."

The Picts were unleashed into the hall. Jack grabbed Thorgil's wrist and said, "We can't fight them."

"I do not fear battle!" cried the shield maiden.

"No, brave warrior," said Brutus. "There will be a time for war, but not here in the heart of illusions. Trust me. I know how these things work." Thorgil spat on the floor near Gowrie's foot, but she put her knife away.

The Picts surrounded them and herded them off.

Chapter Thirty-three

THE PRISONERS

They went down long, winding tunnels. The light grew shadowy, and the noises of the outside world died away. Jack expected to be frightened. His other experience of dungeons had been at Din Guardi, where he'd been locked in a chamber haunted by the cries of sea monsters. But Jack wasn't frightened. On the contrary, he felt better the farther down they went. His mind was clear, and he hadn't realized it had been clouded. Memories came flooding back.

Brude walked ahead with a flaring torch. There was something familiar about him, and Jack suddenly knew what it was. "You were the man at the slave market!" he cried. Brude hunched his shoulders, rejecting any communication. "You bought slaves from Olaf One-Brow. You offered a fine sword for Lucy and a cheap knife for me. I guess I wasn't worth much." Jack smiled ruefully.

"It *is* him," exclaimed Thorgil. "I wonder why I didn't see it before. Between you and me, I should have sold Lucy to him. She's been nothing but trouble ever since. *Hauu nehahwa oueem?*"

"*Hwatu ushh,*" said Brude.

Thorgil laughed out loud.

"You can speak Pict?" said Jack.

"Only a few words. I asked him where the tunnel went, and he told me to eat troll droppings."

"Nice."

"It's my fault we're here," mourned Pega. She'd been crying most of the way.

"Nonsense, lassie," said Brutus. "This is the best thing that could have happened. Those upper reaches are drenched in glamour. It's impossible to think straight. Down here the air is clear." He was right, Jack realized. The air *was* fresh and invigorating, which was odd considering they were so deep in the earth.

"I thought I'd like elves," Pega wept. "B-but they're so heartless."

"Not Ethne," said Jack.

"No," she agreed. "Not Ethne."

Jack thought about the elf lady. The others had been beautiful beyond compare, yet now he couldn't remember their faces. Ethne was still in his mind. "She's more *there*," he said, trying to put his finger on the difference.

"She wasn't laughing at Thorgil like the rest of them," Pega added.

"Who was laughing at me?" demanded the shield maiden.

"No one," Jack said quickly. But he did wonder. Out of all the elves, only Ethne had shown compassion.

In the distance Jack heard a strange sound. It echoed through the winding hall like an animal cry: *Ubba ubba . . . ubba ubba . . . ubba ubba.* Was it a seal? Or an owl? They rounded a corner and came to an iron door, guarded by a man Jack never expected to see again. He was as big as a bear and twice as threatening. He swayed restlessly from side to side, swinging his long arms and muttering, *"Ubba ubba . . . ubba ubba . . . ubba ubba."*

It was Guthlac, he of the large demon possession. Jack thought he'd drowned in St. Filian's Well. From the look of him, the demon was still in possession.

"Back!" snarled the Picts, driving Guthlac against a wall. Brude quickly produced a key and opened the door.

"Inssside," he hissed. "Sufffferrrr."

"And a fine *hwatu ushh* to you too," said Jack, avoiding a blow. The instant the prisoners were inside, the door slammed and the Picts let Guthlac go.

"Gaaaaaa!" he roared, hurling himself against the metal. Jack heard his body thump and his fists pound. After a moment the noise stopped and there was only the monotonous *"Ubba ubba . . . ubba ubba."*

"Good thing they locked the door," observed Thorgil. The room wasn't bad, compared to some of the places Jack had been. The floor was covered with clean straw, and a table held a water pitcher and cups, loaves of bread, and cheese. They wouldn't starve. A small lamp on the table cast a pool of yellow light. It didn't reach far, but it made the center of the room cheerful.

"I thought Guthlac was dead," said Jack.

"It would be a mercy if he were," came a voice from the darkness of a corner. Everyone jumped, and Brutus drew his sword. This was answered by a bitter laugh. "Have you come to slay us?"

"Noooo," moaned a voice from an opposite corner.

"Courage," said the first man. "With luck, you'll only get a few thousand years in purgatory."

Brutus put back his sword. Jack squinted into the darkness. "Why don't you come into the light?" he suggested. There was a pause, and he heard a rustle from the first corner. Slow, painful feet dragged through the straw, and a monk emerged from the gloom.

"I remember you," the monk said. "And *you*, spawn of Satan." He glowered at Thorgil.

"Do you recognize him?" asked Jack.

Thorgil shrugged. "We pillage so many monasteries."

"It doesn't matter. I am but a shadow of my former self. Soon there will be nothing at all." The man tottered to a bench and lowered himself carefully. Then Jack did recognize him. It was the monk who had been bartered to the Picts in the slave market. He'd been fat then.

"I'm truly glad to see you, sir," Jack said. "I thought you'd been eaten by—um, er . . ."

"The Picts?" The monk laughed, which ended in a coughing fit. Another moan issued from the dark corner. "They no longer dine on men, though they're careful to foster the rumor. It makes people fear them, and Picts like nothing better than fear. They have worse habits now."

"There are worse habits than cannibalism?" Jack was concerned about the wretched state of the man before him. His robes hung loosely on his skeletal frame. Coughs racked his body, and there were feverish patches of red on his cheeks.

"They make sacrifices to the demons they worship. That's what happened to the others who were taken with me. First they offered us to the elves as slaves. Those who were rejected were taken under the trees in the dark of the moon. I didn't see what happened, but I heard the screams."

"Nooooo," groaned the man in the darkened corner.

"It can't be nice back there," said Jack. "Why don't you join us?"

"He'll kill me."

"Who? The monk?"

"No! That witch's child, that limb of Beelzebub, that agent of the Evil One."

"I remember those curses," Brutus cried. He strode into the dark and, after a scuffle, reappeared dragging Father Swein by one leg.

"Mercy! Mercy!" shrieked the abbot of St. Filian's, trying to dig his fingernails into the floor.

"This really takes me back," Brutus chortled. "The thrashings, the nights I was forced to sleep in snow, the weeks on bread and water." He propped Father Swein against a wall.

"You're not going to take revenge, are you?" whimpered the abbot. "It was for the good of your soul."

"Just as you tried to improve Guthlac," said the monk. "*He* doesn't seem forgiving."

Jack heard a muffled *"Ubba ubba . . . ubba ubba"* outside.

"That's why the Picts put him there," moaned Father Swein. "To torment me. He has only one thought now, to tear me limb from limb."

"I didn't know he was even alive," said Jack.

"Oh, he isn't. Not really," the monk explained. "He was halfway to the next world, thanks to my colleague here, when the elves pulled him back. Guthlac is stuck between life and death. It would be a mercy to free him."

"Excuse me, sir. I was with you all those days on Olaf One-Brow's ship and never asked your name," said Jack.

"Why ask names of the doomed?" said the monk in a hollow voice. "But in better times I was called Father Severus."

"Severus!" exclaimed Jack and Pega.

"I seem to have achieved some fame," said the monk with a ghastly smile.

"You're the one who rescued Brother Aiden," cried Pega. "He speaks warmly of you. I'm sure he'll be delighted you're alive."

"So he survived the raid on the Holy Isle," murmured

Father Severus. The monk's harsh expression softened. "He was always a good lad, always gentle and forgiving. We must celebrate his deliverance with a meal, even though our own chance of rescue is nonexistent."

Jack almost smiled at the monk's utter bleakness. He remembered it from Olaf's ship.

Thorgil cut up bread and cheese, and Pega poured the water. Most of the food was consumed by Father Swein. Father Severus had little appetite, and the others had just come from a rich banquet. Jack found the water surprisingly good, far nicer than what he'd drunk earlier. It quenched his thirst, while the other had left him unsatisfied.

He absentmindedly touched his staff, and to his amazement, a thrum of power rose to his hand. The warmth of it spread over his body, filling him with joy. "Thorgil, I can feel the life force," he said. The shield maiden's hand flew to the rune of protection at her neck, and she nodded.

"What you feel is the lack of glamour," said Father Severus with a sharp look at the two. "The simple fact of God's world is more powerful than any elvish dream. They think it a vile punishment to live without illusion, but I'd rather eat honest bread and lie on honest earth than wallow in what passes for life in their halls."

"Do you go there often?" said Jack.

"Often enough. They find me . . . amusing. That's why they keep humans, either for slaves or for entertainment. They experience no true emotion and can only watch like beggars at a window."

After the meal Father Swein retreated to his corner. Although Jack thought it must be dreary to hide in darkness, the abbot seemed to prefer not being observed.

Father Severus lit another lamp and gave it to Brutus so they could explore the dungeon. But first he demonstrated a timekeeper made from an old cup with a crack in it. He filled the cup with water and measured how long it took for the water to drip out. "We had hourglasses on the Holy Isle," the monk said, "but this works just as well." Jack had never seen such a device. He privately thought it was foolish. Tasks took however long they needed—hunting, shearing, planting, weaving—and it was pointless to measure them. But the monk said time-keeping was extremely important in monasteries.

"It keeps order," explained Father Severus. "It tells you when to go about your chores, when to meditate, and when to pray. Otherwise, men fall into sloth. From there, they degenerate into other sins." He stared pointedly at Father Swein's corner.

"They had hourglasses at St. Filian's," remarked Brutus. "As far as I know, measuring time didn't keep anyone from sloth—except slaves, of course."

Jack, Pega, and Thorgil explored the prison, with Brutus leading the way. It was very large. Near the ceiling, openings let in a faint breeze. As Jack watched, a mouse fell from one of them and scurried off into the straw.

"The holes must lead outside," observed Thorgil.

"They won't do us any good," said Pega. "I couldn't even fit my arm into one."

"And we are deep under the earth," added Jack.

They found a natural spring that flowed a short distance before disappearing into a hole. A side chamber contained a privy. Straw was heaped near the door for bedding. They avoided Father Swein's corner and found themselves back at the table, where the monk sat with his eyes closed, meditating.

So they walked around the perimeter again, to be sure they hadn't missed anything. But they hadn't. The prison was just as dull as it first appeared. To cheer them up, Brutus told stories about Lancelot and how the Lady of the Lake had given his ancestor the sword Anredden.

"Do you even know how to use a sword?" asked Thorgil.

"As well as Lancelot," said Brutus with a canine grin.

Father Severus stirred from his meditation, refilled the water clock, and began praying.

It wasn't a bad dungeon, Jack thought later as he snuggled into a pile of clean straw. They had bedding and water. Father Severus said the Picts brought food regularly. It wasn't horrible, but it might easily *become* horrible if they had to stay in the dark for days and weeks and months. It was odd how much you missed sunlight when you haven't got it.

Also, Jack thought, Guthlac took a lot of getting used to. His *"Ubba ubba . . . ubba ubba . . . ubba ubba"* went on all night.

Chapter Thirty-four

THE WILD HUNT

Jack woke. He didn't know if it was morning or night, but he felt more rested than he had since reaching the Land of the Silver Apples. His sleep had been shallow and unsatisfying in the hobgoblins cave. Glamour must drain your strength. Perhaps sleep did not exist at all in Elfland, where illusion was strongest. A lamp burned in the privy, but the main room was almost completely dark.

Jack cleared a patch of floor, leaving a small heap of straw, and called to the life force. He didn't need to start a fire. He did it simply because he was comforted by the force's presence, like an old friend. The straw blazed up, and he saw Father Severus sitting at the table. His face was like a skull stretched over by a thin layer of skin. Jack shivered.

"You've learned a trick or two since we last met," said the man. "You do know wizardry is a sin."

Once Jack would not have argued with a monk—Father had filled him with awe for such exalted beings—but much had happened since the days when he was a frightened boy being carried to a slave market. He had stood at the foot of Yggdrassil and drunk from Mimir's Well. "I call to life. Life is not a sin."

The monk laughed. "Hark at you, lecturing your elders! Life is an *opportunity* to commit sin. The longer it lasts, the more evil clings to your soul, until you sink beneath the weight of it. Next you'll be telling me magic is the same as miracles."

"I was about to say that," Jack admitted. "They did miracles every day at St. Filian's, and no one thought twice about it."

"Those weren't miracles," Father Severus said. "Those were vile perversions. They preyed upon the weak and plucked them clean. If I were in charge of St. Filian's, I'd whip those so-called monks into shape. Hard work and fasting for the lot of them. But we don't need to sit here in darkness." He placed a lamp on the table. "None of your magic, please. We'll use honest flint and iron."

To Jack, the appearance of fire from pieces of metal and stone was as much magic as the fire he called with his staff. But he didn't want to argue. Father Severus was a frail, possibly dying, man, and in spite of the monk's gloomy outlook, there was a deep kindness in him. His reverence for "the simple fact of God's world" wasn't that different from the Bard's reverence for the life force.

"Could you fill the pitcher for me, lad?" asked Father Severus.

Jack hurried to obey. He passed Thorgil, who woke up instantly, and Pega, who had burrowed into the straw like a mouse. Jack could see only the top of her head. When he returned, Father Severus was setting out cups and trenchers.

"The Picts will arrive soon." The monk smiled morosely. "Occasionally, I tell time by the rumbling of my stomach."

"Why are they here? The Picts, I mean," asked Jack. "They don't seem to be slaves."

"They're enthralled," said Father Severus. "Long ago, when Romans ruled the earth, they fell under the spell of the Fair Folk. These are not ordinary Picts, but the Old Ones who have turned their backs on God's world. They no longer marry or have children. No mortal woman is good enough for them."

"If they don't have children," said Jack, confused, "why haven't they died out?"

"You don't understand. These are the *same men* who battled the Romans and fled beneath the hollow hills. They have not aged, except for those rare occasions when they must enter Middle Earth."

"How . . . old are they?"

"Hundreds of years," replied Father Severus. "Do not envy them. Long life has not given them wisdom. It has only allowed them to sink more deeply into corruption."

Jack felt cold, trying to imagine so much time. One year

seemed endless to him. One *week* could drag by if you were waiting for something. Pega appeared from the darkness, scratching her head, followed by Thorgil and Brutus. Father Swein was still holed up somewhere.

"I don't hear Guthlac. Does that mean it's morning?" said Pega, yawning.

"Actually, it does," said Father Severus. "The Picts take him for a walk before they bring food. Otherwise, it's too difficult getting in and out."

They heard voices and the sound of the door being unlocked. Brude led the way with a torch. Others brought bread, cheese, apples, and roast pigeons—normal ones with two legs. Brude found Father Swein asleep in a corner and bent over him, whispering, *"Ubba ubba."*

"What? What was that? Don't hurt me!" screamed the priest, leaping up. The Picts roared with laughter.

"You commmme," Brude said, crooking his finger at Brutus.

"No, thanks," replied the slave.

"Ladyyyy wannnts you."

"Ah! That's different." Brutus brushed the straw off his clothes and ran his fingers through his hair. "Duty calls," he told Jack.

"What duty?" said Jack.

"Entertaining Nimue. She must have talked Partholis into forgiving me."

"You're leaving us?" cried Jack, irritated beyond belief by the slave's casual abandonment of his friends.

"Have to, if you want the water back at Din Guardi."

Brutus went off whistling a maddening tune between his front teeth.

Why haven't you already restored the water? Jack wanted to ask, but he knew. The man was having the time of his life in Elfland.

The Picts slammed the door. "Witch's whelp," muttered Father Swein, piling his trencher with as much food as he could manage.

The joy went out of the room with Brutus's departure. Jack was annoyed at him, but the slave's lazy charm had kept everyone's spirits up. A breakfast in prison with a gloomy monk and a half-mad abbot was hardly a good substitute. When Guthlac was returned shortly thereafter (*"Ubba ubba"*), Father Swein retreated to the darkness with his trencher.

Jack, Pega, and Thorgil told Father Severus about their adventures. The monk filled his water clock and listened until it ran dry. "No more," he commanded, holding up his hand. "You have to do things by turns. Otherwise, time will hang too heavily. I personally enjoy prayer interspersed with meditations on sin, but you lack the discipline. Chores are better for young folks."

"How many chores can there be in this place?" said Pega, eyeing the vast, empty room.

"Dozens," Father Severus replied heartily. "You can sweep, wash the trenchers, pick fleas out of the straw, measure the floor by handbreadths—"

"Measure the floor?" cried Thorgil. "What good is that?"

"A great deal if it keeps you busy. It doesn't matter

whether work is useful, only that you keep a worshipful mind while doing it."

"Hel," muttered Thorgil, swearing by the goddess whose icy halls awaited oath-breakers.

"Hell is exactly what we're worried about," Father Severus said. "I've seen what happens to monks who have too much time on their hands. Some of them turn vicious, and some"— he nodded toward the shadows where Father Swein was sucking the marrow out of pigeon bones—"go mad."

Would that be small demon or large demon possession? thought Jack, stifling a laugh.

"I assure you this is a serious business," said Father Severus, frowning. "We might be down here for years. Or *you* might. I won't last."

"Yes, sir," the boy said.

In between chores, the children told stories, exercised, and answered riddles—Father Severus had an endless supply of them. He taught them Latin words and a strange kind of magic called "mathematics." Six times a day he led them in prayer, except for Thorgil, who said it was beneath her dignity to worship a thrall god.

Without that structure, Jack thought he would have gone insane. The days passed monotonously without the least ray of natural light. It was like being buried alive. Jack snapped at Pega, who didn't deserve it, and came to blows with Thorgil, who did. Father Severus scolded him. But the monk understood Jack's despair and set him chores to calm his mind.

Jack was told to capture the tiny animals that fell from the roof and release them into holes in the floor. He didn't know whether they fared better there, but they were certainly doomed if they stayed in the prison. Father Swein delighted in crushing them. If he captured one alive, he took it to his corner, where the others could hear its pitiful squeaks.

The abbot was growing more dangerous. He demanded most of the food and, because he was the largest, got it. He allowed the food he didn't eat to rot. The stench poisoned the air, but no one dared to approach his corner to clean it out. At times he swaggered around, threatening punishment to those who defied him. Then the mood would pass, and he would retreat to his corner, uttering loud groans. Father Severus prayed over him, but it did no good.

Thorgil whispered that if he attacked anyone, she would kill him. Jack's worry was that she wouldn't succeed.

One day—the sixth or seventh after they arrived—Jack asked Father Severus how he'd found Brother Aiden. They had been practicing "mathematical magic" for two turns of the water cup, and Pega had burst into tears over a problem: *If you have ten smoked eels and you eat two the first night and eight the next, how many are left?* "You can't eat eight eels at one sitting," she sobbed. "They're too big."

"Olaf One-Brow could," said Thorgil.

"Anyhow, you can't have *no* smoked eels," Pega insisted. "You can have nothing to eat, but you don't know what it is." She was having trouble with the concept of *zero*. So was Jack.

Father Severus announced it was time for stories, and that was when Jack asked him about Brother Aiden.

"I was living in the forest," replied the monk. "Doing penance, you understand."

Jack remembered Brother Aiden mentioning a scandal between Father Severus and a mermaid. He longed to ask about it.

"It was a grand place," said the monk, the memory softening his grim expression. "I had a hut surrounded on three sides by a giant oak, to keep off the wind and rain. The springwater nearby was as sweet as dew, and in summer the ground was covered with strawberries. In fall I ate my fill of hazelnuts and apples and had enough to store for winter. It sounds lonely, but it wasn't. Deer, badgers, and wild goats played at my door. The branches were always full of birds."

"Doesn't sound like penance to me," observed Pega.

"I assure you, I was suffering," Father Severus said. "At any rate, one night I heard the sound of a chase through the forest—at night, mind you, when all good Christians should be in bed. 'How do they see where they're going?' I wondered. The bushes were thrashing, the hounds were baying. I heard men running and the sound of a horn.

"Then I knew it wasn't a Christian hunt, but something Other. I got on my knees to pray for deliverance, or at least for the courage to bear whatever fate brought me. After a while the Hunt died away. I gave thanks to God for His mercy. And then I heard it."

"What?" said Thorgil, who had been drawn in by the monk's vivid description.

"A child crying. Out there where all was wild and deserted,

I could hear a small boy weeping as though his heart would break. I took my lamp and searched, but the voice fell silent. He was afraid of me. I had a general idea of his whereabouts, so the next day I put out a pot of porridge."

"How did you get porridge in the middle of the forest?" said Pega.

"I was allowed to take oats, peas, beans, and barley with me," said the monk with a slight edge to his voice. "Satisfied?"

Jack nudged Pega to warn her not to interrupt again.

"That night the porridge was gone, and I knew the child was alive."

"By Freya's teats, this is as good as a saga," declared Thorgil.

"I had tamed many a forest creature," Father Severus said, frowning at the shield maiden's choice of words. "A child was no different. Day after day I put out food, and I sat under his favorite tree and told stories. He couldn't understand me—I found that out later—but the sound of my voice must have reassured him. One day he emerged. I didn't move. I merely sat there and continued to speak. And finally, he trusted me enough to come back to the hut.

"Poor, starved, mistreated child! His body was covered in bruises. His bones stuck out. He was half dead, and when I saw the marks on his skin, I understood." Father Severus paused to drink some water. He was an excellent storyteller and knew exactly when to stop.

"Understood what?" demanded Thorgil.

"I'm feeling tired," said the monk. "Perhaps I'll finish the story tomorrow."

"You can't stop now!" said Pega.

Jack noticed a slight quirk at the corner of Father Severus's mouth. It was how the Bard looked when he knew he'd captured everyone's absolute attention.

"Are you sure?" said Father Severus, sighing deeply.

"Yes! Yes!" cried both Pega and Thorgil.

"Very well: The boy had the tattoo of a crescent covered by a broken arrow. Below it was a line crossed by five other small lines, the rune for *aiden*. *Aiden* means 'yew tree' in Pictish. The crescent stood for the Man in the Moon and the broken arrow for the Forest Lord. You probably don't know about them."

"Oh, we know about them, all right," said Jack.

"They're the demons the Picts worship, and that mark meant the child was destined for sacrifice!"

"No!" cried Pega.

"Yes," said Father Severus. "He was the aim of the Wild Hunt. He'd been intended for death, but he'd escaped. I knew he'd never be safe in the forest. The Picts would return, and so I took him to the Holy Isle. I taught him Saxon and Latin, but I didn't have to teach him goodness. He already had that. The boy grew into Brother Aiden and became the librarian of the Holy Isle."

"A wonderful ending." Pega sighed.

"A better one would have been for the monks to go back to the forest and slaughter the Picts," Thorgil said.

"Monks don't do that," said Father Severus.

"That's why they're so easy to pillage," said the shield maiden with a self-satisfied smile.

Chapter Thirty-five

THE BARD'S MESSAGE

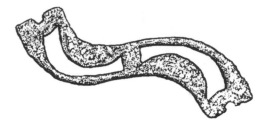

Jack was deeply worried by Brutus's absence. He'd scratched a mark on the wall for every time the Picts had brought food since their arrival, and now there were fourteen scratches. Two whole weeks had passed since Brutus had been summoned back up to the palace! Thorgil had tried to question Brude and been spat on for an answer.

Jack tracked a meadow mouse through the straw and captured it before it got any closer to Father Swein. He held it gently and looked into its bright eyes. The life force was like a tiny spark in its quivering body. It comforted the boy, and he imagined the mouse's family waiting for its return. Then he noticed something else.

It had a flower in its mouth.

It was a daisy, the sort of thing that appeared by the thousands in midsummer. Jack had seen them every year of his life but had paid little attention to them. Now, in the darkness of the prison, this single daisy shone like a star. The mouse had been taking it to build a nest.

Jack released the creature into an escape tunnel, but he kept the flower. He sat quite still, and, unbidden, he heard a voice in his mind:

I seek beyond
The turning of a maze
The untying of a knot
The opening of a door.

Dimly, he saw houses surrounded by green fields. Threads of smoke rose from hearth fires, and John the Fletcher called to his dogs as he strode along the road. Such an ordinary, wonderful sound! It made the vision grow brighter and more real. Women sat in doorways, combing wool for spinning. A girl chased an evil-hearted ewe from a garden. Men fitted sections of a cart wheel together with pegs. Jack could hear the faraway tap of their hammers. And all around, fields of daisies stretched as far as he could see.

But this wasn't where he was meant to be. He turned and found himself in a room. It was a comfortable place with a table and chairs, a brazier for warmth, and beds at the side. A window let in a bar of sunlight, and Jack saw a swallow pecking crumbs from the floor. It looked up at him and warbled, *Chirr, twitter, cheet.*

You see him, too? Clever bird! said a voice. Jack trembled.

Warble, churdle, coo, said the bird.

He does look the worse for wear, but don't worry. He is guarded by the need-fire. The Bard stared at Jack through the farseeing tube formed by his hands. Behind him, Father lay in a bed, pale and unmoving, with Brother Aiden at his side.

You have allies you are not aware of, said the Bard, speaking directly to Jack. *Remember: No illusion, no matter how compelling, can stand against—*

The vision faded. The boy clutched the air to pull it back, but that wasn't how the magic worked. The Bard was powerful enough to allow him a glimpse of the other side. Jack was nowhere near as skilled. He doubted he could calm his mind enough to even begin the charm, what with *"Ubba ubba"* in the hallway and Father Swein's laments.

No illusion can stand against what? thought Jack. The message had ended before that vital piece of information could be given. And what allies did he have in this dark place? Not Brutus, surely! Jack felt absolutely helpless. He could have withstood starvation, beatings, or captivity, but not this false hope. He had no control over anything and no chance of ever escaping. The boy bent his head and gave himself up to despair.

"Come here, Jack," said Father Severus from the table where he was warming his hands over a lamp.

The boy seated himself and prayed he wouldn't lose control.

A long silence followed. "Never forget that there is a purpose to everything under Heaven," Father Severus said at last.

Jack didn't know what he was talking about.

"If I hadn't sinned, I would never have been sent to the forest. If I hadn't been sent to the forest, I would never have saved Aiden's life," explained the monk. "If I hadn't returned to the Holy Isle, I would not have been carried off by Northmen. I wouldn't have met you or Pega or Thorgil. I was meant to be here, because you needed me. And the three of you are meant to be here for a purpose not yet revealed. But purpose there is."

Jack swallowed very hard. "You sound like the Bard."

The monk laughed, setting off a coughing fit. He drank a cup of water to recover. "Don't insult me by comparing me to a wizard. I've heard a lot about your Bard or, as the elves call him, Dragon Tongue."

"You have?"

"He came here as a young man. He'd been gathering mistletoe on an elf hill when Partholis spotted him. She lured him inside and slammed the door. She was smitten by him, you see, or as much as these soulless creatures can care about anyone. It took Dragon Tongue a year to get away. And when he did, he made off with some of Partholon's best magic. A fine trick. *Not* that I approve of magic," the monk said.

Jack was enormously cheered by this. Good old Bard! He'd got the better of that nasty Elf Queen.

"What's that?" inquired Father Severus, pointing at Jack's hand.

"A daisy. A mouse carried it in."

"Really?" The monk looked up at the dark ceiling. "I've often wondered . . ." He paused. "The air is always fresh, and sometimes I've smelled rain. The mice, the voles, the shrews that fall in . . ."

"Are too weak to go deep into the earth," Jack said. "You know, sir, it looked like we were going down when we came here—"

"—but Elfland is full of illusions," cried Father Severus. "Of course! Why has this never occurred to me? A folk who can make palaces appear out of thin air would think nothing of making us think we were going down, when in fact—"

"—we were going *up*," finished Jack.

The two of them gazed at the ceiling. Jack had never considered climbing up because it had seemed pointless. But if they were close to the surface, they could break through and—

The iron door flew open. Jack saw Guthlac pinned against a wall and Brude with his torch. It wasn't time for supplies. The Picts were here for another reason and probably not a good one. Jack grasped his staff and a trencher to throw if it became necessary. Thorgil and Pega appeared from the gloom. Even Father Swein came out of his corner.

Lady Ethne fled across the room and knelt at Father Severus's feet. "I tried! I tried!" she wept.

"There, child," said Father Severus, patting her head. "Tell me what's upset you. I'm sure talking will help."

"Nothing can help," Ethne groaned.

"That's the problem with getting a new soul," the monk said gently. "It's like taking a boat out on a choppy sea. You love too deeply and hate too extremely. You suffer agony from minor slights and are transported by the slightest kindness. It takes time to get used to mortality."

"It isn't *my* soul I'm worried about," said Ethne, looking up at Father Severus with her mouth trembling and her eyes brimming with tears. "It's yours."

"Mine is in the hands of God."

"You don't understand! A messenger has arrived from There. We are all called to Midsummer's Eve."

Jack thought Father Severus couldn't look more ill, but he was wrong. The monk's face turned as white as parchment, and he trembled. "All must attend?"

"I argued and argued with Mother. I begged her to free you, but she's dreadfully frightened. She says *they* get to choose. She says they get angry if they're fobbed off with something second-rate."

"When?" The word was spoken so quietly, it was like the rustle of a candle flame. Jack, Thorgil, and Pega bent closer. It was as though Father Severus had barely enough strength to speak.

"Sssssooon," said Brude, making them all jump. His eyes were shining like a wolf's in the forest. He held the blazing torch high and reached out to touch Ethne's hair.

"Get back!" she cried, leaping to her feet. She turned at once from a frightened girl to the daughter of the Elf Queen. Brude recoiled, holding his hand up as though warding off a blow. "I could have you sent Outside," snarled Ethne. "I could bar you from Elfland. You could spend the rest of your life lying on a cold hillside, begging to be let in."

"Nnnoooo," groaned the Pict, cowering at her feet. Jack was astounded at the change in her.

"Leave us, vile worm!" she commanded. Brude scurried out the door. Ethne immediately reverted to the tearful girl she'd been when she entered. "I shall not desert you," she whispered, bending to kiss Father Severus's hand. She left as dramatically as she'd arrived, and the door was bolted behind her.

"Hussy," said Father Swein, his gaze boring into the spot where the elf lady had stood. "Temptress. Strumpet." Then his attention wavered, and he retreated to his corner, muttering.

"I don't see what the fuss is about. We Northmen enjoy Midsummer's Eve," said Thorgil. "Olaf One-Brow used to make a great, straw-covered wheel, set it ablaze, and roll it down the hill from King Ivar's hall. That was to make the trolls think twice about attacking us. On Midsummer's Eve the mountains open up and the trolls swarm out, looking for a fight. They find it, too, by Thor!" The shield maiden smiled at the memory.

Jack saw she had missed the point of Ethne's visit. It was no innocent party they were being invited to. You had only to look at Father Severus's face to know something dreadful was afoot. He remembered the Bard's words when they were at Din Guardi: *Elves don't welcome visitors except on Midsummer's Eve.* And Brother Aiden's response: *You don't want to be around then.*

"Why is Ethne so upset?" Jack said. "How can there be midsummer, when time doesn't pass in Elfland?"

"It is midsummer when *they* say it is. Time means nothing in Hell," said Father Severus.

"What are you talking about? What's going to happen to us?" Pega said shrilly.

The monk took a deep breath and clutched the little tin cross he wore around his neck. "I must set an example for these young ones," he murmured. "I must not beg for mercy." He looked directly at Jack, Pega, and Thorgil. "Long ago the elves sought to hold back time, but they didn't have the strength to do it on their own. They asked for aid from the powers of darkness."

"Oh! I don't like the sound of that," said Pega.

"For such things, there is always a price. The elves drag out their years, aging only when they leave this enchanted realm. In return, on Midsummer's Eve, they must pay a tithe to Hell. They find a plump, well-nourished soul and bind him over to the fiends. Demons scorn ordinary sinners such as petty thieves. They claim there's not enough meat on them. But nothing pleases them more than a good man who has fallen into evil ways. Or a woman. They aren't particular."

"I've been a petty thief. They won't like me," said Pega hopefully.

"They'd never be interested in you, child." Father Severus attempted a smile. It only made him look more ghastly. "The amount of evil you've done would barely satisfy an imp."

"I won't be chosen," declared Thorgil. "I serve Odin, not a thrall god who can't keep order in his own hall."

"You've done crimes and you will be called to account for them," said the monk, "but not yet. For the Midsummer's Festival the demons prefer the taste of guilt. They say it adds spice to the dish. You, shield maiden, are as shameless as a Roman alley cat. They won't choose you either, Jack. In spite of your wizardry, you haven't used it for evil."

Jack felt a craven sense of relief. He remembered Father's stories of demons with sharp claws. "What about him?" He nodded at the dark corner where Father Swein was mumbling.

"Already in the service of the Evil One. They'll come for him one day, but they prefer to keep their servants on earth to lead others into sin."

"That leaves only . . ." Pega faltered.

"Me," said Father Severus.

"You're not evil!"

"In my youth I committed an act of great cruelty. I won't plead ignorance. I knew in my heart of hearts that it was wrong. Now my sin will drag me down to Hell."

Everyone was shocked into silence. Finally, Pega said, "Did it have anything to do with a mermaid?"

"Be quiet," hissed Jack.

"I must accept my fate, for it is deserved," said Father Severus, ignoring the girl's question.

"Well, we won't let them take you," Pega said. "We'll stand up to those demons and tell them what a good man you are."

The monk smiled slightly. "I take back what I said earlier,

child. You wouldn't even make an appetizer for an imp. Unfortunately, no one can look upon Hell without being struck dumb with terror. There is nothing worse. Nothing."

"You mean, we'll see right into—," Pega began.

Jack shook his head at her. He saw that Father Severus was struggling to appear calm. "Would you like to be alone, sir?" the boy asked.

"Yes! Yes! I must pray!" The monk walked unsteadily into the darkness, and soon there were competing sounds coming from different places: prayers from Father Severus, moans from the abbot, and *"Ubba ubba"* from Guthlac. They made the atmosphere in the dungeon extremely depressing.

But Jack wasn't ready to give up yet. He told the others of his belief that they were close to the surface of the earth. "We must dig our way out," cried Thorgil, seizing the initiative. She immediately dragged the table over to the wall, and the three of them lifted the heavy benches on top.

Jack climbed onto the unsteady heap and began digging a series of holes for them to use for climbing. When he was tired, Thorgil took over. It was slow and exhausting work. Rocks had to be pried out. Dirt fell on their faces. How they would make a tunnel once they reached the ceiling, Jack didn't know. But they had to try.

Pega sat at the bottom and offered advice. "I think Father Severus is too weak to climb," she pointed out.

"We'll carry him," grunted Thorgil, clinging to the wall.

"I don't see how. I mean, it's awkward enough hanging on to those holes."

"I said we'll carry him! He weighs no more than a dead dog," said Thorgil. She attacked the wall with renewed fervor, and the knife clanged against a rock.

"If you're not careful, you'll snap the blade," Pega said.

Thorgil dropped a fistful of dirt on her head. "Next time it'll be a rock," she said.

Jack slumped against the wall, resting. Something was different. Thorgil's knife still hacked at the wall. Dirt pattered down. Father Severus prayed from the left. Father Swein moaned from the right. *"Ubba ubba"* was missing.

Jack jumped to his feet. The hall was full of tramping feet. The door flew open, and the heap of benches collapsed as Thorgil spun around. She landed easily like the good warrior she was, but the benches knocked the knife from her hand.

A mob of Picts swarmed into the prison. They forced Jack, Pega, and Thorgil into the hallway. They dragged Father Swein from his corner, and two more carried Father Severus between them as easily as a dry twig.

"You commmmme," hissed Brude.

"I'd rather stayyyyy," said Jack, dodging a blow, but there was no way he could resist.

It was time for the Midsummer's Eve celebration.

Chapter Thirty-six

SECRET ALLIES

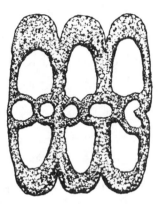

"Are you all right?" Jack asked Thorgil. The bench had struck her a hard blow, and her wrist was beginning to swell.

"I've felt better. By Fenris's fangs, I'm sorry to lose that knife! At least none of these *hwatu shazz* found it."

"Does that mean 'troll droppings'?" said Jack. He guessed from the Picts' scowls that it was an insult.

"*Putrid* troll droppings," said Thorgil.

"I seem to remember Fenris. Wasn't he the giant wolf Thor chained up?" asked Jack.

"Yes. Fenris refused to be bound unless the god Tyr placed his hand in the wolf's mouth. When Fenris realized he'd been tricked, he chewed off Tyr's hand and swallowed it. Hah! That was a merry tale!"

"If you say so," Jack said. He remembered Rune telling the story on the morning the Northmen brought him home. They had camped on a fog-shrouded beach, and Thorgil had given Lucy the necklace of silver leaves. What an ill-fated gift that was! That moment of generosity had led to Lucy's mischief at the need-fire ceremony, the destruction of St. Filian's Well, Father's injury, and now the danger of being dragged down to Hell. All from one little necklace.

Jack turned to get a glimpse of Father Severus. The monk was too weak to walk fast and so was being carried. One of the Picts noticed Jack's interest and shouted, *"Shooff hhahh!"*

Thorgil laughed. "That means 'dog vomit.'"

"You seem to know a lot of their curses," said Jack.

"It's the sort of thing you pick up at slave markets."

Father Severus was right, Jack thought. She hadn't a scrap of shame about the crimes she'd committed. Pega was walking next to the monk, holding Mother's candle against her cheek. Jack hoped it comforted her. He couldn't find anything good about their situation.

They trudged upward—or was it down? Jack closed his eyes and tried to guess. But the farther they went, the cloudier his mind became. He could feel the memories slipping away. A moment earlier Thorgil had reminded him of a fog-shrouded beach, yet now he couldn't say where it had been. Then even that faded. There was only the sense of something gone.

The tunnel changed from a grim mine shaft to a hallway hung with rich tapestries. Torches blazed from jeweled sconces in the wall. The floor was a sheet of gold and made a sweet chiming sound as they walked over it. *Glamour,* Jack thought, both hating and desiring it. Well, why not be surrounded by beauty? Why live in a mine shaft when you could have a palace?

He knew something bad was going to happen, but he couldn't recall what. He asked Thorgil, and she didn't know either. "We're being taken to the Midsummer's Festival," Pega said in a voice made high by fear. "There're going to be demons." Jack was mildly surprised by this outburst. How could she remember when he didn't?

"We Northmen like to go troll-hunting on Midsummer's Eve," Thorgil said. "I hope demons provide good sport." She lost the train of her thought and fell silent.

They came to a doorway, and here the Picts left them. Not for Brude and his warriors was this festival. Elf guards crossed spears to keep them from entering, but they urged Jack and his companions on. The Picts crouched in the hallway, searching one another for fleas.

Jack saw Guthlac in the custody of human thralls. He was wrapped securely in vines, and Jack was unpleasantly reminded of St. Oswald's portrait. The coils around Guthlac rustled and slithered, and a thrall had dropped a hood over his head.

"I wonder what they intend for him, poor fellow," said Father Severus, who was walking slowly and leaning on Pega's shoulder.

"Noooo," moaned Father Swein, attempting to flee. The elf guards at the hall door shoved him back. But Guthlac was unable to see his enemy, and so the abbot was able to edge past.

They found themselves in a vast courtyard under a starry sky crowned by a full moon. In the middle was an enormous bonfire, while at the sides were flower-filled gardens lit by lamps and torches as well as by the fire. Bright shadows competed with dark ones.

Elves were singing, dancing, feasting, playing games, and conjuring up monsters. A giant toad snagged fireflies with its tongue. Jack could see its belly glow as the creatures flew around inside. Then a monstrous black flower grew out of the ground and swallowed the toad. It croaked mournfully as the petals closed. The pet toddlers howled and tried to crawl away, but they were brought up short by their leashes. The elves laughed merrily at their antics.

It was a scene of swirling chaos, a feverish quest for more and more pleasure, and Jack realized suddenly that there was no joy in the celebration at all. It was a mad frenzy, such as came over sheep after they had eaten moldy grass.

"Something touched my face!" cried Pega. Jack whirled around, ready to do battle with whatever had frightened her. But there was nothing. He walked around her to be sure. The competing lights and shadows made it difficult to see. "There *was* something," the girl insisted. "I felt it first in the hallway and now here."

"Did it hurt you?"

"No." Pega seemed unwilling to say more.

"It was probably a bat," said Thorgil. Large, leathery shapes with bodies the size of puppies swooped above the bonfire.

Pega shuddered. "I'd know if one of those bumped into me. This was more like . . . a kiss."

"Maybe it was tasting you to see if you'd be good."

"Thorgil!" exclaimed Jack.

"There's Lucy," said Pega. And Jack saw Queen Partholis and his sister watching a lumpy seedling rising from the ground.

"No, no!" said Partholis. "Branches first, *then* honey cakes!" Lucy stamped her foot, and the seedling died. "I don't know why I bother teaching you glamour," complained the Elf Queen. "You have the brain of a flea."

"Why doesn't it do what I want?" Lucy whined.

"Because glamour needs concentration. Oh, very well. I'll take over." Partholis waved her hands, and the seedling revived, putting out branches, leaves, then flowers, and, last of all, honey cakes. Lucy began stuffing herself with the treat.

"There's our guests of honor!" cried Gowrie, the huntsman who had danced with Thorgil at the party. Elf lords and ladies immediately swept Jack and his companions on to the queen.

"Oh, bother! What's he doing here?" said Lucy, her mouth smeared with honey. Jack felt a pang of grief. After all he'd done to save her, she might at least be glad to see him. But he reminded himself that she might be under a spell. The silver necklace still gleamed around her neck.

"He's here for the ceremony," Partholis said. "He's meant for the—*you* know."

Lucy turned away, bored.

"Let the celebration begin!" cried Gowrie, clapping his hands. Thralls set out chairs, tables, and snacks. Partholis and Partholon seated themselves with Ethne—who threw Father Severus an anguished look—and Lucy.

"Nimue!" shrieked the queen. "Nimue! Come sit with us. This is going to be such fun!" The Lady of the Lake made her way from among a cluster of ladies draped in what appeared to be fish scales.

"I wish I could stay," she gushed, "but I simply must get Brutie-Wootie out of harm's way."

Brutie-Wootie? thought Jack with a sinking feeling. And sure enough, he saw Brutus being fawned over by the same cluster of fishy ladies.

"He *can't* go," wailed the queen. "He promised to sing for me, and besides—"

"You have quite enough humans without him," Nimue said tartly. "I promised to restore the water to Bebba's Town, and I have to admit I miss the dear old swamps and marshes. Now that St. Filian's power is broken, I can go and come as I please."

"You are selfish as always," sniffed Partholis. The Lady of the Lake yawned delicately.

Brutus extricated himself from the crowd of admiring ladies. "Has the sun risen? Have I wandered into the heart of a flower? Or are my eyes dazzled by your ravishing beauty?" he cried, bowing before the queen.

"Oh, *you,*" Partholis said, giggling.

"I assure you, nothing could tear me away from your glorious presence except duty to my Lady," exclaimed Brutus. "Alas, I am in thrall."

"The sooner we get out of here the better," urged Nimue.

"Then I fear I must bid you all adieu," Brutus said, bowing again.

"Wait a minute," said Jack, pulling him aside. "How can you abandon the rest of us?"

"I'm not abandoning you. I'm fulfilling the quest."

"You, Brutie-Wootie, are a vile oath-breaker," said Jack, falling back on Thorgil's deadliest insult.

"You wound me deeply," protested the slave. "My mission was to restore water to Din Guardi. This I shall do. Yet what do I receive for my loyal service? Base ingratitude. But I forgive you, because those of Lancelot's line don't hold grudges."

"Those of Lancelot's line can barely hold a thought for five seconds!" yelled Jack. "You're deserting us! You're leaving us to be dragged down to Hell! How noble is that?"

"Ah! But you have allies you are not aware of," said Brutus with a mysterious smile.

"What allies? What are you talking about?"

"I wish I could say. Unfortunately, the very air in Elfland has ears. I can, however, pass on a gift from them." Brutus fished in a pocket and removed a small leather bag.

Jack looked inside. There was a chunk of flint, a nail of bright metal, and a dried polypore, the sort of mushroom used for kindling. "Fire-making tools!" Jack said, beside himself with rage. "What do I need these for? We've got the biggest bonfire in Middle Earth over there!"

Brutus laid his finger across his mouth to caution silence. "That would be true if, in fact, we *were* in Middle Earth. Nothing in Elfland is what it seems."

"You can't leave us," cried Pega, flinging herself against him. "You can't leave *him*." She pointed at Father Severus.

Even Thorgil unbent enough to tug at his sleeve. "True comrades stay together."

"I have no choice in the matter. The Lady despises humans (except for me, of course). She will not take you," said Brutus, hugging each of them.

"But—but—," said Pega, beginning to cry.

"At least give me Anredden," said Thorgil. "I doubt you even know how to use it."

"Trust me, no mortal sword can defend you. Pega holds the weapon you must use—but I dare not say more."

By now the fishy ladies were calling for Brutus to join them. He blew them kisses. "Now I must go. Water nymphs are so impatient, the darlings!" He stroked Pega's wispy hair. "Remember the gift I passed on to Jack, lassie. *It is real. It does not come from Elfland.*" Then Nimue took him firmly by the arm and led him away. The last they saw of him was his dark head bobbing among a cluster of fish scales in the distance.

"What did he mean, I have the weapon? What can I do?" Pega said. "I'm no warrior. I suppose I could sing."

"Last time your singing got us thrown into the dungeon," Thorgil said.

"Brutus meant nothing. He never does," said Jack, thoroughly disgusted.

Chapter Thirty-seven

THE TITHE OF HELL

By now the elves had ranged themselves in a wide arc around a grassy lawn, with Partholis and her consort at the center. The bonfire snapped nearby and sent a shower of sparks high into the air. They floated golden among the silver stars and did not dim. *Will the demons drag us into the fire?* Jack wondered. *Can an illusion burn you?* He guessed it probably could. The heat was certainly uncomfortable against his face. Gowrie clapped his hands for silence.

Partholis rose to her feet. "It is Midsummer's Eve," she said in a sweet voice. "The moon is almost at zenith, and our guests"—she wavered slightly here—"are soon to arrive. First we must have entertainment, and so I call upon the grim monk"—a titter ran around the gathering—"for one of his amusing sermons."

Jack was startled, but Father Severus seemed unsurprised. He walked slowly, resting his weight upon Pega, until he faced the queen. "Foolish as ever," he said. "You've been given an opportunity for salvation, but you close your ears to it. Time lies in wait for you, false queen. You may hide in this pretty bauble called Elfland, but someday it will be torn from you. You will be cast out on the cold roads to wander until you fade like mist before the rising sun. Not one of your lying tricks will call time back on that evil day. Repent!" His voice suddenly rose, and goose bumps came up on Jack's arms. "Repent! For the hour is at hand when the keepers of houses shall tremble and the strong shall bow down to the earth. All the doors shall be closed and the daughters of music shall be brought low."

As the monk spoke, he straightened up and the marks of illness fell away. Jack had seen the exact same thing happen with the Bard. The old man was sometimes exhausted by the end of the day. Sometimes his fingers were stiff and clumsy. But when he took up his harp, he became a young man again, playing without flaw, with his voice strong.

It was the magic that lay in music. And here, Jack saw, was a different kind of magic. Pega's eyes shone, and Thorgil listened with her mouth open. The shield maiden respected power. Here was power indeed!

But then Jack heard another sound that swelled and overwhelmed Father Severus. It was laughter! The elves roared and hooted and stamped and slapped one another on the back. Partholis was so overcome, Partholon had to signal a thrall to bring her wine. "Oh! Oh! That was good!" the Elf Queen wheezed. "It's like pulling the string on a top. *Whisk!* And off it goes!"

Only Ethne was upset. "Stop it!" she cried. "Don't make fun of him! He's right. We must repent."

"Ethne, you're even more tiresome than usual," said Partholis, wiping her eyes. "It's that taint of humanity."

"Half-human! Half-human! Half-human!" taunted Lucy.

"Now, now. That isn't nice," reproved the queen.

"But it's fun," Lucy said.

The queen put her arm around the little girl and hugged her. "You may be an obnoxious little flea-brain, but you're all elf," she said proudly. And then Jack knew, sure as sure, that Lucy was not under a spell. The necklace had not been responsible for her behavior. It had only awakened her heritage. Lucy was all elf, with the selfishness and cruelty that implied. She had never loved Father and Mother. She had never loved him. She was simply a creature of desire who would one day fade like a rainbow when the night comes on.

It made Jack extremely sad. It also freed him. He no longer needed to worry about her or try to save her, for restoring her to Father and Mother would only bring sorrow to all of them.

Meanwhile, the laughter had drowned out Father Severus's voice. He seemed to shrink before Jack's eyes, becoming frail and sick again. "You *beasts!*" cried Pega, her eyes flashing.

"Beasts would have more honor," Thorgil said.

"La, la, la! Time for the next event," mocked Gowrie. He seemed to be the master of entertainment. He signaled thralls to take Father Severus and the others to one side. A low fence was tricked up out of air, to mark a playing field. Elf lords and ladies stood around the edge armed, Jack noted uneasily, with what appeared to be long tongues of fire. They writhed in the air as though alive, and the elves' eyes gleamed in the light.

Father Swein was tethered to a block of wood in the middle of the field. He stood there, blinking owlishly at the gathering. A gang of thralls dragged Guthlac out, whisked off his hood, and ran for safety. The vines slithered off Guthlac's arms and legs.

For a moment the man simply stood there. A whisper of excitement went round the crowd. *"UBBA UBBA!"* roared Guthlac as he recognized his enemy. He launched himself at Father Swein. The abbot was a strong man, but he was no match for someone possessed by a large demon. He dragged the block of wood to the edge of the field, all the while fending off blows and bites from the frenzied Guthlac. But when he got there, he was driven back by the burning whips.

Back and forth they went, with both of them screaming at the top of their lungs and Father Swein getting the worst of it. He got in a few blows. Guthlac shook them off like fleabites. The abbot's robe was in tatters. He bled from a dozen wounds and was beginning to stagger. Whenever either of the men got close to the edge, the elves drove them back.

Everyone was cheering. Partholon stood on his chair and clapped. Lucy danced madly around the edge. Even Ethne looked flushed and excited. "Stop them! Stop them!" shrieked Pega.

"Shall we throw the little hob-human in too?" cried Gowrie.

"Yes! Yes!" shouted a dozen voices. "Hob-human! Hob-human! Hob-human!"

Gowrie, his handsome face shining with mirth, reached for the girl, and Jack struck his legs out from under him with his staff. Gowrie fell over with a look of absolute amazement. "He *hurt* me!" he exclaimed. The other elves roared with laughter.

"Go on, Gowrie! Get the hob-human!"

The huntsman rose painfully to his feet, and Jack braced for battle, but Father Severus put himself between them. "I'll take the girl's place," he said.

Oh, this was rare sport, indeed! The elves were beside themselves with glee. "Throw the gloomy monk in! Two monks against one demon! What sport!"

"No!" shouted Ethne, jolted from her pleasure in the fight.

"Oh, shut up, you sorry excuse for an elf," said Partholis. "But it really is time to stop. Separate those men," she commanded. "At this rate we won't have anyone left to offer our visitors—and we all know what *that* means."

That sobered up the elves at once. They dragged Guthlac away from Father Swein and tied him up with vines again. The abbot collapsed where he was. The magic fence disappeared as quickly as it had appeared. The elves withdrew to their seats.

Then all fell silent except Guthlac. He shifted from foot to foot, murmuring softly. The bonfire rustled and snapped. The moon moved just that bit closer to zenith. Everyone waited. Jack put his arm protectively around Pega. Thorgil stood with the barely controlled energy of a Northman warrior about to do battle. Father Severus prayed.

From the heart of the bonfire came a distant groaning and grinding of stone being torn apart. The fire brightened. It climbed to the very roof of the sky, licking at the stars. In the distance Jack heard cries that made his heart falter for the fear and pain that lay in them. It was the voices of the damned.

Jack wanted to run and could not. His feet were rooted to the ground. All will, all rational thought fled. He could only stare at the fire and watch the shapes arising within.

They were worse than anything Father had described to him. Father had never seen a real demon. It wasn't only their claws and teeth that were dreadful, but their loathsome bodies half hidden by the flames. Their eyes shone with awful knowledge. They had seen the worst, been the worst. Hate radiated from them like the foulest stench. And stench there was as well. A thousand odors of corruption mixed and mingled in their breath.

Jack covered his nose, but there was no escaping it. Pega clasped her hands. Father Severus fell to his knees. Thorgil bent over and vomited, and she was not the only one. Utter terror swept over the onlookers, elf and human alike. Father Swein lay where he had fallen, gibbering with fear.

A tall shape within the fire reached out a long, long arm and pointed a charred finger, first at Jack, then Pega, then

Thorgil. It hesitated at Thorgil. *Shield maiden,* said a voice like thunder rolling from a distant storm.

Thorgil stared back, unable to move. She had met her match, but even here, where all others were paralyzed, she managed to speak. "I am Odin's shield maiden," she gasped. Jack could see that it hurt her to speak. "I'm not yours."

The Being laughed, shaking the ground. *That remains to be seen,* it said, *but what have we here?* The finger moved and pointed at Father Severus. *I remember you. Do you remember me, when I whispered in your ear about the mermaid?*

The monk was speechless. His hands clutched his tin cross and his lips moved, but no sound came out.

Ah! The exquisite flavor of guilt. The aroma of shame. Other voices hissed and burbled with appreciation in the bonfire.

"Leave . . . him . . . alone," Jack managed to whisper. The finger hesitated.

Defiance. I like that, but it is not as tasty as shame.

"Go . . . away," Pega moaned.

And loyalty. The voice sounded faintly surprised. Then, giving no warning, Thorgil suddenly lunged. She had no weapon, so she brought her fist crashing down on the finger. Lightning flashed. Flame engulfed Thorgil's right hand. She screamed, frantically rolling on the ground to put out the fire. But it clung like a live thing. The Being turned its attention to her, laughing and shaking the earth.

The evil spell holding Jack and Pega wavered. "Pega," gasped Jack. "Hold out your candle."

He understood what the Bard had been trying to tell him

in the vision. *He is guarded by the need-fire,* the old man had told the swallow. *No illusion, no matter how compelling, can stand against—*

Can stand against the simple fact of one true thing. He grabbed the fire-making tools and struck a spark onto the dried mushroom. A tiny flame appeared, pale against the roaring energy of the bonfire. Pega shoved her candle into it.

The candle ignited. Its light was small and humble, but it was *real* where all else was illusion. It came from the need-fire, drawn by the efforts of the villagers on the darkest night of the year. It was pure life force.

The light gently pushed away the sickly dreams of Elfland and the lies that gave Hell its deadly power. First it enveloped Thorgil and dowsed the fire that consumed her hand. The shield maiden groaned and drew herself up into a ball.

The light moved on—it was wonderful how such a little thing could overwhelm such a large space. The bonfire died. The grass and gardens of Elfland faded. The moon blinked and went out. Now the light reached the elves.

Their glorious robes and jewels melted. Their perfect faces grew gaunt; their ever-youthful bodies became what they truly were: the dry husks of beings whose time was nearly gone. Partholis turned into a hag. Partholon was a grasping scarecrow. Gowrie became a weasel-like thug with shifty eyes. Even Lucy, genuinely young, became the crude, selfish creature she really was. The silver necklace had turned to lead.

The whole elfin kingdom was a dirty cave full of rubbish

and bones. But most amazing of all, where the bonfire had been was a gaping hole. Creatures crawled and slithered at its edge like giant sow bugs or the half-decayed things thrown up on beaches after storms.

The Being still inspired terror, though. It was a mass of tentacles boiling out of the hole, the knucker of all knuckers. And it still hissed and bubbled threats. *I will have my tithe,* it said in a deadly voice.

"And I will give it to you!" Guthlac, whose bonds had vanished in the candle's light, seized Father Swein and hurled him into the midst of the tentacles. The abbot shrieked once and disappeared into the seething mass. Guthlac laughed. "A fit feast for my master!" he cried.

You fool, said the Being. *He was mine already and no more toothsome than a crust of dried bread. Come forth and receive your punishment.* Guthlac opened his mouth as if to scream, but a giant sow bug forced its way out instead. It oozed horribly, prying the man's jaws apart until Jack heard them crack. The creature dropped to the ground and was swept up by one of the seething tentacles.

I guess you'd call that large demon possession, thought Jack wildly. He saw Guthlac's eyes clear, and for the first time the man looked sane. And joyful. Then he keeled over and died.

I will have my tithe, howled the Being, rising out of the hole. *One burned-out sinner is not enough. You elves know the pact. If I'm not satisfied, I take one of you!* And with that, it swept up Gowrie.

The elf's screams echoed horribly as the Being sucked him down the hole. The teeming hordes of sow bugs hurried after, throwing themselves into the darkness. Rocks groaned and clashed as they came together again. Thunder shook the earth, going deeper and more distant until at last it died away.

Chapter Thirty-eight

FREEDOM

Elfland was dark. Only the light of the candle revealed the elves huddled in the shadows. They seemed stunned. Jack saw Thorgil curled up in a ball. He hurried to her side and tried to rouse her. "Thorgil," he said, "I don't think your hand is burned."

She turned her face away. Her hand was hidden from him.

"The fire wasn't real," he said, falling to his knees beside her. "Everything was an illusion."

"The fire was real," she said.

"You're in shock. Take hold of the rune of protection. It can heal you."

"I already tried that, stupid, and it didn't work."

"Let me see."

"Go away," Thorgil said, curling up more tightly.

Jack saw Father Severus praying over the body of Guthlac. The monk placed his tin cross on the man's chest and gently closed Guthlac's eyes. Pega was still holding the candle, her eyes wide with shock. At her feet were two almost invisible bulges in the ground. "I really, *really* don't want to go through that again," said one of the bulges.

"If you'd listened to me, Your Noble Nit Brain, we wouldn't have got into this mess in the first place," said the other. Jack's head jerked up. That voice sounded like the Nemesis!

"I had to save Pega," the Bugaboo said.

"I was a fool to come with you," growled the Nemesis.

"A very decent fool," agreed the hobgoblin king. "Oh, Pega! I'm so glad to see you! Mmm! Let me kiss your dainty little feet."

The girl jumped as though she'd been stung. "Stop that!" she yelled.

All around the cave Jack heard movement as the elves began to recover. "We'd better go," said the Nemesis, standing up. "Once they re-create the glamour, we won't know up from down." Jack could see the hobgoblin's shadowy outline in the light of the candle. He was wrapped from head to toe in motley wool and looked like a collection of smudges hanging in the air. Another collection of smudges was trying to hug Pega, but she was keeping it at arm's length.

These were the secret allies Brutus had hinted at—the Bugaboo and the Nemesis had crept into Elfland to rescue

Pega. They must have given Brutus the fire-making tools, but how had they known what to do?

Meanwhile, the elves had gathered themselves together. They held hands and began to sing—softly at first, but gaining strength until their voices rose with heart-stopping power. Jack was spellbound. He had heard that music before, in another world.

It was on the way to Bebba's Town. The tiny band of pilgrims had camped in a wood, and the Bard had played his harp. Father had delighted them with hymns he'd remembered from the Holy Isle. Afterward, they had stretched out under stars shining between the branches of an ash tree.

That night Jack had dreamed of music so beautiful and yet so full of longing and despair, he thought his heart would break. It was the voices of the elves. It was the voices he was hearing now. The music was a distant memory of Heaven, even as the elves themselves were but a fading memory of angels.

Vines curled up from the ground. Flowers blossomed from arbors rising from the earth. Stars reappeared in the sky, and the moon—

The moon!

A wail of anguish rose from the elves. Partholis screamed. Partholon shouted. Even Jack felt afraid. The moon had a bite out of its side! Time had cast its shadow on the Silver Apple.

"Quick! Quick!" bellowed Partholon. "We must repair the damage!"

"And blow out that candle!" shrieked Partholis.

"Run!" ordered the Nemesis, throwing off his cloak. He grabbed Jack's arm and the Bugaboo took Pega's.

"I won't leave Thorgil," Jack cried. The Nemesis cursed him but made a detour and yanked the shield maiden up by her hair. It was brutal and Jack wouldn't have done it, but it had the desired effect. Thorgil stopped moaning and joined the escape.

"Where's Father Severus?" shouted Pega.

"I have him," panted Ethne. She was supporting his weight on her shoulders and was urging him to make haste. The Bugaboo quickly lifted the monk in his arms and carried him along. Jack saw, to his surprise, that Ethne's face in the light of the candle was still beautiful. She was older and her hair had lost some of its brightness, but Jack thought she looked nicer that way.

The elves were too distracted to pursue them far. Jack raised his staff, ready to do battle with the Picts, but he needn't have worried. The Picts were completely undone. They howled like dogs. They frothed at the mouth. The candlelight had aged them dreadfully, and it was a wonder such withered creatures were alive at all. Frail, bent, toothless, they mourned the passing of the time when they had been young and had killed Romans.

Jack found himself climbing up, not down, so the direction of the hallway had indeed been an illusion. But presently, the ground seemed to shift and go down. Tapestries sprouted from the walls, gilded tiles spread across the floor.

"Faster! Faster!" snarled the Nemesis. Try as Jack would to

imagine himself climbing up, the magic was too strong. All his senses told him they were fleeing into the heart of the earth with a mountain of rock overhead. His senses dulled. He stopped, wondering why he was running, but the Nemesis kicked him and forced him to go on.

After a while the walls reverted to dirt again and the floor to gravel. "You can rest," panted the Nemesis. "Glamour doesn't reach here." They all collapsed on the ground. The Bugaboo propped Father Severus against a wall, and the monk gazed at the hobgoblin in utter amazement.

"You aren't—you wouldn't happen to be—an imp?" he said.

"See, that's the kind of slander we have to live with," complained the Nemesis. "Mud men!"

"We're honest hobgoblins," explained the Bugaboo, "*not* to be confused with devils, imps, demons, unclean spirits, or fiends. Or, indeed, with full-blown goblins," he added, warming to his subject. "They're fond of dining on monks, but we'd never do that."

Father Severus felt for his cross and realized he'd left it behind with Guthlac.

"We're good Christians, too," said the Bugaboo.

"You are?" the monk said doubtfully.

"We like nothing better than a good sermon—by the way, I thought your speech to the Elf Queen was excellent."

"It wasn't as good as the one Columba gave the Picts," the Nemesis argued.

"True, but he was a saint," the Bugaboo said. "What a

glorious chase! And what a rescue! I imagine they'll be making poems about us for centuries, eh, Pega? 'The Hobgoblin King and His Bride.'"

"I'm not your bride," said Pega.

Thorgil was sunk in gloom, but Ethne looked radiant. "I'm free," she exulted. "I can hardly wait to become a nun, to wear hair shirts, go without food, and endure public floggings."

"You don't have to go as far as that," Father Severus said.

"Oh, but I want to suffer! I will strive for Heaven like a martyr, welcoming each new pain with joy!"

The monk frowned slightly. "People do better with ordinary goodness—feeding the hungry, caring for orphans. That sort of thing. You shouldn't take pride in suffering."

"Oh, I won't," cried Ethne, clasping her hands. "I'll never be proud again. I'll be the most humble servant God has ever had!"

Father Severus sighed. "We'll work on humility later—if we get out of here."

"No problem," said the Bugaboo. "There's an excellent way out via your old cell. We tried to get to you earlier, but the door was too closely guarded."

They went on, more slowly this time. Thorgil continued to hide her hand, and Pega tried to keep Jack between her and the hobgoblin king. They found the prison door open. To one side was the chain that had been used to tether Guthlac. "If ever I'm tempted to feel sorry for those wretched elves," said Father Severus, "I'll remember what they did to Guthlac."

"Where is he now?" Jack asked.

"Called to judgment, as all of us shall be. I hope Heaven is kind to him, for he suffered much." Once inside, Father Severus lit a lamp and Pega blew out her candle. The light became dimmer, and some of the warmth went out of the room.

"It's so small," mourned Pega, for barely half of the candle remained.

"But it did great service," said the Bugaboo.

Jack found Thorgil's knife under the fallen benches. He handed it to her, certain it would revive her spirits, but she turned away. "You take it. I can never use it again."

"The fire was an illusion," Jack insisted.

"Then how do you explain this?" Thorgil held out the hand she'd been hiding. It was an odd, silvery color. "I can't move my fingers. I'm paralyzed." She laughed bitterly. "Once, Frith Half-Troll threatened to cut off my right hand so I could be a warrior no more. It seems she got her wish."

"We'll find a wise woman. Someone will know how to cure you."

Thorgil looked at him scornfully. "One thing a Northman never indulges in is false hope."

"What in blazes were you doing?" said the Nemesis, looking at the holes hacked in the wall.

"Trying to escape," said Jack. "We figured there was only a short distance between the ceiling and the outside."

The hobgoblin chuckled. "There's an even shorter distance from that spring at the back of the dungeon. Trust mud men to get it all wrong."

"I've been meaning to ask you for the longest time," said Jack. "Why do you keep calling us mud men?"

"Because God made Adam from the dust of the earth, idiot," said the Nemesis. "Honestly! Some people never go to church." He started digging by the spring and soon uncovered a stone circle with a ring in it. He and the Bugaboo moved it away to reveal an opening.

"We go down?" said Jack. "That doesn't make sense."

"It does when you're at the top of a mountain," said the Nemesis. "Elfland lies deep. The tunnel went up until it was high above the earth, but you didn't know it because of the glamour. You'll drop from here into a stream. Then it's a hop, skip, and a jump to Middle Earth."

"I can hardly wait!" said Pega, her eyes shining.

"Me neither." The Bugaboo swept her up in his arms and jumped into the hole. Jack heard a splash not far below and a shriek from Pega.

"I forgot to mention the water's cold," the Nemesis said with an evil grin.

Ethne insisted on going next. "I abandon Elfland," she said solemnly. "I forswear all pleasures and embrace the sorrows of mortality, the better to gain entry into Hea—"

"Enough nitter-natter," grunted the Nemesis, dropping her down the hole. Jack heard a splash and a scream an instant later. Then Jack and Thorgil went.

"Troll spit!" swore the shield maiden. "He wasn't joking about the cold!"

The water was like liquid ice and so was the air. Jack's

breath came out as a plume of fog. "Up you go," said the Bugaboo, lifting them onto the bank. Pega and Ethne were already there, teeth chattering and bodies shaking. The hobgoblin king waded into the stream, and the Nemesis lowered Father Severus into his arms. "Can't get *you* wet, can we?" the Bugaboo said cheerfully. "You're so skinny, you'd freeze like an icicle." The Nemesis came down last.

"Well, what are you waiting for?" he demanded of the humans huddled on the bank. The cold didn't seem to affect either him or the king.

The water rushed past stalactites of ice. Blue light came from an opening not far away, where the stream ended in a waterfall. They edged along a slippery path until they came out onto a shelf of black rock.

"It's daytime," murmured Jack. "It was the middle of the night in Elfland."

"That's how it is when you leave Elfland," said the Nemesis, scowling. "Time is an illusion there. For all we know, they celebrated Midsummer's Eve after breakfast, or even last week. Don't think about it too long," he advised, noting Jack's bewildered expression. "It'll only give you a headache."

Chapter Thirty-nine

THE FOREST OF LORN

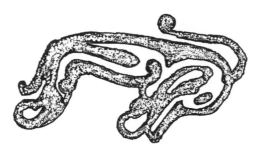

Below was a valley flanked by tall mountains. Its trees were not emerald green. Its fields were not filled with giant flowers, nor was the lake they bordered the brilliant blue of the waters of Elfland, but it was closer to the human heart.

Jack loved every lopsided tree, crooked stream, and marshy meadow of it.

"That's the Forest of Lorn," said the Bugaboo, hunkering down. *The Forest of Lorn!* thought Jack. That was where the Bard had wanted to take them all along.

"It's a bit steep," said the Bugaboo. "Hobgoblins have a head for heights, so we'll carry you down one at a time."

The Nemesis grumbled, but he agreed that mud men

would go, as he put it, "lickety-splat" down the hillside without help. Father Severus and Pega were taken first, then Ethne and Thorgil. Last of all, Jack. He closed his eyes as the Nemesis leaped from rock to rock, crowing with malicious glee. Once, the hobgoblin bounced up and down on a jagged spire, insisting that Jack admire the beauty of the chasm down below. Then he swung dizzily from crag to crag, saying, "Whoopsie!" when he pretended to slip.

"Not bad," conceded the Nemesis when they at last reached the bottom. "Most mud men would have tossed their oatmeal by now." But Jack knew the only reason he hadn't thrown up was because he had no oatmeal to toss.

He was suddenly, ravenously, hungry. The smell of the forest and the cool breath of the waterfall made him feel more alive than he'd been in—well, however long he'd been in the Land of the Silver Apples. And with this sensation came an overpowering desire to eat. Almost without realizing it, he picked a few pine needles and began to chew.

"Stop that! You're not a beetle," exclaimed the Bugaboo.

"It's the effect of Elfland," the Nemesis said. "It's anyone's guess what you were fed there, in the guise of glamour. Earthworms, mud, spiders—could have been anything." He grinned at Pega's horrified expression.

"I never ate their enchanted food," said Father Severus, leaning wearily against a rock.

"You look like it too," jeered the Nemesis. But the hobgoblins quickly set about making camp and gathering wood.

It had been late afternoon when they'd climbed out of the ice cave. Now it was nearly sunset.

"We'll be back in a jiffy," they promised. Jack started a fire, and by the time the hobgoblins returned with trout, apples, giant mushrooms, leeks, and combs of honey, everyone was seated around it, sucking on grass stems to stave off hunger.

The food was delicious. The Bugaboo baked the fish in clay and roasted mushrooms and slices of leeks on sticks. Pega fed Father Severus, who was exhausted but who nonetheless looked extremely happy. "I had forgotten how beautiful God's world was," he murmured.

Ethne refused a honeycomb. "I have turned my back on empty pleasures," she declared. "I eat only to sustain life now."

"Fine with me," said the Nemesis, adding her comb to his heap of food.

"Where did you find the honey?" said Jack, who remembered what a painful chore it was extracting it from Mother's beehives.

"Saw a nest in a hollow tree and helped myself." The hobgoblin stuffed a giant mushroom into his mouth, and juice squirted onto his chin.

"Didn't the bees object?" asked Pega.

"Sure did. Stung me all over. Mmf!" A bulge traveled down the Nemesis's throat as he swallowed the mushroom whole. He slapped his leg with a meaty sound. "Hobgoblins are as tough as tree roots. Even an adder would chip his fangs on us."

The day was coming to an end, and Jack noticed for the first time that a crescent moon was hanging in the western sky. "Look!" he cried. Everyone turned.

"It was near full in Elfland," Thorgil said.

"And is near full still, if I know anything about glamour," the Bugaboo said. "The elves will hold it that way as long as possible, but eventually, shadow will eat away the Silver Apple. Time has leaked into Elfland."

"You mean they'll age?" said Jack.

"Not as you do. The elves still have their powers, but they will gradually fade. The same moon will rise night after night and yet, so slowly you can hardly detect it, a leaf will curl up here, a blade of grass dry up there."

Jack gazed at the silver thread of moon in the deepening blue sky, trying to puzzle it out. "I don't understand," he said. "Father Severus, you were gone from Middle Earth a year. I know, because I was there when you were sold to the Picts. How could time pass for you and not the elves?"

"I often thought about it in my long captivity," said Father Severus. "The dungeon was beyond glamour, and so I aged. But Elfland itself is like an island in the sea. It is always summer there, yet its shores are surrounded by the same storms that sweep us poor mortals from birth to death. Past, present, and future exist at the same time for them. They can, if they choose, step into our world at any moment they please."

"You mean—you mean they could turn up somewhere *yesterday*?" said Jack, now totally bewildered.

"Yes!" interrupted Ethne. Jack was struck by something

familiar about her, something he hadn't noticed in Elfland. Whatever it was, he liked it. "Once, Partholis moved Elfland into the past when she noticed a few wrinkles. It was horrible! We had to repeat everything we'd done before—every moment, every word. I fear, if she is terrified enough, she may force everyone to live the same day over and over again."

"That is a Hell I had not even imagined," murmured Father Severus.

Now that they were full of good food and warmed by the fire, everyone began to yawn. The Bugaboo and the Nemesis, who seemed to know the valley well, went off into the dark and returned with armloads of grass. They made nests for everyone, with extra grass to pile on top.

Jack, Thorgil, Pega, Ethne, and Father Severus crept gratefully into these surprisingly comfortable beds. The hobgoblins, however, were not ready to sleep. They declared that such a victory over the elves deserved to be celebrated. They climbed onto nearby rocks and swelled up like giant bullfrogs.

"Oh, no! Not skirling," moaned Pega, trying to bury herself in the grass.

A most horrible wailing filled the forest as the Bugaboo and the Nemesis alternately swelled and deflated. They opened and closed their nostrils to change pitch. "Listen to this one, Pega dearest," the Bugaboo said. "It's a lament for a prince whose love has gone far away."

"Not far enough," muttered Pega.

"Look on the bright side," said Jack as the hideous skirling broke out again. "Nothing's going to attack us in the night with that going on."

Jack woke up under a heavy layer of dew. The fire had burned down to embers, and dawn reddened a few wispy clouds. Everyone else was asleep. He got up and fed the coals from a heap of branches the hobgoblins must have gathered the night before.

Jack sat close to the fire to dry his clothes. If he hadn't known the others were there, he might have thought he was alone. Everyone was burrowed into heaps of grass. It looked like a collection of haystacks.

The dawn chorus began, first doves, then nuthatches, wrens, sparrows, and a few crows. The first rays of sunlight struck the mountain peaks, making the waterfall shine like fire. He looked for the opening to Elfland, but the waterfall concealed it.

Thorgil threw back her grass cover and came over to sit beside Jack. "I couldn't understand the birds in Elfland. I understand these wretched squawkers too well," she said. Thorgil had never been fond of birds, except when roasted.

"What are they saying?" asked Jack.

"The usual rot: 'Feed me, feed me. I want a beetle, a beetle, a fat tasty beetle.' The rest are threatening their enemies. There's something unusual." Thorgil listened intently.

Jack saw a flock of swallows swooping through the upper air, just below the brightening clouds.

"I can't quite make it out. Something like, 'They're here, they're here, they're here.'" Thorgil turned away from them and poked at the fire with a long stick. Her other hand was tucked protectively under her arm.

"People do recover from injuries," Jack said carefully, watching the shield maiden.

"Many do not," she replied.

"That's no reason to give up."

"I never give up!" she cried angrily. The two nearest haystacks quivered. "I'll admit, when we were on the high ledge, I thought about throwing myself off."

"Thorgil," said Jack, alarmed.

"But I could not. *This*"—she grasped the hidden rune of protection—"prevented me. It sapped my courage. I should tear it off and hurl it into a lake." Thorgil tightened her grip on the rune.

"But you can't," Jack guessed.

"No! The accursed thing won't let me. I can't get rid of it."

"If I understand the Bard correctly, the rune chooses you," said Jack. "One day you'll know it's time to pass it on—just as I knew you were to have it." He didn't say—what was the use?—that he missed it dreadfully and wanted it back.

"Gifts have a way of turning on you," Thorgil muttered, staring into the fire.

Jack said nothing for a while. He thought about Lucy's silver necklace. Sunlight was making its way down the mountain and would soon reach their camp. Mist fumed off a nearby pond, and Jack heard the light splash of a fish.

It was hard to stay depressed in such a place. "Why did you strike the demon who was about to take Father Severus?" he asked.

"What demon? I saw a huge dog."

"A *dog*?"

"It was Garm, the hound that guards Hel. Rune described him to me. He has four eyes, jaws dripping with maggots, and he's covered in blood. He tried to claim me, but I told him I was Odin's shield maiden."

Jack was astounded. It must be the same thing that happened with knuckers. You saw what you expected. "Well, then, why did you strike Garm?"

"I—" Thorgil paused, holding the rune of protection. "I thought he was being unjust. Why should he take Father Severus and ignore oath-breakers like Father Swein and Gowrie? Garm *did* take them later." A satisfied smile flitted across Thorgil's face.

"That's it!" cried Jack, loud enough for Pega to sit up precipitously, scattering grass in all directions. "Remember Tyr? The god who sacrificed his hand to bind the giant wolf? It was a noble deed, to be sung about through all time—and you've done the same!"

Thorgil looked up, and now the morning light reached the camp and shone onto her face. "So I have," she murmured.

"Yes! You'll be known as—what shall we call you? Thorgil Silver-Hand, who fought the Hound of Hel. I'll make a song about it."

"Oh, Jack," whispered the shield maiden. She blinked back

tears, then shook her head angrily. "Curse this sunlight. It's making my eyes water."

Pega got up and began tidying the camp, as was her habit. She brought an armload of branches for the fire. "Are you talking about Tyr?" she remarked. "One of my owners taught me a poem about him." She began reciting it in Saxon:

"Tyr bi tacna sum healdeð
Trywas wel wi æ elingas."

"I know that one," said Jack. "'Tyr is a star. It keeps faith well with princes, always on its course over the mists of night. It never fails.' I memorized that when the Bard was teaching me about stars. I never connected it with the god."

"After Tyr lost his hand, he became the guardian of voyagers," explained Thorgil. "He stands at the roof of the sky, and his is the one star that never moves. We call it the Nail."

"And we the Ship Star," said Jack. He was delighted to see that the despair was gone from Thorgil's face and that she no longer tried to hide her hand. It *was* silvery, as though powdered with metal. The color was clearer in the light.

The Bugaboo and the Nemesis climbed out of their grass coverings and helped Father Severus up. "You rest," the Bugaboo told him. "We'll see about breakfast."

Ethne emerged last, looking cross at finding herself soaked with dew until she realized this was an opportunity to suffer. "I shall not sit by the fire," she declared. "Pneumonia will be good for my soul."

"Dry yourself. Pneumonia isn't good for anything," snapped Father Severus. So Ethne basked in warmth, and the rest of them waited eagerly to see what the hobgoblins would come up with.

They arrived with eels, pignuts, and the inevitable mushrooms. After a leisurely meal they held a meeting to decide where to go next.

"If we could find my ship, I'm sure we could take Father Severus home," said Thorgil.

"Travel on a Northman ship?" the monk said faintly. "I don't know . . ."

"We'd have room for all of you. Skakki hasn't yet loaded up with thralls." The shield maiden grinned maliciously.

"Thorgil," warned Jack.

"The sea's a day's journey that way," said the Bugaboo, pointing east. "There's an opening to the Hollow Road near the beach, and we hobgoblins can go home. You're an honorary hobgoblin, by the way, Pega."

"No, I'm not," said Pega.

"That's the best plan," the king blithely went on. "The pass through the mountains to the west is far too difficult for Father Severus."

The travelers made ready to go, which didn't take long, for they had nothing to carry. Pega took a quick bath in the lake. Jack found a walking stick for Father Severus, and Thorgil practiced using her knife with her left hand. She was in high spirits and demanded that Jack start on her praise poem at once. "Thorgil Silver-Hand. I like that," she said.

The hobgoblins knew every stick and stone of the Forest of Lorn. "We come here all the time," explained the Bugaboo. "The mushrooms are enormous! One chanterelle will feed a family of five, and as for the boletes and morels . . ." Jack stopped listening. When hobgoblins got onto the subject of mushrooms, they went on for a very long time.

They followed a deer trail. Because of the late start and Father Severus's weakness, they reached the mountain pass only at nightfall. It was freezing, and a thick fog brought darkness swiftly. "As I remember, Jack, you had a charm for getting rid of fog," Thorgil said.

"Unfortunately, it also causes rain," he replied. They decided that fog was more comfortable than rain and made as good a camp as possible in a hollow sheltered by rocks. Dampness coated everything. The fire kept dying. Father Severus coughed all night.

Chapter Forty

THE MIDGARD SERPENT

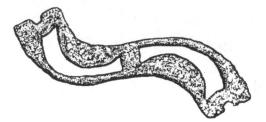

In the morning they could scarcely see three spear-lengths ahead. "I've got a sore throat," Ethne announced. "I do believe I'm coming down with my first illness. What fun!"

They didn't stop to eat, but hurried down the mountain to the warmer air by the sea. "I recognize these trees," Thorgil exclaimed. "That's where Skakki and Rune made camp. There's where Eric Pretty-Face ate a dead seagull he found and threw up. That's the cave Heinrich the Heinous and I—" The shield maiden broke off.

The cave was filled from top to bottom with rocks. There was scarcely room for a mouse to slip in.

"Oh, Freya. The earthquake," whispered Thorgil.

The Bugaboo probed it with a stick, and gravel poured down. "You're lucky you got out alive," he said.

"Where is everyone?" the shield maiden said. "They must have built a shelter. They wouldn't abandon shipmates—but where's the ship?" It was hard to see anything beyond the first few feet of sea.

"This fog might not lift for days," said Jack, looking up doubtfully and gauging how much rain would pour down if he worked a spell. "Why don't the rest of you search farther down the beach? I'll do what I can here."

Jack settled into a comfortable position and reached out to the life force. He sensed, not far away, a sunlit sky. The fog was shallow, and from above, it looked like a cloud hugging the ground. Farther out was the gray-green sea. There was nothing on its surface except a few gulls.

In the sky itself, swallows dipped and soared. They skimmed the upper surface of the fog, and Jack felt the power of their wings. Wonderful creatures! Beyond them, Jack felt other wings. He searched and saw nothing but water, with here and there the white tip of a wave.

It's the wind, Jack thought, surprised. The wind, too, had wings, like a flock of invisible birds. The Bard sometimes called up breezes to cool fields wilting in summer heat or to break up a snowstorm that had gone on too long. But he hadn't taught Jack the skill yet.

I discovered it all on my own, the boy thought proudly. The old man said that once you were steeped in magic, more and more secrets were revealed to you. He also said most of them were dangerous.

Come to me, invoked Jack, intrigued by his new power. *Fly to me, spirits of the air.* He cast his mind out farther and farther, delighting in the gusts and swirls and billows around him. He was flying too, the lead bird, the one who told the others where to go. He was their king. The great air-birds turned and followed him. They were coming!

Jack laughed and held out his arms. A blast of wind shredded the fog. Jack had never seen mist move so fast! It was gratifying and at the same time frightening. A second later a savage blow struck him, sending him spinning across the beach. Water flew through the air, making him choke.

On and on it came, howling and tearing up trees. Waves crashed over rocks; spray blew against the mountain. *Stop!* cried Jack, struggling to regain control. He clung to rocks, to keep from being blown away. *Go back. Lie down. Stop.*

He tried everything he could think of, but the wind kept battering him until at last it lost interest and turned away. That was what it felt like: The wind simply got bored with him. With that, it rose into the sky and wandered off.

Jack picked himself up. He was bruised in a dozen places. He was chilled to the bone, and his clothes were soaked. Trees were scattered like kindling.

"Jack! Jack! Are you all right?" cried Pega, running down the beach ahead of the others.

"I guess so," he said, brushing twigs and mud off himself.

He found his staff jammed between rocks at the entrance of the cave.

"What was that thing?" asked the Bugaboo. The hobgoblin's ears stuck straight out, and his skin had turned bright green with alarm.

"I—I'm not sure," said Jack. The instant before he'd been struck, he'd seen a long white pillar rise out of the sea.

"It was like a giant snake," said Pega, confirming his observation. "It was weaving back and forth between the water and the sky. I tried to warn you, but it moved too fast."

"It was the Midgard Serpent," said Thorgil. Everyone turned to her. "He's one of the children of Loki," she explained. "He was so evil and dangerous, Odin had him cast into the sea. He forms a belt around Middle Earth, holding his tail in his mouth, and when he thrashes, the earth quakes."

"That's what happened here. An earthquake," said the Bugaboo, pointing at the rocks filling the cave.

"Rank superstition," scoffed Father Severus. "Everyone knows earthquakes are caused by Lucifer stamping his foot on the floor of Hell."

"The Midgard Serpent and Thor are enemies," Thorgil went on, ignoring the monk. "Thor likes to fish for him. He cuts the head off an ox to bait his hook, tosses it into the sea, and waits for the stupid beast to bite. The same trick works again and again. Thor pulls up the serpent, but he isn't strong enough to get him all the way out. That's what we just saw— the tail end of the Midgard Serpent being pulled along."

"Sheer fantasy," jeered Father Severus.

"Rune saw it happen in the warm seas to the south, and Rune is not a man who lies," the shield maiden said with a hint of menace.

"No one would ever think that," Jack said quickly. He didn't bring up his own belief, that the waterspout had been caused by the wind. "Now that the sun's out, we can look for the ship."

They all shaded their eyes and looked out to sea, but even Pega, whose eyes were sharpest, saw nothing except a vast, gray-green expanse. Any evidence of a camp had been destroyed by the waterspout. Jack worked to free his staff, which had been wedged between boulders too large for him to shift.

"Let me try," said the Nemesis.

"Don't break it," cried Jack as the burly hobgoblin shoved him to one side.

"Keep your tunic on. I know what I'm doing." The Nemesis rolled a boulder out of the heap.

"Look out!" shouted Jack. He barely had time to yank the staff out of the way before an avalanche of rocks came down. The Nemesis bounced to one side as nimbly as a bullfrog avoiding a crane.

"See? It worked," crowed the hobgoblin.

"What's that?" said Pega, pointing at the mountain above the cave. High up Jack saw figures carved into rock. They were too far away to make out clearly.

"I'll have a look," said the Bugaboo. He climbed easily, having sticky pads on his fingers and toes. "There're three sets of pictures," he announced when he was perched on a high crag. "On one side is a hammer and a branching tree—fairly crude compared with hobgoblin work, but recognizable. On the other are a ship and—I think—a horse, except it has too many legs. In the middle are three triangles bound together."

Thorgil screamed. Jack almost jumped out of his skin. "What's wrong? Are you hurt?" he cried.

"They've gone!" she moaned. "They have gone out over the trackless sea, thinking I am dead." She curled up on the ground as she had after the demon burned her hand.

"You know this?" said Jack, wanting, but not quite daring, to hold her.

"Those are grave-markers," Thorgil said. "The sign in the middle is the *valknut*, the mind-fetter that means someone has fallen in battle. The hammer is for Thor and the tree is Yggdrassil. My symbols. The other pictures stand for Heinrich the Heinous. The horse is Sleipnir, Odin's horse. Heinrich always said he wanted to ride him, but of course you can't do that unless you're dead. Oh, curse Heinrich! He really is dead. He's probably riding Sleipnir right now. And I'm stuck here with a useless hand and no ship."

"You can join me at the nunnery," Ethne said brightly. "We'll have such fun doing penances together."

Thorgil threw a handful of sand at her.

Father Severus knelt down beside the shield maiden, and Jack feared she would attack him as well. But she had an odd respect for the monk, considering that she'd helped sell him as a slave. "There is a purpose to everything under Heaven," he began.

"We call it fate," said Thorgil.

"And it is not given to us to understand its workings. You were meant to be left on this beach. I don't know why. I don't know why I'm here either, but we have work to do in this world. Wallowing in self-pity does no good."

Jack held his breath. If ever there were words calculated to drive Thorgil wild, those were the ones. He saw her face turn pale, then red. Her body tensed.

Suddenly, surprisingly, she laughed. "You use words as Olaf used to use his fists, thrall-worshipper. I can use word weapons too."

"Then I welcome you as an enemy," Father Severus said.

They stayed on the beach for several weeks, to allow Father Severus time to recover. Every morning Thorgil climbed to a high rock and sat looking out to sea. She occasionally helped with chores, but every task reminded her of her useless hand. She would throw down whatever she was working on and return to her perch. Jack didn't have the heart to scold her.

Father Severus lay under a tree. He seemed quietly happy, but Jack worried about his cough and the feverish patches on his cheeks. "Sometimes I think I did not sleep the whole time I was in Elfland," Father Severus murmured. "Perhaps that's why I'm so tired now."

Jack understood what he meant. Glamour seeped everywhere there, so that you didn't know whether you were awake or dreaming. Even Jack's memories of Lucy were confused. Had he actually seen her? Did she really turn against him, or was it only a bad dream? He found it difficult to remember her face.

"Some call Elfland the Hollow Land," Father Severus said when Jack confided these thoughts to him. "It is formed by our desires, but ultimately, it is only a reflection of something else. Do you remember their music?"

That was the one thing Jack did recall. The music seemed to hang in the air like the last thread of sunlight before total darkness came on.

"I listened to their voices night after night, trying to despise them," said Father Severus. "I couldn't." He sighed.

On the beach Pega made an ingenious cairn of rocks that was hollow inside to hold a fire. On top she placed a flat piece of slate for roasting. Jack gathered whelks, sea kale, leeks, and garlic. But the hobgoblins were the champions where fishing was concerned.

They had a unique method. The Bugaboo perched on a rock out beyond the surf line and dangled his foot in the water. The Nemesis waited behind him with a club. Hobgoblin toes were long and wiggly—the Bugaboo could move all five in different directions at the same time. He demonstrated this to Pega, who told him to go away.

From below, the toes must have looked like a clutch of fat earthworms. They were certainly attractive to fish, although it was soon clear that it was important to attract the right *size* of fish. Once, a giant cod swallowed the Bugaboo's leg and the

Nemesis had to knock it senseless before the rest of the Bugaboo followed the leg inside.

"You won't find better than that," proclaimed the king, throwing the fish down before Pega's horrified eyes. It was large enough to feed everyone.

"You're bleeding! That *is* blood, isn't it?" She gasped. Yellow-green drops oozed from a row of holes on the Bugaboo's leg.

"You're worried about me," cried the delighted hobgoblin, turning cartwheels around her and spraying her with sand.

"Worrying doesn't mean I care," retorted Pega, wiping sand off her face.

"Oh, it does! It does! I'm so happy, I'm going to gleep!"

"Don't!" begged the girl, but the hobgoblin was too over-joyed to stop.

Gleeping, Jack thought, moving out of earshot, had to be the nastiest sound in the world. Hobgoblins did it when they were ecstatic, which was far too often in Jack's opinion. It was infectious, too. Once one individual began, others took it up, just as a yawn could spread through a crowd. The Nemesis, never a cheerful creature, gleeped softly as he gutted the fish.

Ethne was hopeless at all chores. Pega tried to teach her to weave baskets, but the baskets fell apart. She let the fire go out and allowed seagulls to steal fish. When Pega sent her to pick fennel, she returned with henbane. "That's *poison!*" shrieked the girl, throwing the plants into the fire. "Don't you know any better?"

"We ate henbane salad all the time in Elfland," Ethne said huffily. "It never did us the slightest bit of harm." In the end she sat beside Father Severus and memorized Latin prayers. Jack was certain she didn't understand Latin, but it kept her out of trouble and entertained Father Severus.

Finally, one afternoon after a meal of roast goose (hobgoblin toes were irresistible to geese, too) the Bugaboo called a meeting. "It is time for us all to go home," he said.

"What home?" Thorgil said. "My shipmates have gone, thinking I am dead. Often when the day breaks, lonely and wretched, I bewail my fate. There is no comrade to whom I can unburden my heart.

> *"The joys of hall are lost to me*
> *And a shadow darkens my spirit.*
> *I awaken from slumber,*
> *Hearing the tossing, foam-flecked sea.*
> *My kinsmen appear—how glad my heart!*
> *But they fade with no word of greeting."*

Jack, always fond of poetry, admired her fine words, but Father Severus cried, "Good heavens, shield maiden! You make a meal out of misery."

"I do not!"

"A true warrior shows gratitude for the bounty God sends him. You could be drowning in the midst of the sea. You could be trapped in a burning building. A thousand devils might be contending for your soul—not that they won't someday—but in fact you're sitting on a pleasant beach surrounded by friends. Fie on this self-pity."

"*I've* lost my home, and I don't have one scrap of self-pity," Ethne announced.

"We really must have that discussion about pride, Ethne," said Father Severus.

"To return to the immediate problem," said the Bugaboo, "when fall comes, this beach will be uninhabitable."

"Can we build a boat?" said Thorgil with a glimmer of hope.

"No!" said the Nemesis. "Hobgoblins never, ever go on boats."

"Is that because of kelpies?" inquired the shield maiden.

"They swim for hours if they smell something tasty," the Nemesis said with a haunted look in his eyes. "They follow you day and night, never sleeping, never giving up. They are tireless."

"Now look what you've done," scolded the Bugaboo. "You've said the K-word." He took his friend for a short walk, and when they returned, the Nemesis was a healthy green again.

"As I was about to say before I was interrupted, it's time to go home. Fortunately, there's more than one cave on this coast," said the Bugaboo.

Chapter Forty-one

THE VISION

Of course. It was so simple, Jack didn't know why he hadn't thought of it before. When he, Brutus, and Pega started on their quest, they had camped in a huge underground chamber full of bats. Eight tunnels branched out from that chamber, like the eight legs of a spider. *Crumbs. I don't like that image,* thought Jack.

The earthquake had collapsed one of them, but perhaps the others were still intact. The Bugaboo assured everyone that there were dozens of branches to the Hollow Road and that hobgoblins knew every part of it. "We know a shortcut to St. Filian's Well," he said.

"Won't it be full of water now that the Lady of the Lake has returned?" said Pega.

"The earthquake opened up the well to the Hollow Road itself. It would take the sea to fill it."

Sunset was coming on swiftly, and the swallows dipped and circled over the little camp on the beach. Pega and Jack had built a bonfire, and they all enjoyed its lively warmth against the cool of the evening. "I keep putting out fish for them, but they won't feed," said Pega, gazing up at the swallows.

"They don't eat fish," Jack said. "I wonder why they're so interested in us."

"Mumsie told them to keep an eye on us. What?" The Bugaboo looked up at Jack's surprise. "Didn't I tell you?"

"You didn't tell them," said the Nemesis. "You meant to, but the thought blew straight through that drafty cavern you call a brain."

"Then there's no time like the present," the king said cheerfully. "Mumsie learned to speak to swallows from the Man in the Moon. Not only that, she learned how to cast her spirit into one. When you went missing, Pega, I was devastated. I thought you were dead until the Nemesis confessed to what he'd done."

"I should have kept my mouth shut," grumbled the Nemesis.

"Ah, but you felt sorry for me," the king said. "Underneath that crusty exterior beats a heart of pure frog spawn. Mumsie sped straight off in the body of a swallow to ask Dragon Tongue's advice."

"You know Dragon Tongue?" cried Jack.

"Well, of course. He's the Wisest of the Wise," said the Bugaboo. "He told us Pega's candle contained the life force of the earth itself. But he warned us that lighting it would move the wheel of the year. Never again would time stand entirely still in the Land of the Silver Apples. We would age—slowly, to be sure, but certainly."

"We held a council. Everyone had to agree," said the Nemesis.

"And they did, Pega, my love." The Bugaboo held her hands in his long, sticky fingers. "They said it was worth it to have such a beautiful, kind queen with such a beautiful voice."

"Oh, Lord," said Pega. "I'm responsible for death coming to your people. I feel so guilty."

"Nonsense, darling. You merely made us step back into the stream of life. We'd been cut off too long, listening to elf music."

Wisps of cloud had turned gold and red. The sea darkened, and the foam caps of the waves stood out more clearly. A breeze quickened the air. The swallows shot away to the mountain, to find roosting places in the hollows of the rock. There was only the sound of the sea and the squabbling gulls.

"What are they saying?" asked Pega.

"They're accusing each other of nest-robbing," answered Thorgil. "Most of them are proud of it."

"You also speak to birds, shield maiden?" the Bugaboo said.

"I tasted dragon blood by accident. Don't ever do that. It almost burned my throat out."

That night they went to bed early, for they would leave at first light. Pega packed the food. The Nemesis, under Thorgil's direction, carved her runes into a tree trunk. "They may return. They may see this and know that I am alive," she said.

Jack waited until all were asleep before rising and facing the fire. He thought about the swallow he'd seen with the Bard when he was in the dungeons of Elfland.

Are you a bard? he had asked Mumsie that last night with the hobgoblins.

Nothing so grand, she had replied. *I've learned a few things from the Wise, but I'm far too lazy to commit my life to such study.* It seemed she was far wiser than she let on.

Jack cleared his mind and walked sunwise around the fire.

> *I seek beyond*
> *The folds of the mountains*
> *The nine waves of the sea*
> *The bird-crying winds.*

It was this beach he had seen when Thorgil, Skakki, and Rune were planning a raid into Elfland. What an insane scheme that was. But if Thorgil hadn't done it, he'd never have seen her again. Perhaps Father Severus was right. There was a purpose to everything under Heaven.

Jack put the thought from his mind. It was interfering with his magic. He walked round and round, chanting softly. Sooner than he expected, the night-dark sea beyond his hands brightened and became a hall lit by firelight. It wasn't King Yffi's. It wasn't any place Jack knew . . . until he recognized a few details: a stained-glass window, an ivory box with the carving of a man being devoured by leaves.

It was the treasure-house of St. Filian's. Torches burned on the walls. Most of the chests of gold and jewels had been moved aside to make room for a feast. Monks were drinking and bellowing songs as sullen slaves moved among the tables with food. Jack remembered the monks as being crude, but he'd never seen them this bad.

Some were collapsed on the floor, soaked with wine or worse. Others reeled drunkenly. Two of them traded flabby punches over some insult. They had given up their home-spun robes in favor of fine linen and wool. The gifts to the monastery had been looted.

At the head of the table was a small man almost hidden by his roistering companions. He alone wore the simple garb of a monk, and only he had a humble meal of bread and water. It was Brother Aiden.

"Please listen," he said in his gentle voice. "We really must go to the chapel." No one paid the slightest attention to him. After a moment he rose, and Jack followed him from the overheated hall down long corridors to the chapel. Brother Aiden lit a candle, revealing the ruinous state of the room. Benches were overturned, dust covered everything, and the cross leaned at an angle.

The little man knelt down to pray. Jack tried to call him, but his magic wasn't strong enough. Finally, discouraged, the boy left the chapel and wandered through the monastery grounds. He didn't know where he was going. He wished he could reach the fortress of Din Guardi and see the Bard, but that wasn't how the vision worked. It showed you what you needed.

A gibbous moon cast a ghostly presence over the ruin of walls and collapsed buildings. Why hadn't these been cleared away? But when Jack stepped through the rubble to St. Filian's Well, he saw that the monks had not been entirely idle.

The opening of the well had been covered. Somehow, with enormous effort, a huge slab of stone had been dragged over the hole. More stones had been wedged into gaps and cemented there with plaster. There was no hope of anyone ever getting out of that well.

King Yffi had never intended to let anyone return. Even when the water was restored, the stone had been left in place. He had no honor, as Thorgil would say. Jack was consumed by a rage so complete, he could have called up another earthquake. But the anger snuffed out the vision, and he found himself on the beach with the waves muttering along the shore.

"The well is sealed? You're certain?" said the Bugaboo. It was early morning, and the sun was still hidden behind a fog bank out to sea. They were all crouched around a roaring fire, trying to warm up.

"I saw it," said Jack.

"Yes, and I saw roast partridges dancing on beds of leeks in my dreams," said the Nemesis.

"Farseeing doesn't lie," the boy protested.

"It's a bard thing," said the Bugaboo, aiming a friendly punch at the Nemesis. "Personally, I believe him. Dragon Tongue wouldn't teach him faulty magic."

"Then perhaps we'd better go through the Forest of Lorn," said Thorgil.

"Father Severus would never survive." The hobgoblins had made a litter to carry the monk, but it would be useless on the steep and narrow trails through the mountains.

"As I remember, the Hollow Road branched in many directions," Jack said. "Are there other exits?"

"Yes," said the Bugaboo. "Most of them go through places you wouldn't like—the Worm Nursery and the Hall of Wraiths, for example. One passage comes up in a deep chasm called Hen Hole. We'd never get up the sides. The only safe exit lies under Din Guardi."

"Under Din Guardi?" echoed Jack, who had a somber memory of dungeons and clashing waves.

"There's a network of caves. The fortress is extremely old."

"Great toadstools and little slime molds! Do you want to get us killed?" exclaimed the Nemesis. "That's where the Man in the Moon committed the crime that exiled him to the sky. The old gods still think it belongs to them. The Forest Lord lays siege to it day and night."

Jack shivered, remembering the Hedge that surrounded the grim, gray walls.

"It's not that bad," the king said. "It was quite a jolly place when Lancelot ran it. Someone else took it over recently. I can't remember who."

"Mud men pirates," growled the Nemesis.

"There! We haven't a thing to worry about. There isn't a hobgoblin alive who can't outwit a mud man—begging your pardon, Jack."

Pirates had indeed taken over, Jack thought, but they were led by Yffi, the half-kelpie. Jack struggled with his conscience for a moment. If he revealed what he knew, the Nemesis would certainly refuse to go. They'd have to travel over the mountains, and Father Severus would fall over a cliff. Others might die as well. Thorgil was clumsy with only one good hand, and Pega wasn't strong. Surely, it was better to protect their lives than reveal an unpleasant (and perhaps unimportant) truth. Yffi might not eat hobgoblins anyhow because he was only half kelpie. Besides, they could ask the Bard for help.

His moral struggle finished, Jack said, "All right. Din Guardi it is."

Chapter Forty-two

YARTHKINS

There were several caves hidden behind vines and trees. All but one were found to be blocked by rockfalls. The last one opened under the sea and was covered by water except at low tide. They had to wait for hours until it was revealed.

It was an uninviting hole, choked with the litter of many storms. A small whale had wedged itself between rocks, and its bones were still draped with decaying blubber.

"We must hurry," the Bugaboo said. "We have to go down before we go up, and if the tide comes in . . ."

We drown, thought Jack, eyeing the slippery rocks beyond. They had made torches for the journey, not good ones and not nearly enough. But the Bugaboo said there would be light farther on. Thorgil went first, brandishing a torch. Then came the hobgoblins, carrying Father Severus. Pega followed with Ethne, who breathed deeply of the odor of rotten whale.

"So that's what decay smells like," she said in wonder. "Nothing like it has ever existed in Elfland."

"If you don't move, I'm going to throw up," said Pega.

"But why?" said the elf lady in honest puzzlement. "It is a strong scent, to be sure. So is the odor of honeysuckle, but I find them both equally enjoyable." And she probably did, Jack thought. How would she know the difference between nasty and nice when nothing in her experience had taught her? Pega shoved her roughly to make her go on.

Jack came last, carrying both Thorgil's knife and his staff. In his experience trouble usually showed up from behind. He looked carefully from side to side and listened for stealthy noises.

The floor sank into pools of brackish, fetid water. Soon they were wading through the muck to their waists. The hobgoblins hoisted Father Severus's litter over their heads, and he clung on grimly. Shadows danced along the walls from Thorgil's torch.

Waves echoed from behind, and now and then a fresh surge of water poured down. Jack's legs itched with salt. His feet were frozen and the air reeked. He tried to appreciate the odor of rotten whale and failed.

A whoosh and sudden rush of water made him stumble. "Run!" cried the Bugaboo. "The tide has turned!"

They hurried as well as they could, sloshing and splashing with curses from Thorgil and even Pega. "What does 'filthy #$@!!' mean?" said Ethne.

"Tell you later," panted Pega. Both she and the elf lady were weighted down with baskets of supplies balanced on their heads. Fortunately, the path began to go up. The floor of the tunnel changed to sand and the ceiling rose until all could walk freely without fear of bumping into rock. They came at last to a level section. Everyone collapsed on the ground, and Thorgil jammed the torch into the sand.

"I haven't been here in ages," said the Bugaboo after a while.

"It's the same old pest hole," grunted the Nemesis. A breeze moved fitfully from ahead, pushing back the remnants of ripe whale.

Jack looked around at the oddly bulbous rocks. They resembled balls of dough glued together. "What kind of pest?" he said.

"Yarthkins, mainly," said the Bugaboo. "The wraiths stick to their hall, except for Jenny Greenteeth. She wanders a bit."

"Why? What's she looking for?" said Pega.

"Don't you worry, my little moss blossom," the Bugaboo said, wrapping an arm about the girl. "Old Jenny's learned a thing or two about bothering hobgoblins since she last—well, I won't go into details."

"I've heard of yarthkins, but what exactly are they?" said Jack before Pega could ask further questions about Jenny Greenteeth's habits.

"They're old gods," said the Nemesis. "They keep themselves to themselves. If you don't bother them, they don't bother you."

Pega passed around cold, grilled leeks as a snack to keep up everyone's spirits. She had smoked fish as well, but the Bugaboo said it would make them thirsty and shouldn't be touched until they found freshwater. Thorgil's torch had by now burned down to the ground, and she lit another one.

The walk was almost pleasant. The tunnel grew larger until it was wide enough for ten men to walk side by side with their arms outstretched. Jack was glad of the space. Narrow, underground tunnels made him nervous. The sand changed to dirt. The air became fresher with a hint of growing things, although nothing green could have lived in such darkness. Still, if Jack closed his eyes, he could imagine walking through a field. There was a liveliness to the air, a feeling that at any moment a leaf might burst out of the soil.

Presently, they came to a spring bubbling up from the ground. It flowed into a brook, and huge, pale mushrooms as tall as a man grew along its banks.

The Bugaboo called a halt. "We've been walking for hours. I'd guess it's already dark outside." Jack realized, with surprise, that it was true. He'd been so interested in this last part of the journey, he hadn't noticed how tired he was.

"You can douse the torch," the Nemesis said. "We won't need it here."

With some misgivings, Jack saw Thorgil reverse her torch and extinguish it. The light went out, and for a moment all was dark. Then—here, there, far, and near—a gentle glow rose like mist. Jack couldn't make out the source at first, but after a few moments it had strengthened enough to cast his shadow on the ground.

It was the mushrooms. Pale green and misty pearl, they shone like veiled moons. Along the ground by their massive trunks crept glowworms. A spark of greenish light flashed from the ceiling and was answered by another flash. Fireflies suddenly filled the upper air.

"We can drink the water here," the Bugaboo said. They were all extremely thirsty by now, and all knelt by the spring with cupped hands. The water was cold and clean with a hint of something green in it.

"If it were not blasphemy, I would say this is the water of life," Father Severus said.

"You wouldn't be wrong," said the Bugaboo. "This was the heart of the old gods' kingdom before people invaded the land. It is this that nourishes the roots of the forest and sweetens the waters welling from the earth. Ancient things still abide here that care nothing for the affairs of mankind. We hobgoblins were once part of it before St. Columba gave us souls."

"God gave you souls," the monk gently reproved him. "St. Columba only awakened you to their existence."

Now they could eat the smoked fish and the pignuts and garlic steamed in seaweed by Pega. It was a jolly gathering in spite of the weird surroundings. Thorgil told several tales of bloodcurdling battles, each ending with everyone getting killed and being devoured by ravens.

"Why don't you give us a poem?" said Jack, hoping to divert her from her depressing sagas. He knew Thorgil was proud of her poetic ability.

"All right," she agreed, smiling.

> *The battlements crumble, the mead-halls decay.*
> *Joyless and still, the warriors sleep*
> *Where they fell, by the wall they defended.*
> *The bright ale cup lies trampled underfoot*
> *And only the gray wolves drink deeply*
> *Of the lifeblood so carelessly spilled—*

"What?" said Thorgil, halting her recitation. The hobgoblins were staring at her in horror, Father Severus was shaking his head, and Pega looked ready to cry.

"Are those men dead?" Ethne said earnestly. "I need to know because I've never seen a dead man."

"It's a poem!" shouted Thorgil. "You're supposed to enjoy it!"

"It's very good," Jack said quickly, "but I think everyone's tired after such a long walk. Perhaps we need something less stirring."

"I'll tell a story," Father Severus said. Jack had no great hopes for the gloomy monk's offering, but he surprised everyone with a tale called:

THE BEST AND THE WORST NAIL IN THE ARK

Long ago (began Father Severus) Noah set out to build the ark, but he was a busy man. He had to gather two members of every creature on earth, and that took time and a great deal of money. So he gave the task of ark-building over to a drunken carpenter. The carpenter nailed a board here and a board there. He worked only when Noah's sons—Shem, Ham, and Japheth— threatened him.

Finally, the ark was done, but there was one flaw. The carpenter had left out one nail at the very bottom of the ship, and so there was a hole for the water to come in.

Now the clouds gathered, the thunder rolled, and the rain came down in buckets. Shem, Ham, and Japheth herded the animals into the ark. Two by two they went, but Noah's sons made a mistake. There were not two, but three snakes. The Devil had decided to sneak aboard in the shape of a serpent.

Noah went around to check all the supplies and animal pens. The Devil hid here, he hid there, because Noah had very sharp eyes and knew the difference between a real serpent and a fake. Finally, there was no other place to hide but that one hole at the bottom of the ship. The Devil went in, and—oh, my goodness!—he was stuck. He could go neither in nor out. He couldn't even wiggle. So there he stayed, plugging up the leak until the Flood was over.

That is why the Devil is called the best nail and the worst nail in the ark.

"That's a fine story," said Pega, laughing.

"I must remember it for the other hobgoblins," said the Bugaboo.

"What kind of seafarer puts out to sea without checking for leaks?" argued Thorgil. "And what were his shiftless sons doing, letting that drunken carpenter slack off? I would have thrashed the lot of them and hired a good shipwright."

Jack realized she had missed the point, but he kept silent. He knew she was still smarting over the reception of her poem.

Last of all, Pega sang. That was how it had been in the dungeons of Elfland and on the beach as well. No one wanted to perform after Pega because she was so extremely good.

Jack had to admit it. He was jealous of her, which he knew was unworthy. After all, she had nothing else but this talent. *I suppose I'm not any different from Thorgil, wanting everyone to admire my poetry,* he thought. He didn't pay attention to Pega's voice, brooding as he was, until she screamed.

Jack leaped to his feet, staff at the ready. Everyone else was huddled in a group. The light was suddenly brighter— now the mushrooms really did look like moons. All around Jack saw that the lumps in the wall, the lumps that had reminded him of bread dough squashed together, had changed. Each one was wrapped in long, silky hair the color of wheat, and inside these cocoons were little curled-up bodies as brown as freshly turned earth. The faces were old beyond imagining, masses of wrinkles so deep, you could hardly believe they were real. And in the middle of each face were two bright black eyes watching Pega intently.

"Yarthkins," whispered the Nemesis. "They're fine as long as you don't upset them."

"What should we do?" Jack whispered back. There were so many of them, all squashed together like cells in a honeycomb. Each one was no larger than a year-old child, but together they might be dangerous.

"Keep quiet," advised the Bugaboo. "If we do nothing, they might go back to sleep." Everyone sat very still. A sigh, soft and high like a little bird twittering, passed over the walls. One of the lumps oozed out of its place and landed with a soft thump on the ground.

Jack saw what appeared to be a tiny man wrapped head to toe in a long beard. He looked as harmless as a pussy willow, but Jack wasn't fooled. He'd had too much experience of otherworldly creatures to trust anything.

Sing, murmured the yarthkin in the same high twittering voice.

Pega cast a worried look at Jack. "I think you'd better do it," he said in a low voice. So Pega repeated the hymn she had just given them. She went on to a ballad and then to a song about gathering flowers in May. She stopped to catch her breath.

Sing, repeated the yarthkin.

"I need some water," said the girl. The yarthkin dipped his long beard into the brook, and it curled up like a fiddlehead fern.

He hopped over to Pega, and she recoiled against the Bugaboo.

"It's all right, dearest. I think he means no harm," murmured the hobgoblin king.

"Yet," added the Nemesis.

Put out thy hands, said the yarthkin. Pega cupped her hands, and he squeezed the tip of his beard. A cascade of water flowed out and splashed over her fingers. *Drink.*

Pega made a face, but she was too frightened to disobey. She drank the water in her cupped hands, and a delighted expression crossed her face. "It's delicious!" she cried.

The yarthkin nodded. *Sing,* he said. So Pega gave them "The Treacherous Knight" and "The Jolly Miller" and "The Wife of Usher's Well." She was beginning to tremble slightly, and Jack realized she was tired. How long would these creatures demand to be entertained? They weren't like anything in Middle Earth—or, rather, they were what lay *under* Middle Earth. They were part of the stones, water, and soil.

Sometimes, when Jack had cast his mind down to the life force, he had felt, among the roots and burrowing creatures, other presences he could barely comprehend. This was one of them. Jack suspected they might want to listen to music for a very long time.

Pega reached the end of a song, and Jack knelt before the yarthkin and said, "She is but mortal, spirit of the earth. She wishes to obey you, but her strength is small."

The creature observed Jack with its bright eyes, and a twittering rustle passed over the walls of the tunnel.

Sing, said the yarthkin wrapped in his cocoon of beard.

"I'll sing," Jack said. "My voice may not be what you're asking for, but Pega can't go on forever."

"Forever is what these creatures are about," the Nemesis muttered.

Jack cast his mind back to all the Bard had taught him about animals, men, trolls, and elves, but he found nothing about yarthkins. Then, unbidden, he saw an image of his mother. In early spring, when the soil was warm enough to plow and the sky had turned from gray to blue, she walked in the fields. And as she walked, she sang:

> *Erce, Erce, Erce eorÞan modor,*
> *Geunne Þe se alwalda, ece drihten . . .*

"*Erce, Erce, Erce . . . ,*" repeated Jack, giving the ancient call to earth in a language so old, no one knew its origin. Perhaps it was what the Man in the Moon spoke. Jack went on in human speech:

> *Mother of Earth, may the all-powerful*
> *Lord of Life grant you*
> *Fields growing and thriving,*
> *Green leaf and tall stem,*
> *Both the broad barley*
> *And the fair wheat*
> *And all the crops of the earth.*
> *Erce, Erce, Erce . . .*

As he chanted, Jack saw his mother in his mind, bending over each furrow, praising it and planting it with seed. The charm was long, and he repeated it nine times. When he had finished, he looked up to see a whole host of yarthkins. They had all dropped out of the walls. To Jack, they looked like a mass of little haystacks, and his heart leaped to his throat. What had he done? One yarthkin had been difficult to entertain. What was he going to do with hundreds?

But the first creature, who stood apart from the rest, spoke: *Thou art a good lad, Jack, to bless the fields. And thou art a fine lass, Pega, to sing as the earth did at our beginning. What shall we do to reward thee?*

"Best not to answer," whispered the Nemesis. But Jack thought that would be ungracious. Besides, he liked the little haystacks, strange though they were.

"We were but thanking you for the kindness you have shown my mother's fields. We ask your permission to travel on to Din Guardi."

A twittering hiss blew through the gathering, like the wind rattling ripe wheat. *Din Guardi is a place of shadows. A ring of Unlife lies about it.*

"It is nasty," Jack agreed, "but, you see, my father's there, and the Bard, my master. I've got to make sure they're all right. Don't worry, we'll leave as soon as possible."

The yarthkins conferred among themselves with many a sigh and hiss and a vague rumble like thunder in the distance. Jack wasn't happy about the thunder. It sounded like anger. Finally, the chief yarthkin replied: *We will not hold thee, but we will not forget thee.*

"Thank you," Jack said uncertainly. He wasn't sure he wanted to be remembered. The yarthkins crept back to the walls and fitted themselves in. It was difficult to see how they managed this without using hands or feet, but they did. Soon they were all tucked into their beds, as snug as peas. The straw-colored hair faded into the wall until it became a collection of brown lumps again.

"I think we should go now," said the Bugaboo, and Jack was surprised to see he'd turned bright green with alarm. It was the first time he'd seen the hobgoblin king afraid, and it made him realize that the little haystacks weren't quite as harmless as they looked.

Chapter Forty-three

THE KELPIES

The tunnel changed abruptly from brown dirt and glowing mushrooms to a harsher landscape of rock. The air had a cold mineral smell, and water dripped from the roof. Jack relit Thorgil's torch.

"Let me take that," said the Nemesis. Thorgil reluctantly handed it over. It was but another reminder that she had only one useful hand and couldn't protect the flame. She fell back to walk with Father Severus, who was looking surprisingly vigorous.

"I don't know what happened," he said, wondering. "I'm feeling extremely well, like a man half my age. Perhaps I only needed time to recover." But Jack thought, privately, that the water in the land of the yarthkins had something to do with it. He felt immensely better since drinking it. The depressing apathy of Elfland had lifted, taking with it the sorrow over Lucy.

Everyone looked happier, even Thorgil. Ethne, of course, was always radiant, finding each new experience fascinating, no matter how disturbing it was to the others. "Those yarthkins are so cute," she gushed. "I could just cuddle them!"

"Never, *ever*, attempt to cuddle a yarthkin," said the Bugaboo.

The Nemesis walked ahead, waving the torch back and forth to avoid drips. "We're near the sea," he called. "Can you feel the waves?"

Jack noticed for the first time a tremor passing through the rocks. A cold breeze stirred and brought whiffs of seaweed and salt. "What's that noise?" he said. Everyone stopped. From far away came a mournful howl.

"That's not Jenny Greenteeth, is it?" said Pega.

"Wraiths are quieter," the Bugaboo explained, "more like heavy breathing in your ear."

"Bedbugs! Just what I wanted to know," said Pega, leaning closer to Jack.

As they went on, the howls became louder. It was clearly the voices of many beings. Some cries were high and screechy. Others were deep like the bellow of a bull. "I've heard that before," the Bugaboo remarked. "Was it wyverns? Or manticores? Ah! I have it! Kelpies."

The Nemesis halted, making everyone bump into one another. "Kelpies! I'm not going a step farther!"

"They're far out to sea, old friend," the Bugaboo said.

"You don't know anything. They could be waiting for us."

"I'm quite sure they're not. You see—"

"Look, I'm willing to follow you anywhere. You're my king. I'm the one our people chose to protect you from your stupidity. Besides, they like you. *I* like you—oh, St. Columba! I can't believe I said that. But, please, Your Royal Ignorance, *don't ask me to go near kelpies.* They eat hobgoblins. They'll eat me." The Nemesis had turned ashen. His ears furled and unfurled, and his eyes blinked so rapidly that Jack was afraid the creature was about to faint.

"I know you like me," the Bugaboo said, grasping his friend's hand. "It's the worst-kept secret in the world. And I absolutely admire and respect you. But I was about to say that the kelpies are howling at the approach of a storm. They can feel the winds building, and it drives them mad. I've seen it before. They're all sitting on islands looking out to sea. More importantly, the wind is blowing from them to us, so they won't smell a thing."

The Nemesis blushed orange. "Are you sure?" he said.

"Just as sure as God made little brown yarthkins."

"Oh my." The Nemesis shivered. "To think I'd have to admit you knew something that I didn't."

"St. Columba would be proud of you," the king said warmly. "He used to say humility was the greatest of virtues."

The group walked on again with the hobgoblins in front. Father Severus said quietly, "They may look like demons, but their soundness of heart puts me quite to shame."

Pega pulled Jack to one side and whispered, "I've just remembered. Yffi is a half-kelpie. We should tell the Nemesis."

"And do what?" Jack said urgently. "Go back? Spend winter on the beach? Father Severus would die."

"But we can't lie."

"Wouldn't you bend the truth just a little to save someone's life? There's Father, too. He needs us." Jack and Pega had stopped. The others went ahead, with the Nemesis holding up the torch.

"I—I suppose you're right," Pega faltered. "Only, we have to find the Bard right away. He'll take care of Yffi."

"That was my idea, too," declared Jack as they hurried to catch up.

They went more slowly now, stopping frequently to listen to the howls. Waves clashed. A cold wind began to whip through the tunnel, blowing the torch flame back. And now a faint light came to them from an opening not far away.

They came out to a rocky shore, wading through a small inlet before climbing up to the trail again. Jack suddenly felt dizzy, like he was about to faint. Then the sensation passed. The sea surged in, sending fountains of spray high into the air. Jack braced himself to get drenched, but the spray never reached him. "How is that possible?" he asked the Bugaboo, pointing at the edge of the water. It stopped abruptly, as though something was forcing it back.

"We've passed into the realm of Din Guardi," the hob-goblin said. "It's protected."

"Protected?" echoed Jack, thinking that it made more sense to keep Din Guardi from threatening everything else.

"Long ago, when this place was taken from the Man in the Moon, a barrier was made to keep him from returning. The old gods still claim the fortress. The Sea God tries to storm it with his tides. The Forest Lord waits on the land."

"Is that the ring of Unlife the yarthkins spoke of?" said Jack.

"The same. They cannot enter either."

"Nothing keeps kelpies out," the Nemesis said. "Keep moving unless you want to be dinner." A line of pillars partly hid them on the left. On the right rose a cliff topped by gray walls so crusted with lichen, they looked as though they'd grown out of the earth.

Jack glimpsed a sunrise between a sky filled with roiling clouds and a lurid sea thronged by dangerous-looking rocks. Tall figures rose and fell as they welcomed the coming of the storm.

"Keep down," the Nemesis hissed.

Jack obeyed, but he couldn't resist another look. He'd never seen kelpies, except for King Yffi, who'd been bundled in clothes from head to toe. Anyhow, Yffi was only half kelpie. The creatures on the rocks were much taller. It was difficult to see much with the light behind them, but they appeared to be covered in fur. More than anything, they looked like huge otters. Their feet—Jack only had a glimpse of these—ended in long, hooked claws. The kelpies' cries were horrible and yet oddly musical. The longer Jack listened to them, the better they sounded. He could use such harmonies in his own music. But first he had to get closer.

The Bugaboo yanked Jack so hard, he fell down and cut his lip. *Do you want to get us all devoured?* screeched the hobgoblin. The others were far ahead, watching anxiously. Jack wiped the blood from his mouth and hurried after the king. When they got to where the trail went underground again, they all sat down to rest. The Nemesis was a pasty yellow, and he kept flinching whenever he heard a howl.

"What was wrong with you?" asked Thorgil. "The Bugaboo had to go back."

Jack looked at the sea. He couldn't see the kelpies, but he could hear them. It *was* a kind of music they made, full of longing and another emotion he couldn't put his finger on. He wanted to hear more.

"Hello? Anybody home?" Pega waved her hand in front of Jack's face.

"That's how kelpies attract their prey," the Bugaboo said. "They make you *want* to be eaten. You'd march right down their throats unless someone stopped you. We should go on before the storm hits." The sun had completely disappeared, and a flash of light, followed immediately by thunder, made the kelpies redouble their howls.

Very little light penetrated the tunnel, and they soon had to halt. "Who's carrying the torches?" said Thorgil.

"I am," replied Ethne. "Oh, thistle fuzz! The water drenched my basket. I suppose it happened when I floated it on that stream we passed."

"Why ever did you do such a thing?" cried Pega.

"I don't know," the elf lady said vaguely. "Perhaps the basket reminded me of the toy boats we had in Elfland. We used to sail toddlers in them, you know, to make them scream. Such fun!"

"I can draw fire from the earth," Jack said before Pega lost her temper. He still had the flint and iron from Elfland, but the torches were so wet, only magic could light them. He made a small heap of kindling from the charred stub of the Nemesis's torch.

"Is this the wizardry you practiced in the dungeon?" remarked Father Severus.

"Yes, sir," said Jack, bracing himself for a lecture, but the monk didn't try to interfere. The boy cast his mind down through the rocks and the water oozing through cracks below. Once, he would have found it impossible to work magic with an audience, but his skill had strengthened with practice.

The rocks were old beyond imagining, although it had never occurred to Jack before that rocks could have an age. They felt *used up*, all the life gone out of them. Trees and grass would never grow here, no matter how carefully you tended them.

Jack realized that he'd seen no garden in the fortress, not even the herbs cooks and wise women grew. Come to think of it, there'd been no women, either.

He reached deeper. The water had a faint radiance as it fell from the sky, but it lost it in the dark channels of the rock. Was this what happened when you banished the old gods? Dangerous and unfriendly they might be, but they ruled the green world.

Jack reached a barrier. He pushed at it, and the barrier pushed back, making his stomach heave and his heart flutter in his chest. He came awake with his skin drenched with sweat and his hands clenched for battle.

"I can't do it," he gasped. The storm was at full strength now. Wind howled in the mouth of the tunnel, and thunder shook the walls.

"Thor's driving his chariot across the sky," Thorgil said.

"I wish he'd go somewhere else," said Pega.

"Nonsense! That's a glorious noise. It means Thor is hurling his hammer at enemies."

"As usual, you are steeped in ignorance," said Father Severus. "God casts down lightning to remind us of the final judgment. It would be best to fall to your knees and implore His mercy."

"A thrall god's idea," sneered Thorgil. "I'd rather shake my fist at Him."

"Stop wasting time," cried the Nemesis, who was dancing from one foot to the other in agitation. "If one of those kelpies sticks his snout in here, you can kiss your drumsticks good-bye."

"He's right," the Bugaboo agreed. "I've been through these tunnels often enough to feel the way."

"What do you mean—," began Jack, and stopped. In the

dim light he saw the hobgoblin king's ears unfurl to their fullest. They were as wide as his outstretched arms, and framing the rims were long, white hairs that stuck straight out like a cat's whiskers.

"I'll have to ask you all to be quiet," the Bugaboo said. "My hearing is painfully keen right now. Join hands, please."

They joined hands, the Bugaboo and the Nemesis in front, followed by Ethne, Father Severus, and Pega. Jack and Thorgil brought up the rear, being the better warriors. Silently, they moved forward, with the hobgoblin king's whiskers brushing the sides of the tunnel, and soon they were in complete darkness.

They wound around pillars and stumbled over rocks. The Bugaboo whispered instructions: "Left now. *Left*. Ow. Sorry. Mind the hole."

The hard floor was unrelieved by sand, and when Jack touched a wall, he was shocked by how cold it was. It was summer outside, but here, it seemed, winter never lifted. An icy chill found its way through his boots. The others must have been affected too, for they began to stumble.

"Almost there," whispered the Bugaboo. "Courage, dearest Pega."

The trail began to go up, and the deadly chill lessened. A light came from ahead. Encouraged, they began to walk faster. Now the grim walls were visible, a blue-black stone that swallowed whatever illumination fell on it. Long shafts of what Jack could only call "lesser gloom" fell from openings overhead.

They passed great iron doors. *Dungeons,* thought Jack. *I wonder if anyone's in there?* They must have come close to the sea again, for he heard a distant boom of waves and the kelpies howling.

"Ah, that feels better," said the Bugaboo, furling up his ears. First the whiskers lay down flat against the skin, then the rims folded over them and rolled up as neat as you please. They looked like fat little sausages when he was finished. "The Nemesis and I will wait here—mud men make such a fuss about hobgoblins. You go up those stairs and come out into the courtyard. Later you can sneak us in through a side door."

"Don't take too long about it," growled the Nemesis, listening to the kelpies out at sea.

"I'll ask the Bard for help," Jack promised.

The two hobgoblins found a recess in the wall and fitted themselves inside. In spite of not having motley wool to conceal them, they blended well into the shadows.

Jack led the way up the stairs. He wasn't quite certain of King Yffi's welcome, but the king was afraid of the Bard. He wouldn't harm anyone under the old man's protection. Once again, Jack felt a twinge of guilt for not telling the Nemesis about Yffi. *The Bard will figure something out,* Jack thought, willing the uncomfortable feeling away.

He couldn't help smiling as he approached the iron door at the top of the stairs. He was back! They could all go home. Father Severus could move into St. Filian's Monastery. Ethne could become a nun. Pega could marry the Bugaboo—here Jack had another twinge of guilt, but honestly, what better opportunity did she have? In the village she'd only be an ex-slave, so ugly that no one would ever ask for her hand. In the Land of the Silver Apples she could be a queen.

And I would have no rival, thought Jack. He was ashamed of himself for thinking it. He'd never been jealous of Thorgil, although she often enraged him. She was a better warrior, but he didn't want to be a warrior. He was a bard. Pega's voice outshone his.

Jack's smile faded. He didn't like finding this ugly motive hidden in himself. Father Severus would call it sinful, and the Bard, whose opinion mattered more to him, would call it mean and petty. *I'll have to overcome it,* Jack vowed.

He was almost at the door. What of Thorgil? He turned back to see her walking behind Father Severus, Pega, and Ethne, guarding them. What was he going to do with her? She wouldn't be welcome at St. Filian's. If she was recognized as a Northman, everyone on the coast would be out for her blood. As for her clothes . . .

For the first time Jack looked at Thorgil the way the villagers would. She was dressed in men's clothes. Her hair was chopped off. She had a belligerent expression, and her manners were crude at the best of times. How was he ever going to explain her?

Using all his strength, Jack pushed open the heavy iron door. Rain blew into his face. A large arm reached through and yanked him outside.

Chapter Forty-four

ETHNE

King Yffi's soldiers had been dragging a scullery boy, caught stealing a chicken, to the dungeons. They'd been none too pleased to be ordered out in such weather, and finding an escapee (as they thought) made them no happier. They threw Jack to the ground. The captain tried to put his foot on Jack's chest, but he twisted out of the way and swung his staff at the man's leg with a resounding *thwack*.

Before the others could react, Father Severus stepped through the door. "Hold!" he commanded, his voice rising above the torrent of rain and wind. Everyone froze—Jack on the ground, the captain holding his injured leg, the two guards grasping the scullery boy's arms, the boy himself, who had been trying to bite. Water splashed all around, pouring off their heads and soaking them to the skin.

Jack recovered first. "King Yffi will be pleased. We have brought back the water," he said, climbing to his feet and holding his staff out to the side. He hoped he looked properly bardlike.

"You're the brat we threw down the well," snarled the captain, rubbing his leg. "Never expected to see you again."

Probably not, since you sealed the well, thought Jack.

Behind the monk, still sheltered in the doorway, appeared Pega, Thorgil, and Ethne. "Who's that?" said one of the soldiers.

"We had no women prisoners," said the captain.

"Begging your pardon, sir," said the soldier, "but that be no mere woman. That be a lady, sure as I'm standing here."

"Aye, a right fair one," marveled the other soldier. "Not a mark of the pox on her or a tooth missing." The scullery boy tried to squirm free, and the soldier banged him on the top of his head.

Thorgil and Pega might have been invisible for all the attention paid to them. The captain hobbled over to Ethne and bowed deeply. "Welcome to our keep, noble fair one. Please forgive this wretched weather and allow us to conduct you to more suitable quarters."

The elf lady laughed, a sound like little silver bells. The captain and his men were enchanted.

"Ratface! Off with that shirt!" barked the captain. Lickety-split, the soldiers had the shirt off the poor scullery boy. They held it over Ethne's head while the captain held her hand to escort her. The only good result was that they forgot about Ratface's punishment and left him to shiver in the rain.

The shirt didn't really protect Ethne, but it was a well-meant gesture. The soldiers and the captain escorted her tenderly, lifting her over the deeper puddles. Thorgil, Pega, Father Severus, and Jack followed, sloshing up to their knees, but no one cared about their comfort.

On the other side of the courtyard they were conducted up and up through a maze of winding hallways to a chamber Jack recognized as the Bard's room. His heart lifted at the prospect of seeing the old man through the open door, but the room was deserted. *Perhaps he's visiting King Yffi,* Jack thought. Very quickly, the soldiers lit a brazier for warmth. Back and forth they went, hauling rugs, tables, chairs, beds, and mattresses stuffed with goose down into the room. They brought food from the kitchen and clean, dry robes for Ethne.

"I'll tell the king you're here," said the captain, blushing when Ethne impulsively kissed his grizzled cheek. "I forgot to ask. What is your name, fair one?"

"Princess Ethne," said Father Severus in his sepulchral voice, before Ethne could respond.

"A princess!" said the captain, impressed. "I should have guessed. No mere lady would be so graceful, so—so—"

"Excuse me," said Jack, before the captain could think up more compliments. "Where's the Bard? And my father? And Brother Aiden?"

"Giles Crookleg is in the infirmary at St. Filian's," said the captain, still staring at Ethne's dimples. "Brother Aiden was put in charge of the monastery, much good that'll do him. Those monks will ride over him like a herd of highland cattle. As for Dragon Tongue, I'm happy to say he's joined them. You could never relax when he was around. Now, don't you worry about a thing, my Princess." The captain turned back to Ethne. "I'll bring you some sweeties, see if I don't."

"She needs a good rest," Father Severus said witheringly. "Not sweeties."

They were left alone, to feast and dry out. Pega was delighted by the food—pigeon pie, roast pork and oysters, bread hot from the oven with a slab of butter. There was also a bowl of apples. "Poor Bugaboo and Nemesis," she said. "I wish I could take them something."

"It would be unwise," Father Severus said. "I, too, feel for them, but they must not be discovered."

"What should we do now?" said Jack. "We need the Bard's help."

"I could go to St. Filian's, but I hesitate to leave you alone. There is evil abroad here."

Silence fell on the group as they ate. Ethne disappeared into an adjoining chamber to try on her new clothes. It was barely past noon, but the sky was almost as dark as nightfall. Lightning forked across the heavens. "I've never seen a storm this bad," Thorgil remarked. "It's as if Thor were casting his bolts at *us*."

"Or God is," said Father Severus.

"No," said Jack as an idea came to him. "I think the old

gods are laying siege to Din Guardi. The Forest Lord and the Sea God seek to enter. Perhaps whoever ruled the sky has joined them."

"*Someone's* definitely having a snit," observed Thorgil, licking grease from her fingers. "Let's hope he—or she—gets tired before we all lose our hearing." Almost as though the "someone" had heard her, thunder shook the walls so fiercely then that plaster fell from the ceiling. Everyone cringed. Having made this statement, the storm withdrew. They could hear it grumbling as it moved out to sea.

"Saints preserve us!" cried Father Severus. Jack saw Ethne dance into the room in the dry clothes the captain had brought her. She was floating as lightly as a dandelion puff, exactly as Lucy had done in the meadows near the village. Ethne's dress glittered with jewels, but the really spectacular garment was her cloak. Jack had never seen the like of it. The rich, creamy cloth was embroidered with grapevines in which animals were hidden. Jack couldn't tell what they were—deer, hunting dogs, or cats, perhaps—but they were as long and graceful as the vines. In the center, hovering over this green world, was a white dove with a small twig in its beak.

"Take that off at once! No! Not the dress," roared the monk as the elf lady lifted her skirts above her knees. "The cloak! The cloak!" Puzzled, Ethne let it drop. Father Severus swept it up before it touched the floor. He sank into a chair and covered his face with his hands. Ethne, taking a cue from his distress, burst into tears.

"Sir, are you ill?" said Jack, kneeling beside the chair.

"It's only shock," the monk said. "Dear Ethne, I'm not angry at you. Please stop crying. I know you meant no harm." The elf lady's tears dried up at once. She smiled and resumed her dance around the room. Her emotions shifted with the eerie swiftness Jack had noticed in Lucy.

"Do you recognize the cloak?" Jack asked.

"It isn't a cloak." Father Severus took a deep breath and smoothed the cloth with his hands. "It's the altar cloth from the Holy Isle. I remember Sister Agnes and Sister Eowyn embroidering it. Poor, gentle ladies, they're both dead, thrown into the sea by those foul, murdering Hell-fiends. . . ."

"How did it get here?" said Jack with a nervous look at Thorgil. She had been one of the Hell-fiends.

"I don't know. Some of the treasures might have been saved. I imagine they were taken to St. Filian's."

Jack said nothing. He didn't have to. St. Filian's existed to fleece the gullible. Whatever treasures the monks there gained were shared with King Yffi. "I swear," Father Severus said slowly, "that if I get my hands on those thieving monks, *they will learn the meaning of repentance once and for all.*"

What Father Severus had in mind, he didn't have time to say, for the captain of the guard rapped on the door. The man had changed his shirt, his helmet had been polished, and his beard was trimmed. "Fair Princess, I bid you welcome to Din Guardi. My master, the king, eagerly awaits you," he cried, giving Ethne a deep bow.

"And the rest of us?" Father Severus said.

"He didn't mention you," the captain replied rudely.

"It would be a dire insult to allow Her Highness to go forth without her retinue. Wars have been declared over less."

Jack admired the monk's skill. The captain had no idea that Ethne was only the cast-off daughter of the Queen of Elfland. Partholis probably didn't even remember her. She certainly didn't recall Ethne's father. Yet Father Severus had given the impression that she was cherished and that an army existed.

He didn't lie. He'd merely said, *Wars have been declared over less* and let the captain draw his own conclusions. It didn't hurt, either, that Ethne fairly sparkled with glamour.

"Of course, of course. All of you must come," said the captain, mesmerized.

An honor guard waited outside. They snapped to attention and followed smartly as the group walked through the halls. Though the storm had gone, the sky was still dark. What little light found its way into the fortress was swallowed up by gloom.

A permanent sadness hangs over this place, Jack thought. He couldn't imagine Lancelot and his knights making merry here, but perhaps they'd been as thick-skinned as Brutus. Brutus was impervious to atmosphere. Come to think of it, where *was* that untrustworthy slave? He was the true ruler of Din Guardi, but Jack couldn't see him ousting Yffi, or even Ratface.

The first time Jack had met King Yffi, he'd been too

frightened to observe him closely. Now the boy looked for signs of the ruler's kelpie ancestry. Yffi was taller and bulkier than his men, and his body filled the gilded throne. His feet were encased in very large boots. What lay inside? Claws? Could the king shift his form? And if he did, what happened to his clothes?

Yffi was swathed from head to toe, and even his head was concealed by a leather helmet that covered his face. The only visible part of him were his eyes, sunk like pebbles in a bowl of oatmeal. The effect was extremely unpleasant.

The creature—Jack couldn't think of him as a man—must have been cold, for braziers burned all along the walls, making the atmosphere breathless. Sweat ran down the soldiers' faces and into their beards.

"The Princess Ethne," announced Father Severus before the captain could speak. A murmur ran round the room.

"Ooh, the pretty thing," murmured one of the men, who was immediately cuffed by his superior. But it was clear they all thought Ethne was extraordinary. She curtsied and twirled around to bestow her smile on the entire company. The men smiled back, not coarsely as they might have grinned at a tavern wench, but with innocent delight. They might have been boys at a fair on a summer day.

King Yffi's reaction was more difficult to guess. He gazed at her steadily, and for some reason Jack was reminded of a toad watching a butterfly. "How did you get into my dungeons?" he said at last.

"We came by the Hollow Road," Father Severus said.

Several men gasped. "That be the way of wraiths," said the captain. "But you be no wraith, Princess," he added loyally.

"Wraiths may not cross our borders," said King Yffi, "yet other things enter by the Low Road." The king's eyes were as emotionless as a spider's. "Some of our prisoners have disappeared from the dungeons. We find their chains empty, though unlocked."

Jack thought of the Bugaboo and the Nemesis hiding down there in the shadows.

"The Hollow Road is used by many, both fair and foul. We have journeyed from Elfland," said Father Severus. The reaction was immediate and gratifying. The men knelt before Ethne, and those who were wearing helmets removed them.

She smiled, dazzlingly. There were times when Ethne seemed human. Jack liked her best then. She was endearing and oddly familiar, though he couldn't think why. There were times when she was fully the daughter of Queen Partholis, such as now. She radiated glamour, and not one of Yffi's men could withstand it.

"An elf maiden! I should have known!" cried the captain. "Such beauty could not be mortal."

"I saw elves dance on the green when I was a lad," a grizzled old warrior declared. "Makes me feel young to think of it."

"I heard them singing," another said wistfully. "I lay out all night in the dew and nearly caught my death of cold. But it was worth it."

"Silence! All of you!" roared King Yffi. The men scrambled to their feet and jammed on their helmets. "This fortress is under siege, and all who enter unannounced are suspect. Why didn't she come by the front gate?"

"Well, you see, Your Majesty, that's a bit difficult with the Hedge," began the man who had listened to the elves singing.

"Silence! She crept in like a thief. How do you know she's not planning an invasion?"

"She could invade my house anytime," said the man.

"Guards! Take this fool out and give him six of the best. No, make that twelve of the best. Any questions?"

"No, sir. No, Your Majesty. Not a word," muttered the men as two burly guards dragged the unfortunate soldier away.

"You've been far too comfortable," the king said to his men. "You spend your days drinking and gambling and have grown careless. *We* invaded this fortress from below. Others could do the same. Elves, kelpies, hobgoblins—"

"Oh, that reminds me. Could you invite our hobgoblin friends in?" Ethne broke in.

"Ethne! No!" cried Father Severus.

"It's nasty down there. I'm sure they'd like this place better," she said with a pout.

Yffi signaled, and a soldier swiftly put a knife to the monk's throat. "Not another word, wretch. The rest of you be quiet too, or he dies. Now, my pretty fay. What were you telling me about hobgoblins?"

"They rescued us from Elfland—Mother was ever so cross when Pega lit the candle. Besides, I have a soul now and want to be a nun. It's ever so exciting! Anyhow, the hobgoblins knew how to get here, but they hid in the dungeon because they weren't sure of their welcome. But I know you won't mind, being a king and all. Or if you do, could you put us out the front door? Although a party *would* be nice."

Yffi frowned, trying to strain the meaning out of Ethne's words. One thing did make itself clear: "You say there are *hobgoblins* in my dungeons?"

Jack started to object, but the soldier pressed the knife harder against Father Severus's windpipe.

"Oh, yes! At the bottom of the stairs."

"Why, I thank you, Princess. Your friends are most welcome," said the king in a soft voice. "I haven't had hobgoblin since— I must prepare a feast! Yes! Yes! It's an opportunity that cannot be missed! Hurry, lads, and fetch me those guests before they leave. We must have wine and ale, cheeses and tarts. Send me the cook and the boy Ratface, if he's still alive. Let me see, hobgoblin stuffed with hazelnuts. Hobgoblin on a bed of mushrooms. So many choices . . ."

Chapter Forty-five

GLAMOUR

The hobgoblins, securely bound with rope, were dragged into the throne room. There had been a fierce fight in the dungeons. The soldiers were covered with cuts and bruises. One man had lost his front teeth, but the Bugaboo and the Nemesis hadn't a scratch on them. Hobgoblin skin, as the Nemesis had boasted, was as tough as old tree roots.

The effect on Yffi was extraordinary. He leaped from his throne and bounced around the pair, uttering hisses of delight that were not remotely human. Suddenly, he threw off his helmet and inhaled deeply. "Ah! The smell of hobgoblins! You never forget it! Oh, the wonder, the ecstasy, the deliciousness of it!"

Pega fell to her knees and the Nemesis fainted dead away, for Yffi's parentage was clear without his helmet. His mouth was a V-shaped slit in bleached frog skin, and his hair clung to his scalp like fur on a seal. The Bugaboo tried to come between the kelpie and his friend, but Yffi danced around so wildly, it was impossible.

"Pega, my dearest, are you all right?" the hobgoblin king asked.

Pega moaned, clasping her hands.

"We're fine, but you, I fear, are not," said Father Severus. "It seems this fortress is ruled by a kelpie tricked out as a man. Did you know that, Jack?"

Jack forced himself to speak. "Yes, sir."

"And yet you failed to mention it. Strange. I suppose you had your reasons."

Jack did and was swept with both shame and horror at what he'd caused. He'd wanted to get home as quickly as possible. He'd lied to the Nemesis—or concealed the truth, which was the same thing—and he'd argued Pega into concealing the truth, too. *The Bard will figure something out,* Jack had told himself. But deep down he had known he was lying.

"We have a saying in my country," the Bugaboo said. "'No use pining for yesterday's mushrooms.' What's done is done, and I hold no grudges." As the Nemesis began to stir, he added, "Courage, old friend." Pega tried to run forward to help the Bugaboo, but she was forced back by a soldier.

"We'll save you," she cried tearfully. "I don't know how, but we'll think of something."

"It makes me happy to know you're safe. As to our fate—why, we'll be able to meet St. Columba. I'm quite looking forward to dying."

"Speak for yourself," muttered the Nemesis.

Meanwhile, Yffi had worked himself into such a state that he burst into song:

> *Scrumptious and savory,*
> *Toothsome and flavory,*
> *Nothing so tasty*
> *As hobgoblin pastry.*
>
> *They're also good fried*
> *With mushrooms inside,*
> *Or in hazelnut stew*
> *With an onion or two.*

There were several verses of this sort, and each one ended with the chorus:

> *Of hobgoblin cutlets*
> *I'll eat my fill*
> *With fennel and parsley and dill*
> *Tra la*
> *Done up in a nice little grill.*

The Nemesis, try as he would to be brave, fainted again.

❖ ❖ ❖

"What a miserable creature I am, lowest of the low!" sobbed Ethne. "I'll starve myself! I'll endure public floggings! No penitent will ever be so abject or suffer more gloriously!"

"You meant no harm," Father Severus said wearily. Ethne had been going on like this for an hour, and they were all thoroughly sick of it. They were huddled in a corner of the courtyard. Soldiers bustled about. Cooks bawled orders to slaves. Ratface slunk by with a bundle of wood. He cast a surly look at the people who had deprived him of his shirt.

Jack concentrated on how to rescue the hobgoblins. He knew he was more at fault than Ethne, but wallowing in self-pity wasn't going to save anyone. He went over the small amount of magic at his disposal. He could call up rain and fog, kindle fires, and make apples fall from trees. Once, he had called up an earthquake. Jack looked speculatively at the fortress walls. He grasped the staff and sent his mind down to the life force, but it was too feeble and distant. He wasn't even sure how he'd done it before.

The soldiers had dug a great fire pit and were constructing a spit for roasting. A mountain of logs was burning down to coals. The Bugaboo and the Nemesis, appropriately, were locked up in the pantry.

Jack tried to estimate how much time they had. Clouds hid the sun and the light was so murky, it was impossible to guess what time it was. On the good side, a constant drizzle threatened to put out the fire.

Pega slumped against a wall with tears rolling down her face. Father Severus was praying, and Ethne was lamenting loudly and creatively. Only Thorgil was alert. She observed the preparations for the feast, the position of the soldiers, the crows sitting ominously on the battlements. Watching her, Jack felt a glimmer of hope. Surrender wasn't a concept she understood. She had continued to fight when she was being carried off in the claws of a dragon.

Jack remembered Olaf One-Brow's advice: *Never give up, even if you're falling off a cliff. You never know what might happen on the way down.* He smiled at the memory of the giant Northman.

"You look cheerful. Have you thought of a plan?" said Thorgil.

"I was remembering Olaf."

The shield maiden frowned as she tried to flex her paralyzed hand. "Once, when Olaf's right arm was broken in battle, he had to fight with his left hand. When the enemy knocked his sword away, Olaf kicked him in the stomach. Then he head-butted the troll over a cliff. Olaf had much battle lore."

"For one thing, he taught us that it's good to have a very hard head."

"He was proud of his," Thorgil agreed. "He was also a master of strategy."

What strategy? Jack thought. As far as he knew, the Northman's only tactic was to run down a hill screaming at the top of his lungs.

"Olaf used to say, 'Even the smallest thing can be used as a weapon. You can bury a castle in an avalanche if you know which pebble to remove.'"

Jack raised his eyebrows in surprise. "Meaning?"

"Yarthkins. They offered you a boon for blessing their land. You should ask them for it."

"What can they do? They're forbidden to enter the fortress."

"You never know what might happen," said Thorgil. "I've seen their like before, in heavy fog and at a distance, but I know they're powerful. Olaf was always highly respectful of them. We call them *landvættir*."

Then, because the shield maiden moved with lightning speed from any plan to action, she immediately turned to Father Severus. "You must remain here with Ethne," she said. "The rest of us will rescue the hobgoblins." Next, she tapped Pega on the shoulder and said, "Be ready." Lastly, she grabbed Ethne and shook her hard. "Stop whining. You know how to create glamour, don't you?"

Ethne hiccupped, and she stared at Thorgil in shock. "Well, do you?" demanded the shield maiden, giving her another shake. The elf lady nodded. "Good. Get over there and perform. I want those guards' wits so clouded, they won't be able to find their backsides with both hands."

Ethne turned to Father Severus for help. The monk smiled slightly. "You've lamented enough, child, and I'm sure Heaven has been impressed. Much will be forgiven if you rescue those noble hobgoblins." The elf lady's face became radiant, all tears forgotten. Father Severus raised his hand in blessing to Thorgil: "May God go with you."

"And Thor and any other god I can get," said Thorgil.

Then, awkwardly, she added, "Thanks," before shoving Ethne into the courtyard.

The elf lady began to dance. She moved like gossamer in a breeze, like sunlight skimming a lake. Her feet barely touched the earth. With each step, she became less human and more elf. First one, then another soldier turned to look at her, and the ground around her began to change.

Flowers grew where no flower had been before. Vines rose into the air. They curled up the fortress walls, covering the gray stone with leaves so green, it was as though a light shone behind them. Strange birds with scarlet wings sat on the branches and sang such music as was never heard in Middle Earth.

"Don't look," said Thorgil, twisting Jack's ear so viciously that he yelped. The pain drove the vision away, and the gray stones returned. He saw Pega huddled against a wall.

"Come on," he said, grasping her by the hand.

"What's happening?" she said.

"Don't look at it. We're going to rescue the hobgoblins."

Any uncertainty Pega might have had vanished. She stumbled after Jack and he after Thorgil until they got to the dungeon door. Guards were standing in front of it, completely hypnotized. Thorgil pushed them out of the way. The three children dragged the heavy door open, and when they were inside, Thorgil had them close it again.

Chapter Forty-six

UNLIFE

They ran down the long stairs and along the halls, passing dungeons that might contain prisoners. Jack remembered King Yffi's words: *Some of our prisoners have disappeared from the dungeons. We find their chains empty, though unlocked.* Whatever lurked down here, it was too late to worry about it now, Jack thought as he passed the grim metal doors.

But he realized another problem as soon as the trail began to go down and the light to fail. "Torches!" he cried. "We haven't got torches!"

"Can you draw fire with your staff?" Pega asked.

"It won't work without something to burn." Jack looked around frantically, but the halls were empty.

"I think I can find the way," said Thorgil. Jack and Pega stared at her.

"It's pitch-black down there and the trail twists around. Even the Bugaboo got confused," said Jack.

"Rune taught me how to remember my way in the dark. It's a little like what he does in the sea."

Jack remembered, long ago when he'd been a prisoner of the Northmen, how Olaf One-Brow had lowered Rune into the sea. The Northmen's method of finding land was to go in one direction until they bumped into something, but they had fantastic memories. A beach, once seen, was never forgotten. Water, once tasted, was never confused with water a mile away.

And Rune was the best. He saw the sea as a good farmer saw his fields. He knew the shape of it, its various colors and moods. He observed how the birds lifted their wings as they felt the currents of the sky. He sniffed the air for smoke and fresh-cut peat, for pine and juniper. He tasted the sea itself, to detect the presence of invisible, freshwater streams or of cold welling up from the depths—the result being that the old man always knew exactly where he was.

"You can do what Rune does?" Jack said.

"I have not the years of experience, but he praised my skill."

Jack looked at the trail going into the dark. It couldn't hurt to call on other powers, in case they never came out the other end. "May the life force hold us in the hollow of its hand. May we return with the sun and be born anew into the world," he said, repeating the Bard's words.

"I shall not return. My hope is Valhalla," Thorgil said.

"And my hope is Heaven," said Pega. Then they all joined hands, Thorgil in front, Pega next, and last of all, Jack.

"Like the Bugaboo, I need silence," the shield maiden said. "I must remember our path."

They went down into the blackness and, worse, the cold. Chill came up from the ground and down from the ceiling. The walls were so bone-numbing, they seemed to burn rather than freeze when you blundered into them. And everyone did that repeatedly. The going was much slower and harder with Thorgil leading.

Sometimes she had to stop and sense the air around her. Jack didn't know what she was looking for. Everything seemed exactly the same, but after a moment Thorgil would choose a direction and pull them on.

Jack began to grow sleepy. He stumbled. "Don't lie down," Thorgil said. "That's how the frost giants trap their enemies."

Frost giants, Jack thought. He remembered the Bard saying something about them.

"I can't go on," Pega moaned. "Leave me. I'll die here."

"It's just what I'd expect from a thrall," Thorgil said harshly. "Very well, die. It's what creatures like you do best."

"I'm not a thrall!" said Pega with sudden energy.

"Good. I feel we are passing close to Niflheim. It is the realm of the goddess Hel, and she has a particular liking for thralls. I wouldn't tempt her with any talk of dying. Now be quiet. I need to think."

They stumbled on. Jack, too, found it difficult to put one foot ahead of the other. They seemed to have been in the dark for hours. Suddenly, he lurched to the side and fell onto something soft.

Well, not soft exactly, but not as flint-hard as the ground. It made a nice bed.

"Get up," Pega said in a panicky voice. She clawed at him, trying to catch his arm. Thorgil returned and helped her.

"I bumped into one of those some distance back and led you around it," the shield maiden said. She didn't explain. The three of them staggered on, and it seemed Thorgil was getting weak too. Her steps became slower and more unsteady.

"I see light," said Jack.

"Not a moment too soon. Hurry," said Thorgil.

Just before the bone-chilling cold lifted, but when the light was barely strong enough to make out the walls, they encountered another strange lump in the tunnel. It was a large, muscular creature covered with fur like a giant otter. Its feet were turned backward, trailing useless claws, and its hands stretched toward the light. But the kelpie had frozen to death before it could escape.

"I suppose they were trying to invade Din Guardi," Thorgil said.

When they came out to the sea, she collapsed on the ground. Jack noticed she was clutching the rune of protection and her face was drained of color. "You should rest," he said, concerned.

"I'm ashamed of my weakness," the shield maiden said. "We were passing close to Niflheim, and I thought if I died there, Odin might never find me."

"Odin would always find you," Jack said warmly. "You don't belong in Niflheim. It would spit you out like a seed." Thorgil smiled weakly.

They all rested, not saying the one thing that weighed on their minds, that time was slipping by and that the fire pit would soon be ready. Finally, heaving a sigh, Pega climbed to her feet. "I feel like I've been beaten all over with a club."

"Me too," admitted Thorgil. "There was more in that tunnel than cold."

Jack did not reveal his theory. He'd been cold many times, but even the ice mountains of Jotunheim were not as terrible as that darkness. Whatever you called it—Niflheim or Hell—that tunnel was the realm of death, not the fate that awaited mortals who trusted in God. It was the utter absence of hope.

They hurried on. The tide dashed itself against the barrier around Din Guardi, and Jack felt queasy as he passed over it again. The country of the yarthkins greeted them with its warm, earthy smells. The air felt green, although, of course, it had no visible color. "I can make a torch now," said Jack, looking around at driftwood and dried seaweed.

"I don't think we'll need it," said Thorgil.

"You think they'll come to us?" Jack said.

"If she sings."

Jack had to fight back a moment of jealousy. His voice was good. It was more than good. It was better than the Bard's had ever been, or Rune's. It had pleased the yarthkins once they had arrived. But it was Pega who had called them.

She sang with the voice of the earth itself, with a power

bards could only dream of. Jack knew then that he would never be the equal of her. He struggled to rise above the bitterness that filled his soul.

"Sing, Pega," he commanded her. "Give them the hymn the angel taught to Caedmon."

She turned toward the warm darkness of a yarthkin tunnel and called, *"Erce, Erce, Erce"* with her arms outstretched. "Come, oh, come," she begged, and then she sang. First it was "Caedmon's Hymn," followed by a Yule song, "The Holly and the Ivy." The next offering was "The Wife of Usher's Well," about a woman who called her sons home, not realizing they had perished under the sea. And the sons *did* return in the middle of the night, covered with seaweed and clam shells.

Jack thought that ballad might be unwise so near to the Hall of Wraiths. He was happier when she changed to a nursery rhyme. But really, it didn't matter what Pega sang. All of it was beautiful.

In the distance Jack heard a whispering and a twittering. The darkness in the throat of the tunnel thickened. Something oozed from the walls and fell to the ground with a heavy *plop*. The hair on Jack's arms stood up. He grasped his staff and placed himself between Pega and the advancing horde. Thorgil joined him.

Along the floor of the tunnel—and the sides and the ceiling—clustered knots of hair as pale as summer wheat. Long, earth brown fingers pulled them along. Bright, black eyes observed the children with a frightening intensity. Thorgil held her knife in her left hand. Jack had no doubt she could emulate Olaf, if attacked, right down to the kicking and head-butting. "Don't do anything," he whispered. "I think they're friendly."

"They're *landvættir*," she murmured. "It is always danger-ous to draw their attention. Olaf used to remove the dragon head from the prow of his ship when he came to shore, to keep from offending them."

"I don't remember that," said Jack, keeping his eyes on the steadily advancing mass of little haystacks.

"You weren't paying attention. It's fine to display the dragon head at sea, but the *landvættir* consider it a chal-lenge. By Thor and Odin! Stop touching me!" By now the haystacks had reached Jack and Thorgil, and the pressure of their bodies brought forgotten dreams to the surface. They were the ones Jack tried to forget the moment he woke up, of sinking into mud or being swallowed by a giant snake.

"I'm not your enemy!" cried Thorgil, hurling the knife away. The ring of yarthkins opened out, and Jack breathed more easily. Pega stopped singing. Her face was chalk white.

One of the creatures stood apart from the mass. Jack assumed it was the same one he'd spoken to before and bowed politely. "Thank you for coming," he said.

How didst thou find Din Guardi, children of earth? the crea-ture said.

"Thoroughly nasty," replied Jack.

And thy people? How were they?

"They weren't even there," Jack said. "My da and the Bard

are at St. Filian's Monastery. So is Brother Aiden. And now our friends are in danger."

"Please, please help us," cried Pega, breaking in. "King Yffi is going to kill the hobgoblins. Please—you offered us a boon before. We're asking for it now. Save them! Save our friends! Destroy their enemies!"

"Be careful what you ask for," murmured Thorgil.

Shield maiden, said the yarthkin, turning toward the girl. All of his followers did the same with a rustling and a twittering. *Thy mother honored us. We do not forget.*

"My—my mother?" gasped Thorgil. Jack knew she hardly had known her mother and had been ashamed of her because she was a thrall.

Thy mother asked us to watch over thee. She does so still.

"How can that be? She's dead! I saw them cut her throat," cried Thorgil.

We will help thee, children of earth, said the yarthkin, ignoring her outburst. The whole group began to move forward, out of the tunnel and into the muted light of late afternoon. Jack, Pega, and Thorgil were forced to go ahead of them. The thought of being overwhelmed by the little haystacks—of being *crept on* by them—was more than anyone could stand.

The sea clashed against the invisible barrier. The clouds lowered as though they, too, were trying to break through. Jack and his companions passed over, with Jack being swept by a familiar sensation of dizziness. They turned to look.

The yarthkins were halted at the border.

"Well, that was a waste of time," said Thorgil.

Pega ran back. "What do we have to do? How can we break the spell that keeps the old gods out?"

Spell? said the head yarthkin. *There is no spell.*

"We were told about it," said Jack. "The Man in the Moon did something bad. I don't know what it was, but he was exiled to the moon, and the rest of you were forbidden to enter his fortress."

The Man in the Moon wished to rule the green world, said the yarthkin in his whispery, twittering voice. *He would have slain all to gain power, and to this end, he made an ally of Unlife. It was we who exiled him. But we have not been able to undo his harm. It is Unlife that keeps us out.*

"I don't know how to help you," Jack cried. "The Bard might, but I can't get to him."

Thou hast the means, said the yarthkin, and his thousands upon thousands of followers rustled their agreement. *Thy staff drew fire from the heart of Jotunheim. It is a branch of the Great Tree.*

"Yggdrassil?" Jack was bewildered. He knew his staff was more than a mere piece of wood, but this? How could he have owned such a thing of power and not known it? And why hadn't the Bard told him?

Lay thy staff across the ring of Unlife that we may pass over.

Jack paused for a moment. He had a feeling he wasn't going to like what was going to happen, and he wanted to keep the talisman he'd unwittingly brought from Jotunheim. It was black as coal but hard as flint. He hadn't used it much, not nearly enough. He didn't really understand it, although once he'd called up an earthquake with it.

"Jack. Remember the hobgoblins," said Pega.

The boy shook himself. Of course. Even now, King Yffi's men might be dragging the Bugaboo and the Nemesis to the fire. He raised the staff and felt the familiar thrum of life within it. Then he laid it across the barrier.

Chapter Forty-seven

THE LAST OF DIN GUARDI

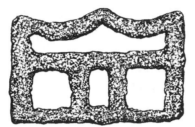

The head yarthkin advanced, pulling himself along by his long, brown fingers. He touched the staff, and Jack held his breath.

The air chimed like a bell. It was as though the sky itself were trembling. The earth answered with a faint thunder. A light as pure as a spring dawn spread over the sea. It flowed up the grim walls of Din Guardi and down into the tunnel. The breeze carried a fragrance that was something like a meadow after a thunderstorm, but much cleaner and fresher.

Green. That was the word for it. The air smelled green, and it made Jack glad to breathe it.

He looked down. The staff that he had won in Jotunheim,

the staff that told the world that he, Jack, was a true bard and the heir to Dragon Tongue, had dissolved into ash. Even as he watched, the silvery dust was lifted by the breeze and blown away.

"Here they come!" shouted Thorgil. The yarthkins flowed over the broken barrier in a vast tide. Rustling and whispering, they swarmed past the children. Jack, Thorgil, and Pega clung to one another, scarcely daring to breathe as wave after wave of wheat-colored haystacks surged past them.

This time the dreams they stirred were good, the kind that Jack wanted to remember and that usually melted away when he awoke. He guessed that the yarthkins had been angry before because Thorgil had threatened them with a knife. Now they were joyful. "You're laughing!" he told Thorgil in surprise.

"You are too," cried the shield maiden, beaming with joy.

"We all are. Oh, isn't this wonderful?" said Pega. "It's like the day I learned to bake bread or when I saw violets for the first time. Or, or—it's like the day you freed me, Jack, the best day of my life!" Pega threw her arms around him and kissed him.

Jack was startled but pleased, and he kissed her back. Then he kissed Thorgil. They all clung together, transported by delight in the sea, the sky, the earth, and one another.

The yarthkins passed them by and disappeared under Din Guardi. The mad joy that had possessed Jack, Thorgil, and Pega vanished. They glanced at one another with extreme embarrassment. Jack couldn't imagine what had possessed him, kissing both girls. And Thorgil *giggling*. They must have all gone insane.

"The clouds have lifted," said Pega, breaking the awkward silence. It was true. The gray mantle that had blocked out the sun was blowing away, and blue sky peeped out behind it. A wave crashed against the shore, sending spray over the three.

"Looks like the sea isn't kept out anymore," said Thorgil. "We'd better run. The tide's coming in, and unless I'm mistaken, it's going to flood the tunnel."

"I don't know if I can face that cold again," said Pega.

"It's either that or drown."

Jack looked up. The sides of Din Guardi were no longer coated in the pearly light that had come over the sea, and the sun was setting. But the darkening rocks were softened by a glorious full moon rising with the sunset. If stones could be said to look happy, these were happy. *Although they're still too steep to climb,* Jack thought resentfully as he followed Thorgil and Pega.

They had a welcome surprise. Nothing was as it had been. Walls were coated with fluttering moss, and the tunnel was lined with the same glowing mushrooms they had encountered before. Not only that, the floor was soft and the air smelled wonderful.

Summer had been let into Din Guardi. No trace of the deadly cold remained. "*Landvættir* are indeed powerful, if they can drive away Hel," said Thorgil.

When they came to the upper reaches, where the dungeons lay, they found all the doors open. No one was inside, although some of the manacles looked as though they had once been attached to an arm or a leg. "Do you think kelpies ate them?" whispered Pega.

Jack doubted it. The doors had been too securely locked. He didn't like the slime trails he saw going up the walls or the way his feet stuck to the floor. *Knuckers,* he thought, but didn't say it aloud.

The door to the courtyard was open, with a red glow coming from the fire pit and torches blazing along the sides. A black spit was silhouetted against the flames. "I can't look. Are they—" Pega hid her face.

"They're all right." Jack saw the Bugaboo and the Nemesis with Father Severus and Ethne. And one more person he never expected to meet. "Brutus!" he cried.

"Welcome to Din Guardi! Or as my ancestor Lancelot called it, Joyous Garde. It's been a while since there was any joy around here." Brutus grinned infuriatingly. He was still dressed in the golden tunic with the scarlet cape that the Lady of the Lake had given him. The great sword Anredden still hung from that diamond-studded belt.

Pega ran to the Bugaboo and hugged him. "I was so afraid! I thought you were—"

"We're right as rain, dearest. Only the better for seeing you." The Bugaboo planted a noisy kiss on top of her head.

"Brutus, why weren't you here earlier? Why didn't you help us?" shouted Jack, longing to wipe the silly grin off the man's face.

"Couldn't, I'm afraid. Old Yffi tossed me into the dungeon as soon as he saw me. Took away my sword, too, but these chaps got it back."

Jack looked around to see that the shadows were full of

many, many dark lumps whose eyes glinted in the light of the torches. "Yarthkins?"

"Mother used to talk to them all the time. Fine fellows as long as you don't get on their wrong side." Brutus signaled, and a very frightened, very repentant Ratface scurried out with a glass of wine.

"I don't think you even know how to use a sword," said Thorgil, torn between scorn and laughter.

"That's not how we Lancelots win battles," said Brutus, winking. "Anyhow, we were waiting for you to show up so they can finish the job." He nodded at the silently watching haystacks. They looked as though they might be settled down for a very long time, perhaps centuries.

"What job?" said Jack.

"Long, long ago the Man in the Moon built this place." Brutus drained his cup and helped himself to a plate of fried chicken held by a visibly trembling Ratface. "Various people lived here after he was driven out, but no one could ever quite *relax*, if you know what I mean."

"Not with Hel in the basement," observed Thorgil.

"Even Lancelot used to look over his shoulder when he went downstairs. Well! Thanks to you, Jack my lad, the ring of Unlife has been broken."

"I'm not your lad," said Jack, who was nettled by the casual way Brutus referred to his sacrifice of the staff.

"All trace of the old fortress must be cleansed," Brutus went on, impervious to Jack's anger. "I hate to see it come down, but there's no way we're going to hold back the Forest Lord. Only the yarthkins have been able to stop him so far. So let us say farewell to Din Guardi. Wine cups all around, Ratface."

The scullery boy ran to the pantry and stumbled out with an armload of metal goblets and bottles.

"Do *they* drink?" whispered Thorgil, nodding at the silent, waiting haystacks.

"Not as we do," said Brutus. "Ah! This is the fine wine of Iberia. That's on the continent, I'm not sure where. Yffi and his crowd had all the best stuff."

They toasted the last hour of Din Guardi, and Jack offered his cup to the one yarthkin who was standing apart from the rest.

Thank thee, child of earth. It was well thought of, though we prefer water, said the creature.

"I didn't want you to feel left out," said Jack.

A rippling sound like pouring sand echoed around the courtyard. Jack suspected he was being laughed at. *Such as we are never left out,* whispered the yarthkin, melting back into the shadows. *We will not forget thee.*

"And now it's time to go," Brutus said cheerfully. "Ratface, you lead the way with a lantern. Thorgil my lad, you bring up the rear." Thorgil smiled, not at all annoyed at being called "my lad."

"Stay close to me," said the Bugaboo, placing Pega between himself and the Nemesis. "I'm not convinced of the Forest Lord's goodwill." They went out between waiting clumps of yarthkins and through the front gate. The Hedge loomed ominously against the stars.

"There's the passage. Don't wander off, anyone. *Nice*

Hedgy-Wedgy," crooned Brutus, almost, but not quite, patting the dark, shiny leaves.

Jack didn't know whether the Hedge was being nice or not. If this was its good behavior, he never wanted to see it on a bad day. The air in the passage was stifling. Thorns and twigs reached out to snag Jack's clothes and skin. Once, a tendril curled around his ankle before—regretfully, it seemed to Jack—slipping away. And the hostility radiating from the leaves made it difficult to breathe. With one shift, the passage could close in, crushing whatever was within—

Don't think of it, Jack told himself.

Then they were through, into the clean air with a swath of twinkling stars above and a full moon cresting the top of Din Guardi. A grinding and a crackling told Jack that the passage had indeed closed. "Wait!" he cried. "Yffi and his men! They're still in the fortress."

"They have earned their fate," said Father Severus. Jack noticed that he had the altar cloth from the Holy Isle cradled in his arms.

"The yarthkins sorted them," Brutus explained. "The rejects were tossed into a storeroom—actually, *all* of them were rejects except Ratface. Yffi tried to fight, but it isn't easy to fight yarthkins. Right, Ratface?"

"N-no," stammered the scullery boy.

"Ratface gave them a bit of a struggle too. I gather it isn't pleasant being felt all over by them."

No, indeed, thought Jack, and he no longer wondered at the scullery boy's terror.

"Let us climb that hill," suggested Brutus. It was a small hill, and Jack found it pleasant to walk through the feathery grass covering it. Crickets chirped and frogs peeped. It was an ordinary, beautiful summer night.

When he reached the top, Jack could see the dark shape of Din Guardi under the full moon. It seemed larger than he remembered. Then he realized that the Hedge was pressed against the walls.

The Forest Lord attacked.

Rocks groaned as they were wrenched from their places. Wooden doors splintered. Iron grills over windows threw off sparks as they were torn apart. The noise was terrifying and continuous. After a while Jack saw that the fortress was *growing smaller.* It was settling into the earth like a snowbank melting into a stream. When it was almost flat, the sounds of destruction died away.

If there had been human voices in that turmoil, Jack had not heard them. His heart felt sore. He couldn't imagine the last moments of the men trapped inside. He regretted the fate of the captain who had admired Ethne and of the man who had lain out all night in the dew to listen to the elves sing. *Be careful what you ask for,* Thorgil had said.

"There passes the glory of Din Guardi," said Brutus, standing tall and outrageously handsome under the full moon. "It was a place of shadows and sorrow, doomed in its grandeur and inglorious in its fall. Still, it's always nice to have a fresh start," he added, spoiling the noble effect of his speech.

"You're going to rebuild?" asked Thorgil. The fortress was

entirely gone now. Only a stretch of lonely rock jutted out over the sea.

"I am its lord, after all. The Lady of the Lake and her nymphs have promised to help me."

"I'll bet they have," said Jack.

"I'm going to stretch out on the grass for a little shut-eye. It's so warm, I'm sure we'll all be perfectly comfortable." Brutus fell asleep at once, and he was soon followed by the others. It had been a long and dreadful day. Once the danger was past, exhaustion fell on everyone.

But Jack sat up for a while, remembering the staff he had carried from Jotunheim and wondering if he was, in some way, responsible for the deaths of Yffi's men. The full moon shone down on the sheet of rock that had once been Din Guardi. Jack wondered whether the Man in the Moon had watched its destruction and what effect it had on him.

Chapter Forty-eight

THE GIFTS OF THE LADY

Jack was the last to wake in the morning. Father Severus was conferring with Brutus, and Ethne was dancing in the meadow at the foot of the hill with Ratface lurking nearby. She looked all elf in the morning light. "I can hardly believe Din Guardi's gone," said Pega, who was watching the sea pensively. "I went down at first light, and there's not a single pebble left. I saw a hole going down into the rock, but I was afraid to get close to it."

"Very wise," said Jack. The flower-filled meadow reached all the way to the shelf of rock. Everything looked as though it had been there for a thousand years. Of the Hedge, there was no trace.

Thorgil pranced up to them on a stocky little pony. She dismounted, then turned it around to show off its dappled skin. "Isn't he handsome? The yarthkins drove the livestock out before the Forest Lord took over." The Bugaboo and the Nemesis had also caught ponies. They clung to their backs like burrs, and the ponies arched frantically to throw off the creatures.

"I d-don't s-s-see what all the f-fuss is about r-riding," complained the Nemesis with his long, sticky fingers and toes digging into the pony's hide. "It isn't f-fun at all!"

"You'd better let it go before it dies of fright," advised Jack.

"G-gladly!" The Nemesis bounced off like a frog, and the pony ran in the opposite direction with its body soaked in sweat. The Bugaboo released his mount at the same time.

"I'm sorry, dearest," the Bugaboo apologized. "I did want to impress you. I suppose I'm not cut out to be a knight."

"That's all right." Pega smiled. "You're a king, which is better."

"I can hardly wait to get to St. Filian's," said Jack.

"Me neither! I miss Brother Aiden."

The Bugaboo was about to say something when Brutus called for them to join him. Thorgil's pony, apparently deciding she was his new owner, followed her up the hill and waited nearby, cropping the grass.

"Are we going to St. Filian's?" Jack asked.

"We must deal with Bebba's Town first," said Father Severus.

"I've been arguing with him," said Brutus. "It seems it isn't enough to be Lord of Din Guardi. I realize there isn't much left of the place—"

"There isn't anything," said Thorgil.

"—but a title should count for something."

"You have to understand," the monk argued. "Bebba's Town has been ruled by scoundrels for a long time. They don't trust anyone. You have to win their support before you attempt to take control of the monastery." Father Severus frowned as Ethne danced to another part of the meadow, followed by Ratface. "For one thing, you must look like a man who could protect them. Yes, yes. I know you're handsome. Battlefields are littered with the bones of good-looking men. But the townspeople expect you to be fierce, a proper warrior like your ancestor Lancelot. It also doesn't hurt to seem irritable, as though you'd cut off the head of the first person who annoyed you."

"I'd never do that!"

"I didn't say you'd have to do it. Just look as if you might. That's how Yffi maintained power and how every leader does it."

"I'd rather rule this field of daisies," said Brutus, smiling.

"Pay attention, you dolt!" Father Severus looked both fierce and irritable. Jack realized the monk would make a far better leader than Brutus, but the job wasn't open for him. "You have a duty to these folk. Great injustice has been done, and innocent people have been plundered and killed. You *must* take control. I have a plan—but before I get to it, would you mind going down to that meadow, good Nemesis? Tell

Ratface I'll turn him over to the yarthkins if he doesn't leave Ethne alone."

"Gladly," said the Nemesis.

After Father Severus outlined his plan, Brutus went off to find the Lady of the Lake—by himself, because (he said) the Lady despised all mortals (except for him, of course). He was gone a very long time.

Jack despaired of ever getting to Bebba's Town. He was hungry, and the meadow had little food to offer. The Bugaboo and the Nemesis found turnips, but raw turnips hardly qualified as food in Jack's mind. When Brutus returned, however, they saw what had taken him so long. The Lady of the Lake had given them wondrous gifts.

For Jack there was a white tunic and a blue cloak embroidered with silver moons and stars—most suitable for a bard, he thought. Thorgil was given a dark blue tunic and a leaf green cloak with vines around the edge. It made her—well, it made her look beautiful, Jack thought, remembering the kiss beneath Din Guardi. He looked away in embarrassment.

Father Severus wore a black monk's robe. To go with it, the Lady had provided a crozier, a shepherd's crook with the end carved like an uncurling fern. "It's magnificent!" cried the monk, waving it about. "Even better than the ones I saw in Rome. All the best bishops have them—good heavens, I've just committed the sin of pride!"

Ethne was radiant in a white gown sprinkled with diamonds. Ratface was dressed as a proper knight's squire, which took away some of his weasel-like demeanor. "There's a heap of swords, belts, and pennants next to the lake," Brutus said. "We can pick them up on the way."

But for Pega and the hobgoblins there was nothing. "I can't go in this," Pega cried, pointing at her threadbare, secondhand dress.

"The Lady must have forgotten about you," Brutus said.

"She didn't forget!" fumed Jack. "She's taking revenge. Partholis must have told her about the candle."

"Don't cry, dearest. It's much nicer to wait here," said the Bugaboo. "Hobgoblins can't go into town anyway. Mud men throw rocks at us."

Pega wiped her tears away. "They are mud men, aren't they? Oh, how I hate them! And the Lady, too!"

"I'll tickle up some trout, and the Nemesis will build a fire. When it's safe, we'll go to St. Filian's and see your Brother Aiden."

"You're so good to me," she said, sighing.

"And who would not be?" the hobgoblin king declared.

It was easy rounding up horses—they seemed relieved to find owners again. Thorgil rode her pony, and Jack found one too. He had never been on a horse, except with King Yffi's men, but he had some experience of donkeys. A pony was exactly the right size to learn on. He turned to wave good-bye to Pega and the hobgoblins. All three were hidden in the grass, and if Jack hadn't known exactly where they were, he would have missed them.

The band set off with Jack and Ratface bearing green pen-

nants that fluttered in the breeze. Jack was pleased with the
new and extremely well-made sword at his side. It was short
and light enough to be used easily. To no one's surprise, Ethne
turned out to be an excellent horsewoman. She had only to
ask, and the beast did exactly what she wanted as though it
understood her speech. Brutus rode a coal black stallion with
neat hooves and flashing eyes. They made a glorious pair,
with Father Severus going ahead to announce them. Ratface
plodded behind on a heavy-footed nag he was afraid of.

"Brutus will charm all the women, and Ethne will charm
all the men," observed Thorgil as she and Jack brought up the
rear. "Perhaps they should marry."

"Ethne wants to be a nun," said Jack.

Thorgil laughed. "You might as well ask a butterfly to haul
rocks. I know little of nuns except that Ethne would make a
bad one."

"She's allowed to try."

"I wonder. In some ways she's like Frith and Yffi—oh,
not cruel or vicious like them. But she's caught between two
worlds. Such creatures often go mad."

"Father Severus will watch over her," said Jack uneasily.

The entry into town was all they could have hoped for.
Everyone was gathered in the market square, for all had
heard that Din Guardi was no more. A pair of shepherds,
looking for lost sheep, had watched its destruction. "It were a
dragon!" one of them told the excited crowd. "All breathing
sparks and whatnot. Horrible noises, just horrible!"

"We daren't stick out a toe all night," the other exclaimed. "Else we'd be gobbled up too. In the morning there was nothing. Not . . . one . . . pebble." The tidiness of the destruction impressed everyone.

It was then that Father Severus rode up on his steed, crying, "Make way for the new Lord of Din Guardi!" Everyone scattered to make room. Brutus followed, cheerfully raising his hand in greeting. "Look fierce," hissed the monk, and so Brutus frowned adorably.

"Coo! He's a handsome one," a woman said.

"What about *her*?" said a man. Ethne made her horse lift its hooves delicately, as though it were dancing. It was a pretty trick that caused many a shout of approval, but of course the prettiest trick of all was the glamour that shone all around.

"You tell me if that looks like a nun," Thorgil said to Jack.

"Behold the man who rules Din Guardi after the death of the vile usurper Yffi!" cried Father Severus, raising his crozier. "In the night, destruction fell on that fortress. All evil was swept away, and now is the time of new beginnings."

"Begging your pardon, sir," said a man who seemed to be a local leader, "you mean a dragon didn't tear the place up?"

"There are no dragons here," the monk said scornfully. "It was the wrath of God that fell on Yffi."

"But He had help, right?" insisted the man. "By the way, I'm the mayor."

"Well, mayor of Bebba's Town, God chooses His instruments where He pleases. Behold Brutus! Rightful heir to his father, Lucius, of the line of Lancelot!"

Again Jack found himself admiring the monk's skill. Not once did he actually lie. God *had* chosen His instruments of destruction: yarthkins. But by proclaiming Brutus, Father Severus left the impression that the unreliable, good-natured, and lazy ex-slave had done it. Ethne's dazzling presence did no harm either.

"Hurrah for King Brutus, Lord of Din Guardi!" shouted the mayor, which was then echoed by the crowd. A feast day was declared, bonfires built, beer kegs rolled out, and unfortunate chickens chased for the festivities. In no time the trappings used for fairs were unpacked. A charming pavilion was erected for King Brutus and (as the townspeople assumed) his future bride, Ethne. Father Severus lost no time in informing everyone that she was a princess.

It was a grand celebration that went on late into the night. Jack worried about Pega and the hobgoblins, but Father Severus said it was better to leave them alone. "The Bugaboo will take care of her," he said. "I hope her heart has inclined toward him since his near escape from death. She's a good child and deserves a better fate than she'd receive here."

But Jack thought about her horror of being underground without the light of the sun.

Chapter Forty-nine

ST. FILIAN'S WELCOME

In the morning they set out for St. Filian's, leaving Ethne behind in case of trouble. A large crowd of townspeople insisted on coming, which was what Father Severus had wanted all along. "Believe me, the real problem lies with the monastery," he told Jack as they rode side by side. "Those monks are little better than pirates, and there's a lot of them. I quite look forward to sorting them out." He smiled ominously.

"You, sir?" inquired Jack.

"Brutus is putting me in charge. Brother Aiden is the most forgiving man in the world. He'd rescue a drowning rat even if it bit him, and would bless the little brute afterward. Father Swein's flock needs a different sort of shepherd."

Jack saw a patch of white beyond a grove of pines on a hill and recognized St. Filian's. Beyond, to his amazement, stretched a large lake filled with reeds. But where before Jack's heart had lifted at the sight of beautiful white walls and buildings buzzing with activity, the monastery now seemed curiously dead. "It hasn't been raided?" he said.

"Not from without," said Father Severus. The grounds that had been carefully tended were now in squalor. Weeds grew everywhere. A rubbish heap was piled outside a door, and a latrine had obviously not been cleaned for a long time. Two monks—or slaves (it was hard to tell from that distance)—lay snoring on the heap. A pig rooted around them for scraps.

Some of the damage had come from the earthquake. Great cracks ran down some of the walls, but they should have been mended by now. "It's like the vision I had," murmured Jack.

"Blow the trumpet, Ratface," commanded Father Severus. Ratface had been taught the skill at Din Guardi, to muster soldiers. What he lacked in musical ability he made up for with zeal. The trumpet shook the air again and again. The monks jumped up from the rubbish heap and ran into each other in panic. The pig dashed for the woods. Cries came from within.

"That should do it, Ratface," Father Severus said. The boy grinned and wiped the spit off the mouthpiece.

"Run! Run!" cried voices.

"No! Fight! Fight!" shouted others.

"It's the Northmen! We're doomed!" one monk wailed.

"If it were Northmen, they'd be inside by now," remarked

Thorgil. Soon a group of slaves armed with cudgels was pushed out the door by cowering monks.

"Tell Brother Aiden we've come to see him," Father Severus called out over the heads of the unwilling slaves. "We bring the new Lord of Din Guardi."

"Hurrah for King Brutus!" shouted the townspeople, who were gathered behind. Brutus rode at their head, as befitted a noble lord. He drew Anredden and brandished it wildly. The crowd cheered.

"Someday he's going to do himself serious harm with that," muttered Thorgil.

"Forward!" ordered Father Severus, and the crowd streamed around the horses. They were thrilled to be part of such a momentous event, and if they punched a monk or two who had cheated them, who could blame them? Very soon St. Filian's Monastery was under control. Brutus rode into the courtyard, beaming goodwill on all sides. Jack looked around until he saw a small man appear from the chapel.

"Brother Aiden! Thank Heaven, you're all right," the boy cried.

The monk's face broke into a smile. "Jack! Brutus! I'm so glad to see you! And—and—it can't be!"

"It is, my friend," said Father Severus.

"You were taken by the Northmen. You were killed!"

"I was sold into slavery, but there's far too much to explain here," said Father Severus. "As soon as I've sorted things out, I'd be eternally grateful for a mug of your heather ale. Oh, and I've come to take over the monastery. I hope you don't mind."

"Such a blessed event has been in my prayers every night!" exclaimed Brother Aiden.

"Good," said Father Severus with a not-so-pleasant smile as he looked around at the subdued monks, some with black eyes and all looking as repentant as one could wish. "I have a few chores to attend to first."

The Bard and Father were in the infirmary, the most comfortable place in the monastery. The Bard had added to the collection of herbs hanging from the ceiling, and he was explaining their uses to Giles Crookleg when Jack and Thorgil came in.

"Jack—oh, my son," cried Father. His leg was still bound in splints and he leaned on crutches, but Jack was delighted to see him looking so healthy. "I thought you'd never return. When Yffi covered the well—" Father straightened up to study Jack. "I swear you've grown, though it's only been a few weeks. And where did you get those clothes?"

"Well done, Jack!" the Bard said heartily. "You've accomplished extraordinary things! Ah, Thorgil, we meet again."

"Dragon Tongue?" the shield maiden said.

"I told you he was alive," said Jack.

"Who is this lad?" said Father. Jack was flummoxed. All along he'd been going over ways to explain Thorgil. He realized that not only Father, but also the townspeople had taken her for a boy. That solved the problem of her refusal to wear dresses. She was still a Northman, however, and would be killed if anyone found out. And then Father made things worse by asking, "Where's Lucy?"

The moment Jack dreaded had arrived. "She's well," he faltered. "She's happy."

"She was never ours, Giles," said the Bard. "From the very beginning, you knew that. I assume she's still in Elfland."

"She didn't want to leave," Jack said miserably.

"Not for me? Or Alditha?" cried Father.

The Bard laid his hand comfortingly on Father's shoulder. "Elves don't think the way we do. You can break your heart on them and they'll only laugh and turn away."

Jack watched awkwardly, not knowing what to do as his father wept. Lucy had never loved him or anyone else. She'd probably forgotten all about him by now.

"Don't you want to know about Hazel?" said Thorgil suddenly.

Father looked up. "Who are you?"

"I'm Thorgil Olaf's—"

"That's quite enough information," said the Bard. "This is someone Jack met on his travels. Hazel is your real daughter, Giles, and last I heard, she was living with a family of hobgoblins."

"Hobgoblins!" Father was suddenly roused from his grief. "They'll eat her!"

"Nonsense. Hobgoblins are good-hearted creatures, and they adore children. I take it Hazel didn't want to leave either."

Jack's heart sank even further. "You see, she's never

known anything else. She thinks she *is* a hobgoblin, and she loves her foster parents. It would have been cruel to kidnap her."

"Although I did think of it," said Thorgil.

"It's a good thing you failed," said the Bard. "Now, we have much to talk about, and Aiden will surely want to hear what happened. Jack, why don't you ask him around for dinner. Oh, and you might take Pega and her friends a basket of food. Tell them they'll be most welcome after dark."

Jack left at once, wondering which bird had told the old man about Pega and the hobgoblins. It was uncanny how the Bard always seemed to know everything that was going on. As he went out the door, Jack heard Father say, "Thorgil is a strange name for a Saxon."

"It's very popular up north," the Bard informed him.

When evening fell, the townspeople went home. They were in a fine mood, laughing and congratulating one another on the victory over the monks. "Father Severus put them on bread and water for a *month*," one of the men said.

"Prayers every four hours and work duty the rest of the time," said another happily. "When they've finished mending the walls, they can start on Din Guardi. Ah, it's good to have a real king again!"

"A fine little princess he's got himself too." The men chuckled and made their way through the darkening fields to Bebba's Town.

Jack listened to them as he lay on his stomach in the long

grass beyond the monastery's perimeter with the hobgoblins and Pega. "Do you think it's safe?" whispered the Bugaboo.

"I hope so. Brother Aiden told me to enter by way of the lych-gate." They crept forward until they reached an opening in the wall around the graveyard. It was completely deserted inside, with weeds growing over sad little crosses marking the monks' graves. A mist drifted in from the meadow.

"All the better to hide us," murmured the Nemesis.

They came to the back door of the infirmary, and Thorgil opened it. "About time," she grumbled. "Dragon Tongue wouldn't let us eat until you arrived."

Jack was used to the strange appearance of hobgoblins, but Father almost fell off his stool when he saw them. "Demons! D-demons! Come to drag us down to Hell!"

"Stay calm, and you, too, Aiden," ordered the Bard. "These gentle creatures are hobgoblins, the kindest folk on earth. Welcome, Pega. I've saved you the best seat."

The girl hung back in her tattered and dirty clothes. "I'd rather stay with the Bugaboo and the Nemesis."

"To be honest, *all* the seats are best because they're all the same," the old man said cheerfully. "You and your friends are guests of honor. Serve the meal, Ratface. You may be dressed like a knight's squire, but we all know you're a scullery boy underneath." Ratface sourly passed around bread trenchers covered in lentil stew and cups of cider.

"To new beginnings!" said the Bard, lifting his cup.

"To new beginnings!" the others echoed. They fell to, and no one spoke until they were finished.

"It's excellent," the Bugaboo said after his fourth serving of stew. "It just needs a tiny handful of mushrooms to improve it."

"As usual, you show deplorable manners, criticizing the food," said the Nemesis. Jack knew the hobgoblins were completely relaxed when the Nemesis started sniping at his king again.

"Thorgil has told us of your adventures, and I, of course, already knew some of them," the Bard said. "You are to be congratulated, Pega. It's no small thing to triumph over the elves. I knew, when you lit that candle at the Yule ceremony, that you were meant to do something important."

"Thank you, sir," she said, looking down shyly.

"And you, Jack, broke the ring of Unlife around Din Guardi. For a long time the life force has striven to enter. It was like a boil that festered and sent infection all around. Now it is healed."

"I lost the staff from Jotunheim," Jack couldn't help saying.

"I know."

Of everyone in the room, Jack thought, only the Bard understood what a terrible sacrifice that had been. The old man looked at him with such sympathy, the boy was afraid he might cry and disgrace himself. "There are other powers that come with sacrifice," the Bard said quietly. "They are known to the Wise, but it takes time to learn them. I knew long ago, at the need-fire ceremony, that you, Pega, and Lucy had set immense change into motion. What I didn't see was Thorgil. She gave what she most valued when she raised her hand against the Lord of Unlife. And gained much that she has not yet realized."

"She?" said Brother Aiden and Father at the same time.

"You got used to hobgoblins. You can get used to Thorgil being a girl," the Bard said. Jack was impressed with how he'd introduced each problem and made it seem like the most ordinary thing in the world. Father was even talking to the Bugaboo, and Brother Aiden had stopped crossing himself whenever he looked at the hobgoblins. Good old Bard! He got the best of everyone.

The door leading to the monastery opened suddenly, and in came Brutus—*King* Brutus, Jack reminded himself—and Father Severus. "Whew! It's been a busy day," exclaimed the new Lord of Din Guardi. "I haven't been able to sit down once."

"Tomorrow will be worse," Father Severus assured him. "We were on our way to bed when I remembered a bit of unfinished business. You can pick out your own beds, by the way. The monks will be sleeping on the floor for a very long time. Dragon Tongue"—he turned to the Bard—"it is time you met someone."

Father Severus stepped aside, and Ethne came into the room, making the candles seem to burn brighter. "Behold your daughter, Dragon Tongue."

For the first time since Jack had known him, the Bard was rendered utterly speechless.

Jack understood now why Ethne had seemed so familiar. When she was elvish, she was like a younger version of

Partholis. But when she was human—and Jack liked her much better then—she had the same blue eyes and even the same smile as the Bard. Some of her kindness probably came from him too. Alas, it was usually swamped by Partholis's influence. Now the human side came to the fore.

"I always wondered who my father was," Ethne said. "I asked Mother and she couldn't remember."

"Elves don't." The Bard finally found his voice. He looked stunned.

"I've heard so much about Dragon Tongue."

"Seems like you made off with more than Partholon's magic," remarked Father Severus.

The Bard cast him a fierce look. "I'll thank you not to spoil this moment. Ethne, believe me, I had no idea of your existence. I wish I'd seen you when I was young. It was sixty years ago when I was in Elfland, and you are young still, but that's how things happen there." The old man smiled sadly. "I haven't much of a place to offer you, but you are most welcome."

"She's going to be a nun," said Father Severus.

The Bard turned on him. "Now, that *is* too much. There's more than one way to step into the stream of life, and I'm perfectly able to instruct her. I won't have her spending hours fasting and turning her back on the beauty of the world."

"But—Father—I *like* fasting," said Ethne.

"It's just a novelty to you. What you need is to be immersed in life, let it flow through you, learn to love."

"I've been instructing Ethne for a year," argued Father Severus. "I'm going to build a nunnery and send to Canterbury for an abbess to run it. Ethne will have companions and instruction. She'll learn to do good works. She'll be taught humility. I'll root out that elvishness and cleanse her soul until the angels will fight over who gets the honor of carrying her to Heaven."

"Oh, dear, dear, dear." The Bard sighed and looked very old and tired indeed. "You have no idea what you're dealing with, and I may not have enough years left to save her."

Jack felt alarmed. He didn't want to think of the Bard dying *ever*, even if it only meant he'd be reborn somewhere else.

"There are many branches on the Great Tree, child," the Bard said gently, taking Ethne's hands. "Christianity is only one leaf."

But the elf lady smiled at him uncertainly. Jack knew she had no idea what he was talking about.

"She's caught between two worlds." The old man looked up at Father Severus. "I don't know whether she can entirely abandon one of them."

"With God's help, she will," Father Severus said.

"Tell me, Ethne, do you truly want to be a nun?"

"It sounds ever so much fun," the elf lady said enthusiastically.

"Very well, I won't stand in your way. But listen, if you ever need help—" The Bard paused, thinking. "I'm going to send you a cat. I know nuns are allowed pets. Treat him nicely and don't forget to feed him."

"This isn't some wizard's trick?" Father Severus said.

"Never!" The Bard's blue eyes fairly blazed with innocence.

"He's a cat I bought from an Irish sea captain who put in to Bebba's Town. His name is Pangur Ban. If ever you feel frightened, my newly found daughter, tell your troubles to Pangur Ban. I often find it very soothing to talk to creatures that cannot possibly—ever . . . in no way . . . by any stretch of the imagination—pass on information."

Ethne bent forward and kissed the old man on the cheek. "I'll remember," she said softly.

Then, because it was very late and everyone had had a tiring day, Father Severus said they should all go to bed. He had even employed a woman from Bebba's Town to look after Ethne. He was a very organized man.

Chapter Fifty

HOMEWARD BOUND

Father's leg healed more swiftly than anyone had dared hope. Even better, the limp was almost gone. "The bones were set badly when you were a lad, Giles," the Bard explained. "Having them broken again was a fine opportunity to straighten them out."

"If you say so." Giles Crookleg grimaced as he put weight on his foot.

"You'd better ride the donkey. It's a long journey."

Father gazed sadly at Bluebell, and Jack knew he was remembering how she had carried Lucy to Bebba's Town. They also had two ponies—gifts from the new Lord of Din Guardi—to carry the Bard and supplies. Jack, Pega, Thorgil, and Brother Aiden would walk. "I wish I could stay here. I've always wanted to be a monk," Father said.

"And I'd say that beating knocked the sense out of you—if you'd had any in the first place," the Bard said. They all turned to look at Bebba's Town, now falling behind, and the empty stretch of rock where once Din Guardi stood. They had said their farewells that morning, and Jack wondered if he would ever see Brutus again. The king had promised to visit the village, but you couldn't trust anything he said.

He and Thorgil had put on their old clothes and packed the beautiful gifts of the Lady of the Lake. There was a small but very good well a half-day's journey from the town. Attached to it was a copper cup on a long chain. No one knew who had put it there—perhaps Lancelot or King Arthur himself. It was for weary travelers to refresh themselves, for the well water was too deep to reach easily. They camped in a small beech wood, and in late afternoon two figures materialized from the trees.

The Bugaboo and the Nemesis were draped in motley wool cloaks and resembled patches of dappled shade. "Welcome," called the Bard. "We've brought chanterelles especially for you." Jack and Thorgil laid out a cloth with the various delicacies they had packed for this farewell feast. Pega, for once, did nothing. She sat by herself looking strained and miserable.

The Bugaboo went at once to her side. "Dare I hope? Are you going to make me happy beyond my wildest dreams?" he cried, grasping her hand.

"Oh, Lord," she said, looking down.

"Do you need more time?" said the hobgoblin king. "I don't mind waiting—well, yes, I do, but I understand if my little moss blossom is feeling shy."

"This is the hardest thing I've ever had to do. You've been so good to me, and I know your people want me as their queen. Saints above! They gave up their immortality for me." Pega drooped still farther and wiped at her eyes. "I feel so guilty."

"It was their decision," the Bugaboo said.

"I always wanted to be beautiful. I went out every May Day morning and washed my face in dew. I even paid a wise woman for a charm, but nothing worked. Finally, I knew it would never happen. But then *you* came along and you liked me—"

"Loved you, dearest," corrected the king.

"The thing is . . ." Pega stopped and looked at Jack.

He was trying not to eavesdrop, but the air was too still. No one else was talking. The night before, Father Severus had gone on and on at her about the suitability of this marriage. He was capable, as Brother Aiden put it, of making a wolf drop a lamb. The mere sight of Father Severus was enough to make the rascally monks of St. Filian's chop wood, haul water, and thank God on their knees six times a day. But he had not been able to move Pega, small and humble though she was.

"The most important event of my life," Pega went on, "was when Jack freed me. 'Freed me for what?' I asked myself. 'For work,' I answered. Just that. To do the simple tasks of everyday life, to care for others, to belong. The Bard once told me my spirit craved a family and warmth. And I replied, 'I'd be happy staying here—and doing chores forever—and just being a fly on the wall.'

"That's pretty much it. I'm not suited to be a queen. I'm most sincerely sorry to disappoint you, and I'd be lying if I didn't admit that I also don't want to live in a cave full of mushrooms. Don't offer to move here!" she said, putting her finger to her lips in warning. "You have a duty to your people. The plain truth is, you belong there and I belong here. I'm sorry."

The Bugaboo's eyes blinked rapidly and erratically. Jack had never seen a hobgoblin weep, and he didn't know whether they could do it, but this probably came close. "I'll visit every summer," he said in a husky voice. "I'll ask whether you've changed your mind. And I'll bring Hazel with me."

"That would be extremely kind," said Pega.

The hobgoblin king rose and bowed to the other members of the group. "It was nice of you to bring chanterelles," he said in the same husky voice, "but I'm not feeling hungry just now." Then he was too overcome to say any more and rushed from the glade.

The Nemesis hurried after him, pausing only to bend over Pega and whisper, "Thank you."

They sat under the trees, recalling adventures and telling stories. When night came, Jack built a fire and Brother Aiden brought out a flask of his special heather ale. Thorgil declaimed gloomy poetry. The Bard entertained them by luring a family of owls to hoot mournfully as a background to her verse. Then Pega sang, and the very trees stopped rustling to listen.

Jack wished the moment could last forever, but time stood still only in the Land of the Silver Apples. And that was a curse rather than a blessing. It was enough to be in the stream of life, to be with good friends and have good cheer. He stretched out on the grass, watching the stars scattered among the leaves overhead.

RELIGION

Many groups of people settled in the British Isles, bringing their gods and goddesses with them. With the passage of time, these old deities were forgotten or were turned into fairy stories. Some of them even became saints. An example is St. Brigid, who was originally a goddess of inspiration and poetry. The line between the old and new religions was often blurred. St. Patrick used a charm to turn his followers into deer to escape their enemies. St. Columba, who surely started out life as a druid, persuaded the Loch Ness Monster to stop eating people. Ravens, after being scolded by St. Cuthbert for vandalizing his roof, made amends by bringing the saint a slab of lard to oil his boots.

How these early missionaries loved to travel! They wandered from village to village, camping out, getting free food, and avoiding nine-to-five jobs. They loved being alone, finding the most remote islands on which to build huts. St. Cuthbert had to be dragged from his to become the abbot of Lindisfarne and was most annoyed about it.

Northern Europe during the fifth to eleventh centuries was a mixture of religions. Worshippers of Odin, druids, wise women, Christians, and people of faiths we can only guess at lived side by side. We don't know what the Picts worshipped. We have only their strange and beautiful carvings—a crescent crossed by a broken arrow, a beast with curled feet and a mouth like a dolphin. I have given them the Forest Lord (also called the Green Man), the Man in the Moon, and the Wild Huntsman as gods. But no one really knows. Nor does anyone know where such beings as the will-o'-the-wisps, hobgoblins, the Lady of the Lake, mermaids, and yarthkins came from. I think they are old gods who lingered on into a twilight with the elves.

As for the elves, the belief that they were half-fallen angels is found in early Christian writings. It was certainly an idea the famous author J. R. R. Tolkien knew about, although he chose not to use it.

ST. FILIAN'S WELL

St. Filian's name is also spelled "Fillian" and "Fillan." There was a St. Fillan's Well in Scotland, where people suffering from insanity were thrown from a high rock into its water. You could call this an early form of shock therapy. In the eighteenth century a minister had the well filled in to stop the practice. In 2005 a construction company called Genesis Properties wanted to remove a large stone near St. Fillan's to make room for houses. Angry locals refused to let them touch the stone because they said elves were living underneath it. Genesis backed down.

DIN GUARDI

The fortress of Din Guardi lies near the city of Bamburgh (Bebba's Town) and across the water from Lindisfarne (the Holy Isle). It is very old, possibly going back to Neolithic times, and was built and destroyed several times. It is now called Bamburgh Castle. It is supposed to be the site of Joyous Garde, Lancelot's palace.

Many interesting things have been discovered buried beneath it, but the most fascinating was a sword. It was probably the finest sword of its time, and even today, scientists aren't sure how it was made. There is nothing like it in existence. The archaeologist who discovered it hid it in his house for forty years, apparently to enjoy its possession in secret. When the man died, the sword was thrown away, but fortunately, his students got there before the garbage collectors.

Of course, this is the sword Anredden, made by the Lady of the Lake. Only she knows how it was done.

SYMBOLS CARVED BY THORGIL'S SHIPMATES

Northmen did not have a good way to record their history. They carved symbols into rock, and through the years some of these evolved into an alphabet. But there is only so much you can say if you have to depend on rocks instead of paper. Most stories were turned into poetry and memorized.

The alphabet symbols were called "runes." Some of these were associated with gods and invoked their powers. Two or more could be combined to make a talisman called a *galdrastafir*.

The symbols carved for Thorgil and Heinrich are as follows:

1. Thor's hammer (*mjöllnir*)
2. The rune of protection; also the symbol for Yggdrassil (*algir*)

These stand for Thorgil. In the middle (3) are the "knots of death" (*valknut*), also known as the "mind-fetter" Odin casts on those warriors he wishes to claim for his own. These are followed by:

4. Odin's rune (*oss*) above the rune for horse (*ior*); this indicates Odin's eight-legged steed, Sleipnir
5. A spirit ship

These stand for Heinrich.

When *algir* (2), the rune of protection, is repeated in the talisman below, it becomes many times more powerful. This is what is carved on the amulet Thorgil wears around her neck.

PICTISH SYMBOLS

Pictish symbols are carved on many stones in Scotland, as well as a few stones in southern France. They are so distinctive and complex, it is certain they had an important meaning. Unfortunately almost no information about Pictish culture has survived. Their language has vanished. Their history is clouded in myth. Their gods remain mysterious.

Their art, however, endures in the Lindisfarne Gospels, the Book of Kells, and many other works. It is clear they were done by master artists. Their animals are drawn with great realism and skill. Thus it is a surprise to find the Pictish beast to be completely unidentifiable. (It is the creature with the curled tail and topknot.) People have called it a dolphin, a horse, and even an elephant. It is a common symbol, and there are tales about it. One (which occurs in the book) describes it as the size of a cucumber when born, and quickly growing to enormous size.

The broken arrow is a common motif in the carvings, particularly the broken arrow crossing the crescent moon.

This has been interpreted as a death symbol for a man, while the comb and mirror are death symbols for a woman. In *The Land of the Silver Apples*, the broken arrow and moon are tattooed on the chest of Brother Aiden, indicating that he is marked for sacrifice. These moons and arrows are often enlaced with vines. I have used them in the book as markers for the three main gods of the Picts: the Man in the Moon, the Forest Lord (or Green Man), and the Wild Huntsman. This is entirely my idea—no one knows who the gods of the Picts were—but the three beings occur in ancient lore all over northern Europe.

Most interestingly, the distinctive comb (which looks almost like a garden gate) and mirror occur in carvings of mermaids. I don't think this is an accident. It is quite possible that the mermaid was a Pictish sea goddess and that these symbols refer to her.

The meanings of all the symbols are guesswork, but here are some possibilities from *The Pictish Guide* by Elizabeth Sutherland, printed in Edinburgh, Scotland, 1997:

A solar disc held by a human.

The broken arrow crossing the crescent moon indicates the death of a man.

The mirror (left) and comb (right) indicate
the death of a woman.

The three ovals connected by a chain may be a bracelet.

The snake crossed by the broken arrow (also called a
"Z rod") may mean renewal and immortality.

The curved, flowerlike design may be a flower
or a horse's harness.

*The arc may be a rainbow, which was
considered a bridge to the other world. This
is sometimes shown with the broken arrow.*

*The double disc crossed by the broken arrow is supposed
to indicate the duality of the sun, which lights this world
by day and the otherworld by night.*

This curved form is probably only a decoration.

The rectangle may be a container for valuables.

*The notched rectangle crossed by the broken arrow
may be a chariot or a fortress.*

Our old friend, the Pictish beast.

*The circle crossed by a line, with two small circles at either
side, may be a cauldron, which symbolized rebirth.*

Another crescent moon crossed by a broken arrow.

Sources

Adalsteinsson, Jon Hnefill, *A Piece of Horse Liver: Myth, Ritual, and Folklore in Old Icelandic Sources* (Reykjavík: University of Iceland Press, 1998).

Adomnan of Iona, *Life of St. Columba,* trans. Richard Sharpe (London: Penguin Books, 1990).

Alcock, Leslie, *Arthur's Britain* (Middlesex, England: Penguin Books, 1975).

Arnold, Ralph, *A Social History of England: 35 B.C. to A.D. 1215* (New York: Barnes & Noble, 1967).

Blair, Peter Hunter, *Northumbria in the Days of Bede* (New York: St. Martin's Press, 1976).

Calise, J. M. P., *Pictish Sourcebook* (London: Greenwood Press, 2002).

Chetan, Anand, and Diana Brueton, *The Sacred Yew* (London: Penguin Books, 1994).

Cummins, W. A., *The Age of the Picts* (Gloucestershire, England: Alan Sutton Publishing, 1995).

Foote, P. G., and D. M. Wilson, *The Viking Achievement* (London: Praeger Publishers, 1970).

Gantz, Jeffrey, *Early Irish Myths and Sagas* (London: Penguin Books, 1981).

Griffiths, Bill, *Aspects of Anglo-Saxon Magic* (Norfolk, England: Anglo-Saxon Books, 1996).

Guthrie, E. J., *Old Scottish Customs* (Glasgow, Scotland: Thomas D. Morison Co., 1885).

Hagen, Ann, *A Handbook of Anglo-Saxon Food: Production and Distribution* (Norfolk, England: Anglo-Saxon Books, 1995).

—, *A Handbook of Anglo-Saxon Food: Processing and Consumption* (Norfolk, England: Anglo-Saxon Books, 1992).

Henderson, Isabel, *The Picts* (New York: Praeger Publishers, 1967).

Hingley, Richard, *Settlement and Sacrifice: The Later Prehistoric People of Scotland* (Edinburgh, Scotland: Canongate Books, 1998).

Hutton, Ronald, *The Stations of the Sun* (New York: Oxford University Press, 1996).

Jackson, Kenneth Hurlstone, trans., *A Celtic Miscellany* (London: Penguin Books, 1971).

Jesch, Judith, *Women in the Viking Age* (Suffolk, England: Boydell Press, 1991).

Kennedy, Charles W., trans., *An Anthology of Old English Poetry* (New York: Oxford University Press, 1968).

Keynes, Simon, and Michael Lapidge, trans., *Alfred the Great* (London: Penguin Books, 1983).

Leahy, Kevin, *Anglo-Saxon Crafts* (Gloucestershire, England: Tempus Publishing, 2003).

Lindow, John, *Handbook of Norse Mythology* (Santa Barbara, CA: ABC-CLIO, 2001).

Matthews, Caitlín, and John Matthews, *The Encyclopedia of Celtic Wisdom* (Dorset, England: Element Books, 1994).

Napier, James, *Folklore in the West of Scotland* (Ardsley, England: EP Publishing, 1976).

Owen-Crocker, Gale R., *Dress in Anglo-Saxon England* (Suffolk, England: Boydell & Brewer, 2004).

Pollington, Stephen, *Leechcraft: Early English Charms, Plantlore, and Healing* (Norfolk, England: Anglo-Saxon Books, 2000).

—, *The Mead-Hall: Feasting in Anglo-Saxon England* (Norfolk, England: Anglo-Saxon Books, 2003).

Rolleston, T. W., *Celtic Myths and Legends* (Mineola, NY: Dover Publications, 1990).

Ross, Anne, and Don Robins, *The Life and Death of a Druid Prince* (New York: Simon & Schuster, 1989).

Rutherford, Ward, *Celtic Lore* (London: HarperCollins, 1993).

Sherley-Price, Leo, trans., *Bede: Ecclesiastical History of the English People* (London: Penguin Books, 1990).

Shippey, Tom, *The Road to Middle Earth* (New York: Houghton Mifflin, 2003).

Simpson, Jacqueline, *Everyday Life in the Viking Age* (New York: G. P. Putnam's Sons, 1967).

Sutherland, Elizabeth, *In Search of the Picts* (London: Constable, 1994).

Webb, J. F., *The Age of Bede* (London: Penguin Books, 1998).

Whitelock, Dorothy, *The Beginnings of English Society* (Middlesex, England: Penguin Books, 1964).

Whitlock, Ralph, *In Search of Lost Gods* (Oxford, England: Phaidon Press, 1979).

Wilson, David, *The Anglo-Saxons* (Middlesex, England: Penguin Books, 1981).